NO PLACE FOR A WOMAN

NO PLACE FOR A WOMAN

Meg Hutchinson

Hodder & Stoughton

First Published in 2001
by Hodder and Stoughton
A division of Hodder Headline

A CIP catalogue record for this title is available
from the British Library

ISBN 0 340 73859 6

Typeset by
Phoenix Typesetting, Ilkley, West Yorkshire
Printed and bound in Great Britain by
Clays Ltd, St Ives plc

Hodder and Stoughton
A division of Hodder Headline
338 Euston Road
London NW1 3BH

Chapter One

'Quite frankly, Laura, I don't want to marry you!'

Sandy hair brushed back from a wide forehead, indiscriminately coloured pale eyes calculatingly cool, Edmund Shaw ran a slow, almost methodical glance over the girl he had known from childhood.

'If and when I marry . . .' he went on, ignoring the swift flush that had risen to her cheeks, 'I shall choose a woman who has, shall we say, more on her side than you have. I will want a wife who will be an asset not a drag, someone with poise and beauty as well as money. You, Laura, have very little of either of those qualifications.'

Moving further into the centre of the small cramped room he ran a longer look over the slim figure dressed in skirts that had been patched several times. What the hell did Jabez think he was doing pushing him into marriage with her! Hiding the quick cold rise of anger the thought had aroused he continued. 'Oh you have Isaac's share of Shaw and Cadman, but that is of little consequence balanced against what I require. You can't be called pretty even in an unenterprising way, though your manners are sufficient for a dirty little town in the Black Country. And that is where they will keep you, Laura, buried up to your neck in dirt and soot; but Wednesbury will not keep me, this town will not hold me down. I want a better life, a life with people who know how to live. I want a fine house and money, more money than Jabez Shaw and Isaac Cadman could ever dream of making; and when I marry I want a wife who is both beautiful and sophisticated, one who knows the best way of furthering her husband's interests. In short, Laura, the sort of woman you can never possibly be.'

Around Laura the world faded. Forgetting to breathe she floated in a world of silence, a world that was unreal. It was not Edmund who stood looking at her, Edmund whom she had known all her life; this cold-eyed man was a stranger, this was a dream from which she would eventually awake.

His own features devoid of emotion Edmund Shaw watched the fingers twisting together.

'I am sorry to have caused you such a shock, obviously you had hoped for marriage to me . . .'

The words chipped away at the edges of her silent world, splintering the barrier that had closed protectively about her.

'. . . but it is better said than to let you go on hoping.' The voice went on, a cold impervious voice that Laura did not recognise.

'. . . better you should know now that I have no intention of marrying you.'

He paused as if only now remembering something. One pale eyebrow lifting in question he asked, 'Has your father spoken of the proposition of marriage between us?'

Her throat frighteningly tight, Laura listened from within that world of silence. It would go away soon. This awful thing, this delusion would disappear and everything would be as it was before.

'Laura . . . !'

It was sharper than the question that went before, more demanding of an answer.

'. . . has your father spoken of marriage between us?'

She did not want to answer. Suddenly it seemed this world of quiet nothingness was where she wanted to be; here she was safe from the pain of words, safe from the pain of those words which, she realised even in her nightmare, were waiting yet to come.

Impatient with her lack of response he turned to leave. 'No matter, I will speak to him myself.'

The last of his words streaming back over his shoulder smashed into the unseen wall, sending its stones falling away, and suddenly Laura's mind was free.

'There . . . there is no need . . .' the words jerked out, '. . . my father has never spoken of my marrying you.'

Pausing at the door he stood with his gaze locked on it. 'At least *he* could see the futility of that, not like . . .'

'Not like me?' Dragging the tatters of her pride together, Laura stared at the man who had so coldly rejected her. 'Is that what you were going to say, Edmund? My father had more sense than to hope? No, you are wrong. My father did have more sense than I, more sense than to believe we should marry. I thank you for telling me what you have, it has prevented a lot of heartache.' Hands clenched at her sides she fought the tears from her eyes but could not keep all trace of them from her voice. 'I will not be a hypocrite by pretending I had not expected one day to . . . to become your wife. I suppose I had expected it since being a child.'

'It is what you were supposed to expect!' For the first time since coming to the house his voice took on a note of heated anger. 'What we were both supposed to expect, our parents . . .' He broke off, his hand reaching for the door handle. '. . . But life does not always give what we expect.'

Laura watched the fingers fasten about the door handle. It was as though they tightened about her heart, squeezing the life from it. 'No, Edmund.' She answered quietly. 'Life is not always what we expect.'

'But it demands to be lived!' Fingers holding the handle tightened even more, jutting knuckles standing out white and hard. 'And I am going to live mine to please myself not to please Jabez Shaw, not to please Isaac Cadman and not to please you,

Laura; my life was given to *me* and I intend to live it for myself!'

'That is your prerogative, Edmund.' The tears suddenly gone from her voice, Laura held her gaze on the man she had known for so many years yet realised she did not know at all. 'Speaking for myself I would not want you to live your life for me and I am certain the same can be said of my father. Perhaps he knew you better than I did, he must have realised your feelings and that is the reason he never spoke to me of marriage to you.'

Opening the door he turned, and for a moment his insipid eyes held a depth she could not fathom.

'Is it, Laura?' he asked quietly. 'Is it?'

'You can't be called pretty . . .'

Tears she had banned in the presence of Edmund Shaw trickled slowly over Laura's cheeks.

'. . . I don't want to marry you . . .'

Biting as cruelly deep as when he had spoken them, the words throbbed in her brain.

Edmund Shaw had no wish to marry her. Laura Cadman could never possibly be the sort of woman he wanted. She would have no idea of the requisite social graces, be no asset to his business, would not know the best way to further his interests.

Her stare glued to the door that minutes before had closed behind the man she had thought someday to marry, she let her tears have full rein.

How long had Edmund thought those things, held such a low estimate of her? She drew a long sob-filled breath. How long before deciding she could never be the woman he wanted . . . why leave it so long before telling her?

But would it have been any easier to bear, less painful to hear had he told her sooner? Lifting both hands to her face she sobbed out the hurt; then when tears would come no more she went into the scullery, wiping her face with a cloth dampened beneath the water pump attached to the sink.

The touch of the damp cloth cooled the flush of colour stinging like nettles against her skin, but it did little to ease the sting in her heart.

But it was said now. Clenching her teeth against the dry sobs still rattling in her chest she walked into the kitchen. Life demanded to be lived. That was something else Edmund Shaw had told her; and she must live hers.

Methodically, every move so long practised it needed no direction from her mind, she reached for a bowl, beating eggs into it. But the aim of banishing further thoughts of that visit proved hopeless, it were as if each word had been branded on her soul.

His voice had been so cold, his face impassionate; speaking to her as if they were strangers. Perhaps he had thought that to be the best way. Adding a spoonful of cornflour to the eggs she folded it in with a fork watching the whiteness swirl into the gold, embracing it, becoming one with it.

As she would have become one with Edmund! The bitterness of it a gall in her throat, she let the fork fall with a clatter against the rim of the bowl. Turning away she reached a cinnamon stick from a jar in the cupboard, dropping it into a pot already half filled with milk, then placed the pot on the bracket above the fire.

Why had he waited so long? The question forced itself once more into her mind. Watching tiny bubbles begin to rise to the surface of the milk, she searched for an answer. Could it have been a kindness on his part, had he thought it better for her that he say nothing until she was past the impressionable stage of those early years? Had he thought that now, nearing the age of majority, she was already a woman with the strength to bear the shock of what he had to say?

Seeing the milk rising fast, she lifted the pot from the bracket and carried it to the table. Whisking as she poured, she tipped the milk into the bowl.

But the waiting had been to no avail. The pot laid aside, she grated nutmeg over the surface of the mixture. The hurt was just as deep, the wound as raw.

Carrying the bowl to the fireplace she set it into the oven to cook. Straightening, her gaze went to the heart of the glowing fire.

She had thought so many times of the ways in which Edmund would propose, dreamed so many day-dreams. Would it be in a summer garden beneath the gentle light of a warm moon, would he present her with a flower as he presented her with his heart? Would it be one wonderful Christmas Eve beside a tree sparkling with the light of candles, while outside soft white snowflakes fell silently to the ground?

But it had been neither of these, none of the ways of her dreams. Instead of the words of love she had so often conjured in the quiet darkness of her room he had spoken words of rejection; cold, hard words that had cut razor deep into her heart.

'My father had more sense than to believe we should marry.'

It had been a lie. She turned back to the table. She had said that out of retaliation, as a way of striking back at the hurt slicing her in pieces, salving some of her own pride by implying that Isaac Cadman did not wish his daughter to marry his partner's son. But that was not true, her father had never once said they should not wed, just as he had never implied they should.

Returning cornflour to the food cupboard she slowly cleared the table, equally methodically spreading it with a clean white table-cloth whose scalloped edge, bordered with bright blue forget-me-nots, she had embroidered herself.

What should she tell her father? The last of the blue flowered crockery in place on the supper table, she stood staring at it. Should she say anything of Edmund Shaw's visit or keep it to herself? Maybe that would be best. Her father was more and more showing signs of tiredness, of the strain of running the business.

The business! Shaw and Cadman Engineering! She had not thought of the business. What of the time when her father was no longer with her, no longer here to take responsibility for the Cadman half of the partnership? Could she work alongside Edmund, knowing what he truly thought of her?

No, she could not! Her legs suddenly threatening to fold beneath her, she dropped into a chair. She could not do that, could not face Edmund every day with the knowledge that he was weighing her against . . .

Against what?

Against beauty? Laura clenched her fingers tight in her lap. There were things went deeper than beauty, meant more than poise and sophistication; there was integrity and respect, the kind of respect she owed to her father. And she would honour that respect in full and gild it in real beauty, the beauty of love a daughter held for her father.

Those would be the qualifications she would bring to further the interests of Shaw and Cadman. She had learned much from the evenings spent together with her father, learned the uses and stresses of steel, the foundries to buy from the ones to avoid, the names of customers and their requirements. But she would learn more, all that her father could impart.

When the moment arrived that he could no longer carry on, she would take his place. Isaac Cadman had no son to carry his name, no son to inherit the business he had slaved to build, and now he would not have the son-in-law he had most likely counted upon having. He and Jabez must have discussed the possibility of such a union. What better way? Unite their children and consolidate their business at the same time. Had Edmund told his father . . . told him this was one wish he would not conform to? Somehow she doubted it. Edmund had never been the man to contravene any wish of Jabez. Yet he had come to her tonight, telling her what he had; would he do that without first telling his father of such an intention?

Colour mounted again into Laura's cheeks. It had been ordeal enough to listen to those words, to hear the man she had thought loved her reject her totally, but now to think of his father having heard practically all of it . . . how could she ever face that!

Embarrassment bringing her to her feet, Laura moved restlessly about the kitchen. Had Edmund told anyone else, had he confided his preferences for a wife to any of the men at the works, had he told them why Laura Cadman did not fulfil that choice?

On the opposite side of the room the kettle lid jigged noisily as water came to the boil, the sudden noise of it jarring Laura's tightened nerves. Disoriented by the thoughts running chaotically through her mind she stared at the steaming kettle for several seconds before the urgency of its call penetrated her brain. Then, still only half aware of her movements, she crossed to the fireplace. Swinging the bracket away from the heat she stared at the fire, letting it once more draw her conscious mind down into its glowing depths.

Edmund had told her why he had no desire to marry her, and more likely than not had informed Jabez of the same; but he would not have discussed her with anyone else. He may not love her but he would surely have more respect for her than to do such a callous thing as talk of her to other men! No, Edmund had never been unkind to her, there was no reason for her to think it of him now. What he had decided was best for both of them and she should be grateful for his courage in accepting that and acting upon it. At least he was not avaricious, not so greedy for the business he would marry her simply to get the half that would eventually be hers. She should thank Edmund.

But as she turned her back to the fireplace a line of silent tears coursed down her face.

Chapter Two

'All of my life you have told me what to do, ordered me here, sent me there; every moment from the time I could understand, and most likely before that, you have dictated my every movement, every action, and now this! But this is one thing I will not do, one thing you cannot make me do.'

'You always was a snivel arse!'

Distaste mirrored on his heavy features, Jabez Shaw looked at the man stood at the foot of his bed. His son! But how he had fathered a specimen like this was a mystery to him. Everything, Jabez blinked, everything he did he had to be pushed into and this was to be no different.

'Perhaps I am a snivel arse, Jabez, but if I complain it is with cause . . .'

'Cause!' Jabez lifted himself on one elbow to glare at his son. 'What bloody cause? You've 'ad the best of everything . . .'

'The best! You call living here in this stinking little town "the best"? You call keeping me clothed little better than the men at the works "the best"?'

Sinking back on to his pillows Jabez stared at the face of the son he had never felt any affinity with. Twenty-six years! Twenty-six years they had lived in the same house, eaten at the same table and yet they could be strangers. He felt no love for the child he had reared, and the child had held no more love for him than the grown man he had become. His only son, the only child Emma had ever borne and it had to be one like this!

'Maybe the reason for that be 'cos you be of no more worth; any one of those men at the works can run rings around you. Call yourself my son . . . pah!'

At the foot of the bed Edmund Shaw's mouth tightened and when he answered it was with a quiet vindictiveness, the enjoyment of at last saying what he had felt for so many years lighting a flame in his cold eyes.

'No, Jabez, I never called myself that . . . you did. Think back, have I ever, since my mother died, called you father . . . ? Did I do so before that, except by her prompting? No, I did not for I have never thought of you as a father.'

Jabez' face relaxed into a sneer. 'That were a bit too much for you were it, your stomach couldn't take that? But it could take my bread, you could bring yourself to take my roof over your 'ead, accept my money for your pocket.'

'Money that was earned twice over!' Edmund snapped. 'You saw to that, you made sure I did twice the work of any other man. You saw to it I stayed at the works long after you left . . .'

'And no more you should! You 'opes one day to own my share of that business, then you should be prepared to work for it; it wasn't given to me on a plate. What I've got I had to strive for.'

Turning away Edmund went to stand to the side of the fire the older man had burning in his bedroom night and day whatever the season. 'Spare me the rest, Jabez,' he said sarcastically, 'the blood and sweat bit, I've heard it all too often before.'

'Ar blood and sweat!' Jabez closed his eyes, the strain of argument draining the strength from him; but in a moment sheer obstinacy had them open again. 'Hard work be what has built Shaw and Cadman, work I put in while you were still piddlin' in your trousers, work I will do again once I be outta this bed!'

'Are you so sure you will be out of that bed?' Staring into the fire Edmund thought of what the doctor had told him out there on the landing; he must be kept quiet, any stress or undue excitement could bring on another attack and should that happen . . . the doctor had shaken his head expressively.

His low chuckle one of sheer spite, Jabez breathed quick, short breaths, each a little more laboured than the one before. 'You be sure of that. I ain't done for yet; you be going to have to pray longer and a bloody sight harder to get what I know you've been wanting for years.'

Yes he had wanted that for years, longed for the death of the man he detested, who had made the life of his mother a torment and his own a mockery. Jabez Shaw had ruled here as he ruled at the works he had helped to build, with an iron hand, and thought for none but himself.

'Don't tell me I be wrong, don't tell me you ain't wished me dead more times than ever you've had hot dinners.'

'I would not dream of telling you so.' Edmund looked up from the fireplace. 'Who would dare tell Jabez Shaw he was wrong in anything?'

Short thick fingers closing about the edge of the sheet Jabez' lids lowered half over his eyes. This was more than he had bargained for; they had argued before but the lad had always backed down, given in before the end of the last round, never standing his ground as he was now.

Eyes sharp beneath the covering lids, he peered at the man he had never brought himself to think of as his son. There was something different in him tonight, something he had not shown before. Spirit? Jabez almost laughed. That was one thing Emma's son would never have. He had no backbone, he was too much a coward to shout 'shit' up a dark entry, and he was too much the coward to stick to his guns now. He had said no, but that no would be yes before he left this room.

'No bugger, that be who!' he grated, watching for the reaction. 'No bugger with any sense would try telling Jabez Shaw he be wrong.'

'Nor any without sense, for what would be the use?'

'None.' Jabez' fingers clutched again at the sheet, his eyes still hooded. 'Therefore there be none in your refusing; you will do what I say. You will marry Laura Cadman.'

Coming back to the foot of the bed Edmund waited several seconds before he answered.

'It might help if you gave me one good reason why I should.'

Eyelids flipping back as though on springs, heavy face flushing angrily, the older man stared back.

'Reason!' The word catching in his throat he choked out the rest. 'I'll give you reason, 'cos I say you will and that be reason enough!'

Knowing that beneath the half-lowered lids the beady eyes watched, Edmund walked slowly to one side of the large bed. Drawing an armchair closer to its edge he settled himself into it. Legs crossed one over the other he leaned into its leather comfort before answering.

'Not good enough, Jabez, not this time. I am finished with doing things simply because you wish it.'

'Wish it!' Jabez' glare was brown poison. 'Who said anything about wishing? It is because I order it!'

Bringing the tips of his own long fingers together, Edmund surveyed the flushed face over them.

'Better still. I am finished with doing things simply because you *order* it.'

'You will do as I say!'

Low and threatening as it was Edmund continued to stare coolly at the figure in the bed. Two strokes in five months. They had taken their toll of Jabez Shaw. The once-powerful barrel chest was sunken, the broad shoulders rounded and the body once strong and virile already showed signs of waste.

Only the eyes were the same. Beady, bright like a blackbird's eyes, and always filled with dislike. But the feeling they displayed so clearly was not exclusive to Jabez; he himself held those same feelings. If ever it were possible for one man truly to hate another then he hated Jabez Shaw.

From earliest childhood Jabez had shown his dissatisfaction

with him, had ridiculed his every effort at pleasing him until at last those efforts had ceased; then at fourteen it was insisted he take employment, starting off as a labourer to the men who made the bolts and turned the threads on the screws. The son of the part-owner of the firm no more than a common labourer! And that was how he had remained. For five years he had fetched and carried for every man employed at the engineering works, skivvied for every last one of them. Oh they had been polite enough in their speaking to him; he was, after all, the gaffer's son even though that gaffer made no secret of the fact he had no love for him. Then when he was nineteen Jabez had installed machinery that could do in minutes what took a man hours to complete. But he, Edmund Shaw, was not allowed to touch one of them except for cleaning it down with an oil-soaked rag. 'They ain't things for bloody fools nor 'alf-baked kids to play with!' had been Jabez' words and the rest of the men had turned away, some with pity in their eyes, others with smiles on their mouths. Not before he was twenty-one had he been instructed in the use of the capstan machines, and when he had the outcome had been that he must produce more bolts than anyone else.

The son of a partner in the firm! Edmund felt resentment settle hard and bitter in his stomach. He would have been more fortunate had he been born to any one of its workers.

'Do you 'ear me?' Jabez glared as he repeated his order. 'You will do as I say.'

His fingertips still pressed together, Edmund watched the flushed face as it lay on the pillow.

'. . . *any stress or undue excitement could bring on another attack . . .*'

The words circling his mind, he smiled a deliberate antagonising smile as he answered. 'Perhaps I did not make myself clear, in which case I will say again: not this time, Jabez.'

Watching the smile play about the younger man's lips Jabez' eyes narrowed still further. What was the game he was playing, what did he hope to gain by refusing to marry the Cadman wench?

Isaac Cadman was his partner in the business, his share would go to his daughter; marry her and the lot would belong to Shaw. For all there was no love lost between them he knew Edmund not to be such a fool that he could not see the benefits of that, so what was it had him refusing?

'But why?' Jabez demanded. 'The wench be presentable enough to look at, and her manner be docile; besides which you ain't had nothing to say against her all these years.'

'Nor anything to say *for* her.'

Aggravation growing every moment Jabez tried to push himself higher on the pillows, his fingers clenching angrily when strength failed him.

'That wench will make you a good wife, not that that matters, what matters be that her will bring Isaac's share of the business with her. Take her and if it turns out her ain't what you desires in the bedroom then women can be got cheap and plenty in any town you cares to visit.'

For long seconds Edmund stared at the man he detested, the only sound the quiet hiss of the gas lamps whose yellowy glow sent shadows sliding over heavy, dominating furniture, slithering silently over papered walls.

'That, of course, is your main priority.' He spoke at last, his tone holding an acid fit to burn flesh from bone. 'To bring the whole of the business under one roof.'

'Of course it is.'

'That roof no doubt being yours.'

'To begin with, ar, that roof will be mine, but in time roof and business will come to you.'

Time! It was only a matter of time. Edmund's smile died. Lowering his hands to his knees he felt the rough worsted cloth beneath his palms; the cheapest that could be got but then the cheapest was all he had ever got. Time! His thoughts acrid, he watched the face on the pillows. Would time ever end his misery, would the time ever come when he was free of Jabez Shaw?

'What makes you think the girl will agree to marry me?'

Seeing the question as acquiescent to his order, Jabez' fingers relaxed their convulsive clutching at the sheet. Slightly misshapen from the effect of the second stroke that held the left side of him in an immovable embrace, his mouth became a grimace as he tried to smile.

'Agree? What the bloody hell do it matter whether her agrees or not? The wench will do as her be bid.'

'And who is it will do the bidding?'

Jabez' fingers twitched. 'What do you mean?'

'I mean who will tell the girl what she must do? Will it be Isaac Cadman or Jabez Shaw? Is the man so much under your thumb he will even sacrifice his own daughter to your greed?'

The fingers opened and closed spasmodically and in his heart Edmund smiled.

Jabez' breathing became more rapid, each breath a struggle. 'You be talking shit as usual. Isaac Cadman will see it as I do, beneficial to the business.'

Still seemingly relaxed in the chair's comfort Edmund felt his whole body tense. Everything was inferior to this man's business, nothing mattered except its well-being; not the happiness of his son, not the life of another man's daughter. All must be given, all must be offered up on the altar of the only god he knew, Shaw and Cadman Engineering!

Contempt clear in his eyes, he answered, 'That has always been your philosophy, hasn't it? The business first and to hell with the hindmost.'

'And that hurts your delicate sense of right and wrong does it?' Laboured as his breathing was, Jabez managed a sneer. 'Well let me tell you summat. The right of anything be to finish on top, the wrong of it be to work your guts out every day and then to finish with nothing; that be the biggest sin in life but it's one Jabez Shaw don't intend to commit. Marrying you to that wench will bring the whole of that works into my hands and that be exactly what you be going to do.'

Leaning a little forward in his chair Edmund let his stare hold the other man's before saying softly, 'No, Jabez, that is exactly what I am *not* going to do.'

Anger bubbling the words in his throat, Jabez dragged air into his lungs. 'What be you after . . . why the play-acting all of a sudden? You ain't never shown no indifference to the wench afore.'

'Nor any preference.' Edmund's reply sounded almost pleasant, bringing the reaction it was meant to.

'Preference!' Jabez spluttered. 'Preference! What the hell does preference 'ave to do with marriage? The wench don't please you in bed you gets yourself another one; preference ain't no reason not to wed.'

'Especially not when the bride brings half of an engineering works with her.' Edmund smiled, his tone still pleasant.

'Ar, especially then!' Jabez spat. 'P'raps if you had worked night and day to build yourself a business you would know what it means . . .'

'But I have worked night and day, Jabez,' Edmund interrupted, the smile still playing on his mouth, hiding the tension that gripped his veins as he leaned once more into the back of the chair. 'From the moment I reached fourteen years of age you made sure of that. You worked me harder than any man and you have gone on doing so ever since.'

'And if I did it were for your good! You will be the one to benefit in the long run; it will all come to you lock, stock and . . .'

'Wife!' Edmund interrupted again and this time the smile was gone. 'It will all come to me provided I marry Laura Cadman.'

Fingers plucking at the sheet, his face red with anger, Jabez stared at the figure sat beside his bed. Why had Emma never had more children . . . why couldn't she have died years before she did? Then he could have married and got more children; he could have raised a different son, one worthy of taking over his business.

'Why all the bloody fuss?' he rasped. 'It was you chose her.'

'No, Jabez.' Edmund shook his head. 'You did.'

Fury leaving little scope for breath, Jabez glared. 'What be the difference, you'll marry her just the same!'

Watching the shades of anger play over the older man's features the tension faded from Edmund's body. His own breathing slow and even he allowed the smile to return, sure for the first time in his life that his would be the final word. Every syllable soft and perfectly clear he answered.

'If it is so important to you that Laura Cadman becomes part of this happy little family, Jabez, then *you* marry her.'

Slumped against the pillows, Jabez narrowed his eyes to the merest slits. The bastard was defying him! The wench couldn't be that abhorrent to him, whenever they met he had been civil enough to her, so why this now? He had something in mind otherwise he wouldn't be trying his arm. Well if he thought to best Jabez Shaw then he could think again . . . better men than this one had tried that and failed.

Sheer strength of will forcing the anger from his voice he relaxed against the pillows. Waiting a little, taking time for his breathing to become easier, he pushed his twisted mouth into a smile though his fingers refused to give up their spasmodic twitch. Allowing his lids to lift he played the full brightness of beady eyes over his son, feeling the dislike of him hot in his chest.

'That be the best idea you 'ave ever had,' he said, 'I *will* marry the wench myself and nine months after there will be another Shaw, a son to take your place, a son worthy to follow after me. You can pack your bag and bugger off now, for you will get nothing of what is mine. Tomorrow will see a new will signed and no sooner I be up out of this bed than this house will see a new mistress.'

Drawing a long, slow breath Edmund Shaw pushed to his feet, staring silently at the figure in the bed. Strange, he had not before realised the equality of himself and Jabez Shaw, always feeling the child to the man. But that was not so any more; the child was now equal to the man.

'What makes you so sure she will have you?'

Jabez' eyes glittered. 'Be you so sure she won't?'

Running his glance downward over the suddenly wasted

figure, Edmund wondered again why never before had he noticed age creeping over this man, how easy it would have been to step into his shoes. Had he realised sooner he would not be standing here now listening to an old man's demands, he would have been the one giving the orders.

'That caught you by the tail, didn't it?' Jabez slurred his tongue, unused to the twist of his mouth. 'That set you thinking. But it be too late. Nobody tells Jabez Shaw no, least of all you. Take yourself out of my sight and out of my 'ouse, for as soon as I be out of this bed I marries Isaac Cadman's daughter!'

It was no empty threat. Edmund's pulse quickened. The man was not given to making empty threats. It was already too late to say he would marry Laura Cadman, he had already burned his boats there, and tomorrow the inheritance he had slaved almost ten years for would be gone, wiped out with the stroke of a pen and even should there be no other child born to Jabez Shaw, any hope of his own would be lost; Laura Cadman would be the sole owner of Shaw and Cadman Engineering.

'Listen, Jabez, I shall not be taking myself anywhere.' The words glided from his mouth, soft and sibilant as a serpent, his pale eyes never leaving those bright beady ones.

'You bloody well do as I say!'

'No, Jabez.' He took a step forward. 'Like I told you, not this time. This time you are going to do what I say, and I say you will not re-draw your will, nor will you marry Laura Cadman and, sadly, neither will you be getting up from that bed.'

'I said before you was talking shit and I tell you so again. You heard what I intend and there be nothing you can do to stop me.'

'For once, Jabez, you are wrong.' Coming close to the head of the bed, Edmund smiled clear into those glittering eyes. 'There is a great deal I can do, such as this for instance.'

Snatching the pillow from beneath the other man's head he whipped it over his face. The same ice-cold smile burning in his eyes he pressed hard down.

'Goodbye, Father,' he whispered.

Chapter Three

'There is no need for you to do that, Laura love, I will see to them in a while.'

'I've almost finished, another five minutes will see the books done for this month.'

Laura Cadman ran a finger down the column of figures, squinting a little in the poor light. She had checked this particular page several times but each time the result was the same, and that did not tally.

Her lips moving soundlessly she counted again. Four deliveries of steel bars, one barrel of machine oil. The invoices for each checked with the delivery date recorded in her father's neat handwriting. Her glance moving to a book placed beside her on the living-room table, she frowned. Four deliveries of steel but five payments made. Could her father have made a mistake?

She glanced to where he sat, his chair drawn close against the hearth. He looked so terribly tired. She had not told him of Edmund's calling, of what he had said; and now, as she watched the face which until two years ago had always held a smile for her yet now so rarely wore one, she felt glad of her silence. Her father seemed to have worries enough. He had always worked too hard, even as a child she remembered his coming home long after she had been put to bed. He thought her asleep when he came quietly into her room, touching a hand gently to her hair before kissing her brow, but somehow she had not managed to sleep before her father was home, it was almost as though she feared his not coming home again.

Why? Watching the tired face, the hands twitching restlessly against the wooden arms of his chair, she asked the question she had asked herself so many times before, and as always, she could find no answer. But as she returned her eyes to the columns of figures she felt a touch of fear, a fear that had no explanation yet left her trembling.

'Put the books away, girl, I can finish them tomorrow.'

Pushing to his feet Isaac Cadman crossed to the table.

'There is just this one.' Forcing away the shivers Laura rested a finger on the page she had spent so long on. 'I . . . I think there might possibly be a mistake.'

'Mistake?' He frowned. 'Where, child?'

Moving her finger slowly, giving him time to follow with his eyes she pointed to each separate entry.

'You see, Father,' she explained as he bent closer over the book, 'four deliveries but payment for five. I have gone over it several times . . .'

The hand he had rested on the table clutched into a tight fist, then just as quickly relaxed.

'No, girl,' he straightened, 'there be no mistake. I . . . I had the steel returned to the mill, the order were for hardened steel and they sent mild.'

'Shall I delete the payment then?'

'No need.' Closing each of the books Isaac picked them up. 'The new load will be at the works in the morning, no call to mess up the books with crossings out.'

'Now you are not to go taking those books upstairs!' Laura smiled, love soft in her eyes. 'I know you, Isaac Cadman, you will go over every figure to see if my accounting is correct; but it is, I had a good teacher.'

Beneath the tiredness Isaac's face was gentle. 'You were an apt pupil and the best child a man could have. Anything you do can be trusted.'

'Then trust me to put those accounts away.' Waiting for no argument she folded the ledgers in her arms, marching with them to the heavy sideboard adorning one wall of the small room and placing them in a drawer.

'There!' Turning her back she leaned against it. 'Tomorrow will be soon enough for those to come out again, but now you are going to have a hot drink and then to bed.'

Across from her Isaac tipped his grey head slightly to one side. She was the one thing life had given him that he loved with all his heart. Sarah had been his wife but there had been no real love between them, no heart-stopping breathlessness, no passion, just a mutually quiet respect. Nor had it been real love with that other one, the one who had flattered and smiled and beckoned with her eyes; not a beautiful woman nor yet plain, but one who used him for her own purposes, and when it was done . . . but he could not say that she ended it, for him it was over long before . . .

'Here we are, Father, drink it while it is hot.'

Jerked from his memories Isaac blinked then took the heavy pottery mug held out to him. His gaze taking in the face looking at him with eyes that might have been pieces left over from a summer sky, he felt the guilt that had become a part of him. She had paid all these years, paid for a folly she had no part in; paid with her patched clothing and tired little house. She should have had more, a better life than he had given her . . .

'It won't do you any good unless you drink it.'

Folding the guilt back into his heart Isaac gave a rare smile. 'You know, my dear, I never would have dreamed you would turn out as you have.'

'Oh.' Forcing her mouth to smile Laura raised her hands, resting one on each hip. 'And how have I turned out?'

As he took a sip from the mug his tired eyes suddenly found a little of their lost light. 'To be a bully . . . you turned out to be a bully.'

'Really!' The smile remained, continuing the pretence that nothing was amiss. 'I wonder who it was gave me lessons in that?'

Shaking his head in mock sadness Isaac lowered his gaze to the mug held between both hands. 'I have often asked myself that same question . . . who taught my little girl to be such a bully?'

'Father!' Despite the unhappiness in her heart she laughed at his teasing. 'I don't really bully you, but if I do it is because you have to be bullied.' Her hands dropping away from her hips she leaned towards him, planting a kiss on one cheek. 'That is the only way I can tear you away from your work; if you are not at the factory you are sitting here into the small hours keeping the books. I wonder Mother put up with you.'

Covering the hand that rested on his arm Isaac pressed it gently, the light already dead in his eyes. 'I wonder too,' he said almost to himself. 'I wonder too.'

There was a sadness in it that tugged at Laura, a sadness that grew a little every day. But what was it, what had turned her father from a happy, laughing man into an almost silent shadow of himself? It had happened some six years ago; not a gradual change that could have been attributed to work or even to worry over the illness that had killed her mother, for that had not begun until two years after. No, it had been a quick, almost cataclysmic occurrence.

His drink finished, Isaac rose slowly to his feet. Laying his cup aside he picked up the cheap enamelled clock turning its key with weary fingers.

'You should go to bed too, child.' Returning the clock to its place he dropped a kiss on her forehead then, without another word, walked from the room.

Laura's eyes followed and as the door closed behind him the pain that had been so tightly held inside her rose searingly in her heart.

What had happened to each of them, to her father to cause him so much heartache? Whatever it was, it had been so marked in its happening she could clearly remember the day.

Gathering the cups, her mind wandered back to that time as she took them into the kitchen.

It had been one of their many trips to the Shaw house. They had taken tea in the pretty garden of the house Emma Shaw was so proud of. Four times the size of the one belonging to her mother and father, it always had some new piece of furniture or new ornament Emma delighted in showing off. But that particular day it had been Jabez who had a prize to show. 'A sunken garden,' he pronounced proudly, 'like them there Hi-talians 'ave.' But Laura had not wanted to go look at it.

Drying the cups on a huckaback towel scrubbed almost to extinction, Laura replaced them on the old pine dresser. Everything in this house was old, every stick of furniture second-hand, yet her father and Jabez were equal partners, so why did one have a grander home than the other?

One more question besieging her brain, she turned the key in the lock of the door that gave on to a tiny cobbled yard. No pretty sunken garden to Isaac Cadman's house. Turning off the gas lamp she returned to the living room.

Edmund too had not wanted to go look at the new garden. Laura's heart twisted at thought of him, of the happiness she had thought to share with him. Together they had wandered off to the brook that ran some distance from the house, an obedient fourteen-year-old following the tall sandy-haired youth six years her senior. Laura's heart twisted at the memory.

She had looked back as they had walked away. Laura held the cushion she was plumping, her inner glance on a man and a woman, she leaning forward, her hand resting on the man's arm as she talked. Emma Shaw and her father; left behind, they were deep in conversation.

But there was nothing strange in that. She set the cushion back on the chair. Yet every time she tried to analyse the change in her father, tried to pin-point the time when the hurt that was inside him began, it always came back to that day. Had there been words between her father and Jabez on his return from that garden? She might never know, for she could not shame her father by asking his partner so personal a question; as for Isaac, he would probably never tell her.

Turning to the black cast-iron grate she pulled out the damper, closing off the updraught to ensure the fire smouldering until morning. Then, casting a final glance about the tidied room, turned off the gas lamps.

At the top of the stairs she paused at her father's closed door as had become her habit; it was as if she must reassure herself that all was well. All was well! Laura felt the sadness within her. Would all ever be well again with her father, or with herself?

In her own small bedroom set at the rear of the house she undressed, washing her hands and face in the large flowered china bowl set on the washstand before slipping into a cool cotton night-gown. With her long wheat-coloured hair released from its plaits she pulled a brush slowly through its thickness.

Had she been married her father might have left the business, lived with her and Edmund . . .

The brush stilled in her hand, she felt a warm flush spring to her cheeks. Edmund did not want marriage with her, did not want her to become his wife. But they had been together from being children, seeing each other almost every week! Laura's heart cried out in pain. She had thought it could only be a matter of time before Edmund said something, just a matter of time before he spoke. And now he had, and there would be no marriage.

He wanted a woman with beauty.

Laura stared at the reflection regarding her from the mirror set above the washstand.

Tears thick in her throat she watched the tide of hot colour rise in her face. Why had she not realised it before . . . why had she been so blind? She was not the woman Edmund wanted, not the woman any man would want. Beneath the cheap cotton night-gown her small breasts heaved as she drew a long sobbing breath. Why could she not have been born beautiful?

Blinking the almost blinding moisture from her eyes she set the brush back in its place. How would it have felt to be held in Edmund Shaw's arms? Walking slowly to the bed she tried to dispel the thought that only added to the hot flush in her cheeks, but despite the effort it refused to be dismissed.

Turning back the covers she climbed into bed.

The nearest she had come to that was the time he had lifted her down from the branch of a tree she had climbed against his warning that she would get stuck. His hands had closed about her waist and as he lowered her to the ground he had held her against him, steadying her. She had thought many times of that happening, wondering at the lack of emotion other than relief. There had been no rush of feeling, no breathless magic, no quickening of the heart. But in fairness to Edmund she had to remember she had been only twelve years old, far too young to know the emotions that heralded love of a woman for a man.

Turning off the lamp she drew the covers up over her breasts. But she was no longer twelve years old. She was nearing twenty-one, almost of age and a grown woman, yet Edmund had not attempted to hold her since that day; never touching her, never taking her hand even on the few occasions they found themselves alone together. It had not really given her cause for thought and certainly not concern; she had seen it as natural reticence on his part, an idea that such was a familiarity that must wait until after they were married. No, she had not seen anything unusual in his behaviour, but then what did she really know of behaviour between two people in love? Truth was she knew nothing but dreams, dreams filled with a rapture that in her childishness she wanted to last for ever. But she was no longer a child, she could no longer allow herself to get lost in fairy tales; romance was for stories, love would come after marriage. And marriage to Edmund Shaw would have proved a solid basis to her life even without the heady excitement of her dreams, and she would have been satisfied with that.

Crooking an arm over her eyes Laura felt despair wash over her. All she had hoped for was gone, and she was left with nothing.

But that was not true. She had her father and he held half of Shaw and Cadman. They would work together until finally she would be ready to take the burden from his shoulders.

Clinging to the thought, using it as a shield against the coldness of despair, Laura dropped into fitful sleep, a sleep filled with a detached, empty voice.

'. . . you can't be called pretty . . . the sort of woman you can never be . . .'

Slowly the fingers clutched about his wrist gave up their struggle to hold on. Moment after terrifyingly long moment he held the pillow down, leaning all his weight upon it. Beneath it the muffled cry had been silenced as its softness filled mouth and nose, and now the threshing of the one leg that held movement was weak, almost still, the pressure on his wrist lessening.

Bent double over the bed Edmund Shaw jerked breath into his lungs, blinking perspiration from his eyes. Hold on! He must hold on! What if someone came now, came into the room with that figure in the bed not yet dead? A ripple of fear ran through him, jangling his nerves like bells on a string. But they would not come! He jabbed the pillow hard down, they would not come . . . they would not come!

Everything was still. The hand that had clutched on to his wrist, that had clung stubbornly to life, fell back on to the covers.

His own hands locked tight on each side of the pillow, tiny spots of moisture dripped from his jaw on to its surface, spreading small damp patches. But he did not release the pressure of it, did not straighten, only stood listening to the rasp of his own tortured breathing.

It was over!

He stared down at the pillow.

At last it was over!

His glance slid sideways to where the arm lay motionless, the fingers still partly curved like a claw.

His life of jumping to this man's every little word was over!

Sucking air in short, hard breaths he relaxed his elbows, letting his whole tight body rest on his wrists.

He was free! From this moment he was free. Never again must he run to anyone's bidding. Edmund Shaw was free, free to be his own man.

A spot of perspiration fell from his chin on to the back of his hand, the touch of it making him start. He must take care, make everything appear normal.

Gingerly, fingers still gripped tightly into the folding softness, poised to do again that which he had done moments before, he raised the pillow.

Breath snatched into his mouth was locked in his throat, and his stomach lurched. Tongue half in, half out of the gaping mouth, eyes wide and filled with the horror of understanding stared back at him.

Jabez Shaw was dead!

For a moment he wanted to run, to get away from this house, away from this body in the bed. But that was all it was, a body . . . a dead body. He forced himself to release the breath from his throat, willed himself to look once more at the face grimacing up at him. Jabez Shaw was no more than a carcass on any butcher's slab and, dead, he could tell no tales nor could he marry Isaac Cadman's daughter. There would be no other son to take his place!

Edmund laughed, a short wild laugh that echoed in his throat, running into the shadowed corners of the room, folding itself away in their purple depths.

The man who called himself his father was dead and he was free!

Perspiration trickling down the path it had made from brow to chin he laughed again, but this time it was softer, more controlled, the wildness of hysteria replaced by cold calculation.

Dead men did not speak. He looked more carefully at the features crying out in death. The red flush of anger was already beginning to fade, the eyes glazing over.

No one would suspect. If he were careful no one would suspect.

'. . . *It could happen again at any time . . . no one can predict . . .*'

Words the doctor had spoken after that first stroke five months ago whispered from the dark caverns of his mind. No one could tell, no one could predict. Pushing upright he breathed long and slow. Who was ever to know he had killed Jabez Shaw?

A smile curving his thin lips he plumped the pillow held in his hands, smoothing the indentations on either end, wiping out the hollows where his fingers had gripped it.

'You won't tell will you, Jabez?' He laughed softly. 'You won't tell and neither will I.'

Leaning forward he grabbed the wealth of brown hair, only the temples were touched with grey. Twining his fingers into it he snatched the head towards him. Replacing the pillow he released his fingers, the smile on his mouth deepening as the head flopped backwards.

Blinking perspiration from his eyes he drew another steadying breath. One thing at a time, check everything, he must check every detail; nothing must look out of place, everything must appear ordinary.

First the body! The smile fading, he hesitated. Chest tight with breath once more locked inside it, he looked at the dead face, the open mouth screaming silently up at him, the accusing eyes condemning him.

It had to be done. If he was to be safe it had to be done!

Swallowing hard, lids squeezed tightly down over his eyes, his hands balled into fists.

It had to be done!

Eyes flicking open, breath still caged, he reached forward. One hand still screwed hard, the other trembling, he reached towards the dead face.

Middle finger and thumb hovered . . . *it had to be done* . . . his stomach lurching again he jabbed finger and thumb on to the cooling eyelids, drawing them down over those unbelieving, panic-lit eyes, breath juddering from him as he touched the dead man.

Good, that was good! Dragging his forearm across his brow he wiped moisture away with his sleeve. But it was not done with yet. At any moment someone might knock at the door, someone might come and find them like this. Revulsion rising like sickness, threatening to choke him, Edmund forced his hand forward again.

Turning back the bed clothes he straightened the leg that had bent in its thrashing, then, uncurling the fingers that had curved in on themselves as though even in death they sought to keep their hold on him, he laid the arm alongside the body and replaced the covers. Finally, teeth gritted, he placed his hand beneath the jaw, lifting it closed.

Standing upright, breath rasping from him, he ran a glance over the bed. All was smooth, all as it ought to be, except . . .

Turning, he crossed quickly to the heavy old-fashioned washstand Jabez insisted upon keeping. Taking up the hairbrush kept beside the bay rum Jabez was partial to using as a hair dressing he returned to the bed.

Confidence building with every move, the smile returned.

From tonight Edmund Shaw would be master in this house, and from tonight he would be master at Shaw and Cadman. Come morning every man and boy would run to his orders, and that would include Isaac Cadman. There would be one master and one only; and that one would be him. 'Thank you, Jabez,' he murmured, 'thank you for the legacy.'

Bending over the bed he drew the brush over the bushy hair, tidying the strands tousled by the pillow.

'We must have you looking your best, Jabez.' He laughed, the sound issuing from his lips soft and sibilant, completely devoid of remorse. 'It is not your wedding you are going to but still we can't send you off looking anything but your best.'

Returning the brush to the washstand he stood looking at the figure lying peaceful now with eyes and mouth closed. All looked as it should. Sheets unrumpled, pillows smooth and body relaxed; there was nothing to say Jabez Shaw had not died naturally in his sleep.

'no one could predict . . .'

His smile pure satisfaction he walked slowly back to the chair, drawing it even closer beside the bed. Sitting on its edge he folded one arm beside the motionless body, lying his head on his sleeve. Reaching his other hand to where that of his father lay beneath the covers he closed his eyes. The dutiful son would be found comforting his father to the last.

Chapter Four

'You be worrying over-much wench, your father be tired that's all, just tired.'

Her hands in the baking bowl, Laura Cadman remembered the words of the elderly woman who had sat in this kitchen a little over a year ago. Abigail Butler had been a neighbour and a friend of her mother for many years and to Laura she had been like a second mother, forever ready with a word of practical advice and when necessary a word of comfort; and it seemed of late those words had become necessary more and more often.

'P'raps there be a bit of a rough patch at the works,' Abbie had gone on. *'According to what I hears in the town it be hard all over, folk be talking of the sack.'*

'Father has not spoken of there being anything wrong at the works and certainly not of men losing their jobs.' Laura remembered her answer as she dusted flour from her hands then reached for the dish she had already greased.

Abbie had watched her line the dish with the soft pastry, her head nodding approvingly.

'There you be then, it be like I said, the only thing wrong with Isaac Cadman is that he be over tired.'

But that had been a year ago. Laura filled the lined dish with meat and potato then covered it with a pastry lid. A year in which he had shown no sign of improvement. He did spend too many hours at the works and when at home he did not rest enough but sat into the small hours keeping the books.

Brushing a film of milk over the pastry crust, Laura smiled at the thought of what Abbie had said when she had told her that.

'*They should have a man paid to do a job like that, a what you calls 'em . . . a countin' man.*'

'*An accounts clerk.*' She had hidden her smile as she had said that. Abbie became indignant when she was corrected over what she termed 'high falutin' fancy words that meant nothing'.'

'*Ar, one o' them!*' The answer had been sharp.

'*There was a clerk employed to keep the accounts,*' she had replied. '*But he was dismissed six years ago. Father did not say why but since that time no other clerk has been appointed, Father has done all of the book keeping himself.*'

Carrying the pie across to the fireplace Laura balanced precariously on one foot, using the toe of the other to release the latch on the door of the oven and swing it open, remembering the woman's caustic reply.

'*I've no doubt there ain't been no man given that job nor do I doubt old Jabez Shaw will go on letting Isaac do it. I don't see that one sitting up 'til the devil squeals, least not with no counting books I don't!*'

The pie in the oven, Laura took a corner of her apron to protect her fingers as she closed the door then pressed the latch into place. There were many differences between her father and Jabez Shaw, the keeping of accounts being one of the least of them.

'*Then there be that son of his.*' The thoughts ran unchecked in her mind, bringing back memories. '*Why ain't it he can't have the adding up of figures, he do have a brain don't he?*'

Back beside the table Laura gathered remnants of pastry, squeezing them into a ball. Setting it on an enamel plate she carried it to the oven, slipping it on to a shelf below the pie. This was a regular practice, she liked watching the birds gather in the yard to feed from it.

'*Edmund too works long hours.*' Her defence of Edmund Shaw circled her mind as she straightened. She had always been quick to defend him . . . but what now, now that he was no longer the man she thought to marry? But that must not cause a difference, it must not give rise to rancour. She must be as fair in her dealings with him as he had been in his dealings with her. So the answer was yes: supposing he were wrongly spoken of, she would defend him.

'*I ain't denyin' he does!*' Abigail had persisted as Laura's thoughts persisted. '*But I warrant they don't be near the length of them as Isaac Cadman keeps. I've no doubt Edmund Shaw sees his bed enough hours to rest his body!*'

As she did now, Laura had piled cooking utensils into the large earthenware baking bowl and carried them into the scullery for washing. Not to be put off, Abigail had followed behind.

'*Edmund will see to it that changes are made once he inherits his share of the business, he will insist Father does not do so much.*'

Returning to the kitchen to fetch the kettle filled with boiling water, the thought of how quickly she had once more jumped to Edmund's defence edged into Laura's mind.

Pouring the hot water into a white enamelled bowl stood in the shallow brownstone sink, she cooled it with water fetched from the pump. Reaching a bar of Sunlight soap from a shelf she held it in her hand, whisking it in the bowl of water until a skim of bubbles danced in ripples on the surface.

'*So Edmund is to be put in charge of the works . . . . ?*'

Abigail had put her question as Laura had proceeded to wash the crockery.

'*. . . and when be this to come about?*'

Plunging the mixing bowl into the warm soapy water Laura scrubbed at a patch of dried potato just as she had that day, trying to avoid having to answer; but, as it had then, the answer came.

'*Edmund has not said exactly, his father has not set any definite date.*'

The older woman had taken the bowl from her, balancing it expertly in one hand while rubbing the drying cloth over it with the other.

'*Edmund Shaw in charge of them works. Not while his father lives. Jabez*

Shaw be too fond of holding the reins to pass the cart to another. His son might well have been promised a lot of things but what Jabez will give could prove summat different entirely.'

Carrying the enamelled bowl into the yard Laura tipped the water into the channel that carried it away. Edmund had once said much the same thing and there had been such anger in his voice, so much hostility, it had made her stop and stare at him. But then he had given one of his rare smiles and said he was simply joking. But the look in his eyes had said otherwise.

The rest of the dishes dried and the towel draped over the length of line strung across the scullery, Abigail Butler had watched her replace the bowl in the sink; not all of her questions had been asked.

'*This idea of Edmund Shaw taking his father's place . . .*' she had said bluntly, '*how do Isaac take to the idea of the son becoming the partner?*'

It had made her think, and now all these months later the memory of that question brought the same reaction. Gathering the cutlery into the earthenware bowl, Laura's brow furrowed as she carried them back to the kitchen. Edmund had made no mention of that and neither had her father, in fact the more she had thought about that the more she realised how little she had been told.

'*I have not asked.*' She had answered truthfully then turned away, not wanting the perplexity that suddenly rose to her eyes to be seen by the other woman.

Now, alone in that same kitchen, Laura felt again that niggle of uncertainty. There had been a time when her father had told her all that transpired at Shaw and Cadman, discussed matters arising at the works openly with her, seeming so often to value her opinion.

Putting each utensil in its place she tried to drive away the memories of that discussion but, like the phantom of some unpleasant dream, they refused to be banished.

She had turned away yet somehow she knew Abigail had not missed the frown or the puzzled tone of her answer. Placing the kettle she had refilled in the scullery on the bracket above the fire, she had turned to Laura.

'*You ain't asked!*' It had been said quietly but the underlying emphasis held a deep concern. '*Then mebbe you should, or failing that ask what is to be done with Isaac Cadman's share!*'

Laura had turned about this time, the puzzled look going unveiled in her wide eyes.

'*I . . . I don't understand . . . what do you mean?*'

'*Put them cups down and listen, a cup of tea will taste all the better for the waiting of it.*' Taking the cups from Laura she had put them on the table, then taking her hands had almost pushed her into one of the two chairs drawn each side of the hearth before settling herself in the other and talking quietly.

'*Sit you still for a while, Laura wench, for there be summat as I have to say and say it I be going to, no matter if you tells me I be putting my nose where it ain't wanted.*'

The frown that had settled over Laura's brow deepened.

'*You know you can say anything to me, Aunt Abbie.*'

Laura remembered the smile that had come to the woman's mouth at her use of the courtesy title. It had always pleased Abigail to be addressed as such.

Then the smile had faded and the older woman had shaken her head. '*You says that now but chances be you will pipe a different tune when you hears what it be is biting my tongue.*'

She had waited for no answer. Glancing at the chair Laura seemed to see the figure of her friend sat there, her shoulders hunched as she leaned forward, her lined face set in firm determination.

'*Laura wench, you be a child any man would be proud to call his own and a daughter any mother would hold as precious. But that be it . . .*' She had tossed her head then in a kind of hopeless gesture. '*. . . that be the whole crux of what has played on my mind these many years, ar and played on your mother's mind the same. You be a wench, a daughter. Isaac Cadman has no son. He may leave all he has, everything he has worked a lifetime for to you but it can only be yours until you wed, for on that day not only do you give*' *yourself to the man you marries, but you gives to him every last thing you owns. Think of it. Every penny your father and your mother have put aside for you will go to your husband. We might be approaching a new century but the year 1900 won't bring much in the way of change for a woman, they will still belong heart and soul to the man they marries. Ask yourself, Laura, do you want that man to be Edmund Shaw? Ask it and ask it well, for once done it cannot be undone. A marriage vow be for life!'*

She had asked herself that question once Abigail had left and repeated it often in the months that followed, and each time the answer had been roundabout, never an unthinking yes. But she need ask it no more. Unaware of having crossed to the hearth, she sank into a chair. Edmund had answered and his answer had held no hesitation. He did not want the money her parents must have put aside for her, he did not want Isaac Cadman's share of the business and nor did he want Isaac Cadman's daughter!

'It be no business of mine.' The memories went on dancing through her mind like flames in the fire. *'But that don't mean it don't give me concern. You have been like a daughter to me since you was in swaddling clothes and I could not feel more for you if you had been born of me, that be why I risks our friendship by speaking as I do . . . that be my reason for saying think on what you do and think even more on the son of Jabez Shaw.'*

'It . . . it was always understood . . . our parents planned . . .'

Abbie had shaken the grey head vehemently, her faded eyes growing bright with truth. *'No, wench, your mother never planned that. We was friends from being babies, your mother and me. We two had no secrets from one another and this her told me many times. Though her would not say it to your father, her held no faith in Jabez Shaw and none in his son. Deep was the word she used of that lad. I don't know, Abbie, her would say to me, I don't know why but I don't trust that lad of Jabez Shaw, he is deep . . . deep and secretive. No, Laura, if it were planned you be given to that man then it were no doing of your mother's!'*

Those words had returned to haunt her many times since their saying and the shock of them never lessened. Even now, knowing what she did, they still shook her. She had never once thought . . . never guessed . . .

The answer, though in her mind, seemed to ring in the quiet warmth of the kitchen and her hands twisted together as they had that afternoon, the same emotions pulling at her heart.

'*But my mother liked Edmund. She welcomed him whenever he came here and she was always pleasant to him each time we paid a visit to his parents' house.*'

Laura watched the kettle begin to steam gently above the fire but her inner eyes saw the older woman push the bracket aside then lean forward to touch her hand.

'*Good manners teaches we be pleasant to all folk, lessen they gives cause to be otherwise. Jabez and his son never give your mother cause, least not any spoken cause and your mother's manners called for no teaching. You knows that as well as I does. But being pleasant to a lad don't necessarily mean you holds faith in him and Sarah Cadman . . . God rest her . . . held none in Jabez Shaw's lad. It were summat her could not rightly tell, summat her never could put her finger on but in her own heart her knew . . . Edmund Shaw was not entirely what he seemed, he did not show all of himself to the world.*'

Why had her mother not said anything to her? Even as the query rose in her mind it was dispelled. How could her mother talk of such a thing to an impressionable fourteen-year-old girl?

'*Then . . . then my mother did not want me to marry Edmund.*' Once again memory invaded her thoughts.

'*I ain't said that, nor would I!*' Abigail had withdrawn her hand and sat upright, though her eyes had stayed on Laura's. '*Your mother wanted what you want, same as I does. Your happiness was her only concern, same as it be my reason for speaking out now. Your mother would never have spoken. The choice must be Laura's was what her said, and if it were yours entirely then no word of her need be spoken. Sarah Cadman never went against her husband in anything, only in this was her prepared to speak. But her was gone long afore you could make your choice, long afore her counsel could be given; for that reason and for the esteem in which I holds her friendship I tells you again, think well afore you makes your promise.*'

Turning her head Laura stared about the empty room as if looking for the mother she had loved and the woman who had been her friend.

'*But I thought they both wished Edmund and me to marry, that they had always hoped we would.*' Thoughts drifted back into her mind, meeting their answer in its silent sphere.

'*Isaac . . . maybe.*' Abigail had risen then, her dark skirts brushing the stone floor as she fetched the tea caddy from its shelf on the dresser. '*And Jabez most certainly. With you married to his son then he will own Shaw and Cadman down to the last screw.*'

Her mother had held no faith in Edmund. Half-stunned by what she had heard Laura had watched the other woman's deft movements, spooning tea into the pot then scalding it with water from the bubbling kettle. Her happiness was all her mother wanted even should her daughter's marriage to Edmund Shaw cause herself heartache.

'*No he would not, my father would still own half.*'

Out of the shadows that veiled the past Laura saw Abigail Butler pause to look at her, her eyes filled with ancient wisdom. Carrying the teapot to the table she had set it on a delicately wrought iron trivet, stirring the contents before she looked across the room once more.

'*Ar, Isaac will hold what be his, but only so long as he lives. On the day he dies then all he had comes to you and remember that this country don't allow no woman to run things for herself, not while her has a husband, nor do I suppose the day to come when it ever will. So you ponder well who you gives his portion to; it don't be so bad when the man be one you loves truly, but do you love Edmund Shaw . . . really and truly love him?*'

How could she have answered that! Over the fire steam hissed from the blackened spout of the kettle but the sound went unheard, lost in the turmoil of Laura's thoughts. How could she have told if she loved Edmund, how could she really tell now? What was love . . . what did it feel like? There had never been any wild beating of her heart when she saw him, no catching of her breath when he smiled, no feeling of loss or emptiness when he left, no pain of parting until last night . . . But were all or even any of those feelings significant of love? No one had ever told her as much, so were they simply fruits of her own imagining, did none of those emotions occur and, if not, was it of any consequence?

One question followed another, each chasing an answer that was not there.

Abigail had seen the uncertainty in her face and her own had shown sympathy. '*I knows you be all at sixes and sevens.*' She had handed out a cup of hot, sweet tea. '*You don't be really knowing what it is your heart be wanting but I tells you this. If it don't be as it has told you you want Edmund Shaw more than you want tomorrow's sun to rise then it don't be true love you holds for him, not the love a woman holds for a man her be willing to give her life to. Your mother said the choice of a husband should be yours and yours alone, but be sure you knows your own mind sufficient to make that choice!*'

The words had weighed heavily between them as the older woman had resumed her seat, the silence almost oppressive as it was now. Outside in the street a hawker called his wares but Laura remained unmoving, memories her only reality.

'*Has he spoken yet?*' Abigail had asked, sipping her tea. '*Has Edmund Shaw asked you become his wife?*'

Laura had shaken her head and, though there had been no answer, the lined face clearly showed the thoughts flicking through her friend's mind. Jabez Shaw's son must be all of twenty-five years. Most men in Wednesbury were wed by that age. If it was that Jabez and Isaac had settled on their children marrying, why had it not been done before this . . . was it a part of their strategy or was it something else?

Laura shifted in her chair, embarrassment tingling along her nerves. That was not all she had seen reflected in those old eyes. She had seen another, more crucial, question. Could it be due to Edmund Shaw himself, was it possible he did not want to marry Laura Cadman?

'*If he ain't asked then there be no need of any rush to answer.*' Abigail had broken the silence. '*All I be advising is this. Listen to your heart afore you speaks any word, listen to what it tells and you won't go wrong.*'

She had asked herself all of those questions over and over

again. Laura swallowed as her mind became still. Asked them, but learned nothing new. Surely what she felt for Edmund had been love, what else could it be?

But now Abigail, as well as her mother, was dead. There could be no more questions asked of them. But then there was no need of questions, what did it matter what she felt for Edmund, he himself had put an end to questions. He did not love her, he did not want her for his wife! But that knowledge did not ease the hurt, did not stop the pain. Listen to your heart, Abigail had said.

Her fingers gripping tightly together Laura closed her eyes, holding in the surge of emotion.

She had tried listening. But how did you listen to silence?

Chapter Five

Seated in a tiny room, its dusty glass windows looking on to the workshop Isaac Cadman ran a finger down the page of the accounts book. There was no real need to check the figures, Laura had a good grasp of book keeping and her knowledge of arithmetic was more than adequate; there would be no mistake in the totals. But it was not whether the columns of figures tallied that had him bent over the book, it was that one entry, the one for steel he said had been returned. Laura had spotted that but was it the only one of its kind she had spotted? It had to be; had she gone over the figures for previous months she would have found others of its ilk. But one would be enough if she mentioned it to Jabez, spoke to him of a load of steel bars that proved to be non-existent. Holding his head in his free hand Isaac closed his eyes against the damning figures. Why had he allowed this thing to happen . . . why had he given way?

But he had and now the evil of what he had done sat like a demon on his shoulders draining him of all he had hoped for, draining him of life.

Everything would be for Laura. That was what he and Sarah had decided when they were told the child would be the only one born to them. There would be no son to take his place, his partnership in the firm; but they would give their daughter all of the education a son would have, Isaac would teach her all he knew of the business. Except for the turning of a screw his daughter would have as much experience as Jabez Shaw's son; enough knowledge of the business to help make it grow. For that reason they had lived simply, a small house sparsely furnished, Sarah making her own clothes and those of the child. 'It will all be worth it,' she had said, 'put all you can into a bank and let it lie 'til our daughter be a woman.'

And he had done that. Week upon week he had laid most of his wage aside, profit shares being ploughed back into the business, a business of which half would be his daughter's, one that would see her comfortable for life.

But that bank account had long been emptied and now he was robbing the business he had worked so hard to build, stealing to pay . . .

The pen dropping from his fingers rolled off the book, rattling noisily across the table that served as a desk. Breath almost a sob in his throat, Isaac covered his face with his hands. He couldn't go on with this, yet neither could he end it. Life held him in a vice, a vice of his own forging. To tell his daughter would break her heart; worse still, it could destroy any hope of a suitable marriage. Secrets were dreadful things to hold in your heart, they brought misery to your days; but to divulge what was in his would be to shatter not only his life, that was as good as destroyed already, but it would shatter all of their lives, and most of all it would shatter Laura's. That must never happen.

Pulling in a ragged breath he ran his hands over his hair, the act of a man caught in some invisible trap. How much longer, how long before Jabez asked to see the books, how long before he found out his partner was a thief? Closing the ledger Isaac stared at it, the calls of workmen resounding off the glass of the dusty windows but finding no passage to his brain.

It was said a man's sin had a way of catching up with him. Breath shuddered again into his lungs. Isaac Cadman's sin had certainly done that. He had been such a fool! It wasn't as if he had been a child. He had been a man grown, a man in complete possession of his senses . . . yet where had been the sense in letting such a thing happen?

He had never told Sarah. The sin was his, he must bear the consequence of it alone. He could not mar her life with its burden nor would he let the shadow of it touch his daughter, not even should her protection mean the taking of his own life.

'Mr Cadman . . . Mr Cadman . . .'

The voice called from a long way off but Isaac blocked it out, wanting only the seclusion of his thoughts.

'Mr Cadman . . .'

It spoke again, louder, forcing consciousness to recognise it.

'It be the steel, Mr Cadman, you said to let you know when it got delivered, well the cart be 'ere now.'

Isaac's hands fell away from his head as he struggled to bring his thoughts back to the moment.

'Oh yes . . .' He touched a hand to the book lying closed in front of him. '. . . yes, the steel. I . . . I want to see it . . . I . . .'

'Be you all right Mr Cadman?' The workman took a step further into the room, concern on his sweat-streaked face. Isaac Cadman had not looked well for months, all the hands had remarked upon the fact; a man looking as sick as he did should be home in his bed.

'What!' Isaac frowned, rising unsteadily to his feet. 'Yes, Jonas, I be all right, just bent over the books a little too long. Tell the carrier I will be along directly. I want to see the quality of the steel the foundry has sent, I'll have no rubbish.'

'Right you be, Mr Cadman.' Jonas touched a finger to the peak of a dirty flat cap. 'I'll tell 'im what you says, there'll be no tipping of them bars 'til you says so.'

Watching the door close behind the man Isaac felt a terrible weariness descend upon him. What a pleasure it would be to walk out of this place, to take Laura and leave Wednesbury for ever. But that was a blessing he knew he could not pray for; no matter where he went or how far he travelled his sin would follow after him.

Placing the book in a drawer set into the table, he locked it with a key which he slipped back into the pocket of his waistcoat. Going out to the yard he checked the delivery. Nodding to the men to unload the horse-drawn wagon he turned back into the works, halting as a high-pitched voice piped his name.

Beyond the tall wooden gates held open by a heavy stone set at the base of each, a tow-haired lad waved his hand above his head as he called.

Eyes narrowing against the sun, Isaac peered towards the running figure. That were Amy Boswell's lad, young Tommy Boswell, but what had him running here?

'They be lovely, I likes 'orses I do.' The boy's breathing was hard as he raced into the yard, drawing to a stop beside the pair of great Shire horses.

''Ere, you be off, this be no place for you!' Jonas reached a hand to the collar of the boy's ragged coat, jerking him away from the horses.

'Tommy ain't 'arming 'em, Tommy likes 'orses.' The boy wriggled, trying to break loose.

'I don't give a bugger what you likes,' Jonas held on, 'you do what I says and take yourself off or I'll tan your arse for you!'

Bringing his foot sharp backwards against Jonas's shin the boy danced away as, with a shout of pain, the man released his hold.

'You don't be going to tan Tommy's arse, Jonas Small, ain't nobody going to tan Tommy's arse, you hit me and I won't tell what I been told to tell.'

'You ain't been told owt, you lyin' little toad!'

'Wait!' Isaac came back to the yard as Jonas began unbuckling the broad leather belt that circled his waist. 'Mebbe the lad has something to tell.'

'Don't go payin' no 'eed to him Mr Cadman, that one tells more lies than he takes breaths.'

'Tommy ain't lyin'! Tommy *was* told summat.'

'Oh, ar!' Jonas glared at the boy. 'Who by? The fairies were it, or p'raps it were the man in the moon?' He turned to Isaac. 'Don't pay no mind to him, everybody in the town knows he be five pence short of a tanner. Mutton-headed that's what he be, thick as a grorty puddin'.'

The lad was light on brain but he was not stupid. Isaac raised a restraining hand then smiled at the boy, his trousers several inches above his ankles, basin-cut yellow hair blowing across bright eyes.

'Did someone tell you to come here, Tommy?'

'Tommy likes 'orses, Tommy do.' The boy smiled, Jonas's threats already faded from his childish mind.

Isaac walked forward, his smile remaining. 'So do I, Tommy. You can stroke them if you like.'

''Orses don't shout, and they don't hit you neither, 'orses be nice.'

Pity for the lad, who at fourteen or more years should have been making a living for himself but instead was locked inside the mind of a five-year-old, welled inside Isaac. What sin had he committed to be so punished?

Standing beside the grinning youth Isaac raised a hand to the back of one of the animals, running it over the smooth coat.

'Tommy.' He spoke gently. 'Did someone tell you to come here to these works?'

Tommy nodded vigorously. 'Ar, Mr Cadman.'

Giggling like a young child Tommy touched his nose to the cheek of the horse. 'Somebody . . . somebody told Tommy.'

'Let me ask 'im!' Belt in hand, Jonas made for the boy but a swift shake of Isaac's head halted him, a backward gesture telling him to return to the workshop.

'Tommy.' Isaac waited until the bright eyes were turned to him. 'Tommy, have you ever had a ride on a horse?'

'Tommy ain't got no 'orse, so Tommy can't ride one can he?'

The answer contained more sense than ever the lad was given credit for. Isaac continued to let his hand play over the great smooth back.

'You could ride on this one, Tommy, all the way from here to the High Bullen.'

The bright eyes sparkled like sunbeams on water. 'Could Tommy ride one . . . could he truly?'

'Truly, Tommy.'

'All the way . . . all the way to the Bullen?'

Isaac smiled, reassuring the lad. 'All the way, Tommy.'

'Tommy would like that, Mr Cadman, Tommy likes 'orses.'

'But you have to be very sensible if you are to ride a horse.' Isaac's hand stilled, the velvet softness warm beneath his palm. 'You have to remember what you are told.'

'Tommy can remember what he be told, Tommy can remember lots of things.' The boy beamed.

'That's good, lad, that's very good, but you have to show me you can remember.'

'How?' Tall as Isaac, the youth jigged with childlike excitement. 'How can Tommy show you?'

'Hmmm!' Isaac pursed his lips, pretending to search his brain for a way. 'I know,' he said as the jigging threatened to get out of hand, 'if you can tell me who sent you here and what it was you were to say then I would think you sensible enough to ride on Caesar here.'

The grin faded from the boy's mouth but the jigging continued, though now it seemed to be more a dance of apprehension than of joy. 'That be two things to remember,' he pointed out, his lower lip jutting over the top one. 'Tommy has to remember two things!'

'There are two horses, Tommy.' Isaac's smile was steady. 'You could ride Caesar up along Dudley Street then change over and ride Emperor the rest of the way.'

'It were 'im up at the Shaw 'ouse.' The words fell from the lad's mouth, pushed out by the thrill of the promised ride. ''Im who does the gardens said to tell you to go see 'im.'

Enoch Baxter had said for him to go to see him at Jabez'

house! Isaac frowned. Perhaps it was as Jonas said, the lad lied without understanding what he did. Enoch Baxter would send no such message.

'Tommy.' He tried again, keeping patience in his voice. 'Tommy, are you sure it was Mr Baxter told you?'

The tow head bounced up and down. 'Tommy is sure, Tommy remembers. Tell 'im the master says for 'im to come right away, be sure you tells that to Mr Cadman his very own self. That was what Mr Baxter told Tommy to say, and I said it ain't I, Mr Cadman . . . Tommy remembered didn't he?'

Finding it hard to swallow against the nervous lump that suddenly blocked his throat, and even harder to hold on to his smile, Isaac nodded.

'Yes,' he murmured. 'Tommy remembered.'

There would be no more questions!

In her bedroom overlooking the yard Laura knelt to pull open the bottom drawer of a plain wood chest.

Abigail Butler would come to this house no more and there was no other to question her about Edmund . . . except, of course, her father.

The last coming as a sort of shock, she sat back on her heels. She had been so wrapped up in herself she had forgotten he too would have questions to ask.

And what did she tell him? Edmund Shaw does not wish to marry me, I am not pretty enough to become his wife. Or, perhaps, we have both decided that we would be happier not married to each other; that, anyway, was only half a lie for Edmund at least would be happier that way.

Would her father be unhappy at what had happened, would he understand Edmund's reasons or would he be angry? Angry enough to dissolve the partnership between himself and Edmund's father?

They could leave this house, leave Wednesbury. Find a new place to live, a place where no one knew them. Her father could make a new start . . .

No! Laura checked her thoughts. Her father was too old, too worn out to make a new start. He had poured his whole life into Shaw and Cadman, she could not let him throw it all away just to save her face; and that was what it would amount to, they would be leaving simply because she might find it too hard to face the truth.

There was bound to be talk. Folk in the street, the men at the works, they must all have expected the children of Isaac Cadman and Jabez Shaw to marry and when they did not there would be speculation and gossip, and not all of it kind. Could she face that, could she ignore pointing fingers and possible snide remarks? She would have to. She took a long breath as if already screwing up courage. She would face anything to save her father worry.

Reaching into the drawer she touched a hand to a damask table-cloth, its woven design gleaming like threaded silver. Abbie had taken her to Birmingham rag market, there they had spotted the remnant of cloth. 'Take a needle to it and it will make a cloth fit for a lord's table,' she had said after paying tuppence for it. Well Edmund Shaw was not a lord, and this cloth was no longer destined to cover his table.

Running her hand deeper into the drawer she rifled through cloths and pillow-slips, each beautifully hand sewn, each laid aside against her wedding day. But now there would be no wedding day, and this linen . . .

Closing the drawer abruptly she stood up. There was no sense in mooning over what was not to be. Life had to be lived! Was that not what Edmund had said? Then best to put the past behind her, for from where she stood it looked as though the future would hold as much misery as she could handle.

'*Isaac will hold what be his but only so long as he lives . . .*'

Downstairs in the kitchen Laura paused, a half-peeled potato in her hand. To put the past behind her was an easy decision to make but a very difficult one to carry out. Try as she would to block her thoughts, to prevent the images of yesterday returning to plague her, they somehow managed to slip into her conscious mind as this one had.

Everything that had been her father's would one day be hers. Giving up the effort to shut out all such thoughts Laura let them run freely. That would include his holding in the business. She, not her father, would be the Cadman in Shaw and Cadman.

How would Edmund take to that?

When he had stood in this kitchen last evening he had given her more than the decision not to marry her, he had given her a peep at an Edmund she had not seen before; a cold, almost callous Edmund, a calculating man who had no sympathies or interests other than his own, a man prepared to do anything and stop at nothing in order to benefit himself.

The potato forgotten, Laura stared in front of her, seeing nothing but the figure of Edmund Shaw.

She had not allowed herself to think such things. Even during the long sleepless hours of the night when she had dissected his every word, his every look, she had not allowed such thoughts access to her mind; yet now she knew they had always been there, buried deep in its darkest chambers but nevertheless there.

Edmund had always been kind to her. She had owned that much. But then he had always been first. His had been the decisions. Even when she was a child his had been the decision which flower to pick, what walk to take or which topic to talk on. Not that she had minded or seen any reason for things to be different. Edmund was so much more grown up than she was. So grown up he could not see things through her younger eyes? See her desires as well as his own . . . or too caught up by the need to dominate?

As a child she had not seen, as a woman she had been blind! Edmund Shaw had been kind to her as a child because she had been no threat to his authority, placed no obstacle in the path of his decisions.

But she was no longer a child. One day she would be his equal at Shaw and Cadman. Her voice would be heard, she would have equal say in policy. And if her word was different to that of Edmund . . . if her decisions did not coincide with his?

Returning to peeling the potato Laura felt a faint coldness touch her spine. She had been given a peep at an Edmund who had not shown himself before and he was one she did not wish to encounter again.

It had been only a brief look but it had been enough to force her to face reality. Edmund Shaw was not the man she had dreamed him to be, not one to take kindly to being opposed . . . or to deferring to a woman.

As he had faced her across this kitchen she had refused to recognise that brief glimpse, refused to admit that Edmund might not after all be the caring, gentle boy of her past.

Dicing the potato into a pot Laura felt her stomach tighten. Somehow she felt the doors to Edmund's true character, if flung wide open, would show a very different picture, one that could damage both their lives.

Was that what her future held? One day she would know, it was only a matter of time!

Chapter Six

Why had Jabez asked for him to go to the house?

Isaac Cadman's mind churned as he walked. What was so important it could not wait until evening? He had called at Jabez' house every night since the man had taken ill, called to discuss the day's business, keeping his partner informed of every detail.

Every detail! Isaac felt his nerves quicken. Not every detail. He did not speak of the so-called deliveries of steel for which payment was entered in the ledgers yet never settled in any account with a steel foundry, the oil it seemed was ordered then paid on delivery but never was, the bolts and screws sold and the money never shown.

It was lies . . . all lies! And every lie covered a robbery.

Crossing the market square he paid no mind to the hurrying women with baskets on their hips who clucked agitatedly at children hanging on to their skirts. He turned left into Spring Head which would lead him directly to the Walsall Road, and once there he could cross into Squire's Walk.

The houses there were spacious and airy with fine high-ceilinged rooms and large gardens. The one Jabez had built ten years ago even boasted an indoor privy.

How Sarah would have loved the luxury of that. No more trailing through all weather to the one they had at the bottom of the yard. But there had been no luxury in Sarah's life, he had given her no large house filled with costly furniture, no fancy shop-bought gowns. Instead they had made do with the two-up two-down in Great Western Street. She had never complained. Isaac's steps slowed against the rise of ground. Never openly compared what they had to what Jabez and Emma had, never questioned his reasoning, only ever agreeing that the money they took as his share of the business profits be laid aside for their child.

Yet that too had become a lie!

Hesitating before a fancy wrought-iron gate set between two stone pillars that stood half as high again as he did, Isaac swallowed hard. So many years of deception, so many years of waiting for the blow to fall and now at last it had. Jabez had found out about his thieving, his falsifying the accounts; why else would he send for him from the works?

He had left Jonas Small in charge there. Rightly it should have been Edmund. Isaac rested a hand on the decorative iron latch that held the gates. The lad knew the engineering business inside out, and so he ought for Jabez had seen to it he worked at every aspect of it; and that longer and harder than any hired hand and his output scrutinised even more closely. One wrong move had Jabez roaring like a bull. But even following the stroke of five months ago he would not countenance his son having any part of managing the works. Was there a reason for that, a reason deeper than the jealousy of an older man for a younger? Sarah had said that sometimes a man becomes jealous of his first-born son, resentful of the love his wife devotes to it, but Isaac could never quite accept that for how could any man be jealous of his own child, his own flesh and blood . . . !

Pushing against the gate, he felt the guilt that was never distant from him rise like a cold tide flooding his heart. She had suffered so much, he had seen it often in her gentle eyes, but not once had she complained, never asked for more than he gave and he . . .

The door opened almost at his first knock, the maid whispering that the master would see him 'in there', pointing to what Jabez proudly termed his study, though the only thing Isaac had known him to study in that room had been the various brands of whisky he had come to drink more and more.

Jabez had not come into the hall to greet him as was his usual practice . . . but then it was not his partner's usual practice to call him away from the works.

Guilt giving way to speculation then speculation to fear, he followed the neatly uniformed figure towards the study.

A timid tap to the door that gave on to the shared yard brought Laura up from the dark depths of yesterday. She had not spoken of Edmund's visit to her father but it had not left her mind for a moment. Why . . . why had Edmund let her go on thinking . . . ?

A second tap followed by hushed voices clearing the remnant of thought, she laid aside the pan she was scouring, drying her hands on the rough cloth and flinging it back over the length of line stretched across the scullery.

Outside in the yard small voices piped in disagreement.

''Alf that 'appenny be mine, I run that errand same as you so I should 'ave a say in the spendin' of it . . .'

'You'll 'ave what I say you'll 'ave or you'll get nowt!'

'I wants a bull's eye . . .'

'You'll get a bloody black eye if you keeps snivellin', now shut up!'

Running her hands over her hips Laura smoothed the apron she had scrubbed as often as the drying cloths, an echo of a smile touching her mouth.

The Bailey boys had miraculously found a way to earn themselves a halfpenny and now they were itching to spend it, buying themselves sweets. But, just as they ever did when paid a farthing or a halfpenny, they did not carry their prize to the market place where it might buy half a broken meat pie or a loaf of three-day-old bread; they brought it to 'Missis Laura'.

'If I don't get a bull's eye I'll tell Mother on you, our Alfie, then you'll get a lampin' for not 'anding that halfpenny over to her.'

'Oh, ar . . . !'

Laura crossed to the door, listening to the reply as she went.

'. . . so I'll get a good hiding and you'll get no suck! Neither a bull's eye nor nuthing else, 'sides which your arse will sting as much as mine 'cos I'll leather it first chance as comes . . .'

Smothering the smile that at best had been only a hint since Edmund had called, Laura opened the door, her gaze falling on the two boys whose red hair flamed the colour of fire.

'Oh it is you boys!' She pretended confusion. 'Now I could vow I heard an insalubrious use of language.'

'A what, Missis?'

Eyebrows pulled together over a nose deluged with freckles, the younger boy stared up at her with puzzled brown eyes.

'Subrious.' The older boy looked scathingly down his own freckled nose at his brother. 'You don't know nuthing! Subrious means cussing don't it, Missis Laura?'

Folding her hands in front of her, hiding her amusement, Laura regarded the older boy. 'It does indeed mean swearing, Alfie and I did hear, but who was it?'

'Must 'ave been the rag man.' The one she knew had been christened Edward but answered to nothing but Teddie smiled, an angelic innocence filling large toffee-coloured eyes. ''E was here a minute ago but we told him to go 'cos 'e was being subrious and me and Alfie don't like that, does we, Alfie, so we told him to go, didn't we?'

A perfect imitation of his brother's innocence painting his own pert face, Alfie nodded, his unhesitating answer displaying a consummate skill practised from earliest childhood.

'We did, Missis Laura, we told him to bug . . . be off, that you wanted no swearing outside your door.'

'Thank you, Alfie,' Laura answered, felling the smile twitch in her throat.

'That's all right, Missis.' Teddie grinned, showing a row of small square teeth. 'We don't like bloody cussing neither, do we, Alfie?'

Her mock primness completely destroyed Laura giggled, then turning back into the scullery pretended not to hear the older boy's expletive as he caught his brother a cuff about the ear.

Following her inside the house, the six-year-old holding a hand to an ear already turning crimson, they waited for Laura to speak.

Removing her apron and folding it over the length of line, she looked at faces alike as peas in a pod. They all knew the procedure, it was one they had played out many times before.

'We was wondering, Missis Laura, was there anything we could 'elp out with . . . p'raps an errand you wanted running . . .' Alfie said after she asked what she could do for them.

'Or mebbe some rubbish shifting,' Teddie piped up, 'we can tek it to the tip.'

'No, thank you.' Laura shook her head, as expert in the charade as both boys. 'But it was very thoughtful of you to call and ask, and so kind to send that awful rag and bone man on his way.'

'We told him . . .'

'Shut up, you pillock!' Alfie pushed a closed fist against his brother's shoulder blades. Then to Laura, 'We knowed you wouldn't want his kind hanging around the yard. You can't trust 'em to keep their hands in their pockets, and with your dad not bein' home . . .'

'It was fortunate for me you two came by when you did.' Laura lifted a hand to her throat in pretence of alarm, though it was an effort to suppress the giggle that still lurked there. 'I really must thank you both again.'

'Well if there ain't no way we can help . . .' Alfie turned away, then on a well-rehearsed afterthought swung back to face Laura, '. . . afore we goes p'raps . . .'

Thought of the treat that lay ahead being too much for Teddie, he broke in. 'What our Alfie be going all around the Wrekin to say be this, Missis Laura, we wants to buy a happorth of suck and me, I wants a bull's eye.'

'I've told you once . . .' Alfie's closed fist found its target, pushing Teddie off his feet and causing him to stumble, '. . . you play your face and you'll get nowt!'

One hand steadying the boy as he fell against her, Laura intervened. 'Now isn't that a coincidence, I made a few bull's eyes only last evening but they did go very quickly.'

Once more finding his feet Teddie wiped a ragged sleeve under his nose. 'Not all of 'em, Missis Laura, did they . . . ain't you got just one left?'

Lids shielding the smile in her eyes, Laura shook her head slowly. 'I really think the last one went to Cissy Porter, her mother bought it . . .'

'Sod it!' Teddie's lips curved downward. 'I told you, our Alfie, I told you to come to Missis Laura's right away 'stead of waiting to earn another halfpenny which we ain't been paid!'

'Tek no notice of 'im, Missis Laura . . .' Alfie treated his brother to another disdainful stare. ''E's just a snivel, 'e blarts at the least thing.'

'I ain't blarting!' An angry glare widening his brown eyes, Teddie shot his left foot sideways landing a heavy boot against his brother's ankle.

'Of course Teddie is not crying.' Laura stepped strategically between the two.

'We minded the man's hoss like he told we to, we even took it to the trough so it could take a drink; he promised to pay a halfpenny but when he come out of the Turk's Head he took off wi'out paying . . .'

Laura listened to Alfie's explanation, continuing to hide her smile as the younger lad broke in.

'Rode off wi'out a word he did . . . the tight-arsed bugger . . .'

'Teddie!' Laura lifted a hand to each hip, her glance falling on the younger lad. 'I may not have a bull's eye but I do have a tin of mustard, some of which I will spread on your tongue unless you stop your swearing.'

'But it is his fault ain't it, Missis Laura?' Teddie sniffed the tears collecting in his throat. 'It be our Alfie's fault; if he had come when I asked 'stead of arsin' . . . 'stead of 'anging about then I would 'ave had that bull's eye you sold to prissy Cissy.'

Unable to hold the smile any longer, Laura turned towards the kitchen. 'Well maybe it was not the last, come with me and we will see.'

In the kitchen the two boys stood close together, afraid to walk over quarries freshly scrubbed.

Carrying a large tray from the pantry, Laura laid it on the table. 'You can hardly decide from the doorway,' she said, watching two small tongues slide over drooling lips. 'Come and choose while I find something to wrap them in.'

'Won't 'ave to wrap mine!' Teddie darted to the table, one hand fingering his scarlet ear while his eyes feasted on the sweets laid like jewels before him.

Gleaming brown brandy balls, tiny ruby-red cherry lips, raspberry drops showing pink through a coating of white sugar, each more enticing than the other they held the children's gaze.

Returning again from the pantry, Laura felt a tinge of pleasure at the rapt faces. It was always like this when the local children came with their precious halfpennies to buy her sweets; the delight on their faces more than making up for the cost, for the halfpennies were never enough to cover their making.

'*You be daft giving them sweets away,*' Abigail had often told her, but the happiness on those small faces was all the payment she wanted.

Watching a few seconds longer she walked to the table, setting down a shallow enamel plate.

'You did 'ave one after all, Missis Laura, you did 'ave a bull's eye left.' Jigging from one foot to the other, the boy grinned his gratification, his glance swinging to the brother still regarding the tray of sweets. 'I wants that, our Alfie, I wants the bull's eye.'

'We only got a halfpenny.' Alfie's eyes roved the tempting display. 'You'll 'ave to do wi' what it buys . . . we 'ave to share. I know you, once your bull's eye be gone you'll blart until you gets what I bought for the others . . .'

'Well why not both choose, perhaps a halfpenny will be enough.'

'I choosed already!' Teddie's lips firmed mutinously. 'I wants the bull's eye.'

'Better give it him, Missis Laura.' Alfie sighed exasperatedly. Older by only two years he was used to a lifetime of handling the boy who had been passed into his care long before he passed into trousers. With three more even younger, his mother left him to look after Teddie.

'And what will you have?'

Another deeper-felt sigh issued from the boy's lips as he wiped a grubby sleeve over them. 'I'll 'ave some dolly mixtures if it be agreeable to you, Missis Laura, the young 'uns will like them.'

He was spending the whole of the precious halfpenny on his brothers and sisters, choosing nothing for himself. Laura scooped dolly mixtures into paper she had twisted into a cone. The look on his face told he longed for a sweet, any sweet, but Laura knew from talks with their mother that what he got was taken home for the younger children.

Handing over the cone-wrapped sweets she took the half-penny, dropping it in a drawer set in the table. Then as the boys turned away, the bulge in Teddie's cheek showing the bull's eye to be safely stowed in his mouth, she said, 'There is something you can do for me. I have just remembered I have a few things I would like taken to the tip and I really do not have the time to take them myself. Would you wait while I get them?'

Drawing the sweet-tasting saliva noisily on to the back of his tongue, Teddie could only nod, leaving Alfie to say yes they would wait.

Running quickly to her own room Laura collected a dress she had made from a length of brown worsted. There were years of wear left in it and she could scarce afford to give it away. But Mary Bailey's needs were greater than her own. Snatching a cotton petticoat from a drawer she bundled the two together, carrying them down to the kitchen.

'There are also a few stale bits and pieces in the pantry I would rather went out today,' she said, handing the bundle of clothes to Alfie. 'But if you cannot carry them . . .'

'We can carry 'em, Missis Laura.' Alfie's eyes lit up at sight of the dress. 'Teddie be only little but he be strong, ain't that right, our Teddie?'

Another noisy whoosh of saliva his answer, Teddie nodded vigorously.

'In that case I will get them.'

Inside the cool pantry Laura filled a basket with freshly baked mutton pie, a small left-over joint of pork and a wedge of cheese, topping it over with a sweet-smelling crusty loaf. Back at the table she covered it all with a piece of cloth.

'I should have thrown this lot out yesterday.' She smiled, holding out the basket and waiting while Alfie shoved the bundle of clothes into Teddie's hands. 'But I never got around to it.'

His eyes gleaming, Alfie tried to hide his delight. 'I knows 'ow it is,' he said solemnly. 'Mother says the same, there ain't enough hours in a day to do all as needs doing; but me and Teddie will get rid of this lot for you.'

Taking the halfpenny from the drawer Laura pressed it into the boy's hand. 'Will you return this to your mother with my apologies. I found I paid her a halfpenny short for the sausages she bought from the town the other day.'

Eyes wise as the ages, the boy nodded. 'I'll tell her, Missis Laura, and I'll bring the cloth and basket back.'

Leading the way into the scullery, Laura opened the door to the yard. 'Yes, please, I do not mean for that to be thrown on to the tip; but there is no hurry, tomorrow will do.'

Listening to the thud of boots as the two boys raced away, Laura felt the pleasure drain from her and heaviness returning to settle like a stone in her stomach.

Mary Bailey had a hard life, but she had a husband who adored her. Two days ago she herself had thought to have if not a husband who adored her, then at least one who would respect and care for her.

'. . . I want a wife who is beautiful . . . the sort of woman you could never be . . .'

Tears pricking warmly against her eyelids, Laura returned to the sink. Picking up the pan she had left off scouring, she stared hard at the plain, dark enamel.

Plain as everything in her life was plain. Plain as she herself was plain.

Has Jabez found out? Isaac stood as the maid tapped on the study door. Had he had Edmund bring the accounts ledgers home, had he studied them . . . found the amounts missing every month? But how could Edmund have taken the books without his knowing?

Like moths around a candle flame the thoughts flicked around in his head. Unless Edmund had gone to the works late at night, taken the ledgers from the office, returning them before the men turned up for work next morning . . . That must be it, there was no other way, just as there was no other reason for Jabez to summon him to his house.

'The master said for you to go in, Mr Cadman, sir.'

Bobbing the trace of a curtsy the maid looked at the man she had shown into the house so often, but never once in dust-ingrained moleskin trousers and muffler. Perplexion in her eyes she turned away across the hall, leaving Isaac to enter the study.

'So, you finally got here!'

Looking around from closing the door Isaac frowned, the

tightening of his mouth adding to the drawn quality of his features.

'Edmund . . . ?' He glanced about the room which boasted no book-lined shelves or writing desk, holding instead several leather-upholstered wing chairs with accompanying side tables and a pair of imposing rosewood cabinets whose contents, Isaac knew, consisted of nothing but an assortment of alcohol and a range of drinking glasses. '. . . Is Jabez not here?'

Sandy hair thrown straight back from a deep forehead, adding to long, too-thin features, Edmund Shaw raised a laconical eyebrow as he stared at the tired looking grey-haired man whose face was streaked where thin lines of perspiration had trailed through black dust.

'Does it look as if he is here?'

'But the maid said the master was in here.' Isaac sent another glance about the room.

'She was perfectly correct.' Edmund made no attempt to rise but sat with fingers spread on each arm of his comfortable chair.

Thin eyebrows drawing together more in irritation than perplexity, Isaac gave a half shake of his head.

'Look, lad, I have no time for the wasting and neither should you have; you should have been at the works hours since. If Jabez has gone back to his bed then I'll go see him in his room, and you, lad . . .'

Pale, almost colourless eyes glinted like spears of sunlight on winter ice and long fingers gripped at soft leather upholstery.

'No, Isaac, not "lad"! Not "lad" ever any more!'

Edmund's voice was low and lethally even.

'As for having time for the wasting . . . time is my own to do with as I please.'

'You'll jig a different measure when Jabez be back on his feet,' Isaac warned, turning to the door. 'Now whatever bug be biting you I advise you scratch it and then get yourself off to the works afore Jabez catches you hanging about the house; you know how easily he is riled and the doctor said . . .'

'I know what the doctor said.' His tone no less icy, Edmund continued to stare blandly at the man he had not invited to sit. 'But there is no need to worry on Jabez' account, he will not become riled; as for your advice, I do not thank you for it and I do not need it.'

'That be your answer, then I'll leave you with it, I have business with Jabez . . .'

'You have business with *me*.' The words rapped out, bouncing off the cabinets like ricocheting bullets.

'Not yet, Edmund,' Isaac reached for the door handle, 'you are not master here yet.'

'Short-sighted as always, Isaac.' Edmund laughed softly, a cold, vituperative laugh that barely cleared his throat. Letting the terseness of a moment ago fade from his voice he continued to stare at the spare, slightly bent figure against the door. The round wooden door knob cradled against his palm, Isaac felt a flicker against his spine and a new worry close threateningly about his heart. Turning to face Edmund, the dislike of him he had always tried to hide showing clearly in his faded eyes, he asked quietly, 'Where is Jabez?'

'Where you thought him to be,' one hand waved an indolent gesture, 'in his bed.'

Allowing one second for his gaze to rest on the face that featured neither of his parents, Isaac answered with a voice which, though quiet, disguised none of the aversion that rose in him.

'Then I will speak with him there, I always find it best to discuss matters of business with the master rather than the employee, be he son or no son.'

A swift pallor giving the only sign the barb had struck home, Edmund smiled.

'In that case you have no need to leave this room. You see, Isaac, I *am* master here; there will be no more conducting of business with Jabez, nor indeed of anything else. Jabez Shaw is dead . . .'

The shock of those words encompassing his mind, closing it off to the world, Isaac failed to hear the rest. Only when Edmund repeated his name in sharp succession did he return to the reality of the room and the man who was speaking to him.

'. . . that leaves me. But I am not your partner, nor am I any longer an employee. There are to be changes made at Shaw and Cadman, and not all of them will be agreeable to you, Isaac.'

Chapter Seven

The red-haired boys had returned the basket and cloth within the hour, relaying their mother's message of thanks. Laura smiled at the memory of those mischievous eyes and quick tongues. Mary Bailey need have no worries for those two, they were already wise to the ways of Alfie; rich men they might never be, but they would hold their own. But try telling Mary that! Laura's smile faded as she spooned dumplings into the pot of stew simmering over the fire. Like any mother uncertain where the next meal was coming from, and without a halfpenny to spend on anything but food, Mary Bailey worried for her brood.

Fetching the flat iron from the scullery Laura stood it on its end, the flat surface to the bars of the fire grate, then placed a shirt on the piece of old blanket folded across the kitchen table as an ironing pad.

At least that was one worry she would be spared. Now there was no prospect of marriage to Edmund, the prospect of a family of her own was also gone, she would never know the troubles of raising children. Nor the joys! The thought twisted like a knife blade in her chest.

'. . . *you can't be called pretty . . .*'

The words that had plagued her attempts to sleep all during the long hours of the night returned to mock her again. Edmund wanted a beautiful wife, and she could not be that woman.

Swallowing the lump that rose in her throat she picked up the iron, the weight of it heavy in her hand. Wetting the tip of one finger she touched the flat base, testing its heat. Her life had changed. In the space of a few minutes it had changed for ever. But it had not ended!

Wiping the hot iron over a scrap of clean huckaback to check that no dust from the fire clung to it, she ran it determinedly from tail to shoulder of the cotton shirt.

Life did not depend upon Edmund Shaw. She would go on as she had before, keeping house for her father, sharing his life . . . and when he was gone . . . ? Pausing, the iron in her hand, Laura stared at the window with its shutter of cotton lace closed against the street. What would her life be when she was left alone? But she would not think of that now! Placing the iron flat on the up-turned saucer next to the scrap of huckaback she folded the shirt, forcing her mind to remain on the task in hand. She would *not* think of that.

The laundry ironed and returned to its several places, Laura carried the flat iron back to the scullery, lifting it on to a shelf that ran along the wall. She might as well fill the coal bucket whilst she was here, it would save her father a task when he got home.

She was still in the yard when she heard it. The door to the street closing. It was Edmund! He had come back to tell her it was all a horrible mistake . . . that he did love her, he did want to marry her!

Straightening, she listened for his call. Any second she would hear his voice and surely now he would take her in his arms, hold her as he whispered his love. But the house remained locked in its own silence.

A tingle of apprehension running the length of her spine, she carried the coals into the scullery, setting the bucket beside the sink.

Why did Edmund not call her name . . . why did he not come to the scullery to find her? But Edmund never had come into the scullery, the same as he had never entered the house that way; yet no one else she knew ever called by coming in through the street door.

Reason dispelling the tingle, she rinsed her hands quickly. He was waiting in the kitchen, hoping to surprise her. A smile touching her lips she ran both hands over her hair, self-consciously smoothing wisps from her forehead.

Maybe she could not feign surprise but the happiness he would see in her eyes would be no pretence.

Coming into the kitchen her glance went immediately to the centre of the room where Edmund would be standing, apology darkening his pale eyes. Only Edmund was not there . . . no one was there.

But she had heard the click of the door! Laura frowned, then her glance taking in the rest of the neat little room she stiffened, her breath catching in her throat.

The funeral would be on Thursday. Three days was long enough to have that dead body in the house. Edmund flicked through the sheaf of papers he had taken from a drawer in his father's room. Having the interment take place so soon would doubtless give rise to gossip but that would not worry him, he would be no slave to convention; he had at last been given his own life and he would start as he meant to go on, by doing things to suit him rather than other people.

And that was what he had done today. He had done the thing he had wanted to do for years, what he had long dreamed of doing, he had begun to pay back the pain he had suffered.

The papers becoming still in his hands he stared at the fire blazing in the fireplace. He had sent for Isaac Cadman and watched that gaunt face as he had broken the news of his partner's death, watched the shadows first of guilt then of relief flicker in his eyes. With the death of Jabez a load had lifted from the other man's shoulders, but the weight of that load was as nothing compared to the one waiting to take its place.

His eyes watching the flames leap and dance into the chimney, Edmund's mouth curved in a cold smile.

Isaac Cadman's thieving would be made public knowledge. The whole town would know that for years he had systematically defrauded the books and robbed his partner, deceiving the man who trusted him most.

The smile deepened as Isaac Cadman's protests echoed in his mind.

'. . . I did not do it for myself . . . I ask you not to divulge to the public . . . think of Laura . . .'

But he would not think of Laura, nor of anyone ever again. From now on only his own feelings and welfare had meaning for Edmund Shaw.

He had listened to the other man, listened to the dozen and one excuses but the outcome had been decided from the beginning. Isaac Cadman would no longer play any part in the running of Shaw and Cadman Engineering!

He had watched the other man leave. Old already from the adversities of life and hard-grinding labour, he had aged half as much again as the decision was given him. He had shuffled from the house like a man in a trance. For the first time in years Edmund laughed with full enjoyment. A man in a trance! An apt enough description, for Isaac Cadman had certainly received a revelation, and soon many more would be given the same.

The man's thieving had been a double blessing for Edmund Shaw. He returned his glance to the papers in his hand. He could use that as an excuse for not marrying Laura, should one become necessary; secondly, and most important, it had given him virtually full control of the business.

Leafing slowly through page after page Edmund felt the balloon of exhilaration begin to deflate. He was sure it would be here, but then Jabez Shaw had not been exactly open with him, never a father to share his confidence with his son; nor his secrets!

Just what had Jabez carried with him to the grave? Not that it mattered.

Edmund turned another page, his glance flicking over the elegant, flowing copperplate of Jabez' handwriting. What mattered was what he had left behind. Left for his son to find! He almost laughed again at that. If only Jabez had known, known his end was so close, then no papers, not one iota of information of any sort concerning the business, would have been spared the flames.

Provisions merchants, butcher, coal, gas and wine merchants. Edmund frowned as the stream of bills paid and ones awaiting settlement went on; everything of no importance and none of what he was searching for. But there had to be one, it had to be somewhere. He had searched that bedroom from floor to ceiling and the same with the study, but had found nothing.

Impatience flaring, he threw the papers aside. Jabez could not have known. For all the dislike so evident between them he could never have guessed a son would murder a father. Yet the papers he searched for were not in this house. Had Jabez distrusted him so much as to place them elsewhere?

That must be the case. Jabez' deed of partnership with Isaac Cadman had been deposited either with his solicitor or at the works.

Ignoring the scattered bills, Edmund strode from the room. It was an irritant having to go and look for the agreement but no more than that. Yet he would find it, and be fully conversant with the terms laid down before Jabez' will was read.

Outside the large red-brick house that had been built to Jabez' own design, Edmund lifted his face to the pale April sunshine. His father's will!

Everything would be his. Dislike him as Jabez had, there was no other son or even a daughter to leave his worldly goods to. No, apart from maybe the odd bequest, the house, the business and everything else that just last night had belonged to his father was now his, and the thought was a pleasurable one. As pleasurable in its way as was the other locked in his mind. He had told Isaac Cadman the fiddling of the works' books would be broadcast to the town. What he had not mentioned was the fact that robbery had an even more serious consequence. The penalty a thief must pay was a term of imprisonment and, in such a case as this, possibly a very long term.

The sun warm on his face, Edmund smiled.

And Isaac Cadman would serve that sentence!

'Father?' Breath held for seconds rushed out, carrying the word with it. 'Father!' Laura ran to the chair drawn against the hearth, sinking to her knees beside the figure slumped in it, his head resting in his hands. 'Father, are you ill?'

A shake of the grey head her answer, Laura fought the panic rising inside her. She had never in her life known her father to come home from the works at this hour; and with the way he was sitting, his face was hidden from her. Something had to be wrong, badly wrong, and if it was not that he was ill then what was it?

'Father, what is wrong? Tell me, please.'

'Jabez.' The answer was quiet with shock, the tone one of disbelief. 'Jabez is dead.'

'Dead!' Laura gasped. 'When . . . how . . . ?'

'Last night is when.' Isaac's voice shook. 'As to how, it seems he passed away in his sleep . . . another stroke. The doctor said as how that could happen.'

Sitting back on her heels Laura let the news sink in. Edmund had made no mention of his father feeling unwell again, but then perhaps a stroke gave no indication of that sort, perhaps it struck without warning.

'Did Edmund tell you at the works?'

'No.' Dropping his hands to his knees, Isaac stared at the kettle steaming on the bracket. 'He . . . he sent for me to go to the house.'

'Poor Edmund.' Her immediate thoughts for the man who such a short while ago had told her he would not marry her held only pity. 'It must be terrible for him, such a shock.

Perhaps we should go to him, Father, he will need support.'

'No!' Isaac's glance swung to her, his mind searching for an excuse. 'He will be best left alone for a while, get the worst of his grief over in private; a man does not care to be seen in tears.'

'But we are like family, you and Uncle Jabez were such friends, surely Edmund would want you beside him . . .'

'No, Laura, let things be for a while at least.' Reaching for her hand Isaac held it between his own callused ones. 'If Edmund wants my help he will ask for it.'

If! Laura frowned. *If* Edmund wanted help! Her father made it sound as if the offer were already refused. But that was impossible. Edmund had refused marriage, he had not refuted friendship.

Kissing her father's cheek she stood up. 'This has been a dreadful shock for all of us, Father, as much for you I think as for Edmund. Why not go upstairs and rest for a while? Surely there is no need for you to return to the works today, Jonas Small can manage until tomorrow.'

His glance swinging back to the steaming kettle, Isaac drew a long breath, and when he answered the tremble was back in his voice. 'Jonas Small is going to have to manage for a lot longer than today.'

The frown still nestling between her brows deepened and the earlier feeling of panic gave way to a more solid, colder fear. 'I don't understand, Father, what do you mean? Why must Jonas manage for a lot longer than today?'

A long sigh escaping his lips, his head slumping back against the chair, Isaac closed his eyes. Watching the shadows of pain cross features dark with weariness, Laura felt the nerves of her stomach contract. What had happened at the works . . . was it only the news of Jabez' death which had her father looking and sounding so depressed or was there more . . . something her father had not told her?

Behind her a coal fell from the grate into the hearth, the slight noise causing her nerves to quicken further.

'Sit down, Laura.' Isaac's eyes opened but his head remained resting against the chair back. 'There is something I have to tell you. The news of Jabez' passing was not all of what Edmund Shaw said to me today, he also said it would no longer be advisable for me to be part of the works' management.'

'But . . . but that is absurd!' Wide eyes darkening in disbelief, Laura stared at the tired face. 'You are a partner in the firm, half of it belongs to you; how can Edmund say it is inadvisable for you . . . ?'

'Laura . . . Laura, listen . . .' Isaac's eyes rested on hers. '. . . He was right, Edmund was correct in what he said.'

'But he can't be . . .'

'Laura child, listen to me. Today I was as good as given my tin; like any other employee who proves unsatisfactory I was dismissed.'

'But why . . . for what reason?'

Either not hearing the question or else ignoring the asking of it, Isaac continued to speak.

'I thought it was Jabez sent young Tommy Boswell to ask me to go up to the house but when I got there it proved to be Edmund. He was different somehow. He has never been what you might call a pleasant lad but today he was . . . I don't know. To say he seemed happy is an unkind thing given the circumstances, but it is the nearest I can get to the truth of what showed in his face, happy that his father was dead and happy to be giving me the sack.'

Fingers twisting together on her knee, Laura bit back the reply rising quickly to her lips.

'He must have hoped on this day for a long time, longed for the moment he could be sole master of Shaw and Cadman even if it be in name only; and that is what he will be from now on. He bided his time, waiting like a cat waits for a mouse and now he has pounced. He knew about the books, and I think you knew something too, Laura, knew of the payments for non-existent deliveries. But you did not know how long the embezzlements had gone on. Years, Laura . . .' His mouth twisting with the pain of what he said, he held his breath for a moment then went on. '. . . for years I have stolen money from the business and now I am found out. Should I try to return to the works or to have any more to do with it then the town will know of the fact that your father is a thief.'

'That's not true!' Flinging herself from her chair Laura was once more on her knees beside her father. 'There has been a mistake made in the accounts. I will go through them myself, I will find it . . . I will prove Edmund is wrong and that you are no thief.'

'No, no, Laura, there is no mistake!' Isaac rolled his head sideways against the chair back. 'The books *will* show discrepancies, it will do no good to deny it. I am a thief and have been for many years.'

Her father a thief. The words dinned in her brain. Stunned and confused Laura sat on her heels. But why would he steal . . . and from the business? It was like stealing from himself.

'Why, Father?' she asked at last.

Eyes shut once more, Isaac made no answer, only the workings of his tightly closed mouth attesting to the emotions raging through him.

There would be time for questions later, time for explanations. Pushing to her feet Laura reached for the prettily enamelled tea caddy sat on the corner of one shelf of the dresser. A cup of tea had always been her mother's first approach to solving a problem and one Aunt Abbie had sworn by. Spooning tea into the pot she scalded it with water from the kettle. Leaving it to mast she set out first the cups then the sugar bowl, finally fetching a small jug of milk from the scullery.

Glancing at her father as she lifted the earthenware teapot from the hob she saw he had not moved, not opened his eyes and none of the pain was gone from his face.

'Drink this, Father, then go and lie down for a while. We can talk later.'

'The time be past for putting things off, Laura.' He took the tea, his hand shaking. 'What has to be said be best said now. I took that money . . .'

'But what for!' Laura's cry came despite her intentions not to question. 'What did you need that money for? It has not been spent on furniture or on anything in the house!'

Opposite her Isaac laid aside his cup, and when he looked at her his faded eyes swam with tears.

'It went on . . .'

'No!' Her sob filled with anguish, Laura knelt beside him. Her arms around his waist, her face hidden against his chest, she hugged him with fierce protectiveness. 'I don't want to know what the money was for . . . what you spent it on, I only want to know how much. How much you have taken from the firm's accounts so it can be paid back.'

'It can't be done, wench.' Isaac touched a hand to her hair, stroking it as though it were he seeking to give comfort. 'It be too much. I could never earn enough to pay back what I took.'

Close against his chest Laura felt the sobs shake through his slight body. Whatever it was had turned her father into a thief, he would not live under its shadow for ever.

'We will pay it back, Father,' she murmured, tears filling her own eyes. 'We will do it together. Edmund will get it all . . . every last penny.'

She had meant what she said but now, hours later and preparing for bed, Laura realised the emptiness of those words. How could she hope to earn enough money to settle such a debt? She had no skills, all she had ever done from leaving school was keep house for her father. That would be of little use in trying to earn the sort of money needed now. True she might secure a post of scullery maid somewhere in the town but that would bring no more than eight, possibly ten, pounds a year.

Her hair plaited and tied with a ribbon she stared at her reflection in the mirror. Had her father's thieving been the true cause of Edmund not wanting to marry her, had he known of it yet not said it so her feelings would be spared? Or was the truth of it that he really found her plain?

'You know that to be the reason,' she whispered softly, 'and it is a plausible enough one. Edmund was right, you are not even pretty, Laura Cadman.'

Lying in bed she stared hard against the shadows clothing the walls of her small room.

'. . . *It be too much, I could never earn enough to pay back what I owe . . .*'

Out of the darkness her father's words returned and in the shelter of that same darkness Laura's mouth tightened. Her looks had denied her a marriage and a possible way of helping solve her father's problems, for as a son-in-law would Edmund not have helped put matters right? But that was not to be. Laura Cadman must find some other way to help her father.

Over seven hundred pounds! Ten pounds every month for more than six years! Her heart had sunk when he had told her how much he had stolen, and it sank again now. The sum was enormous. Even with a post of scullery maid . . . even with ten pounds a year it would be impossible, it would take a lifetime to repay.

But repay it she must. She had seen the torture in her father's eyes, felt the sobs wrack his body, and in that moment she had known that no matter how, no matter what it took, she must lift that burden of guilt from his shoulders, remove the blight that threatened to destroy him.

Turning her face into the pillow she closed her eyes.

Laura Cadman was not beautiful, but she was a woman who kept her word. She had said the money would be returned to Edmund Shaw and it would, every last penny!

Chapter Eight

Stood at the corner of Great Western Street, Laura hesitated. Perhaps she was wrong, perhaps she should not go to see Edmund, at least not yet.

'I wouldn't stand in the horse road if I was you, Missis Laura.'

Still trapped in her thoughts Laura was only vaguely aware of the voice beside her.

A hand on her arm pulled her backwards, out of the way of a cart rumbling past, the driver flicking the reins and calling encouragingly to the horse which shied nervously as a blast of a steam whistle from the nearby railway station shrieked through the air.

'I told you not to stand there!' The hand released its hold. 'Only last week old Ben Forman were knocked flat by one of them. Carters along of this way stops for nobody.'

'I ... I was not thinking ...'

'I don't be surprised, the scream of that whistle be enough to drive the senses from anybody's head, but don't let it frighten you none, it be just a train.'

A train! If only she and her father were taking that train, leaving this town with its memories and its sorrows.

'I suppose you be headed for the station. We will come with you, we ain't scared of them trains am we, our Alfie?'

Her mind clearing, Laura looked down at the flame-haired

boys, each the image of the other. 'I am not going to the railway station but I thank you for offering to go there with me, I really do not care for trains . . .'

'Oh they won't hurt you, Missis Laura, they be like me dad on a Saturday night, all wind and noise but nothing at back of it.' The older boy smiled.

'One day I will ride on a train.'

'Oh, ar!' Alfie looked scathingly at his brother. 'And I'll ride in me own carriage . . . Pah! Some hopes we both have of that, Teddie Bailey!'

'I *will*!' Teddie kicked truculently at an empty carton dropped from the rear of the carter's wagon. 'I *will* ride on a train, just you wait and see.'

Taking a cautionary step backwards taking himself out of reach of his brother's boot, Alfie surveyed the freckled face beginning to flush with the first signs of argument.

'You know, Missis Laura, our mother be right about him. Her says he would need live to be an 'undred to do all the things he talks of doing and he would an' all.'

'Teddie will do whatever he sets out to do.' Laura smiled placatingly at the irate Teddie. 'Which is more than I can say of myself if I stand here much longer.'

'Be you going to Brummagem?' Anger forgotten, Teddie was his usual inquisitive self.

'No.' Laura shook her head. 'I am not going to Birmingham. Why do you think that?'

''Cos you be all tarted up in your Sunday clothes and it don't be Sunday so you must be going somewhere special, don't her, our Alfie?'

'You shouldn't ask things as don't concern you. You'll get your arse tanned when Mother hears you've bin poking your nose!' The older boy's tone was sharp but his bright brown eyes showed he too wondered why Laura was dressed in her best while it was just midweek.

'You looks very pretty, Missis Laura.' He smiled an already

well-practised diplomatic smile. 'I would say you looked a picture . . .'

''Cept he ain't never seen no picture!' Teddie's face gleamed with one-upmanship but he kept well clear of the fist clenching at his brother's side.

'It was very courteous of Alfie to say so anyway.' Reaching into the bag hung about her wrist Laura withdrew a silver sixpenny piece. 'If you are not on an errand for your mother perhaps you would do one for me.'

'You knows we will.' Two faces, each drenched with freckles, smiled up at her, antagonism forgotten in the hope of earning a halfpenny.

She really did not want any errand performing but then neither did she want the Bailey boys to see her going into the works; tongues would wag soon enough without her giving them a head start.

Handing the coin to Alfie she said, 'I want you to go to Mrs Distumal on the High Bullen and ask for a pint of her best blue peas and then . . .'

'I knows, Missis Laura, I knows . . .' Teddie hopped from foot to foot, his brown eyes gleaming like newly minted pennies, '. . . then we goes to Mother Grant along of Oakeswell End for two pennorth of faggots.'

'That's right.' Laura drew the string tight, closing her bag.

'We'll do that.' Alfie tossed the sixpence in the air, catching it expertly. 'And I'll say to put extra gravy on them faggots.'

'You want we to do anything else, Missis Laura?'

She could not help but catch the hopeful gleam in those bright eyes. They ought to be in school, all children of that age should be in school, but already these two were masters in the art of dodging the school board inspector, the 'whipper in' folk here-about called him and all helped each other in the deceiving of him; children could not help to earn a living by sitting in a classroom.

'Well . . . !' Laura pretended indecision. 'If Teddie could

manage to carry them I would like two large crusty loaves from Purslow's bakery on Bridge Street and a halfpenny worth of oil of peppermint from Jackson's chemist.'

'Course I can carry 'em.' Teddie's chest expanded proudly. 'I ain't no babby!'

'In that case you will need more than sixpence.' Delving into her bag Laura withdrew a threepenny bit, handing it to Alfie.

'That will leave a penny change.' He took the coin, the mathematics of the job already calculated.

Laura nodded. 'It will, that is a halfpenny each for you and Teddie.'

'Halfpenny each!' Teddie's eyes were huge. 'Ta, Missis Laura, we'll get everything . . .'

The rest was lost as Alfie, afraid another purchase might be added and thus reduce their payment, yanked the younger boy away.

Relieved to be left alone, Laura turned towards the works several streets away. Why had she dressed in her Sunday clothes . . . was it to impress Edmund . . . did she hope that seeing her in her one acceptable coat and bonnet he would change his mind about not marrying her?

The thought brought a tinge of pink to her pale cheeks. Let Edmund believe so if he wished, but the truth of it was she would not visit her father's business premises in patched skirts and with a shawl over her head. Her Sunday best was not the fine clothes that Edmund's mother had worn but at least it would not let her father down, it would lend some little credence to the fact that he was their employer.

'You've 'eard the news, miss?' Jonas Small came hurrying from the shop floor as he glimpsed her crossing the yard.

'Of Mr Shaw's death? Yes I have, Mr Small.'

Jonas seemed to grow an inch in stature. Isaac Cadman had always taught his wench to be polite and to use a man's name when they met, even if it were a man with the most menial of jobs. Ay, the difference there had been between the two men who together owned this bolt and screw works; now one of them was gone, and the man left to take his place looking to be a right bastard!

'It be a sorrowful thing his passing, when it seemed he were getting better an' all; goes to show you can never be sure of anything, a man never knows what be round the corner.'

'No.' Laura answered quietly. You could never be sure what fate had in store, what other tricks like the one it had played on her father. He was a thief, that he had confessed. But what had driven him to such lengths? That she did not know.

'Is Mr Edmund at the works?'

She had called at the house but Edmund was not at home. Somehow she had expected he would be with so much to be taken care of. But the works, too, needed taking care of and with her father not being there . . .

Only half listening to the man's reply Laura followed toward the small brick-built room that was the works' office. Here or at his home she could give Edmund her condolences and ask her questions. Perhaps, just perhaps, he may be able to shed some light on the reason her father had stolen money.

'Good afternoon, Laura.' Edmund's pale coloured eyes widened, slight surprise etching his long features as she was shown into the office. 'Had you sent a message I would have called on you, this is no place for you.'

Had she imagined it or had there been a particular emphasis on the last of the sentence? Accepting the chair Jonas Small dusted with a rag, Laura waited until he left.

'I called at the house to express my sympathies in your loss but seeing you were not there . . .'

'This place needs management, too.' His reply was terse as if answering some admonishment. 'And since your father is not here . . .'

'That is another reason I came here to the works.' She lifted a steady glance, letting it remain on his face as his eyes shifted. 'I understand you have given my father reason to believe his presence here is no longer desirable, nor acceptable. Might I ask why?'

'Hasn't he told you?'

'I am asking *you*, Edmund.'

Turning his back he stared out of the dust-caked window. Beyond it men worked, shoulders hunched over long bench-like tables, not one head lifting from the work in hand.

'Perhaps it is not my place to tell you.'

Holding the bag on her knee Laura's hands tightened, anger rising like gall to her throat, but still she kept her tone even.

'It was not your place to tell my father he was dismissed but you did it.'

'You don't understand!'

'Then make me understand!' Staring at the narrow figure, Laura felt anger turn to sudden disgust. How could a man her family had known and loved since babyhood behave this way? What had happened to the Edmund she knew; or was it an Edmund she only thought she knew?

'Leave it, Laura, go home; I've told you this is no place for you.'

'No place for my father and no place for me; both of us dismissed! Is that what you want, Edmund, for both of us to be no longer involved in the works, for it to be solely your concern?'

'I said for you to go, Laura.' He turned quickly, indiscriminate eyes hot with anger. 'You have no right here.'

The look on her face deceptive, hiding the disgust stubbornly staying with her, Laura kept her gaze on him.

'Then neither have you! Our fathers are equal partners, both will pass their share of the business to their children, those children being you and me, Edmund . . . you and *me*. As my father's heir I have equal rights with you, *equal* Edmund! That is the way things are and the way they will stay. If my father no longer wishes to return . . .'

'If . . . *if!*' He strode forward, banging a fist on to the dusty desktop. 'There is no if, Laura. Isaac Cadman will never come back here, he has no further part in this business.'

Easing the string of her bag over her wrist Laura held tight to her self control.

'Was that your father's word or yours? Whichever, it makes no difference. My father still owns fifty per cent of Shaw and Cadman, and when he is gone a Cadman will still own half; that Cadman being me, Edmund.'

'You!' He ran an openly disparaging glance over her. 'What the hell do you know of engineering!'

'As much as yourself, maybe even more.'

'A woman? Pah! Whoever heard of a woman running an engineering firm?'

Hands resting at her sides Laura watched the anger in his pale eyes change to contempt.

'Maybe as of now no one. But if my father does not resume his work here then they soon will.'

'You want him to come back here, to face folk after what he has done?'

She knew what her father had done, but the reason for it . . . 'What has my father done, Edmund, just what is it you think gives you the right to treat him as you might any one of those men out there?'

'Any one of those men out there doing what your father has would be behind bars now.' Edmund flung the words at her. 'Isaac Cadman is a thief. He has robbed this firm of over seven hundred pounds. *That* is what he should have told you.'

'Seven hundred and eighty as it stands now!' She answered calmly. 'The figure stands at seven hundred and eighty pounds. You see Edmund I do know as much about the business as you do.'

'Then why ask?' he snapped. 'Why ask if you know so much?'

'I did not come here to ask how much my father has taken . . .'

'Stolen.' Pale eyes glittered. 'The word is stolen!'

'If that pleases you.' Laura gave a brief nod. 'I came to ask why, why did he take that money?'

A half-laugh breaking in his throat Edmund stared at her. 'What makes you think I have the answer?'

'I thought perhaps when your father discovered what was happening he would have discussed it with you.'

'As Isaac discussed it with you!' His mouth curved but even in disparagement it could not be called a smile. 'Jabez did not discover what was going on.'

The contempt on his face showing clearly, Laura had to force herself to face him. 'Then it was you.'

'Yes, it was me. I found your father's thieving and it is my decision he will no longer come here; Isaac Cadman is finished at this works.'

'That decision is not yours to make.' Laura's chin lifted defiantly.

'He is *finished*.' The hand coming sharp down on the desk only emphasised the softness with which he spoke, the menace of the words leaving his curved mouth. 'The alternative being that every man in this town will know he is a thief, that he robbed his partner of seven hundred and eighty pounds.'

Beyond the windows tools screeched on metal clamped in vices, the sound creeping in past the dust-covered panes.

'Three hundred and ninety pounds to be precise.' She saw the fleeting frown draw his brows down then release them. 'My father took the money from the firm's account therefore as part-owner he took half of it from himself; that leaves him to have stolen three hundred and ninety pounds from your father.'

'Seven hundred and eighty or three hundred and ninety, where is the difference? Isaac Cadman is still a thief and being so I will not have him on these premises again.'

'The money will be repaid, however in the meantime you too must face the alternative, Edmund. You will not act in partnership with Isaac Cadman, then you will do so with his daughter. From now on no business transaction will be undertaken, no steel purchased and no bolt or screw delivered without my say so.' At the door she paused and when she looked back it was to see livid anger wipe the contempt from his mouth, leaving it caught in a thin white line. 'There is just one consideration I will make. I give you the choice. Do you relay that to Jonas Small, or do I?'

She had not found the answer. She still did not know the motivation behind her father's stealing. Her fingers shaking, Laura removed her bonnet, putting it carefully back in its box.

'. . . *He bided his time, waiting like a cat waits for a mouse . . .*'

The words of yesterday returned, stinging her mind.

She had not believed her father when he said Edmund must have hoped on the day, longed for the moment he could be sole master of Shaw and Cadman. But listening to him in that office, watching the emotion on his face, how could she not believe.

Isaac Cadman had robbed him of three hundred and ninety pounds; he, it seemed, was set to rob Isaac of his life's work. But that would not happen, she would not allow it to happen.

Removing her Sunday suit, hanging it in the cupboard stood opposite her bed, she reached for her patched skirt. Letting it down over her head she thought again of Edmund's look as she had delivered her ultimatum. She had given him no time to reply but walked quickly from the small room, her heels soundless on the earth floor as she followed Jonas Small from the workshop.

The money will be repaid. She had said it with absolute confidence, but here in her own room she faced reality. How could she repay that money, what could she do to earn it?

The answer no clearer now than it had been twenty-four hours ago, she stared at her reflection in the mirror.

'*You were right in one thing, Edmund,*' she thought, '*I am not pretty but neither am I an idiot. For a reason known only to yourself you want what my father has worked hard for. It is not the return of that money alone you intend to have but the works itself, all of it, even if you destroy him in the getting of it. But you reckoned without me, Edmund.*' Teeth clamped firmly together she walked downstairs to the kitchen. '*You reckoned without me!*'

'I have been to the works, Father.' She looked at the figure sat hunched in a chair beside the hearth. She had never lied to her father and to do so now would be of little help. 'I spoke to Edmund.'

Isaac looked up, the lack of sleep marked clearly on his face, his eyes heavy with anxiety.

'Has he . . . did he say . . . ?'

'He told me Jabez did not know of . . . of your embezzlement, that it was he, Edmund, who found out about the discrepancies in the accounts.'

'Did he tell you why, why it is I have robbed Jabez for six years?'

'He did not know, Father.' Already busy with teapot and cups Laura realised Edmund had not specifically said he did not know. He had in fact made no direct answer to that question; which in turn meant he truly did not know, or he would have thrown that at her as he had thrown the rest. He had made no apology, made no effort to soften the blows of what he had said, not like he might once have done.

Pouring milk into the cups Laura's hand shook, sending a few white droplets sprinkling into the pretty blue saucer.

Her whole world seemed suddenly composed of questions. Why had her father turned to stealing? What had turned Edmund into the cold, almost vicious man she had spoken to not an hour ago?

'He did not know? Edmund Shaw said he did not know?' Behind her, Isaac's voice trembled with incredulity.

'All he said was, "What makes you think I have the answer?"'

'Then I must . . .'

'No, Father.' Setting the teapot back on the hob Laura cut him short. 'There is no need to say any more. I have told Edmund the money will be returned in full, there is no need for anything more to be said.'

'But how, child?' Isaac took the cup she offered, his mouth trembling. 'I don't have a penny; what was set aside for you has long since been swallowed up, and without the works . . .'

Stirring sugar into her own tea Laura asked emphatically, 'Who said anything about being without the works?'

'But that's what he be about, I know it. Edmund Shaw wants my share; I've guessed that for a long time and this be the chance he has waited on, he won't waste it. He will see to it I never goes into that workshop again.'

'That will have to be your decision, Father. Should you decide you cannot return then, as I have already informed Edmund, I shall take your place. So you see he will not remove you completely. What Edmund Shaw wants and what he has are not the same thing.'

Resting the cup and saucer on his knee, Isaac looked at the daughter he loved. She had never asked for the finer things in life, satisfied always with what was given, though that had been less and less as money flowed away to . . .

'What about you, wench?' he asked. 'Does Edmund Shaw have you?'

The bluntness of it catching her off-guard, Laura swallowed the hot liquid, scorching her throat. Coughing a little she laid her cup aside. 'If you mean are he and I contemplating marriage then no, Edmund Shaw does not have me.'

Slumping back into the chair, sending tea slopping into his saucer, Isaac's face creased deeper with pain.

'Oh Laura, Laura my little wench. I'm so sorry . . .'

'For what?' Reaching forward she removed the cup and saucer from his hands, laying them beside her own. 'Because I am not about to marry Edmund, or because you think that in some way the reason is to do with the business of the accounts? If so, Father, you are wrong. Edmund and I never once spoke of marriage either between ourselves or with anyone else.'

Maybe this could be construed as a lie but Laura experienced no guilt in the speaking of it. Sufficient was as good as a feast, so Abigail would say, and her father had feasted well, she would add no more than necessary to his worries.

'Then you don't want to marry Jabez' son?'

The element of hope in his voice cut into Laura. 'No.' She shook her head. 'I do not want to marry Jabez' son.'

Thinking of that exchange as she washed cups in the scullery she found herself wondering at the look of relief that had flooded her father's eyes, at the almost sob in his voice as he had answered, 'Thank God!'

Why thank God? Bringing a bowl of peas to the table she began to shell them, wondering again at the heartfelt vehemence of that reply. If he had wanted a marriage between her and Edmund, as Abigail Butler had seemed to believe, then why that answer, was it a sudden change of heart and if so then what had given rise to it?

But he had made it clear now. Union between the families was not what he wanted. She would not have the worry of her father feeling disappointed on that score. But what of that other? Would she be a disappointment in that? Her father had not reacted with the same contempt as Edmund had shown when she had said she would assume the responsibilities of a partner, but that did not necessarily mean he thought her to have the ability to carry it through. Would she have? Adding a spoon of sugar to the peas in the pot she gathered the empty pods, setting them aside for soup-making. She had as much knowledge of the administration as Edmund, she also knew the grades of steel and all the theory, but when it came to the actual process of making a bolt or a screw she had no practical experience.

But that should prove of little drawback, though Edmund would doubtless argue otherwise; but it was the men at the work benches did the making and she could spot inferior work every bit as well as he could: her father had taught her well.

Looking across to where he sat staring into the fire, she felt her heart twist. He looked so tired and drawn. Those years of misappropriating the funds, of worrying every minute that he might be found out had taken a dreadful toll, and all the time she had thought the cause to be overwork. But why had he done that terrible thing, why steal money he could not be seen to have spent? She had told him the reason was unimportant to her, that she did not want to know. But was that the truth, was it really the truth?

She had wrestled with those thoughts since he had told her of his actions but still she did not have the answer.

Her father's thieving . . . the almost complete change of behaviour in Edmund. The whole thing was a mystery, one she could see no logical answer to.

Chapter Nine

Why the hell couldn't she have waited? She had been to the house, she could have left a message but instead . . .

Edmund Shaw stared at the food in front of him.

A woman in the works at all was bad enough, but when that woman was Laura Cadman!

'Will there be anything else, sir?'

'What!' Edmund looked up, only now aware of the waiter at his elbow.

Dressed in black with a white heavily starched shirt that made him look like an out-of-place penguin, the man bowed, a slight deferential movement that left Edmund feeling awkward. 'I could not help but notice, sir, you have not eaten. May I change the dish for some other of your choosing?'

'Dish?' His thoughts not entirely collected Edmund looked blank.

'Perhaps Steak Bordelaise is not sir's preference this evening, perhaps a little fish . . . if I might suggest a Sole Meuniere . . .'

'No, no, this will do.' Unused to dining out and completely baffled by the culinary terms, Edmund glanced back at his plate. Why had he come here at all? He could have taken his meal at home as usual. But things were not usual, there was a corpse laid out in the study. He had had Jabez put there rather than in the front parlour and let folk make of it what they may, the idea of a dead body in his mother's favourite room was more than he was prepared to give.

To give! He snorted angrily and the waiter moved away, the hoped-for tip dismissed from his thoughts.

To give! He continued to stare at the steak garnished appetisingly with mushrooms, an attractively laid salad set at the side, but his appetite was not for food.

Why should he give that man anything when all he had received from him had been hard words and contempt, why afford him respect when he himself had never been shown any!

And what respect had she shown, coming to the works like that? A woman in the works, pah! I will be taking my father's place, she had told Jonas Small. Over *his* dead body!

Thought spilling into movement, he shoved the plate away.

There was no place there any more for Isaac Cadman and there was none for his daughter.

The eyes of the workmen had followed him across the workshop, the unprecedented fact of his leaving before them adding to the talk already buzzing from Jonas Small's news. Oh he had told them all right, there need be no doubt of that; told them Isaac Cadman was retiring and his daughter taking his position. Well let them talk . . . let the tongues wag but it would be Edmund Shaw had the last word!

'Your pardon, sir.'

Edmund looked up, a quiet apologetic cough calling his attention.

'The dining room is rather well attended this evening . . . the tables . . .'

'What Mr Mills is saying is there are no tables unreserved,' a rather more sophisticated voice interrupted, 'therefore he cannot accommodate me unless you would have the goodness to allow me to share yours, that is unless you are expecting company.'

'No, I'm not expecting anyone.'

'Then may I?'

Sage-green eyes regarded him below brows so well defined they might have been painted on to the handsome face that smiled, waiting for an answer.

'Yes . . . yes, of course, I . . . I was just about to leave anyway.'

'No, please do not leave, I must not inconvenience you.'

The figure straightened, dropping a long-fingered hand from the chair it had reached for.

'No inconvenience,' Edmund replied politely, while thinking it could not have been more so. He preferred to be alone, he needed to think.

'Then if you are sure . . . but only if you will take a glass of wine with me.'

The smile in those sage-coloured eyes deepened and, despite himself, Edmund could not look away. Handsome was not a word that truly described the man seating himself opposite.

'Thank you, Mr Mills.'

Edmund watched the courteous nod of the head and the none the less dismissive wave of the hand that told the manager of the White Horse Hotel his presence was no longer required.

'What will you have, Chateau Tayssier St Emilion or perhaps Pouilly Fuisse Vinaton?'

It had been Jabez who was the drinker and if not whisky then claret had been his choice; he did not recognise the words let alone what drink they named.

'Would you allow that I make the choice?'

Edmund felt the faint colour rise to his cheeks. The man had seen the confusion in his eyes, guessed he did not know wine from water, same as that waiter had guessed he did not recognise the fancy sounding names of the food.

Ignoring the wine list offered by the ever-attentive wine waiter, the man spoke quietly to the waiter whose slightly disdainful smile vanished, replaced by a respectful half bow as a bottle of Canard Duchene was asked for.

'The White Horse is not too bad a hotel when a man must

dine out but, like waiters in most places, these do tend to go a bit overboard with the phraseology; I must admit I quite enjoy giving them a taste of it themselves . . .'

The man's smile became suddenly intimate, almost conspiratorial, leaving Edmund wanting more.

'. . . me . . .' He leaned forward across the table, dark brown hair glinting as it caught the light of overhead chandeliers. '. . . I say call a steak a steak and a fish a fish.'

But he had not called a wine red or white, he had rattled off words Edmund could only guess referred to one or the other.

'Then why don't they?'

'Standing.' He drew back, sitting straight in his chair as the wine waiter returned, cradling a bottle in a snow-white linen serviette and displaying the label for approval.

'Standing.' The wine sampled and poured into sparkling glasses, the smoothly modulated voice continued, 'and of course, competition. The George Hotel in Union Street runs this one very closely, therefore every effort is made to attract custom.'

'But like you said, why not call a fish a fish, why Sole Meuniere? It makes no difference to the taste.'

'The ladies.'

Opposite Edmund the man laughed, a soft musical laugh. 'The ladies like it and what the ladies like . . .' he shrugged expressively, 'is sure to bring the clients and clients are business, which in turn means profit.'

Touching a hand to his glass he let it remain standing. 'I shall drink to your health in any case, but I would prefer to drink it after having introduced myself. My name is Sinclair, Sheldon Sinclair.'

'Shaw,' Edmund responded. 'Edmund Shaw. How do you do, Mr Sinclair.'

'Not Mr. Please!' Eyes gleamed jewel-like as the man raised his glass, holding it slightly towards Edmund. 'Sheldon. Friends call me Sheldon.'

✻

Edmund opened his eyes then closed them quickly as the ceiling of his room began to spin. His head felt thick and heavy, his stomach queasy. Why . . . what had caused him to feel this way? He had eaten . . . he groaned, covering his eyes with his hand, as memory of the night before rushed in on him. It wasn't what he had eaten, it was what he had drunk! Wine, glass after glass of it.

Why had he accepted it? Why hadn't he left when he said he would?

His head throbbing he sat up, breathing deeply before swinging his legs from the bed.

He should never have gone to the White Horse or any other hotel, but while that corpse was in the house . . .

The thought bringing other memories of last night, he dropped his head into his hands. Hearing him fumbling with his key after alighting from the hansom that had brought him home, Jabez' manservant had opened the door to him. Taking his coat he had suggested helping him to bed, but he had shaken off the man's hand, going instead to the study.

On each side of his head Edmund's hands pressed harder as if trying to close out the scene which formed so clearly in his mind.

He had lurched across to the open coffin, his hand closing over its edge to prevent his falling over.

'You didn't see him did you, Jabez?'

He had bent over the stiff figure, light falling on the waxen features from the candles that would burn constantly until after the coffin left the house.

'You didn't see him, see his fine clothes or hear the way he spoke. Well that is the way I am going to be . . . you hear me, Jabez?' He had leered into the face, the eyes closed beneath two pennies. 'That's the way I am going to be, I will have clothes like that, I shall know the fancy names given to food, the wines you could never dream of let alone pronounce. That is where your precious engineering works will go . . . sold, Jabez, sold and the money spent giving me the life you denied me, you and your precious partner . . .'

How much more had he said? Pushing to his feet he walked unsteadily to the bathroom. How much more had he shouted at that dead body? Splashing cold water on his face he tried to remember, but all that he could recall was Jabez' man pulling him away and helping him up the stairs.

Had he said anything more . . . the business . . . Isaac Cadman . . . ? So what if he had! The whole town would know soon anyway.

Dressed and feeling somewhat better, but refusing breakfast, he analysed his movements of the day before. Jabez' bedroom and the study he had already searched but he went through cupboards and drawers again. There had been papers, endless bills and receipts but not the paper he was searching for.

He had been going through those kept at the works when she had walked in. Laura Cadman had come into the office as bold as brass. Partner! Take her father's place! Edmund's mouth tightened. Not if he could help it. There had to be a way of getting rid of both her and her father. But how watertight had the contract between him and Jabez been, had it been properly drawn up by a solicitor?

That was one place he had not looked. Ignoring the morning post laid beside him on the breakfast table, he strode into the hall.

'Will you be at home this afternoon, sir?' The manservant held out Edmund's coat.

Easing the coat across his shoulders and fastening the buttons Edmund shook his head.

'But the undertaker, sir, you remember he is to call at four o'clock today to arrange any last-minute requirements you may wish for the funeral.'

He had forgotten the funeral. It was unfortunate he had ordered it take place so quickly, he should have given himself more time; he might have known Jabez would not make things easy, that hiding that one paper would be another of the man's ways of showing his dislike.

'*But it doesn't matter any more, Jabez!*' The thought flooded his mind, lighting it like sunbeams in a shadowed room. '*You are dead and I am alive. I will find that contract and when I do then I will find a way to break it. There is going to be just one to spend all that works will fetch, and that one will be me.*'

'Will I tell Mr Webb you will be home at four, sir?'

'No.' Edmund stepped through the door held open for him. 'You deal with it . . . Jabez had more time for you than he had for me. I return the compliment!'

Set on the rise that was Squire's Walk, the house overlooked the town spread around its foot. Edmund gazed at the forest of chimneys each breathing black smoke, colliery winding wheels, the tracery of their structure a dark silhouette against a sky ablaze with the scarlet of the first of the day's opening of furnaces that spewed molten iron and steel.

Walking down the hill his glance swept the whole vista. Streets of tiny houses huddled around every foundry, the little open land that remained was criss-crossed with scars of open-cast mining, and everywhere the buildings were coated in soot and dust. Coal and steel, the town lived on coal and steel and now it was choking in its waste.

Edmund felt distaste rise like bile in his throat. So much dirt. The town was drowning in soot. The Black Country! How well it was named. But the last of its dirt had settled on Edmund Shaw; from now on he would lead a life totally divorced from the one Jabez had given him, he would live the sort of life that Sheldon Sinclair had, a life he would enjoy.

That man had been so different, dress, speech and manner, so elegant. Yes that was what Edmund Shaw wanted and that was what he would have . . . and finding that contract would give it to him.

✷

'I am sorry I could be of no help to you, Mr Shaw. Your father did use our services in some transactions, all of which I have explained to you, but as for a contract between himself and Mr Cadman, I am afraid I was not called upon to draw it up.'

'Thank you, Mr Messiter.' Followed by the short, balding solicitor Edmund walked along the narrow corridor that led to the door of the musty-smelling chambers.

'I hope my services have been such that you will continue your father's patronage.'

Quick mincing footsteps echoing on the patterned floor tiles irritated the silence of rooms hushed as sanctified ground. Edmund made no answer; once Jabez' will was read he would have no need of Frederick Messiter's services.

Lower High Street throbbed with traffic busy with the day. Carts coming from West Bromwich, some feeding goods to Bilston or Wolverhampton, others travelling in the opposite direction, rumbling away up Holloway Bank. But it was not the carts or the people that held Edmund's attention. It was the church, its blackened spire rising like a beckoning finger. Jabez' beckoning had come and tomorrow he would be laid in that churchyard. Edmund drew a long, satisfied breath. May the Lord he had professed to believe in treat him as Jabez Shaw had treated his son!

Crossing the street, passing the church, he turned right on to the Holyhead Road. Ernest Knowles had his solicitor's practice there, maybe Jabez had left his copy of the contract with him.

Half an hour later and back on the street, Edmund ground his teeth with anger. Wherever Jabez had placed that paper he had hidden it well. It was in no solicitor's office, not in the house nor yet in the works' office. But wherever it was, he would find it.

Isaac. The thought came swift and certain. Isaac Cadman was a full partner, whatever one had the other would have the same. He could not find Jabez' copy of the contract; then he would look at the one held by Isaac.

Not so clever after all, Jabez! Solution to the problem giving a spring to his step, Edmund walked quickly to the house set among others grouped back-to-back in squares about communal yards, wrinkling his nose as he knocked at the door. He had little enough affection for Wednesbury as a whole but here, so close to the noise of steam trains and the shouts and clangs of steel and coal being loaded on to barges crowded into the canal wharfs . . . Why on earth had Isaac Cadman chosen to live here?

Surprise registering on her face, Laura held the door open to his knock. Edmund had always just walked in, but after their meeting yesterday . . . !

'Please come in.' She stood aside for him to pass as any visitor might.

'I have come to speak with your father.'

Laura's heart leaped. He had come to tell her father that the whole sorry business had been a mistake, to ask him to resume his work at the factory, that there had been no robbery. But her father had admitted to theft. Elation fading as quickly as it had flared, Laura glanced at the man who had so easily wrecked her life.

'You know where the parlour is. If you will wait there I will ask my father to join you.'

Turning away she took the few steps that carried her to the kitchen. Isaac sat next to the hearth, his shoulders in the droop that was becoming so familiar.

That had to be the reason for Edmund's visit. Laura felt the dry tears block her throat as she looked at him. It had to be that her father was wanted back.

'Father.' She smiled as the grey head turned to her. 'Father, Edmund is here, he wishes to speak with you.'

'Edmund here?'

For a moment it seemed fear flashed into his faded eyes, then his glance had dropped away.

'He is in the parlour. I thought it would be more private for you there.'

Was that truly why she had asked him to wait in that room?

If she were so sure things were back to normal, that he had in reality come to apologise to her father and ask him back to the works, why had she not taken him to the kitchen where they usually sat?

'Did . . . did he say why he has come?'

Going to him Laura folded her arm in his. 'I think he would prefer to say that to you. Everything is going to be all right now, Father, I just know it is.'

Settling him in the parlour, she turned to Edmund. He had not yet seated himself and when she looked at him his glance slid quickly sideways. Yesterday was the first time in their lives that harsh words had passed between them; even on that evening he had told her they would not marry he had been civil, cold but civil. But what had passed between them then was done, she wanted no more than he was about to give now: recognition of her father's rightful position as partner in Shaw and Cadman.

'I will leave you to talk.' She turned away. 'I will bring some tea in a few minutes.'

The door closed behind her and Edmund faced the older man. 'I have been going through Jabez' papers.' He spoke quickly and to the point. 'I have been looking at those to do with the business . . .'

Isaac remained silent, only the fleeting emotions touching his mouth testifying to his listening.

'. . . but there is one that I have not found.'

'You have a lot on your mind.' Isaac spoke at last. 'It is easy to overlook a thing, dealing as you are with your father's funeral. No doubt you will come across whatever it is once the stress is over.'

'How do you come across something that isn't there!' Edmund brought his hand palm-open against his thigh. 'I have searched carefully and very, very thoroughly but there seems to be no trace of what I'm looking for.'

Laura was wrong. Isaac felt his spirits drop. It was not going to be all right. Whatever Edmund Shaw had come to this house for it was not to make things right between them.

'It is not in the house nor is it in the works' office . . .'

Isaac interrupted wearily. 'If you cannot find it in his study then I suggest you try his solicitor.'

Study! Edmund almost smiled. Private saloon would be a more accurate description, for the only thing studied in that room was the rate of drop in a whisky bottle!

'I have seen his solicitor,' Edmund rasped. 'In fact I have seen both of those that practice in Wednesbury. Do you know of any other he might have consulted in another town?'

'No.' Isaac shook his head. 'But it must be in a safe place, Jabez would not leave his will in the works' office where it is liable to be seen by Jonas Small or even myself.'

'It is not Jabez' will I am looking for. I am looking for his copy of the contract you and he made together when you started Shaw and Cadman.'

Brows folding together, Isaac looked away.

Impatience riding his nerves, Edmund swung away but as quickly returned to stand over the older man. 'You heard what I said and you know full well I mean to have it. You and Jabez signed a paper when you set up that business, I want to see what it contains.'

Taking fully half a minute before answering, Isaac looked into the face staring down at him. 'Did Jabez tell you that?'

'Did Jabez ever tell me anything!' Edmund laughed sarcastically. 'Everything of any importance I had to find out for myself, the same goes for that contract.'

'Why is a piece of paper so important to you?'

Edmund's eyes darkened, his mouth tightening until it seemed to pull his long features out of shape.

'It's useless to prevaricate, Isaac!' he hissed. 'That is what you have done for half of your life. I mean to see that agreement and one way or another I will . . . perhaps Laura . . .'

'There is no contract.' Isaac looked up sharply. 'Jabez and myself . . . we never signed no paper.'

It wasn't true, Jabez was too shrewd to partner a business without a contractual basis. Edmund stared at the lined face. Isaac Cadman was lying . . . to save his daughter's inheritance? Was there something written in that contract that would take the business away from her once her father was dead?

Watching for the slightest reaction he said, 'I can't believe that, Jabez wouldn't be fool enough . . .'

'Jabez Shaw was no fool!' Isaac's tired voice suddenly crisped.

'Wasn't he, Isaac, wasn't he!' Again that sarcastic laugh fell like a sword between them. 'Maybe not in business but in other things . . . but then we both know about that, don't we?'

'Edmund.'

'Don't bother going over old ground!' Edmund turned away, irritation taking on a deeper note. 'Just show me the paper, I know you have one. Like I said, Jabez would not be fool enough not to have a contract drawn up.'

'One thing, at least, you and I have in common,' Isaac's voice was once more dejected, 'we both know Jabez Shaw was no fool, but he was a good friend, God rest him. It was as friends we began that business, we needed no paper between us, a handshake was our contract.'

No contract, no signed agreement. Edmund breathed long and slow. Then neither man had claim on the other and neither had full claim to the business! Thoughts bounced in his mind like dried peas in a baby's rattle. That meant it was open to the strongest. To the victor the spoils. Losing the tightness, his mouth relaxed into a half smile. He intended to be the victor.

Turning slowly about he faced Isaac, and when he spoke irritation had given way to triumph.

'Then you were nothing more than Jabez' employee, no more than any other workhand.'

'You know that be a lie, I put my share to his!'

Looking into the faded eyes, Edmund laughed quietly. 'Oh I believe it, Isaac, but will a court of law believe it? You see, to prove what you say is truth you will need to go to law, that can be very expensive, very expensive indeed; I hope you have the money to pay for it.'

'We were partners, half that business is mine . . .'

'Prove it!' Edmund spat. 'Prove it like I had to prove . . .'

He broke off as Laura entered, a laden tea-tray in her hands.

'I hope I am not too early.' She smiled. 'You will take a cup of tea, Edmund?'

Glancing from her to Isaac he gave a brief shake of his head. 'No, no tea thank you. I have all I want from this house!'

Chapter Ten

Edmund had said that! Watching her father, his hands trembling despite the warmth of the kitchen fire and the rug she had spread over his knees, Laura felt a cold, hard anger such as she had never felt before. Edmund had said her father had been no more than an employee of Jabez', that Isaac Cadman had no claim to the business.

'I never thought . . . I never dreamed . . .' Isaac continued brokenly, 'nor did Jabez; neither of us expected such a thing. A verbal agreement, the word of one friend to another was enough for us, that was how it always was.'

But not any more, Laura thought, remembering the look on his face as Edmund had refused her offer of tea. There was no longer any friendship between them. Or had it all been merely pretence, had Edmund truly ever felt real friendship for her family or had it all been a carefully hidden pretence? Either way, it was over now.

'It's all my fault.' Elbows on his knees, Isaac covered his face with his hands. 'It was to be for you, it was all to be for you and now there is nothing. Edmund Shaw knows I don't have the money to fight him . . . Oh my God!' He drew a juddering breath. 'One moment, one stupid moment, that is all it took . . . one moment to lose everything!'

'It is not your fault,' Laura answered quietly. 'We both

thought Edmund was our friend, we both trusted him.'

'Were it just myself I wouldn't mind so much, I would say it was no more than I deserved for what I have done; but it is you, Laura, I mind for you.' He looked up, his hands falling to his lap. 'You would have been comfortable, you could have moved from this house, but now . . .'

'I don't want to move from this house.' Going to kneel beside him she took his hands in her own. 'And I am comfortable just so long as I have you.'

'That is easy to say.' He shook his head slowly. 'But where will I find work, who will give work to a man who robs his employer? No one will, Laura, no one. That will mean no money coming into the house, nothing for us to live on. How long can you be comfortable with that?'

'If there was no agreement then it is Edmund's word against yours.'

'He said much the same,' Isaac answered. 'He said that to prove my claim I would have to go to law. He knew I had not money enough for that. We have to face it, Laura, Edmund has won. He intended to take the business from me and he has done it. I have lost everything, and because of me so have you.'

'If you mean Edmund then don't worry.' Laura pressed her cheek to the hands she still cradled. 'I told you last night I . . . we never discussed marriage. In that respect you have lost me nothing, as for the works . . . Edmund has not won yet.'

'Stay away from him, wench!' Freeing his hands Isaac tilted her chin; the eyes that met hers were dark with anxiety. 'Edmund Shaw has shown what he is capable of. He has waited too long to be master to let go easily. Seeing him today, listening to him, to the poison stored inside him, I feel he could not be trusted to behave reasonably . . . not even with a woman.'

'I can scarcely credit the change in him, he seems like a different man.'

Looking into that upturned face, Isaac's mouth firmed with determination. 'Laura,' he said quietly, 'Laura, it be time I told you the whole story, the reason behind doing what I did. It goes back a long way. Jabez . . .'

He broke off as a knock sounded to the street door. Laura pushed to her knees with a feeling almost of relief at his being interrupted. She wanted to help her father to ease the pain of all this, of course she did, but in a strange adverse way she did not want to hear, did not want to hear the hurt in her father's voice, see the shame on that beloved face.

'That will be the Bailey boys.' Her gesture purely automatic she raised a hand, smoothing hair drawn tightly back from her brow. 'They went to the market for me earlier.'

'Do they always come to the front?'

The question took her unawares. Caught in the emotions felt for her father, the direction of the knock had not registered on her brain. Now, as he queried it, she was suddenly puzzled. The Bailey boys had never once called at the front door, neither did anyone else in these streets! Yet it had to be either those boys or Edmund . . . but Edmund would not be calling on her again.

'I suppose it is some new game they have devised, you know what boys can be sometimes.' She smiled quickly but did not allow her glance to meet the one she knew was filled with apprehension. Already crossing the kitchen, she said lightly, 'I will give those two a piece of my mind, they will not come knocking at the front door in future!'

Leaving the kitchen she blinked against the shadows gathered in the tiny parlour. Windows that looked directly on to the street were already purpling behind their veils of lace but she had no need of lighting the lamp that stood in the centre of the cloth-draped mahogany table, every inch of this room was as familiar to her as her own hand.

Reaching the door, whose bolt had never once been slipped into its socket, she opened it, the reprimand she promised already leaving her tongue.

'Alfie Bailey, you should know better than to . . .'

The rest of it silent on her lips she stared at the figure stood on the doorstep.

Face shrouded in gloom, a man raised his hand!

Breath sounding in her throat Laura stepped back, grey evening light picking up the fear in her eyes.

'Evening, miss.' The hand touched against a temple, then lowered.

'Sergeant Potts!' Laura's laugh was tight with relief as she recognised the figure stood watching her.

'Does your father be home?'

'Yes, yes, he is at home.' She stepped further back, holding the door wide. 'Come in.'

She had known Sergeant Potts since her earliest days, he had always given her a smile, but tonight there was no smile peeping above his bushy whiskers; and the front door . . . he had never called at the front door!

'If you will wait a moment I will light the lamp.'

She turned, reaching for the box of matches stood behind the gilt clock on the mantel shelf.

With pale yellow glow spreading itself on the room Laura looked again at the man, the brass buttons of his dark blue uniform gleaming in the lamplight.

'Father is in the kitchen, will you . . .'

'Not tonight, Laura wench . . .' The sergeant apprehended the rest of the sentence, his tone gentle with apology. 'I'll be seeing your father in here, it . . . it be business.'

Setting the lamp back in its place, a sense of perturbation deepening, she walked the few steps to the kitchen, each footfall sounding like a drum in her brain. Why see her father in the parlour . . . what business could Sergeant Potts have in this house?

'It . . . it is Sergeant Potts, Father, he wishes to speak with you.'

'Have him come in, have you forgotten your manners?'

She tried to smile at her father's pretended admonition but it would not reach her lips. 'He asks to see you in the parlour, he . . . he says it is business.'

In the jaundiced light shed by the oil lamps still used in both bedrooms Laura saw the pallor heighten in the lined face and the new worry spring to already anxious eyes.

'Business?' The word came quietly, his voice seeming too heavy to lift. 'What business can Walter Potts have with me?'

She had asked herself that question. Taking the rug from his knees as he stood up, Laura could not help but see the shake of his hands.

'It must be something amiss at the works. I hope there has not been an accident.'

'No.' Isaac shook his head, his steps slow as he left the kitchen. 'It will be no accident, were that the case I would have heard of it long afore Walter Potts.'

Inside the parlour the police sergeant still stood but now the round pill-box cap was in his hands, his fingers moving self-consciously over the stiff shiny peak.

'You wanted to see me, Walter?'

Isaac pointed to a chair but the sergeant shook his head.

'This don't be a social call, Isaac.'

'So Laura told me, but you taking a seat can't be breaking any law.'

Obviously uneasy the policeman settled his burly frame on to a chair then, his glance still on his cap, said, 'You might want to hear in private, the girl . . .'

'Will stay where her be! There be no . . .' He broke off, a frown fleeting across his brow. 'Say what you have to say, Walter.'

Standing beside the chair Isaac had taken, Laura rested a hand on his shoulder. Opposite her the sergeant's bushy beard twitched as he searched for words.

'There were a complaint . . .' Stubby fingers stroked the shiny peak of his cap. 'It were made at the station an hour ago.'

'Oh, ar! And what be this to do with me?'

'See here, Isaac . . . Laura wench . . . !' The sergeant looked up, his glance going from one to the other. '. . . I knows there can be no truth in this that be why I have called myself, duty is duty and that means when a complaint be made it has to be looked into. I'm sorry to have to bother you, but you understands.'

'Of course I understand and it is no bother. Say what it is you must, then share a glass of ale with me . . . if you can forget duty long enough.'

'Nothing I shall enjoy more, the law can turn a blind eye for a minute or two.' The policeman's face relaxed in a relieved smile. 'Isaac Cadman and me have been friends for too many years to let owt bar us from taking a tankard together.'

There had been a complaint made. In the kitchen Laura set two glasses on a tray then filled a jug with ale fetched from the scullery. But how could that have anything to do with her father or herself?

Carrying the tray to the parlour she set it on the table between the two men. Taking one glass the sergeant drank deeply. Then wiped his hand over his beard.

'It be this way, Isaac.' He cleared his throat, delaying the moment. 'There were a complaint, I had to . . .'

'It would be easier if you came right out with it.' Isaac watched the other man's face. ''Tis obvious the complaint concerns me for Laura could offend nobody, and whatever it is you can't be held responsible, Walter, the friendship you spoke of won't suffer for you doing what you gets paid to do.'

'Then I'll say it.' Walter touched a finger to the gleaming badge set at the front of the cap resting on his knee. 'An hour back a man came into the station. He said you had robbed him of a sum of money.'

'No!' Laura's gasp filled the tiny room.

'I questioned him for I knew there had been a mistake made but he remained adamant. Isaac Cadman was the man had robbed him and he wanted an arrest made. I'll have to ask you to accompany me along of the station, Isaac.' He looked at Laura's stricken face. 'It won't be for long, wench, just to get things cleared up; your father will be home in time for supper.'

Laura's hands tightened on her father's shoulders. 'Who?' she whispered. 'Who has laid this complaint?'

Rising to his feet the sergeant replaced his cap then eased the black leather belt secured about his middle, the embossed brass buckle glinting gold in the light of the lamp.

'I think we know the answer to that already, Laura.' Lifting a hand to his shoulder Isaac pressed it over hers.

Eyes on the bearded face she answered quietly, 'I want to hear it, Father . . . I want to hear it said.'

Uncomfortable beneath her stare the policeman shuffled his feet. 'It were your partner's lad.' Released at last, the words came clear and definite. 'It were Jabez Shaw's son.'

Edmund! Laura felt the earth reel beneath her feet. Edmund would do this to her father . . . to her! Not satisfied with taking their livelihood, with taking the business, he had accused her father in public, brought in the police. How could he? What more could he gain by doing such a thing?

Her movements trance-like she brought her father's coat, helping him on with it before wrapping herself in her shawl. He would be repaid. She followed the two men out into the street. Edmund would be repaid every penny, she had told him that. But it had not been enough, for some reason Edmund Shaw wanted more than his pound of flesh and he wanted the world to watch him take it.

'I am glad we have met once more.'

Sage-green eyes smiling above the rim of his wine glass, Sheldon Sinclair watched the face of the man sharing his table at the White Horse Hotel. Edmund Shaw was a discontented man. A discontented man with an inheritance! He had made discreet enquiries and what he had learned was interesting; and Edmund Shaw was interested in *him*, that he needed to make no enquiry to find out, it glowed in the man's eyes!

'Are you in Wednesbury for long?'

Looking into those velvet eyes Edmund knew he wanted the answer to be yes.

Covered by thick lashes the eyes lowered, following the glass to the table. 'Just a week or so, I am winding up the estate of an aunt of mine. She died a few weeks ago and left her property to me, but I have no wish to settle here so I am selling the house and all that goes with it. The whole thing has taken more time than I expected so I shall not be sorry to return to Birmingham. But you . . . your home and family are here in this town?'

Picking up his glass, Edmund took a swallow of the rich red Bordeaux Sinclair had ordered. It tasted good on his tongue.

'I have no family.' He watched the other man refill the glass, silently admiring the long fingers with their well-manicured nails. 'And following the funeral tomorrow my house too will go up for sale.'

'Funeral?' Sheldon Sinclair's brow creased slightly.

'My father.' Edmund supplied the information gladly. He enjoyed this man's company, the longer he could remain in it the happier he would be. 'He passed away several days ago, a heart attack brought on by a second stroke.'

'You have my deep condolences.' The low, musical voice seemed to caress. 'I know how you must feel your loss, especially so if you have no other family. We have not known each other very long so forgive me if what I say is unwelcome to you, but if there is anything I can do to help, anything at all, then please call upon me to do so. A friend can sometimes help where a fiancée could not.'

'I have no fiancée.' Edmund draped a snow-white serviette across his knee as he had seen Sheldon Sinclair do the evening before. 'There is nothing to keep me in Wednesbury. Like yourself I intend to sell the house and the business and then move away.'

The business! His glance following the knife with which he cut a piece of the tender T-bone steak that smothered the fine, white china plate, Sheldon Sinclair gave no outward sign that he was already familiar with knowledge of the engineering works, or that it was held in partnership with another man. That could prove a stumbling block.

'Selling a business; ah, now that could be a problem.' He raised his glance. 'Unless, of course, the board would be willing to buy you out.'

'The board?'

'The other men with interests in the business, partners,' Sheldon answered as Edmund took another swallow of wine.

'There is only one partner . . .'

Sheldon held his glance steady, though the answer was something of a blow. It would have been more conducive to what he had in mind had there been no other man involved.

Edmund chewed the meat, emptying his mouth before answering. 'Isaac Cadman and my father were in partnership but that partnership no longer exists. What was Shaw and Cadman Engineering is now only Shaw. He has no claim upon it.'

'You intrigue me.' Laying aside knife and fork, Sheldon touched his serviette to his lips. 'How can a partner not be a partner?'

'When he is fool enough to forego drawing up a contract.'

'No contract.' The laugh was short and held in the throat. 'I can hardly believe that.'

Edmund tipped back the contents of his glass into his mouth, feeling the glow of it reach past his stomach, feeding his confidence.

'Neither could Isaac Cadman.' He smiled, the effects of the wine weaving it across his thin mouth. 'He couldn't believe it either when I told him his so-called gentleman's agreement might not be enough.'

'But if there was no legally signed document between your father and this . . .'

'Isaac Cadman.'

'. . . this Isaac Cadman, then you have no more claim to the business than he.'

'My word against his.' Waiting while wine was tipped into his glass, Edmund drank it off in one gulp. 'I told him that an' all. He could take the case to Court, let the law decide, 'cept he don't have the money to pay and seeking justice can be pricey.'

Helping Edmund to yet another drink Sheldon Sinclair raised his own glass, but where Edmund swallowed a mouthful he merely touched the liquid to his lips.

'So this man resigned his claim?'

Eyes slightly glazed, the smile wide on his long-drawn features, Edmund laughed again.

'Not in so many words, but he will after tonight.'

'Why tonight in particular? What is special about tonight?'

With the dinner plates removed Sheldon surveyed a laden sweet-trolley, waving it away when Edmund loudly refused dessert, ordering instead two large Cognacs.

'What's shpecial?' Edmund slurred, fumbling the words around his tongue. 'I'll tell you what is shpecial. Isaac Cadman can't go to the law so I sent the law to him. Tonight Isaac Cadman will find himself behind bars.'

'Arrested?' Sheldon smiled. 'Surely you cannot have a man arrested for failing to seal a business arrangement with a legal document.'

'He won't be arrested for that, not because he held no contract. Isaac Cadman is to be arrested for thieving. He stole seven hundred and eighty pounds from the firm's account. Once that be local knowledge he will be only too glad to make no further demands regarding the business. From this night that works belongs solely to me!'

Solely to him. Sheldon Sinclair watched the brandy slide away down the other man's throat.

'This man you say has robbed you, does he have any family?'

Wine and brandy mixing potently, Edmund blinked as the

room tilted. Still smiling, Sheldon Sinclair took the brandy goblet from his fingers.

'Laura . . .' Edmund frowned, searching for words that seemed to slip away. '. . . he's got Laura.'

'You have your father's funeral tomorrow.' Sheldon changed the subject abruptly. 'And here I am keeping you talking. Forgive my thoughtlessness, Edmund, and allow me to call a hansom.'

'I don't want to go back to that house, that corpse . . .' His mouth firming truculently, Edmund slapped a hand to the table, setting the fragile glass bouncing. 'I hate that house same as I hate Jabez Shaw . . .'

'Then why go there? You are welcome to spend the night in my house.'

Already on his feet, Sheldon steadied the swaying Edmund as he pushed from the chair, his drunken smile restored. Holding his arm as they made their way from the hotel, helping bundle him into a waiting cab, Sheldon's mind raced. How much money was this man about to inherit, who was Isaac Cadman and who was Laura? He seemed to think he had them neatly erased from the picture . . . but had he? Only the man was liable for prison, that left the woman. In the dark recess of the hansom, he smiled.

A woman was as easily dealt with as Edmund Shaw would be.

Chapter Eleven

Beyond the window the shriek of a steam whistle calling the change of shifts at the Lea Brook Colliery blasted through the quiet streets. Laura glanced at the clock set on the shelf above the kitchen fire. Five o'clock. She must wait another five hours. Ten o'clock Sergeant Potts had told her after shutting her father in that awful cell. The magistrate would hear the case at ten o'clock the next morning.

She had begged the policeman to let her bring her father home but, sympathetic as he had been, Sergeant Potts had said a warrant for arrest meant what it said and though, were it left to him, he would be glad to let Isaac return home it could not be done. '*The law be the law, Laura wench,*' he had said solemnly, '*and though we might not like what it dictates we 'ave to abide by its ruling.*'

She had asked then at least to be allowed to stay with him, but again Sergeant Potts had said no. Isaac needed sleep he had said, and he wouldn't get it worrying about her sitting in a chair all night.

'*You 'ave known me long enough to believe when I tell you your father will be all right here at the station. You go home now and get your rest. By tomorrow noon this whole mistake will be cleared up and Isaac will be home.*'

He knew her father was no thief, that he did not deserve to be in jail . . .

Yet he had confessed to stealing that money!

Laura stared at the embers of the fire lying low in the grate.

Her father had owned to taking money, half of which he had known to belong to Jabez Shaw, so how could he not be called a thief? Sergeant Potts was a lifelong friend, a man willing to believe Isaac was no true criminal, but would the magistrate believe that . . . and even if he should could he allow that to interfere with the demands of the law?

Taking the poker she raked ashes from the dying fire, her steps slow and laboured as she forced herself to fetch the bucket of coals kept beneath the sink.

The demands of the law or the demands of Edmund Shaw?

Having tipped coal on to the fire and returned the bucket to the scullery she sank listlessly to the chair.

What did it matter which, each could be as vicious as the other and either way her father would suffer. Edmund must have known that, planned it so her father would not be able to hold his head up in Wednesbury again.

Prison! She stared at the flickering flames bringing life back to the fire. It might as well be Isaac Cadman as Jabez Shaw being laid in that churchyard today, for a term in prison would kill him.

Maybe it was not too late! Hope rising in her veins she stood up. Maybe if she asked once more, called upon the friendship they once shared, then maybe Edmund would withdraw the charge. He could have the works, she would pay back every penny, work as a servant in Edmund's house for the rest of her days; anything . . . she would do anything he asked if only he would withdraw the charge against her father.

'Was I alone?'

Edmund resisted the urge to put a hand to his aching head.

Discreetly placing a glass of frothing Eno's Fruit Salts in front of his master, the manservant hid a grim smile. Serve this bugger right if he never got rid of that headache, he had shown no respect at all for his dead father, and these last two nights he had come home drunk.

'No, sir.' He took the glass Edmund had drained. 'There was another man in the hansom.'

'Another man?' Edmund winced as his head came up sharply.

'He gave his name as Sinclair, he said you would know him. Will you take breakfast now?'

'What? No . . . no I don't want any breakfast.'

'I think you should, begging your pardon . . .'

'It doesn't matter what you think!' Edmund snapped. 'I don't want your bloody questions, just answer what I ask!'

Fingers tightening on the tray that held the glass, the manservant bit his teeth together. Jabez Shaw had often come home the worse for drink and sometimes his words had been sharp, but the next day the apologies had come just as quickly; never once had he insulted his staff deliberately. But this son of his seemed set to prove himself a different kettle of fish.

'Mr Sinclair, did he say anything else?'

'Nothing as I remember . . .'

'As you remember . . .' Edmund's voice rose to a squeak of anger. '. . . Christ, man, it wasn't a thousand years ago! You can't be so far gone as not to remember what you heard only hours since.'

'That is just it, the man spoke very quietly, I could not swear to being right about what he said.'

Exasperation increasing the throb at his temples, Edmund loosed a short breath. 'Then if your mind be so bloody feeble you can't be sure what you heard tell me what you *think* you heard.'

The few seconds he took to realign the glass on the tray a ploy to mask his growing resentment, the servant answered. 'It was something about his thinking that after all you would be better sleeping in your own bed.'

His glance meeting Edmund's head on, holding back nothing of his thoughts he went on, 'Will there be anything else?'

Almost smiling as Edmund turned his back, he added, 'May I remind you, the funeral is at two o'clock.'

He hadn't forgotten *that*! Throwing aside his chair, Edmund strode from the dining room. The fool of a man could not remember what he had been told last night but he could remember a funeral.

Slamming the door angrily as he left the house, he looked at the vista spread before him. Had the sky ever been blue or had it always been shut away behind that pall of dark smoke; had there ever been a time when the land had not festered with belching chimney stacks or writhed beneath the wounds of open coal pits? He drew a long breath, tasting the soot-laden air on his tongue.

Did Sheldon Sinclair live like this, surrounded by soot and smoke, people scratching at the earth's bowels to make a living? It wouldn't matter if only he and Sheldon . . .

Edmund snatched at the thought, pushing it back into the dark reaches of his mind, but on the surface of his memory the handsome face continued to smile.

'*Then why go there?*' Sage-green eyes seemed to smile. '*You are welcome to spend the night in my house . . .*'

But he had not been as good as his word, he had not taken him to his own house, he had brought him back to Squire's Walk. He had left no message, no promise to call or any word where he might be found. Or had he? Edmund's steps faltered as the seeds of suspicion sprouted. Had Sheldon Sinclair given a message that had gone unheard . . . or was Craddock keeping something back?

But why should he, why should the man withhold anything? But then Craddock had never liked him, and now he was master of the house it seemed the fellow liked him even less. But the Craddocks of this world mattered not at all. Edmund resumed the walk down the hill. He could be gotten rid of as could any that incurred the displeasure of Edmund Shaw, as Isaac Cadman had been gotten rid of.

'Edmund.'

The call dispelling his thoughts, Edmund glanced further down the hill.

'Edmund, I'm so glad I caught you before you . . . I was going to call at the house . . .'

It was not the voice he had hoped to hear, the voice he wanted to hear. Edmund felt the irritation of minutes ago return. Lengthening his step he swept past the figure half-running to meet him.

'Edmund . . . Edmund, please I have to speak to you.' Laura stared after the retreating figure.

'About what?' He turned suddenly, his face displaying all the anger inside him. 'I have heard all I want from the Cadmans . . . both of them!'

'Edmund, listen to me, please . . .' She ran to him. 'The police . . . Sergeant Potts came to the house last night . . . they took my father away, he is in the cells at the station, they would not let me bring him home.'

'So?' He raised a slow eyebrow.

'Don't you understand, Edmund, Father has been arrested.'

'What did you expect of a thief?'

Stunned by the coldness of it, Laura stared. Only a week ago this man had been her father's friend, now it seemed he detested him.

'Edmund, you know there must be a reason for his doing what he did, my father is not a thief . . .'

'Then what is he, what do *you* call a man who steals from another, a man who lies to cover his own misdoing?'

'I . . . I can only think he did it for someone else.'

'Someone else!' The sharp, deriding laugh spread itself on the morning. 'Who, Laura, who did your father steal for, was it for you, did he give that money to you?'

'No.' Laura's glance fell.

'Then who else . . . ?'

'I don't know!' Her strangled cry following after the laugh and joining it in the smoky air, Laura twisted the corners of her shawl between her fingers. 'I don't know, Edmund, but I promised you would have the money returned to you and you will, only help my father now. Withdraw the charge you have laid against him.'

His brows drawing together, Edmund looked at the girl his father had hoped for him to marry. Pale hair peeped from beneath a shawl that framed a face almost filled by eyes ringed in mauve shadows, high cheekbones accentuating its drawn mouth. Not even pretty! Jabez had wanted to marry him to a woman who was not even pretty!

'Withdraw.' The word came stone hard.

'Tell the sergeant there was been a mistake, that you do not wish my father brought before the magistrate.'

'You are asking me to cover the truth, to lie as Isaac Cadman has lied . . .'

'It would hurt no one.' Reaching out, Laura touched a hand to his sleeve. 'You and Father are the only two people involved and if the money is returned then where is the harm?'

'The harm is blinding yourself to the truth.' He glanced over her head, seeming suddenly to be a long way away. 'In thinking that to hide what has been done makes it unimportant. But what Isaac Cadman has done will not be hidden . . .'

'Why?' Laura almost sobbed. 'What has my father done to turn you against him?'

It seemed to take Edmund a long time to drag himself back from where his mind had taken him, and when he did he shook her hand from his arm.

'I can't stay any longer, I must go to the works and see to things there before the funeral.'

The funeral. That was something her father could not miss, he would never forgive himself if he did not pay his last respects to such an old friend.

'Edmund.' Her boots crunching on the dry ground she ran to catch up. 'Edmund, I beg you, please withdraw the charge. You can have the business, we will make no claim upon it, and I will keep my word to repay the money . . . please, Edmund, please, I will do anything . . . work as your unpaid servant, anything only please withdraw the charge before it is too late.'

Coming to a halt he looked down into her face, his think mouth becoming a straight line. 'It is already too late for Isaac Cadman. As for you, Laura, like I told you before, I have already had what I want from you.'

He would not withdraw the charge. He would not prevent her father being brought before the magistrate, humiliated . . . shamed.

Standing there half way along the hill Laura felt the world close in around her. Her father had not denied the claim Edmund Shaw had brought against him, he had not denied the offence when Sergeant Potts had read it out to him at the police station and he would not deny it before the magistrate. One hand clutching the shawl beneath her chin, she walked blindly down the hill towards the police station. Her father would speak the truth and that truth would put him in jail.

'The nature of the crime to which you have freely admitted is such that I cannot but impose the sentence upon you . . .'

Seated in the upstairs room of the George Hotel that served as a courtroom, Laura caught her breath.

'. . . to rob one's friend, a man who set his trust in you is a diabolical act and as such incurs the heaviest punishment. Isaac Cadman, I sentence you to be detained in Her Majesty's prison . . .'

'No..o..o!' Laura's agonised cry rang across the room, bringing the magistrate's glance swinging to her.

'Any disturbance in my courtroom will be severely dealt with, Sergeant, remove that woman before she too is sentenced to a month in prison.'

'The girl meant no offence, your worship.' Walter Potts moved quickly across to Laura, his hand clamping warningly to her shoulder.

'You know the woman, sergeant?'

'Since her was born, your worship.'

'What is your business here, girl?' Eyes keen over horn-rimmed glasses, the magistrate questioned Laura direct.

'Speak up, Laura wench, but take care against what you says.'

The sergeant's whisper in her ear, Laura glanced to where her father stood, a police constable on each side.

'I . . . I came to be with my father.'

'Your father.' The magistrate's voice rose slightly. 'And just what is your father doing here?'

Trembling fingers losing their grip on the shawl so it fell to her shoulders, Laura lifted her head high as she brought her gaze to the magistrate.

'He is being tried for theft.'

Glancing at the papers before him then back to Laura, he removed his spectacles, holding them between finger and thumb.

'The man in the dock is your father?'

'Yes.'

'Then I can understand your disagreeing with my findings. On those grounds, and for this one time only, I will overlook your disturbance but let me warn you, if ever you find yourself in a courtroom again, bind your tongue unless asked by a magistrate to do otherwise. Now tell me, young woman, why should the accused not go to prison?'

Involuntary steps taking Laura towards the magistrate's table, he lifted a dismissive hand to Sergeant Potts as he reached to draw her back.

'My father is no real criminal.' Eyes wide and bright with tears, Laura's voice caught on a sob. 'He took that money, half of which was his to take.'

Grey eyebrows drew together as the magistrate glanced at Isaac.

'Half of that money belonged to yourself . . . why did you not say so?' Receiving no answer he returned his glance to Laura. 'What you say intrigues me, and as the accused has said nothing

124

in his own defence the court is willing to hear you before sentence is passed.'

Looking to her father, his head slumped to his chest, Laura realised this was her last chance to help. Every breath trembling, shaking the words from her tongue, she told all she knew of the affair, finishing with, '. . . I saw Edmund again this morning, I told him he could have the business, we would make no claim upon it, that I would repay every penny and become a servant in his house for the rest of my life.' She glanced up, tears spilling freely now. 'I meant all I said, I am willing to sign papers to that effect.'

'Were you privy to any of this?' The magistrate turned to Edmund's solicitor.

Rising to his feet the man shuffled, obviously ill-at-ease with the answer he was forced to give.

'Not with the last, your worship. My client said only that a theft had been committed.'

'For which guilt has been clearly established.' The magistrate replaced his spectacles, looking over the top of them at Laura. 'What you have told us has our sympathy. However the problem of who or who does not have title to that engineering works is not the business of this court, therefore it cannot be allowed to have bearing upon sentence.' Taking the gavel in his hand he held it poised in the air.

Breath held tight in her throat, hands clutched at her sides, the earth suddenly became a vacuum in which she floated isolated from sound or movement. The magistrate's lips moved, her father's head lifted, turning to her, the police sergeant's hand closed over her elbow but none of it was real, nothing was real . . .

'Laura, hold on, Laura wench!'

The hand shook her elbow, bringing her back to reality.

'. . . sentence the law allows . . .'

The breath would not come . . . she could not breathe.

'. . . for theft of the sort to which you have confessed is twenty years' hard labour . . .'

Laura felt the hand on her elbow tighten, saw the look in her father's eyes.

'. . . however, given that this is a first offence, grave though it undoubtedly is, and taking into consideration the blamelessness of your conduct to that moment the court is prepared to combine mercy with justice. Isaac Cadman,' the gavel rose, 'you have been found guilty as charged. It is my duty to pass sentence accordingly. You will be detained in Her Majesty's prison for a period of fifteen years.'

The gavel coming hard into its wooden cradle, the magistrate's keen glance played over Laura's stricken face, then as he rose to leave he added, 'The prisoner will be allowed one quarter hour with his daughter before sentence commences.'

Breaking free of the sergeant's hold Laura flew across the room, throwing herself into her father's arms.

'It's all right, Laura, my little girl.' Isaac smoothed the pale hair, imprinting the softness of it on his heart. This was all he would ever have of his daughter. They would not live in the same house again. Fifteen years in prison! He would not live to see them pass. 'It's all right. Something will come along . . . I will be home soon, you'll see.' The lie cold on his lips, Isaac pressed them to the head held tight against his chest. Edmund Shaw had waited long to see this day. God be thanked Jabez had not lived to witness it.

'Laura, child, listen to me.' He tried to hold her at arm's length but she clung stubbornly to him. Folding both arms about her he went on softly. 'Today Jabez Shaw will be taken to his rest. I had not wanted him to go without my respects being paid but that is now beyond hope; so I ask you, Laura, go to that church in my stead, give Jabez what is due to an old friend. Promise me, Laura . . . promise me.'

Words drowning beneath sobs, Laura could only nod.

'One more thing you must promise.' Determination lending strength to his arms he managed to release her grip, holding her so he could see her face.

'Stay away from Edmund. Let him keep the business, that will more than reimburse him for the money I took. He has visited his spite upon me, that I can bear; but I cannot live with the thought of his visiting it upon you and he will if you cross him, Laura. Forget what he has done . . . forget it and give me peace.'

'Time be up, Isaac.' Walter Potts stepped forward.

'Remember, Laura.' Isaac looked at her as the constables came for him. 'Have no more dealings with Edmund Shaw . . . tell me I can go in peace.'

Looking into the faded eyes brimming with tears, Laura sobbed. 'I love you, Father, I love you, I will . . .'

But the door had already closed. Her father was gone.

Chapter Twelve

The church of St John rose from its surrounding grave stones, its spire a black finger pointing to a heaven obscured by never-ending drifts of smoke.

Standing at the edge of a group of curious onlookers, Laura watched the coffin being set down beneath the Lych Gate, the plain deal unadorned by wreaths.

'Who be it?'

She heard the whispers pass from one to the other, curiosity offset by pity.

'Ain't got no idea, but whoever it be inside that box it don't seem as how anybody think a flower be due.'

'Poor sod! Surely a flower wouldn't be too much to ask.'

'That be right an' all. It don't be seemly to send anybody off wi'out a token, no matter who they be.'

Laura pulled the shawl closer about her head as the whispers flitted to and fro. In her troubles she had forgotten about a wreath and Edmund had not cared to provide one. Did his spite reach out to Jabez as well as it had to her father?

From the door of the church the priest, with book in hand, walked slowly down the path, April sunlight reflecting off his white lace-edged surplice, a gold crucifix gleaming against his chest. On each side of her women crossed themselves, Laura following suit as the priest came level with the coffin then turned to lead it into the church, his voice intoning prayers drowned by the rumble of a passing steam tram.

'Eh up! See who that be?' A woman nudged her neighbour.

'That be Jabez Shaw's lad,' the woman answered.

'An' the one in the box be his father.' The first woman sniffed disapprovingly. 'What kind of son brings his father to his rest with not so much as a flower to brighten his way? Disgustin', that be what I calls it, disgustin'.'

'Don't show respect that be certain. I tell you were he a lad of mine I'd kick his arse into his ear'oles!'

'My Jack 'as worked at that place his father set up along of Potters Lane from its first starting, he says there never seemed to be no love lost atween the two.'

The other woman turned away as the coffin was borne towards the church followed by its solitary mourner.

'Mebbe not but you would 'ave thought whatever feelings rode between them they would 'ave been put aside for this day. I mean look at him following! Could be he don't possess no black suit, that be understood, but he ain't even tied a black band to his arm. No respect . . .' She moved off, muttering as she went. '. . . I don't know what this world be coming to . . . no respect.'

'I had not wanted him to go without paying the respect due to an old friend.'

The words her father had spoken returned to her mind and in her mind she answered. He would be given her father's respects, and hers too.

Her boots crunching on the gravel pathway caused Edmund to turn. For a moment he stared at her then strode to stand in front of her.

'What do you mean by coming here?' he demanded. 'You are not wanted!'

Over his shoulder Laura saw the coffin disappear into the church.

'My father asked I pay his respects.'

'Hummph!' His mouth thinning in a sneer, Edmund glared.

'A respect he felt so deeply in Jabez' lifetime? A respect so strong it could not prevent his robbing him!'

Though parting with her father, watching him being taken away by the police, was still a searing hurt inside her, Laura tried to understand. What she was feeling must be being felt by Edmund; he too must be heart-broken at losing a parent, that was the reason behind this new outburst.

'Edmund . . . Edmund, I know what you must be feeling at losing your father . . .'

'Do you!' he snapped, anger bringing a vibrance to his pale eyes. 'Do you know what I am feeling? I doubt that, I doubt that very much. Lose a father and a man loses a best friend, that's the best laugh I've had in my life. Jabez Shaw was no . . .'

He paused, the struggle to bring his emotions under control visible on his long features, and when he spoke his voice was flat and cold.

'The ceremony is private. That is all the respect required of Isaac Cadman.'

Turning on his heel he strode away without a backward glance.

Edmund wished the ceremony to remain private. Laura stared at the smoke-grimed building. She could not intrude upon that. But how could she tell her father she had failed to do the one thing he had hoped to do for himself? How could Edmund behave this way, what devil was driving him?

Her steps slow, she returned along the path passing beyond the Lych Gate and into the busy street. They had been such good friends her father and Jabez, and her father held it a duty to pay respect at a friend's passing.

'*A respect so strong it could not prevent his robbing him?*'

Edmund's contempt stung again.

Perhaps he was entitled to that. She pulled her shawl over her head, holding it tight beneath her breasts. After all her father had robbed Jabez; but then was that not what Edmund Shaw had done to her father? But it was no seven hundred and eighty pounds he had stolen, not just a business or even a man's pride; Edmund Shaw had robbed her father of his life!

Quickening her steps she walked rapidly along Lower High Street, past the Shambles, turning left into Union Street.

Yes, Edmund had robbed her father of everything but he would not rob him of the privilege of knowing Jabez had been given his respect.

Half an hour later, breath coming in short, laboured gasps from running back along the street, she stood in the churchyard as the priest led the coffin to the freshly dug grave, the simple bunch of white freesias she had purchased from Mary O'Connell's flower shop clutched in her hand.

Drawing behind a tall stone plinth of a carved angel, wings partly unfurled at its top, Laura watched as Edmund passed by. She would wait until the churchyard was empty before placing the flowers on that coffin.

'I am the Resurrection and the Life . . .'

The words drifted over the churchyard, the noise of tram and cart seeming to halt, leaving the street in a quiet hush of tribute to the dead.

'. . . he that believeth in me . . .'

Laura felt the tremble that shook her hands. Her father had believed, believed that if a man led a good, honest life he would have no trouble . . . But then he had not been honest, he had committed theft! But God would forgive where Edmund Shaw had not.

'. . . Ashes to ashes, dust to dust . . .'

A sob trembling on her mouth, she peeped from behind the stone memorial. At the head of the grave the priest intoned the last of the funeral rite, his hand raised in a final blessing as the coffin was lowered into the earth. From one side of the priest the church warden stepped across to Edmund, holding out a small shallow box filled with soil.

For a moment he looked at the proffered box then, lifting his hand, shoved it away. Stepping to the edge of the hole that held the remains of his father he stared down at the wooden box.

'Here is all you cared for, Jabez.'

His voice, loud as it was cold, rang over the churchyard. Withdrawing a hand from the pocket of his jacket he held it poised over the gash in the earth.

'Take them with you to hell, Jabez, for they are the last that will ever come from Shaw and Cadman!'

Her eyes glued to him, her ears catching his mocking laugh, Laura caught her breath as he drew his hand slightly back before hurling a handful of screws and bolts on to the coffin. Then without a word or glance at the priest he turned away.

It was as he strode past the stone memorial that the breeze caught the edge of her shawl.

The movement catching his eye Edmund glanced sideways, the sight of Laura bringing him to a sharp stop.

'I told you to leave!'

Looking into a face pinched and white with fury, Laura felt her earlier trepidation fade completely. Her own face reflected the calm that settled upon her. She was here to do what her father would have wanted, not to do as Edmund Shaw ordered.

'. . . I told you the funeral service was private!'

Priest and warden passing back towards the church glanced curiously at Laura, she answering their nod of greeting with a quick bob of her head.

'And I observed that privacy.' She watched the two men disappear inside the building. 'I did not go into the church neither did I approach the graveside whilst the service was still in progress. But the service is over now and the churchyard is public ground. You have no jurisdiction here, Edmund. I shall pay your father the respect you could not show.'

'I said leave!' he barked. 'It's over!'

Glancing at the flowers tied with their broad band of purple mourning ribbon, she touched a finger to a delicate white petal.

'Yes, it's over,' she murmured, then raising her glance stared directly into his pale eyes. 'It is all over, Edmund, the friendship

I once believed we shared, the future I thought we might have together.'

'I never gave you cause to think my future would be spent with you!'

'No.' She smiled. 'No, you did not. That was girlish imagination, but like any feeling I once harboured for you that is completely gone. But my feelings for your father are not.'

His mouth screwed so tight with anger words could hardly pass his lips, he glared down at her but Laura did not lose her smile.

'Jabez will stay in my heart, Edmund, long after I have forgotten you exist.'

The words almost a physical blow, Edmund's head jerked on his neck. Then his mouth relaxed into a slow, contemptuous smile.

'No, Laura.' The words slid out easily now, quiet and heavy with threat. 'That is something I can guarantee will never happen. No matter where you go, no matter how long you live, I vow you will never forget Edmund Shaw. Take your flowers to Jabez if you must, pay Isaac's respects, the respect you think due, but I say . . .'

'It does not matter what you say, Edmund.' Laura's head lifted, the smile dying on her lips. 'Nothing you can ever say will affect me any more.'

Behind his eyes an indefinable shadow dulled the glint, but in a moment it was gone.

'Don't believe that, Laura,' he breathed, 'whatever else you hold to, never believe that!'

'I think a change of scene might be good for you.'

Edmund Shaw looked at the handsome face smiling at him from the sofa set beneath the window of the sitting room. He had thought never to see Sheldon Sinclair again. There had been no word, no sign of him since the evening he had escorted him home from the White Horse.

'I won't say I am not tempted.' He watched the smile deepen in those remarkable sage-green eyes.

'What fun is there in temptation if you do not give in to it at least once?' Sheldon leaned against the tapestried sofa, crossing one elegantly sheathed leg over the other.

'There are things I have to do. Since the funeral . . .'

'Ah yes, your father. A sad business but one that must be gotten over, you cannot let sorrow rule your life and whatever it is you have to do cannot possibly come to any harm by your taking a few days' rest. Do as I say, come back with me just for a little while, you will return feeling better I promise you.'

The sale of the works could wait, there was no immediate rush. Edmund ran the idea around in his mind. Jonas Small could run things until he got back and there would be no interference from Laura Cadman.

Fifteen years! That was what the magistrate had given Isaac. Edmund's pale eyes darkened. It should have been life!

Across the room Sheldon Sinclair could see the interest he had aroused disappearing behind a stronger emotion. If he hoped to keep the man in tow he must make his move now. His movement unhurried he rose, brushing a hand against a braided lapel.

'I must leave. Like yourself, I have things I must do.'

'The property your aunt bequeathed you . . . it's sold?'

'A week ago; I was glad to see the back of it. Holding on to property can be such a drag on one's life, do you not find it so?'

The glance holding fast to his held a deeper question than Sheldon Sinclair had given voice to, but Edmund could read it clearly. Why be saddled with a life he did not want when a new one was within his reach?

'There is nothing now to keep me here and since my aunt is no longer with us, and her estate disposed of, I shall not be returning to Wednesbury again. That was my reason for calling upon you today, to say goodbye and wish you well for the future.'

Holding out his hand, his smile becoming a faint shadow about his mouth, he slid a slow glance over Edmund's face as if storing every detail in his heart.

'I have enjoyed your company, Edmund, what little there was of it.' The hand clasping Edmund's tightened slightly, the voice softening to the velvet of those compelling eyes. 'I wish we could have had more time together, but that is a selfish wish, you have a business to run. Yet even so . . .' The softness of his eyes intensified, seeming to draw everything into their endless green depths. '. . . I feel we could have had a truly wonderful time . . . together.'

Together! The word drummed in Edmund's mind as his hand was released. It had been two weeks since he had last been in this man's company, two weeks in which he had thought of him every minute, looked for him on every street and in every hotel. Now he was leaving this town for good, chances were he would never see him again.

He had invited him to stay, to be with him at his home. He could accept, take the chance while it was offered. Indecision clear on his face, Edmund followed the other man into the hall. Just three days, that was all! Three days and he would return . . . but . . .

Easing his long fingers into doe-skin gloves, Sheldon accepted the tall silk hat Edmund held out to him. His smile holding just the right amount of pathos he said quietly, 'So then it is goodbye, Edmund . . . I shall treasure the memory of our short acquaintance, what a pity it could not have been longer.'

'It can.' The words tumbled out. 'I shall do as you say, I shall take a few days' rest. If your offer of hospitality is still open . . .'

'But of course.' The green eyes glowed. 'Nothing could be more of a delight to me than to have you as my guest.'

Climbing into the waiting hansom Sheldon raised a hand. 'Until tomorrow.'

Driving down the gentle slope of Squire's Walk he leaned into the leather upholstery.

A few days. He smiled. There would be more than a few days, and at the end of them . . . ?

The smile widened.

'Mother said we was to come see as you was all right.'

Laura looked at the two children stood at the scullery door. Red hair pointing in all directions, eyes bright as new pennies, they smiled up at her.

'Yes, thank you, Alfie, I . . . I am quite all right.'

'You sound like our mother when her says her be all right and we knows her ain't 'cos her be half cryin'. You be half cryin', don't you?' The younger boy caught her hand.

It would be easier were she left alone. Having to talk to people made the tears more difficult to hold. But everyone in Great Western Street had been so kind, so understanding. Like the Baileys they meant well, wanting only to help.

'I am half crying, Teddie but then I always am when I have been peeling onions.' It was a refuge from further questioning and though it was only part truth she took it.

Cocking his head on one side the six-year-old's face held a wisdom beyond his years. 'Ar, our mother says that an' all, her says it when we ain't had no onions for a week!'

'Well I have got onions, a panful over the fire and you, young man, can take the peelings to the heap for me.'

'Best let me do that, he will only leave a trail of them across the yard for you to pick up in the morning.' Ever the man, Alfie stepped forward, taking up the bowl of vegetable remains from the board adjoining the brownstone sink. 'Mother says if ever you wants a mess making then give our Teddie a job to do, he can make a bigger mess of a thing than anybody else her knows.'

'I can make a mess of your nose, Alfie Bailey!'

Fists doubling as he released Laura's hand, the boy made to follow his brother into the yard.

'There will be none of that here.' Her quick reaction catching him by the coat collar, Laura held on to the wriggling form. 'I thought you came to help me, not to brawl in my yard.'

'You be right.' Teddie stopped wriggling, his arm reaching up to her. 'I got the rest of the day to knock our Alfie's 'ead off.'

'I emptied the bowl and swilled it out.'

Laura's smile of gratitude was weak but no less well meant as Alfie joined her and Teddie in the kitchen.

'You didn't leave no ring round it did you?' Teddie demanded.

'I am sure Alfie washed the bowl thoroughly.' Laura stepped in swiftly, the role of peacemaker between the two being nothing new to her. Inside she wanted to smile. These two argued with each other but the bond of brotherhood was strong; the one would fight tooth and nail for the other were the need to arise.

'Mother said to do anything you wanted doing.' Alfie glanced at the pot simmering above the fire, trying not to sniff the appetising aroma of frying onions.

The meal she had prepared would be enough to share. She pretended not to notice the glance. Somehow she could not yet bring herself to make a meal big enough just for herself; day after day, deep within, she prayed her father would come home, would walk into the kitchen as she served the meal, just as he had always done.

'Would you reach me a basin from the dresser, Alfie.' She pushed the hopeless wish aside.

'What can I do?' Eyes shining like newly minted pennies, Teddie wiped a hand beneath his nose.

'You can fetch me the ladle, you will find it hanging on the inside of the pantry door.'

Their separate tasks quickly achieved, the boys stood beside the table watching Laura fill the basin with boiled potatoes, laying several slices of cooked liver on the top then smothering it over with fried onion and gravy.

Spreading a clean white cloth she placed the basin on it before drawing two corners together and tying them into a knot.

Repeating the process she tied the remaining corners over the top of the first, forming a carrying handle.

Handing it to Alfie she smiled briefly. 'Take that to your mother, tell her I made more than I could use.'

'We didn't come here for you to give us your dinner.'

Alfie stepped away, his grin suddenly gone. 'Mother said to see if we could be of help and that was all.'

'I understand and I appreciate your mother thinking of me and you for coming.' Laura felt her own embarrassment match that of her young visitor. Mary Bailey must have drummed it into her sons not to take food from her now that she was alone. It was probably a wise move on Mary's part. Laura rested the basin again on the table. The time would soon come when the money she had put by from the weekly housekeeping would be gone, then meals would be hard to come by; but until then, until she absolutely had to make changes, it was somehow vital to her that things remain as they had been before.

Before her world had toppled, before her father had been taken from her, before Edmund had turned his back on her!

Fingers tightening about the cloth handle she felt the tears, hot and stinging, slide beneath her closed lids, her mouth tightening on the sobs that shook her body.

'Don't cry, Missis Laura . . .'

Teddie flung himself forward, both arms going about her middle, his freckled face pressing against her waist.

'We'll look after you, we won't let nobody hurt you. We love you, Missis Laura, me and our Alfie we love you and we'll look out for you 'til your father be home.'

Until her father was home!

Laura's hand rested on the basin the children had refused to take.

They would look out for her until her father was home.

The thought should have been a comfort to her, the thought that one day this nightmare would be over and they would once more be together.

The words she whispered each night after her prayers came now, soft and whispering.

'It is only a matter of time.'

But there was no comfort in the words, they were empty as her days were empty.

'Father . . . oh, Father!'

Her cry resounding in the quiet kitchen, she sank to her knees beside his empty chair.

Time would be too much for Isaac Cadman.

Chapter Thirteen

The handle of the heavy basket digging painfully into her arm, Laura rested it on the platform, the indignant tut-tutting of people hurrying to and from Birmingham Snow Hill Station undisguised as they pushed roughly past her. Behind her the rush of steam and the blast of a whistle announced the departing train.

It was so unlike the railway station at Wednesbury. There people smiled and the station master was ever ready with a kindly word and a helping hand. But here no one smiled, no one cared.

But then why should they! Laura chivvied herself. They probably had problems of their own, why ask a stranger for hers!

'Excuse me . . .'

Drawn out of her thoughts, Laura looked at the woman who stood a little way from her.

'I couldn't help but notice you stood there, you be the same girl I seen visiting Winson Green prison a month ago.'

Laura's colour rose quickly and she glanced at the bustling figures making their way along the platform to the exit.

'It's all right.' The woman smiled briefly. 'Ain't nobody here cares you be going to that place . . . ain't nobody here cares if you be going to hell! But it might be safer if we goes on together, that be if you have no objection.'

Safer. Laura thought of her first visit a month before. She had asked directions of several women but when she had mentioned

Winson Green prison they had hurried away, their mouths tight, their fingers clamped firm on their bags and purses as if she were some pickpocket accosting them. Then she had asked that man. Shuddering at the memory she picked up the basket, clutching it against her stomach.

He lived not far from the prison he had said, and since it was time for his dinner and he was going home, he would show her the way. She had murmured her thanks, trying not to look at the yellowed teeth or the clothes steeped in grease and dirt.

She had followed through the streets, narrow and twisting as a rabbit warren, along alleyways darkened by buildings that almost met overhead and leading off in all directions.

He had stopped in a deserted street, grinning when she had said surely this could not be the place she wanted to be.

'*But it be the place I wants to be.*'

The memory of those words and the rough hands grabbing her, forcing her into a foul-smelling house, filled her throat with sickness. Swift as a striking serpent, he had pushed her backwards on to that filthy floor, laughing as he snatched at her under-clothes, forcing her legs wide as his vile-smelling mouth closed over hers.

The flesh crawling on her bones, Laura caught her breath, her inner gaze fixed on a scene only she could see.

She had cried out as he had released her mouth, but his hand catching her a fierce blow to the face had knocked her almost senseless.

He had taken his time then, easing open the buttons of her blouse one by one, his hateful lust-filled eyes fixed on her face. Just as slowly he had undone the fastenings of her chemise, a breath of satisfaction loud as he pulled it apart.

'*I've 'oped for such as this for a good long time . . .*'

He had fastened a hand on each of her breasts squeezing the delicate tips.

'*. . . now I got it . . . and I be going to enjoy it . . .*'

Dropping on to her sprawled beneath him, he closed his

mouth over one breast, closing his rotting teeth about the nipple, pulling it savagely.

Remembering the pain and the horror Laura whimpered, her knuckles white where her hands gripped the basket.

It seemed he lay across her for ever, the foul odour of his body drifting into her nostrils. Then he had lifted himself and she had cried out with relief. It was over, he would go, leaving her alone.

'I likes that . . . I likes it when a woman cries out for more . . .'

Her eyes had sprung open, fear a bright beacon in their depths.

'. . . well you be going to get more, girlie . . .' He had leered, both hands stroking her smarting breasts. *'. . . I be going to give you the best bit right now . . .'*

His legs straddled across her, he knelt upright, dirt-ingrained fingers releasing a wide, buckled belt.

'. . . you don't have to 'elp, girlie . . .' He had grabbed her hair with one hand, twining his fingers in it so it pulled at the roots. Grinning as she had cried out with pain he went on, *'. . . Bull Benton can tek his own trousers down, 'specially for a girlie like you.'*

'Please! Please let me go!' Laura remembered her own begging and the coarse, gravelling laugh that had bubbled in his throat.

'O'course I'll let you go, once you've had this . . .'

He had lowered himself, his hand seeking her breast, his mouth once more closing on hers, the hardness of his flesh throbbing against her thigh.

'. . . Bull Benton likes to satisfy a woman . . .'

'An' that be all Bull Benton likes to do . . . he don't like to do anything else, the idle bastard . . .'

Laura heard the shout, felt his body jerk as a boot came hard against his bare backside.

Another swift kick helping him to roll off her, Laura saw the woman stood over them, her plump face red with fury, a broad-bladed knife raised above one shoulder.

'Bull Benton thinks he can treat me same as he's treated all the others who have worked to keep 'im.' The knife blade had caught the drift of light

seeping through the open doorway, glinting as the woman raised it higher. *'Well we'll see 'ow he satisfies 'em once I be through with 'im; he'll be a bull all right . . . a bloody castrated bull!'*

He had rolled away from her, scrambling to his feet as the woman had bent to her. Laura felt again the great sweeping wave of relief, her cries of thanks as with one hand the woman hauled her to her feet.

'And you . . . you bloody doxy . . . you get yourself gone afore I slices them pretty tits off! You won't keep your customers long once they sees you got none.'

She had shoved her towards the street, the knife still threatening above Laura's head, then in the doorway had brought it slashing down.

Watching it fall towards her hand, Laura had screamed while every muscle of her body became paralysed with the fear of what was happening. The woman intended to mutilate her!

Her eyelids pressed hard down, Laura heard again the swish of that blade descending towards her, and a whimper broke from her lips.

The woman had laughed in unison with that terrified cry, then the knife had sliced through the strap of the bag still hanging from Laura's wrist.

'You can leave this behind.' Catching up the purse, the woman had waved it in her face. *'It will pay for the services you've just had.'*

'I asked if you had a fancy go on to Winson Green along of me, but if you don't I'll be on my way.'

Swept back to the present, Laura's eyelids lifted.

Threadbare brown coat stretched taut even over her pathetically thin body, the woman who had spoken earlier still stood on the platform.

Her senses not yet completely her own, Laura stared wordlessly.

'Well don't never say I didn't offer!' The woman turned towards blackened stone arches that gave on to the street. 'But if a bit of advice ain't above your acceptin' you best mek a move or the tram to Handsworth will be gone and 'alf your visiting time gone with it.'

'A tram!' Laura half ran, catching the woman as she passed beneath a high curved arch. 'Is there a tram runs to the prison?'

The woman winced, lifting her foot to brush away the stone caught in the hole that mostly ate away the sole of her boot.

'Not to the jail exactly.' The stone gone she walked on rapidly, the tap of almost bare feet slapping against the pavement. 'But near enough. Saves a body a fair walk and p'raps a fair bit o' worry an' all. It don't be too sensible a thing for a woman to walk some of these alleyways by herself, not that I be saying all of the folk of Brummagem be rogues and vagabonds, but there be a few I wouldn't want to meet up with on a foggy night . . . no nor a clear one neither.'

She had not known about the tram. Her feet kept rhythm with the woman hurrying beside her, but Laura's thoughts slid into the past.

The thought of her father waiting for that monthly visit the only thing holding her together, she had stumbled from that house, fastening her clothing as she went. With no idea in which direction to go she had caught the conversation of two women passing the end of an alleyway. They were talking of Winson Green prison. Praying that was where they were headed she had followed.

'Three 'alfpenny return, Handsworth.'

Laura seated beside her on the wooden bench that ran both sides of the tram, the woman held out two coins to the conductor who clipped a pink ticket in the machine held in one hand, his eyebrows raising as he glanced at Laura.

'Ain't seen you afore,' he said sourly, 'you another going to Winson Green jail? Bloody criminals, 'ang the lot of 'em I says!'

'It ain't every criminal be in Handsworth jail, some of 'em be conducting on Handsworth trams!' The woman held the coin she had been given as change on the flat of her palm. 'I be due a 'alfpenny this be only a farthing. You be a bigger bloody thief than my old man and a richer one if you does every woman down by slipping her short in her change.'

'It were a mistake, it can easy happen when the tram be full.' Edged about by whiskers, his narrow face pink as the ticket he had clipped, the conductor fumbled through coins held in a leather bag fastened about his waist with a stout strap, as the chorused assent of several passengers ran the length of the tram.

'Ar, too bloody easy!' The woman grabbed the extra farthing handed to her, stuffing it inside a purse every bit as shabby as her too-small coat. 'But you try it once more on me, mister, and you'll feel my boot against your arse!'

Watching as Laura was handed another of the pink tickets the woman grabbed her hand, running a quick eye over the change from her sixpence.

'You 'ave to watch some of 'em,' she glanced at the conductor retreating rapidly along the body of the tram, "specially so when you be on your way back. Most of the women be in tears then, all upset at leaving their menfolk they don't pay so much atten-tion to what they be given. That be when the like of that one makes his money.'

'Thank you. I will be careful.'

Fifteen years! Laura felt despair flood into her. How could she stand fifteen years of this, terrified of being caught by another man intent on raping her, of others hoping to rob her . . . ?

But she had to stand it.

Following the woman from the tram, hearing the quick ring of the bell that sent it trundling away, she looked up at the high red-brick wall surrounding the body of the prison, its own walls punctured by mean, narrow slits of windows barred against the world.

Yes, she would stand it. She would face whatever she had to for the father she loved.

✶

How did men endure this? Laura followed behind the group of women, a uniformed prison guard leading them along a passage that smelled of damp and despair. On each side walls rose bleak and bare, seeming to Laura to be held together by a wretchedness that was born out of the miseries of human life.

This was where Edmund Shaw had caused her father to be sent, where he had condemned him to live for fifteen years.

'Prisoners will be through in a minute.' The guard ushered them into a huge, square, empty room, keys rattling as he re-locked the door.

This was where she had met with her father a month ago, here in this room, with every other prisoner who had a visitor; one hour per month was all they were allowed, and that here among all the others. Not that there had been all that many. She remembered some of the stricken looks on the faces of men ordered back to their cells when no visitor arrived for them. She would not let that happen to her father, but to see him here, where every word was listened to by guards! Even the cell she knew he shared with three other men would have offered at least a pretence of privacy.

On the opposite side of the room keys rattled in the lock of the one door. Around the walls the assembled warders drew thick wooden truncheons, holding them significantly across the open palms of their hands as the door opened and prisoners shuffled through in single file, some faces lighting up as they paired with their visitor, others falling dejectedly as they were herded back through the door.

Where was her father? Laura's glance roved over every face.

Why had he not come, he would surely know she would let nothing prevent her being here?

Checking each man's face again she glanced more keenly at them. In that horrible prison clothing it would be easy to miss her father.

But he was not here!

At a loss she turned to the guard who had accompanied them

since they stepped through the massive wooden gates that closed Winson Green prison to the world.

'My father, he . . . he is not here.'

'What name, miss?'

'Cadman . . . Isaac Cadman.'

'And you be?'

'His daughter. I am Laura Cadman.'

'Wait here a minute, miss, I'll see what it is has kept him.'

Giving a quick, not unkind, smile the guard signalled to one of his fellows then let himself out of the room.

All around the buzz of voices hushed beneath the sentinel gaze of warders brushed against Laura's ears. Time, those precious minutes were ticking away; why had he not come with these others?

Fear edging the worry seeping cold into her mind, she tried to find an explanation but all that would come was . . . why?

Keys sounding in the heavy lock she saw the sympathetic look on the face of the returning guard, but her glance passing beyond his burly figure found no trace of her father.

'Where is my father . . . why don't you bring him?'

The anguish of the cry brought several stares from the prisoners standing together with their womenfolk but any sympathy they had was soon lost beneath their own need to talk to loved ones.

'Come with me, miss.'

The guard stood to one side, indicating Laura to step out of the visiting room. Locking the door behind them he spoke quietly to another guard posted in the corridor then, heavy boots ringing on the stone floor, led the way to the end of the passage and on up a steep flight of stairs.

'Wait here, miss.' He stopped before a door marked Governor.

Why had he brought her here? Fingers twisting together, Laura kept her eyes on the closed door. Every nerve tuned to it she started visibly when it opened and the guard called her in.

Seated behind a large desk on which a heavy metal stand supported a pair of glass ink wells, a man rose politely as she entered.

'Good afternoon, Miss Cadman, I was hoping you would visit today . . .'

'Please!' Laura interrupted, forgetful for once of her good manners. 'Please, all I want is to see my father.'

'And you will.' He signed to the waiting guard to bring a chair to the front of the desk. 'But first I must speak to you. Please, be seated.'

Didn't he know how long she had waited . . . didn't he know that all the time she was allowed with her father was one hour in a month?

'Miss Cadman,' the Governor began as she opened her mouth to speak, 'I am afraid I have some unfortunate news . . .'

Her father! Laura felt the room spin. Something had happened to her father!

'Are you all right, Miss Cadman . . . a little Sal Volatile perhaps?'

'No.' It was only a whisper but Laura's answer was firm. 'No, thank you. I need only to see my father.'

'Yes, yes of course. Your father is in the infirmary.'

The colour draining from her face, Laura half fell against the desk. Her father was in the infirmary . . . he was ill.

'Allow me, miss.'

The guard who had brought her to this room caught her elbow, lowering her gently into the chair.

Eyes wide with fear of what might come next, Laura forced her lips to move.

'What is wrong with my father . . . is he ill?'

Grey head nodding, the Governor looked at her. This was the daughter of a condemned thief, a self-confessed embezzler, but the love she bore so obviously saw only the man not the deed.

'I am afraid he is, Miss Cadman.' He answered compassion-ately, a pity for the girl softening his tone. 'Your father suffered a fall some three weeks ago . . .'

'Three weeks!' Laura gasped. 'My father suffered a fall three weeks ago and you sent me no word.'

'Miss Cadman.' His reply stern despite the sympathy that still showed in his face the Governor leaned forward, his hands on the desktop. 'This is a prison, a place of punishment for offenders against the Crown and against its subjects. It is not, I regret, an establishment formed to cater for or observe the wishes of a pris-oner's dependants. I called you here out of a desire to spare you any unnecessary distress, to assure you your father will be cared for to the best of the prison's ability.'

'Thank you.' Fumbling for the handkerchief she had placed in her pocket before leaving the house, Laura touched it to her quivering mouth. 'Forgive my outburst, I meant no rudeness. It . . . it is just . . .'

'I understand, Miss Cadman, you need say nothing more. The guard will conduct you to the infirmary.'

'There is little more than five minutes of visiting time left, Stephen.'

His presence unnoted until now, a tall dark-haired man dressed in a deep-grey thigh-length coat trimmed with black and worn with black trousers, stepped from the further side of a tall cabinet.

Looking up at him Laura caught her breath.

'We meet once more, Miss . . . Cadman?'

Laura watched the elegant rise of a dark eyebrow as the question that required no answer was posed.

'I take your point, Travers.' The Governor gave a brief nod before glancing at the guard stood behind Laura. 'Miss Cadman is to be given a full fifteen minutes, see to it, Slater.'

Fifteen minutes! Much as she wanted every possible moment with her father, Laura's look betrayed her apprehension. The rest of the prison visitors would have gone by then and the tram also;

that would mean finding her way to the railway station alone, with a strong possibility of losing the way through those awful alleyways. Much as the thought terrified her, she would not sacrifice the time she had with her father. Murmuring her thanks, she rose.

'Miss Cadman.'

The tall man paused as she turned to face him.

'You will no doubt be returning to Snow Hill Station once your visit here is concluded. If you would allow, I would be pleased to take you in my carriage; I too will be travelling from that station.'

'Thank you. That is very kind of you but there is really no need.' Dipping a slight curtsy she turned towards the door, but as the guard opened it the tall man called again, his voice soft with a hidden smile.

'Miss Cadman, call it my second good deed.'

Her own smile brief, Laura let her glance fall before that of the dark-eyed man who had helped her once before.

Chapter Fourteen

'Father . . . I did not know . . . I would have come.'

Sentences broken up by sobs she tried so hard to hold back, Laura took the thin, cold hand in hers.

'No use in that, child,' he wheezed, 'they . . . they wouldn't have let you inside.' He smiled, a thin, heart-broken smile. 'They wouldn't let you in and they won't let me out.'

'But surely if you are ill!' She lifted his hand pressing it to her cheek.

'Not even if a man be dying.'

The answer jarring every nerve, Laura could not prevent the fear showing in her eyes as she looked at him.

Taking his hand to rest on the coarse grey blanket Isaac kept his hold on that of his daughter, his faded eyes never leaving her face. This fifteen minutes in the month was all that kept his heart beating, all that kept him alive.

'Don't fret, my little wench,' he drew a short, rapid breath that rattled wetly in his lungs, 'I don't be going to die, not for a long while yet. I intends coming home, to walk with you across the cornfields as I did when you were naught but a babby; I want to watch you pick golden kingcups and weave them into a crown for your pretty head, same as your mother often did. I wish I could give you a true golden crown, my little wench, for you be a princess to me . . .'

Laura tried to laugh but listening to the cough that wracked his thin frame she could only set her teeth into her lip and fight back her tears.

'Whatever would I do with a golden crown? I would make a strange picture shopping in the Shambles with a crown on my head, I would look like the Queen of the May.'

'You . . . you be a queen any time of the year,' he squeezed her fingers, 'you be your father's queen and he's proud of his little wench.'

Her heart bursting with love and emotion, Laura pulled her hand free. Pushing up from the chair she looked the length of the narrow room, skimpy iron beds almost foot to foot leaving little room to pass between. From two of them the interested eyes of other prisoners devoured her every move.

'You ready to leave, miss?'

The guard that had walked her to the infirmary came to the bedside.

'I want to be taken back to the Governor . . . I must take my father home, he is ill . . .'

'Afraid it don't work that way, miss.' The guard smiled kindly. 'Here he be and here he'll stay 'til his sentence be served, that be the law.'

'But you can't keep him here, he needs medical attention, he needs nursing.'

'The prison doctor calls once a week, miss, he has seen the prisoner a time or two and reckons there be nothing to be feared of, a cold on the chest be all apart from a broken leg, and the prisoner ain't likely to die from a broken leg, now is he?'

The awfulness of the bare room, its only decoration the patches of damp climbing the walls, the beds with musty-smelling, grey blankets, the men's night-shirts bearing the seal of convicts, all combined to overwhelm Laura.

'The prisoner!' she sobbed. 'My father has a name the same as you, he is a man, can't you treat him as one!'

Disconcerted by her tears the guard shuffled his feet, the

sound of his heavy boots loud on the stone floor.

'We ain't allowed to call the prisoners by name, miss, there be regulations and we has to observe them.'

'Laura . . . Laura wench . . .'

She turned to her father as the words wheezed quietly on to the dank air. Taking the hand he raised to her she sank back to the hard wooden chair the guard had found for her on first entering the dreary ward.

'. . . It's no use to argue.' The tired voice wheezed, the faded eyes clinging to hers. 'What he says be right, there is no way I can be released, not until my time be up.'

'But, Father . . .'

'Better listen to 'im, miss.' The guard produced a watch concealed in a breast pocket. 'The bit of time you have together is fast being used up and once it's gone I have to see you out of the building.' His face softening he returned the watch, buttoning down the flap of the pocket. 'Think on it, a month be long enough for you to wait but for a man locked away behind prison walls . . .'

The rest of the sentence unsaid he turned away, the watching prisoners sliding lower beneath their respective blankets as he came to stand at the foot of their beds.

'Father, I can't . . . I can't!' The cry breaking from her lips she threw herself forward, her face resting on his chest. 'I can't leave you here like this!'

Touching a hand to her head Isaac closed his eyes, wanting only to hold her, to feel her in his arms as he had when she was a child; but knowing it to be a luxury he could not afford, he tried to lift her from him. When stubbornly she clung to him, he whispered, 'There is something I have not told you. I should have spoken of it a long time ago . . .'

'Not now, Father.' Laura pulled him tighter into her grasp as if to release him was to lose him completely. 'There is nothing to tell.'

'But there is!' He coughed, air wheezing in his lungs.

'Then tell me next time I come, it will keep until then, it does not have to be said now.'

Stroking his hand over her hair Isaac opened his eyes, staring at the drab, damp-stained ceiling. That was what he had told himself for so very long, that what he had to tell would keep. But he had already kept it locked away too long, she had to hear the truth, no matter the pain to himself. He stared at a dark spot above his head; dark as the secret hidden in his heart, dark as the truth that lay in his soul.

'No, Laura wench, it won't keep,' he said quietly, 'I want you to hear it now, hear that which I should have spoken of years ago. I did not mean to be disloyal to Jabez, I wanted no secret from him . . .'

'Time be gone, miss.'

Feeling the touch on her shoulder, Laura's arms clung protectively to her father.

'Regulations, miss.' The guard touched her shoulder again, a little more pressure in his fingers. 'We guards don't make 'em, we just have to see them kept. Sorry, miss.'

'Tell me next time.' Unhappiness a living thing throbbing along every vein, Laura kissed her father's lined cheek but try as she did she could not bear to look into eyes she knew were filled with the same pain as pulled at her. 'I love you, Father,' she whispered, 'I love you very much.'

Following the guard out of the ward she heard the soft, broken cry reach after her.

'Laura . . . Laura, my little wench!'

He had been in this house for a week yet in those seven days he had lived more of a life than in all of his twenty six years. Glancing at his reflection in the tall standing mirror of the dressing room, Edmund Shaw ran a slow appreciative look over the finely tailored cashmere jacket, its rich chestnut colour lending depth to his sand-coloured hair, the touch of the cream Shantung-silk hand-stitched shirt exotic against his skin.

Sheldon Sinclair had opened a new way of life for him, shown him a world he never dreamed existed, and it was one he wanted to keep.

Glancing at the selection of cravats laid out for his choice he took a warm peach silk, holding it first against the jacket. Even as a boy he had never been allowed colours such as these, Jabez had insisted on dark, serviceable clothing.

Fingers still a little clumsy at the unaccustomed task, he knotted the delicate fabric about his throat then stood again surveying the finishing touch in the mirror.

What would Jabez say now? Slow and rancorous the smile spread, but the pale hazel eyes held no humour. Jabez would never say anything again, Jabez was dead. Dressed in his dark, serviceable clothes Jabez was dead and he, Edmund, was alive . . . alive to enjoy all that Jabez had denied, to spend all that he had hoped to keep.

'But you didn't keep it did you, Father?' Lips curling back from his teeth he gloated softly, his eyes still on the reflection his father would not have recognised. 'You could not take your money with you, there are no pockets in a shroud, Jabez. But I have pockets and I will fill them with every penny you were set to give to Isaac's daughter and I will spend it all, including what I get for that works you were so proud of.'

Isaac's daughter his father's wife!

Edmund was still smiling vindictively as he walked into the elegant sitting room.

'There you are, Edmund.'

Sheldon Sinclair laid aside the newspaper he had been reading and reached for a small envelope lying on a side table set beside his ivory-velvet chair.

Edmund ran an envious glance about the room. The sitting room that had been his mother's favourite room in the house at Squire's Walk had, he had always thought, been elegant but compared to this it was a pauper's room.

Tall windows sparkled behind Venetian damask which fell in graceful folds, echoing the colour woven into the huge, ivory, Bhukara carpet that almost covered the entire floor, complementing the delicate Hepplewhite furniture.

He had not known the pedigree of any of the beautiful items in this room or those that furnished the remainder of this house, but he had listened to the almost casual descriptions Sheldon had given and he was learning, he was learning fast.

'I have had a note from Sandon, he has received an offer for the Gallery.'

The envelope held between finger and thumb, he paused.

'I thought Sandon had agreed to wait.'

'To wait yes, but that was five days ago. Philip Sandon is a nice enough chap but patience is not the greatest of his virtues; besides, one cannot blame him if he takes what is, after all, money on the table.'

'I suppose not.' Edmund tried to think. A few days ago he had been offered the chance to buy the antiques gallery, a chance to become one of the circle inhabited by Sheldon Sinclair and his like, to shake off the image of Wednesbury and Shaw and Cadman engineering works. But until that works was sold the money he had was not enough.

Jabez' will had given him control of all. Edmund felt his nerves tighten. Money in his private account, the house and all that went with it . . . but the works . . . !

'I tell you what . . .'

Laying aside the envelope Sheldon rose, his movements a fluid synchronisation.

'. . . why don't you take a later train home? That way we can go see Sandon now, together we might get him to wait a little longer before taking that offer.'

'Do you think he might?'

Velvet green eyes smiling, Sheldon placed a hand on Edmund's shoulder. 'We won't find out by standing here.'

The drive to the club where Sheldon was sure the other man

would be lunching was pleasant enough, but Edmund's thoughts were not on the passing scenery.

Jabez's will had clearly stated '*the engineering works held in partner-ship with Isaac Cadman . . .*'

Partnership!

Teeth pressing viciously together, he stared out of the carriage window.

If that will should ever be seen by anyone else . . . even as it was it was known to Jabez' solicitor and they were not always the reliable people they made themselves out to be. What if he told Isaac Cadman the works were to be sold? Cadman was in prison but would those bars keep out a solicitor?

'You are very quiet, Edmund. Don't worry, I am sure we can persuade Sandon.'

Beside him in the carriage Sheldon placed a hand on Edmund's thigh. The touch of those long, almost feminine fingers electric through the fine cloth of his trousers, Edmund felt the nerves of his stomach leap. It was the same each time this man touched him, each time he smiled, each time those wonderful green eyes looked at him.

He had to sell those works! He let the hand stay where it rested. He had to buy the Gallery.

'The Periwig Club is just around the next corner.'

Sheldon withdrew his hand, stroking it slowly down to the knee before lifting it.

'The name is as quaint as the inside of the building, full of Georgian pretension; but the service is impeccable. A lot of busi-ness is transacted there, privacy being guaranteed.'

The carriage coming to a halt Sheldon climbed out. Nodding to a doorman attired in palest green breeches, a matching velvet jacket heavily adorned with gold braid and frogging, a tall powdered grey periwig on his head, he led the way into what would have passed for a large early Georgian private house.

Inside the dimly lit reception hall Edmund blinked against the blaze of a large crystal chandelier, its numerous candles reviving the elegance of a past generation. Following Sheldon towards the dining room he breathed deeply. The whole atmosphere of the place reeked of money and he wanted a share.

'Good to see you, Shaw.' Philip Sandon raised a hand, silently calling a waiter dressed in a replica of the doorman's livery. 'Join me in a spot of luncheon.'

Waiting until the glass of each of his guests was filled with wine, Sandon smiled at Sheldon.

'Why not bring Edmund along to the Gallery this evening?' He sniffed at the mauve-edged white carnation tucked in the buttonhole of his jacket.

It was identical to the one Sheldon had attached to his lapel before leaving the house.

'There is nothing I would enjoy more, but Edmund tells me he simply must return to Wednesbury tonight.' Sheldon laid a lace-edged linen serviette across his knees as he was served with Vermouth-poached rainbow trout circled with a shallot sauce.

Mouth half-filled with a forkful of dressed crab, Philip Sandon shook his head. 'You will miss a good evening.' He swallowed, clearing his mouth. 'There are some fine pieces on offer.'

Spreading his own serviette, Edmund glanced at the dish set before him. As yet still unsure of the food which lay behind the elaborate headings he had selected a plain grilled sirloin with button mushrooms.

'It is a pity Edmund will not be with us but business must come before pleasure, you know that very well, Philip.'

'Tiresome thing, business.' Philip Sandon lifted another forkful of crab to his mouth. 'Gets in the way of a man's pleasure.'

It was getting in the way of his. Edmund sliced into his steak. Given the Gallery he could combine one with the other.

'Couldn't you put it off for one night?'

Edmund looked up. Sandon was watching him over the rim of his glass.

'Edmund is returning home to see to the sale of his engineering works.' Sheldon answered for him. He took a sip of wine, savouring the bouquet on his tongue before adding, 'Edmund had considered the possibility of acquiring the Gallery but . . .'

Sandon set the glass down, holding on to the stem as he spoke. 'But what? The Gallery is a fine business house. I wouldn't be selling it were it not for the sake of this pesky earldom.'

'Philip's uncle, the Earl of Conroy, died recently leaving no offspring so Philip here, being the only remaining relative, finds himself the next Earl.'

'Damn pesky I calls it; but then the family line an' all that . . .' He raised his glass, emptying the contents at a throw.

Lowering his glance to the contents of his plate Sheldon sounded nonchalant. 'Sandon, you have no pressing need of the money the Gallery will fetch, and before you answer I know the adage about business being business, but Edmund here is a friend and between friends couldn't we come to some arrangement?'

'Arrangement?' Philip Sandon paused in the refilling of his wine glass. 'What sort of arrangement?'

'Oh . . . let us say Edmund pays you half the asking price now and the other half shall we say a month from now?'

'A month!'

His mouth already open to refuse the suggestion, Edmund caught the almost imperceptible shake of the head and the sharp no couched deep in those sage-green eyes, and remained silent.

'What is a month?' Sheldon returned his glance to the other man. 'You will hardly have settled into your very stately new home by that time.'

'Damn you, Sinclair, you always could charm the ducks off the water!' Sandon laughed, raising his glass. 'A month it is then, Shaw.'

The Gallery was almost in his hands. Edmund raised his own glass, touching it to that of Philip Sandon. All he had to do now was find the money to pay for it.

Half! Leaning back in the carriage returning them to the

house, Edmund felt the tremors of trepidation increase. Half of twenty thousand pounds! It was an impossible sum for him. The house and the works together would bring nowhere near a half of it. He would have to tell Sandon, apologise . . .

'If you are worrying about finding that money, then don't . . .' Sheldon's hand came again to his thigh, sending the blood pounding through Edmund's veins.

'. . . I can arrange for you to borrow it.'

'Ten thousand!' Edmund swallowed, the lump in his throat caused more by the other man's hand than his offer of the loan of money.

'Ten . . .'

The hand moved slow and sinuously toward his crotch, stifling the breath in Edmund's lungs.

'Ten, twenty . . . whatever it takes to keep us together.'

It was the second time this man had helped her. Seated in the hansom that had waited for him beyond the gates of Winson Green prison, Laura fumbled in her purse. Holding out a small gleaming coin, she said shyly. 'I was hoping to be able to return this and to thank you for assisting me that day at the railway station.'

'I need no reimbursement, being able to help was enough.'

Laura saw the smile but could find none of her own to reward it with, the sorrow of seeing her father so pale and thin in that infirmary still raw inside her.

'The help was kindly given but nevertheless I must pay what is owed.'

'I said to call it my good deed.'

Still holding out the coin Laura nodded. 'That was most certainly what it was, had you not lent me the money to take the train I don't know how I would have got home.'

'I did not term it a loan.'

In the changing light of early evening Laura caught the flash of grey eyes. This man had not said anything to her as he had pressed the half-sovereign into her hand that awful day, except to call over his shoulder as he strode away to his train, 'Call it my one good deed!'

'No, sir, you did not,' Laura answered quietly. 'But that is how I viewed it. Now I wish to repay it.'

'If you feel you must then I suppose you must.' He shrugged his shoulders, accepting the coin. It was nothing to him but to the girl he had seen on that platform, her shabby grey coat carrying all the marks of having been rolled on a dirty floor, a bewildered, almost bemused look on her face as the station master had told her loudly no ticket no travel, it must have meant a great deal. He had been a fool to part with his money he had told himself as the train had carried him home. The girl was probably a prostitute who had gotten herself roughed up by an irate client. But beneath the self reprimand the feeling had lurked that he was wrong, that the girl was no prostitute, that she was more a victim, that somehow the marks on her coat were the marks of an assailant rather than a lover. Now, looking at the gold glinting in the palm of his hand, he was certain. Whoever this girl was she was honest and that characteristic was not often found in the stews of any city.

'I apologise for not thanking you earlier in the Governor's office, but I was so worried when my father did not appear in the visiting hall.'

'Your father?' He slipped the coin into his pocket.

For a moment Laura felt a pang of something like shame, then her head came up and she looked straight into the grey eyes fastened on her face.

'My father,' she said quietly but with a firmness that held no shame, 'is a prisoner in Winson Green prison. I had visited him there on the day you so kindly helped me. I was visiting him again today.'

You had to give the girl top marks for guts. Rafe Travers smiled inwardly. Not every girl he had known would have had the courage to stand up and say that.

'And today you have your purse and you are without dried mud on your coat.'

Colour sweeping warmly into her cheeks, Laura glanced at the small drawstring bag looped about her wrist.

'Last month I . . . I had an accident.'

'An accident!' The answer, dry and clearly disbelieving, further deepening the colour riding her cheeks, Laura turned her glance to the window. She had tried so hard to fight off the memory of that attack, defying the demand of sleep, afraid of the terrible nightmares that travelled in its path.

Opposite her Rafe Travers felt a keen anger bite into him, but it was an anger directed against the unknown. It must have been obvious to all and sundry who had met this girl that day in Birmingham that she was at a loss as to her whereabouts and someone had taken advantage of that knowledge.

Had the someone taken more of an advantage? The dirt on her clothing had suggested she had been lying on filthy ground.

Pushed there? Knocked down by some lout?

Watching the face turned away from him, he felt the anger bite more sharply.

Had the girl been attacked . . . had she been raped?

The question stayed with him as the hansom brought them to the station, staying in his mind as he watched her into a third-class compartment of the train for Wednesbury, and as he turned away he knew it would plague him for long days to come.

Chapter Fifteen

Edmund was no book-keeper. Following the dismissal of that accounts clerk Isaac Cadman had the job of keeping the firm's books; but looking at the last year's figures for the Gallery he was highly impressed.

Antiques! 'Bloody clapped-out pieces of rubbish' was what Jabez would have called the items on display in that building. Edmund smiled to himself. It seemed selling clapped-out pieces of rubbish was exceptionally profitable.

'Well . . . what do you think?'

Closing the ledger Sheldon Sinclair set it aside before taking up a walnut humidor exquisitely inlaid with silver. Holding it open he offered a cigar to Edmund, smiling as it was refused, then took one for himself, lighting it with a silver lighter.

'It appears profitable enough.' Edmund watched the stream of lavender-grey smoke curl from the tip of the cigar.

Parting his lips Sheldon let cigar smoke drift languidly, watching it spread a gossamer veil above his head.

'Were it not more than just profitable, I would not have advised you buy it. We are friends, after all, are we not?'

Edmund let his glance slide from the handsome face, his thoughts twisting and turning.

Why him, why a man who knew nothing but bolts and screws, a man who had never stepped outside of Wednesbury in his life before this, a man who knew nothing of a way of life that was natural to these men? Why had Sheldon Sinclair chosen to befriend him?

'I might have purchased the business myself but I am an extremely lazy creature . . . why bother myself with all of that? Beside which, I do not have that much money.' Inhaling from the cigar he watched Edmund through the haze that drifted from his lips. 'And to be truthful, I can find far more pleasurable ways to occupy my time.'

Had it been intentional? Edmund felt the heat of blood in his veins. That voice was musically soft at all times but as he said those words it became thick and husky, playing across the senses in a sensual, inviting wave.

'Sandon is none too pleased at the prospect of losing so agreeable and prosperous a business but, as he said, he cannot combine that with running such a vast estate as Conroy.' Sheldon blew a fresh cloud of lavender smoke through carefully posed lips. 'But then one man's loss is another's gain they say, but only if the other is quick to snatch it.'

Borrowing ten thousand pounds was a risky venture. Edmund felt the palms of his hands moisten. At most he could probably only raise half of that.

'Of course, if you did buy the Gallery it would mean you having to live there . . . you would have to leave Wednesbury. Travelling daily between the two would be exhausting.'

He had played a trump card. Sheldon leaned into the depths of the Hepplewhite chair. Now Edmund Shaw must show his hand.

'It could be some time before I could raise the money and even then I could not raise it all.'

Stubbing the cigar in a heavy crystal ashtray Sheldon smiled affably. 'You are worrying over nothing, but if it will set your mind at rest we could set up a syndicate, buy the Gallery between a group partnership, with a few friends I know would be interested but . . .' He paused, eyes twinkling like green gems.

'. . . you will have to run it on your own, Edmund, for like I told you I am an extremely lazy fellow.'

Part ownership, a group purchase. He could manage that. He could leave that smoke-hole of a town, have the life he had promised himself. The business would be his to run but, best of all, he would be close to Sheldon Sinclair.

Rising from his chair Sheldon came to stand over him, those wonderful eyes reaching into the depths of his stomach, playing every nerve like violin strings.

'Well . . . ! Can we be . . . partners?'

The eyes seemed to smoulder, charring his soul, burning away the last of his doubts. Sheldon Sinclair was offering more, much more than a part-share in an antiques shop.

Lost in that wonderful gaze Edmund only knew that was what he wanted.

That man had been very kind, not only in letting her ride in his hansom to Snow Hill railway station, but in staying beside her until she was actually seated in the compartment.

He had volunteered no further information about himself. From the shelter of the railway carriage she had watched him walk away. Tall, dark head held high, his body movements matching the grace and fluidity of a stalking cat, he had disappeared from her sight. But not from her mind.

Leaving the train at Wednesbury station Laura smiled at the station master, answering his enquiry as to her father's health, thanking him for his suggestion of a cure for what he called a bronichal chest.

In the street beyond the station she glanced along the way that would bring her home, then turned instead toward Dudley Street. If she bought the things she needed now she could make a linctus tonight, that way it would be matured enough for her next visit to Winson Green.

The thought of the prison brought back thoughts of the man

she had met there. He had not said his name nor made mention of what brought him to the Governor's office. But she should not think that unusual, why would he reveal such to a perfect stranger?

Turning into Griffiths Green grocery shop Laura saw in her mind those gleaming grey eyes watching from a strong handsome face and somehow it seemed it was not the face of a stranger.

'How do, Laura wench, how be that father o'yourn?'

Coming from the living quarters adjoining the shop Henry Griffiths smiled a welcome.

'My father is not well, Mr Griffiths. It seems he suffered a fall some weeks ago.'

'A fall you says.' Henry Griffiths wiped a hand around a fine crop of whiskers. 'Be it bad?'

'A broken leg.'

'What was that . . . a broken leg?'

Never one to pass up the chance of a gossip, the ample figure of Mary Ann Griffiths appeared from the back room.

'It be Isaac.' Henry continued to fondle his whiskers. 'Laura here says he's had summat of a tumble.'

'Eeh, wench!' Concern genuine on her chubby face Mary Ann stepped from the doorway, coming to stand beside her husband behind the counter. ''Ow did that happen?'

Laura shook her head, only now realising no one had told her how her father's accident had occurred and that she had not asked.

'I . . . I can't say. I was so worried seeing Father in that awful place I forgot to ask.'

'That be understandable.' Mary Ann nodded her dark head sympathetically. 'But painful though a broken limb can be they heals, given time. This be hard for you, I know, 'specially so when you don't have the caring of him yourself, but try not to fret, wench, could be next time you sees him your father will be well along the road to mending.'

'It is not so much his broken leg, bad as that is.' Laura felt in her bag for the florin she had placed in it before leaving for the prison. 'It is the cough he has. Father's chest was never strong and that prison is so damp and cold.'

'You has to watch a cold on the chest, you never can tell what it might turn to.'

Catching the wife's warning glare, Henry turned to the display of apples arranged in a triangular tray set on a sloping board at his back.

'You take along a jar o' goose fat with a bit o' wintergreen mixed in and rub that on his chest, then wrap him about wi' a length o' red flannel, that will put paid to any chesty cough,' Mary Ann went on. 'My old mother swore by that remedy and I have to say it's always worked on Henry.'

'It be good I warrant you.' Catching Laura's eye he winked roguishly. 'But I reckon it be the stink as is the true cure, you get a dollop of that lot on your chest and you be frightened to cough lest you gets another dollop on your back!'

'It has always worked for you, Henry Griffiths, stink or no stink!' Mary Ann retorted sending him another sharp stare. ''Sides it be better to stink for a week than suffer for a month!' Turning her glance back to Laura, softening it as it touched the girl's face, she let loose a long-suffering sigh. 'But then you can't expect a man to think like that, you don't get brains growing in concrete! You wait here, Laura wench, I have a jar o' fresh rendered goose fat in the larder, do with it like I've told you when next you sees Isaac and he will be over that chest in no time.'

Watching the figure of his wife, black skirts sweeping the floor, as she disappeared into the family living quarters Henry grinned. Whiskers bobbing he whispered, 'Isaac may well be over his chest but the rest of them prisoners will be away over the wall, the stink of that goose grease giving a lift to their legs.'

Catching sight of the returning Mary Ann he ran his hands over the sack tied about his middle for an apron, the grin mysteriously vanished from his face as he asked loudly, 'Now then, Laura, what can I be getting for you?'

'Could I have six large lemons, please?'

The grin was gone but Laura caught the twinkle of bright eyes. 'You can, Laura me wench, you certainly can.'

'You can't be carrying them as well as a pot o' goose grease in that fiddlin' little bag.' Mary Ann set the pot on the counter, fussing away to the back room and returning with a basket. 'Set your things in that, you can let me have it back when next you be passing.'

'Thank you, Mrs Griffiths.' Laura smiled her gratitude. Watching the lemons being placed in the basket beside the goose grease she held out the florin, slipping the shilling change into her purse.

'Now you remember and give Isaac our wishes for his speedy return to health.'

Turning from seeing Laura from the shop, Mary Ann Griffiths shook her head. 'Isaac Cadman be paying a sorry price, Henry, and it be my guess that what they say he did was done for another.'

What he did was done for another. The woman's voice, never exactly muted, had followed Laura into the street. Certainly her father had not spent the money on himself or on her, neither had he kept it or he would have returned it to Edmund instead of being sent to prison. But where was it? Laura walked slowly on towards Jackson's chemist shop. Just what had happened to the seven hundred and eighty pounds her father had embezzled?

'We guessed you would most like be coming home about now, though we hadn't thought to see you in Dudley Street.'

The voice paused and when it resumed it was on a note of enquiry. 'Be you going for anything special? If you ain't then me and our Alfie can fetch what you be wanting.'

Forcing her mind into focus Laura glanced at the boy falling into step beside her, ragamuffin hair blown across a freckled face, trousers inches above his ankles revealing the worn-through toes of his boots.

'Thank you, Teddie, but I am almost there, I need some more oil of peppermint and two ounces of herbal essence.'

Beside her the lad jigged excitedly, his boots clattering on the uneven sets of the road.

'Eh, Missis Laura, you be going to make Tigs Herbal . . . I love Tigs Herbal!'

'You likes any kind of suck!' his elder brother said scathingly, snatching him on to the narrow footpath out of the way of a cart rumbling its way to the station.

Alfie was not wrong in that, his brother did like all sweets. Laura glanced at the two boys already locked in battle over who was to blame for the near-accident with the cart.

Alfie the unbeaten champion, he held the squirming Teddie by the collar, brushing dust and dried horse manure from his ragged clothing.

'Watch where you be going next time!' The warning leaving his lips, Alfie pushed the younger boy ahead. 'That be all he thinks of, Missis Laura . . . where be the next suck coming from.'

'One could come from my kitchen, supposing you two let each other live long enough to come for it.' Laura came to a halt outside the chemist shop and immediately Teddie's nose was pressed against the bull-nosed panes, exclaiming as his glance roved over round-bellied flagons and tall-necked bottles, their blues and greens glinting in the gas light.

Taking a threepenny piece from her purse Laura looked at Alfie. 'Would you go along to Mr Ward's cottage in Trouse Lane and ask for a jar of his best honey?'

The coin clutched in his hand Alfie glanced at his brother still entranced by the coloured glass. 'He'll be all right there, Missis, I can be along of Ward's and back again afore he lifts his nose from that window.'

Nodding as the boy set off at a run Laura turned into the shop, setting the bell above the door tinkling, summoning the owner from the small dispensary set behind a shoulder-high, wood-panelled partition.

Mr Jackson taking his time to measure out oil of peppermint and herbal essence into separate small containers and even more time to chat meant Alfie had already returned from his errand when Laura at last emerged from the shop.

It had been dusk when she had arrived back at the station, now it was quite dark except for the pool of yellow light shed by the one gas lamp stood on the corner of the pavement where the roads crossed.

After placing the honey in the basket, carefully avoiding the delicate phials of oil, Alfie took it from Laura and hooked the handle over his arm, a shove at his brother's shoulder bringing the boy jogging at their heels as Laura began to retrace her steps towards Great Western Street.

Coming to the Pack Horse Inn she hesitated. The rumble of men's voices drifted through the part-open door. She had never once set foot inside a public house but tonight she had to.

'Hold up!' Teddie's voice shrilled in surprise. 'I ain't never knowed you to take a half pint, Missis Laura.'

'And you will not know me do so tonight, Teddie.' Laura turned her face away from the inquisitive stare of a man leaving the tap room. 'I need a gill of brandy.'

'Eh, Missis Laura, that be powerful stuff! I've seen men fall down from drinking that.'

'I am not going to drink it.' Laura smiled, aware of the concern backing Alfie's warning. 'I want it to make a linctus for my father's cough.'

'Then let me fetch it!' Alfie pushed the basket into his brother's arms. 'It be all right, John Turley knows I often fetch drink for the men working over at Bagnalls and the like, he'll serve me with what it is you want; might be best.' He glanced at Laura's face, an ancient wisdom on his own. 'There gets a few rough ones in there at times.'

Hesitant at first Laura agreed, breathing a sigh of relief when the boy appeared carrying a small cream-painted pottery jug loaned by the landlord.

'I told him he could have the jug back tonight.' The boy grinned. 'That way he don't charge the farthing for the loan of it.'

A raucous laugh floating out into the night air set Laura's nerves on edge. *He* had laughed like that. He had knocked her to the floor, laughing as he tore at her clothes.

A shiver rattling her spine she turned quickly, the boys trotting to keep up as she half ran towards the safety of home.

If only he had not spent all that money on clothes. Edmund fingered the satin-lined, wine coloured velvet waistcoat, diamante buttons winking in the light of his bedroom. This alone had cost more than a Shaw and Cadman man could earn in a year.

Shaw and Cadman! His hand closed hard about the lovely fabric, crushing it between his fingers. Was there after all a signed paper somewhere, hidden away where he might never find it? But why hide it? . . . Unless Jabez had known after all, known and . . .

He swallowed hard, rage draining the colour from his cheeks.

Think calmly! He sank to the edge of the bed, his eyes staring into the collecting shadows beyond it. He must think things through calmly.

He had found nothing among the papers in the house, nothing lodged with a solicitor nor with Jabez' bank, and nothing with the books at the works. He had searched everywhere and everything but had found no document.

Yet common sense said there had to be one! He snatched angrily at the garment in his hands, tearing off one of its buttons. Jabez Shaw had been too shrewd a businessman not to have seen the necessity for such an agreement and Isaac Cadman . . . he stared at the button gleaming in his palm . . . Cadman too was nobody's fool. Gentleman's agreement, pah! That had been a lie, a ruse to throw him off the scent; there was a document, there had to be. But Isaac was in jail, he could not easily be questioned there . . .

Fingers closing over the button Edmund's mouth relaxed to its usual thin line. Isaac was in jail . . . but Laura was not, and what Isaac knew Laura would also know!

Chapter Sixteen

'Lost a button?'

Edmund had watched the trim, almost slender figure walk across his room, collar-length brown hair glowing with the barest trace of Macassar oil; and had seen the smile of friendship that played about that full mouth becoming something more as it rested in the summer-green depths of swallowing eyes.

As long fingers traced over his palm, touching skin to skin, the warm and sultry look that lingered on his eyes had Edmund catching his breath.

'A button is nothing compared with what *I* am losing, Edmund. Had I known . . . had I realised the danger, I would not have asked you to come here.'

'Danger!' Edmund felt the hairs rise on the back of his neck, but it was not fear that suddenly had his pulses racing.

'Yes, Edmund, danger. The danger of the feelings I hold for you.'

The look in his eyes changing to wistfulness, Sheldon Sinclair laughed, a short unhappy-sounding laugh, as he took the button and turned away.

'You are shocked, Edmund. That one man can have such strong feeling for another fills you with disgust. Perhaps that is as it should be, who can tell.' He paused, catching his breath with a sharp jerk. 'All I know is that for me it is a beautiful concept, a wonderful natural love. But you will hear no more of it.' Dropping the button into the pocket of his coat he turned to face Edmund, sadness lending his handsome face an appeal that caught at the throat. 'I ought not to have confessed my feelings, Edmund, I am sorry I have done so. I know they can never be returned so, with your permission, I will keep this button as a warning not to embarrass you ever again by voicing what is inside.'

'I'm not embarrassed.'

At the door Sheldon Sinclair halted.

'Sheldon, I am not embarrassed nor am I disgusted, unless I am disgusted with myself.'

Sheldon turned slowly, his question softly asked.

'You, Edmund, why should you feel disgust with yourself?'

'Because . . .' Edmund faltered, a flood of colour suffusing his narrow face, 'because I have those same feelings.'

'You also, Edmund? Then you must know a little of the pain they can bring.' Lowering his lids Sheldon Sinclair hid the quick gleam that had sprung to his eyes. 'I wish you happiness, my friend; whoever it is your feelings are for is a very lucky person.'

Not moving from the bed Edmund looked at the handsome figure still stood beside the door, and when he answered his voice was low.

'I am the lucky one, Sheldon, lucky that you feel that way for me.'

'Edmund!' It was a breathy gasp as Sheldon took a step forward, then he was still once more, the velvet-soft glance that lifted to Edmund's face empty of the glint of triumph. 'You . . . you are sure? We have known each other such a short time.'

'A matter of time.' Edmund smiled. 'What is time, what are a few days counted against a lifetime? And that is what I want, Sheldon . . . a lifetime spent with you.'

His glance never wavering, Sheldon Sinclair walked slowly back to the bed. Taking the waistcoat from Edmund's hand he let it slide slowly to the floor.

✳

Placing the basket on the table Alfie Bailey caught the sob that broke from Laura's lips. His quick brain long ago registering where matches were kept, he had no difficulty locating them in a kitchen dark with the shadows of night.

'I'll have the lamp lit in a jiffy, Missis Laura, you get your coat and hat off while Teddie and me sees to the fire and brews you a cup o' tea.'

A sniff all the answer she could give, Laura held the match flame to her oil lamp then made her way upstairs.

In her bedroom she pressed the knuckles of one hand against her mouth, trying to stem the tide of fear. It happened so often, day or night, the memory of that attack would come rushing in on her, the rank smell of that man's body, the foul breath in her face, the touch of his hands as he laughed. It was the sound of that laugh that haunted her, waking her in the blackness of the night, so real it seemed he was there in her room.

And tonight in the street . . . a shiver traced again along her spine . . . thank God the Bailey boys had been with her.

Setting the lamp on the tiny chest alongside her bed she unbuttoned her coat, hanging it in a tall cupboard.

But the Bailey boys would go home she would be alone, alone in a house empty of all but memories . . . memories and night-mares.

Sunday clothes exchanged for her every-day brown dress she poured a little of the cold water from the jug, sluicing her hands and face, washing away the fear. Running her hands over her hair she drew a deep breath. The terror that stalked her was not washed away, it was merely dampened. In the night when she was alone it would return in all its dark reality.

'Be you going to make Tig's Herbal, Missis Laura?'

Teddie turned with his question as she entered the kitchen. Tying an apron about her waist she gave a shake of the head.

Teddie's pert little face fell. 'You ain't? But you bought herbal essence!'

'So I did, I thought to make some herbal soothers for my father, they will help with his cough.'

'That be what the brandy is for.' Alfie turned an imperious all-knowing look at his brother then turned to Laura. 'It makes better linctus than any you can get from a chemist shop, so Mother always reckons. You going to take that for your father an' all?'

Bird-bright eyes watching her every move, Laura set about collecting the necessary utensils and setting them on the kitchen table, its surface white from repeated scrubbing.

'When all that be done then will you be making Tig's Herbal . . . or brandy balls!' Teddie's eyes gleamed even brighter. 'I loves brandy balls!'

'I stoked the fire for you, Missis Laura, and set a fresh bucket of coal 'neath the kitchen sink; be there anything else we can do?'

They should be going home. Laura spooned the jar of honey into a cast-iron saucepan. But would they? Chances were they would hang about the streets in the hope of picking up a half-penny for running an errand or minding a horse; at least here in this house they could come to no harm. Or was it her own comfort she was truly thinking of? The fact that whilst the boys were here she was not alone.

'You should be getting along home, Alfie, your mother may want your help.'

Standing the spoon in the jar she caught the longing look on the small face watching from the other side of the table. A quick smile touching her mouth she handed the jar to the boy.

'I told Mother where we would be and her said to stop as long as you wanted.'

Laura glanced at the older boy as he licked the spoon once then gave the whole treat over to his brother. If only she had brothers and sisters, someone with whom to share this dreadful time; but she had no one, no family at all. Edmund would have been her family . . .

Catching the thought before it could spread, she took a knife from the drawer set in the table and began slicing each of the lemons in half.

'I want to help an' all.' Teddie ran a pink tongue over sticky lips. 'I wants to do summat.'

'Half an hour then.' Laura compromised. 'You may stay half an hour then it is home, home without touting for jobs in the market place . . . agreed?'

Alfie let out a resigned breath but his eyes shone. 'If you says it, Missis Laura.'

'I do say it, Alfie, and remember a man's word is his bond.'

That was how it had been with her father and Jabez, a word of agreement that had been a bond between them, a bond Jabez' son had broken.

Laying the well-scraped jar aside, giving one last lick to a spoon already devoid of any trace of honey, Teddie sniffed, wiping a hand beneath his nose.

'You have my . . .' He paused, the unusual word gone from his mind.

'Bond.' Alfie supplied the word laconically. 'It means promise, you have to promise to do what Missis Laura says!'

'O' course I promise, cross me heart and hope to die!' The younger lad grinned widely, his freckle-covered face turned upward in the lamplight, gleaming with anticipation.

'In that case,' Laura made a pretence of thinking, 'there is something I could do with having help with, but it needs very clean hands.'

Turning their palms over and back both boys surveyed their hands.

'I'll wash mine, I'll even use soap,' Teddie volunteered quickly, seeing the promise of a brandy ball begin to fade.

'There is more, Teddie.' Laura sliced the last lemon. 'You may not want to do it.'

'He ain't frightened of nothin'. You tell him what it be and he'll do it.' Alfie defended his brother's courage.

''Cept spiders.' Teddie's grin retreated rapidly. 'I don't like messin' with spiders, they gives me the creeps.'

'Don't be a babby!' Alfie retorted scornfully. 'Spiders can't hurt you.'

Seeing the younger boy's shamed look Laura gave an exaggerated shiver. 'Please, let's not talk of spiders, they frighten me, all those spindly legs and hairy bodies.'

Relief that someone else could be shouldered with the change of subject, Teddie's grin returned in all its splendour. 'What else is it I have to do?'

Hiding the smile that begged to be loosed Laura laid the halved lemon beside the rest on a large plate and fetched a glass lemon squeezer from the dresser.

'Hands washed first!' Pushing his brother towards the scullery Alfie's voice dropped to a whisper as both boys removed their jackets, but it was clear to Laura that the older was giving the younger a set of strict orders.

'Be that clean enough?'

Alfie spoke but both boys held out their hands for inspection as they returned to the kitchen.

'Excellent.' Laura nodded.

'He made me use the scrubbing brush!' Teddie darted an accusing glance at his brother.

'Well the result is very good.'

'So what is it he has to do?' His own glance one of 'I told you so' Alfie looked at the assembled crockery and ingredients.

'You have to wear an apron, Teddie.' Laura watched the satisfied grin disappear and a look of horror take its place.

'A pinna!' Teddie almost choked. 'You mean one of them things that prissy Cissy wears, all frills and flounces!'

Across the table Alfie chortled, his brown eyes glistening with mirth. 'It'll suit you, you'll look a right little pansy in that!'

'You too, Alfred!'

Caught between the devil and the deep Alfie stared at the apron held out to him.

'. . . and the first one to say anything will get an apron with flowers as well as frills!'

Still holding the smile inside as both boys struggled into the aprons, Laura turned to the task of making cough linctus for her father, both children following her instructions to the letter. But busy as she was she kept an eye on the clock above the fireplace, and the thirty minutes being up she told them to prepare to go home.

Making sure Teddie was firmly buttoned into his ragged coat she reached for the basket Mary Ann Griffiths had loaned her, handing it to the smaller boy; then taking a penny from her purse she held it out to Alfie.

'A workman is worthy of his hire.'

Alfie's brow creased. 'You what, Missis Laura?'

'It means I am very pleased and satisfied with the help you have both given me this evening,' Laura smiled, 'you have earned your wage.'

'Well we ain't taking it!' His mouth setting in a firm line the lad caught his brother's arm, drawing him towards the door. 'We didn't help you for any wage. We . . . we come here because we love you an' that be all about it!'

But it was *not* all that could be said about it. Laura felt a lump, hard and choking, in her throat. These boys loved her not for what money they could get from her but loved her for herself; apart from her father they were the only people on earth who did.

'But the basket . . .'

At the door Alfie turned. 'We know who the basket belongs to and we'll see it be returned.'

'Wait!' Laura called as he opened the door to the yard. 'You can refuse your own penny but Teddie . . .'

'Teddie don't want one neither!'

Laura had seen determination on the face of many people but as she looked at the eight-year-old boy she realised she had seen none more determined than him.

'Very well.' She acknowledged defeat with a smile. 'But if you will not accept my money then at least accept my sweets.'

'I'll have a bull's eye.' Teddie squirmed free of the restraining hand.

The door latch in his hand, Alfie's mouth relaxed. 'All right, Missis Laura, better give him one.'

Sprawled backward across the bed, his senses pounding, every nerve tingling, Edmund sucked in a great gulp of air as long fingers moved slowly over bare flesh.

Beside him Sheldon Sinclair smiled. 'You will not be sorry . . . afterwards?'

Trying to answer but choking on the words Edmund closed his eyes, spreading his parted legs wider.

Bending over him Sheldon trailed his lips downward along a stomach held tight with desire, following the fingers into a warm crotch, smiling as he heard the long-drawn gasp.

'This is what you came for, Edmund.' He ran the tip of his tongue over testicles hard as stones, while Edmund's body jolted. 'This is what you wanted . . . this,' he ran his tongue once more over hardened flesh, '. . . isn't it?'

'Yes!' The word tearing itself between teeth cemented with passion Edmund arched upwards towards the teasing mouth.

'Then say it.' Easing away Sheldon smiled down at the man beside him, at a face twisted with the pain of its own desires. 'Say it, Edmund, so we both know where we stand.'

'This . . .' His whole body jerking as a finger traced his pulsing flesh, Edmund drew a sharp tortured breath. '. . . This is what I came for.'

Laughing softly to himself Sheldon lowered his lips to the taut stomach, his fingers closing about the throbbing penis.

It had been what he wanted. It *had* been what he wanted.

Eyes closed, Edmund lay in the hot perfumed water. He had

wanted Sheldon Sinclair to make love to him, yet if he had wanted it why now did he feel sick with shame?

'It is often that way the first time,' Sheldon had told him once it was all over.

The first time. Edmund felt the blood rise to his face. Would there be other times, did he want that exquisite joy when it was followed by such feelings of degradation? Why put himself through such self-reproach when he could experience that same elation with a woman and suffer no censure? But in all his adult years no woman had had the effect upon him that Sheldon Sinclair had, no woman had ever had him gasping for her touch as he had gasped for that man's.

The very thought arousing fresh passions Edmund slid lower into the water. It could not happen again. What they had done together was against nature, it flew in the face of all he had been taught. It would *not* happen again! Tomorrow he would return to Wednesbury and that would be the end of it.

Tomorrow he would return to Wednesbury. But as his head slipped beneath the warm water he knew it would not be the end.

Wrapped in a huge towel Edmund looked towards the tap sounding discreetly at the bathroom door.

'Mr Sinclair asks you wear this buttonhole in your lapel this evening, sir. I will leave it in the dressing room.'

Hearing the door close Edmund waited several minutes, holding the towel tight around him. Did Sheldon's manservant know what had gone on in that bedroom, did he perhaps guess? The colour returned to Edmund's face, then drained rapidly as the next thought came. Had it happened before with some other man?

The thought leaving a kind of sickness in its wake, he forced himself to walk into the dressing room. Glancing at the rack of jackets and trousers he touched a hand to the soft velour and rich velvet. So much money! How could a jacket and trousers cost so much . . . how could he justify spending what he had?

But he had spent it. He dropped the towel, leaving it behind as he walked along the rack. He had spent it and he did not have to justify it to anybody!

Dressed in carefully selected cream-coloured trousers and matching silk shirt he ran an eye over the half-dozen cravats he had also purchased. Choosing one he held it against a mulberry mohair jacket. Satisfied it was of much the same shade he tied it about his throat, then slipped into the jacket.

He had hesitated whether to buy this with its lapels cut to hip level, but Sheldon had assured him it was quite the London fashion.

Looking at himself now Edmund saw the change it brought about; lending depth to his insipid hazel eyes and richness to pale sandy hair it emphasised his height. Taking the carnation he held it to his nose, inhaling the delicate bouquet. Touching a finger to purplish-red frilled cream petals he smiled. They matched his outfit perfectly. It was almost as if Sheldon had known what he would choose to wear. But then Sheldon Sinclair seemed to know so much more of his tastes than he knew himself.

Setting the flower in his lapel he glanced once more at his reflection.

'*Bloody pansy, dressed up like a paycock!*' That is what Jabez would have said seeing him now. But what had Jabez ever known apart from bolts, screws and a whisky bottle?

But he would know. He would sample all the delights Jabez' money could buy, and that included what could be got for that damned works!

Chapter Seventeen

The jars of linctus stored on the pantry shelf, Laura sprinkled sugar on a sheet of greaseproof paper, folding it in half across itself.

The Bailey boys would have enjoyed this part. She smiled, the faces of the tousle-haired lads seeming to smile back across the table. Teddie and his bull's eyes! Heaven would have to be full of them to be paradise for him.

Taking the thick earthenware bottle she had fetched from the scullery she pounded the sugar.

They were such kind boys, so full of fun. Edmund had never seemed to be full of fun yet, to be fair, he had been kind. She stared at the paper with its filling of sugar. What had changed him? Almost overnight he had become a different person. Never an outgoing man he had become moody and withdrawn, and when he did speak it was with a sharpness that could cut or a cynicism that burned the heart.

'*You are not even pretty . . .*'

Tears collecting in her eyes, Laura blinked them away angrily. There was more to a woman than beauty, one day Edmund would find that out for himself.

Leaning her weight on the bottle she rolled it several times across the paper.

What he had done to her father she could never forgive; the

heartache and suffering he had caused was more than enough, yet she felt there would be more, much more for both herself and for Edmund Shaw before he made that discovery.

Unfolding the paper she spooned up the powdered sugar, sifting it over the herbal sweets set to harden on a tray. Alfie had chosen to take a few of the sweets even without the coating of sugar. She forced her thoughts away from Edmund. In fact he had chosen sweets in place of the penny she had offered, that was as baffling as the sudden change her life had taken; for Alfred to refuse a penny was strange indeed.

Gathering the utensils she had used she carried them into the scullery, returning for the kettle of boiling water.

There were not many pennies left, the box that held the housekeeping money was almost empty. Drying the crockery she had washed she carried them into the kitchen, putting each in its place. Putting aside the fare needed to get her to Winson Green and back there would be barely enough to last another week, but the visit to her father must come first; no matter what she must go without, that visit would be made.

Making the honey linctus and the herbal soothers had eaten more deeply into her meagre funds than she liked to admit, but getting her father well, giving him what little comfort she could, was more important than her own well-being.

Staring down at the try of sweets she felt a new sadness. This was a task she loved doing: thinking up fresh flavourings and new recipes, seeing the delight on the faces of neighbours' children whenever they were given a toffee or a bull's eye.

'I loves a bull's eye.'

The refrain that was as much Teddie as his roguish grin echoed in her mind. But there would be no more bull's eyes, no more sweets of any kind; from now on she would need every penny, a halfpenny of it to live and a halfpenny of it to pay back to Edmund Shaw.

*

'Ah the carnation, you remembered.'

Sheldon Sinclair ran an approving eye over the man coming into the sitting room. He had not been mistaken in his expectations of Edmund Shaw, nor would he be in the weeks ahead; not that there would be too great a number of them, Shaw was already half-way destroyed by his own hand . . . or was it his own mind?

'I'm glad.' He went on, grass-green eyes smiling, 'The button-hole will be necessary if you are to be allowed into the Gallery this evening.'

'Allowed?' Edmund frowned. 'But I thought . . .'

'The Gallery was open to the general public?' Checking the time on a gold hunter Sheldon tucked the watch back into the pocket of his satin brocade waistcoat. 'So it is, but tonight there is to be a private showing, a special collection for a few . . . shall we say connoisseurs, men who appreciate art in its many forms.'

'Well I know practically nothing about art,' Edmund answered truthfully.

Leading the way into the spacious hall Sheldon shrugged into the coat held for him by his manservant, taking gloves and tall silk hat in hand as Edmund donned his own coat.

'It might be better if I stay behind.' Far from sure of himself among a group of men talking paintings and all the rest of the paraphernalia Jabez would have called bloody clapped-out pieces of rubbish, Edmund tried to make an excuse not to go.

'Nonsense!' Sheldon's smile deepened. 'As the prospective new owner of the Gallery of course you must come, how will you ever learn to run a business like this one if you refuse to attend a simple function!'

'Perhaps I should read a few books.'

Nodding to the manservant Sheldon walked from the house to the waiting carriage. Edmund seated beside him, he took the reins.

'Of course you should read, Edmund, books are an invaluable asset to learning, but then so is the practical approach; one is complementary to the other but both lose something if they are not used in conjunction.'

The words themselves baffling to Edmund he remained silent. He could hold his own with any man discussing the pros and cons of a steel bolt, but a painting or a statue? He wouldn't know an old master from old junk.

'Stafford Lawton will be there and so will Unwin Thorne and Melville Hutton. Those are the men I spoke to you of, the ones who might possibly be interested in a part share of the Gallery; but don't talk of business tonight, these men take their leisure as seriously as they do their business and they do not like their pastimes infringed upon.'

So what do I talk about? Edmund stared from the carriage, seeing nothing in the darkness that raked the drive leading from the house.

'Don't worry.' Sheldon touched a hand to his thigh. 'The evening will soon pass and we can come home to a pastime we both enjoy.'

Edmund felt the tremor shoot into his loins as the fingers pressed gently. Yes, he had enjoyed what they had done earlier, enjoyed it but somehow regretted it. It had left him feeling sick at his own behaviour, yet wanting the same thing again. He should have gone home . . . now he doubted he could if he wanted to.

Lost amid his apprehensions he stayed silent, little of what Sheldon said entering his mind.

He wanted a different life and a different world. Well the world that Sheldon Sinclair had shown him was all of that; fine houses, rich men and beautiful women. It was there in plenty, there for the taking and Edmund Shaw would take his share.

'The Gallery.'

A nudge from Sheldon had him look ahead. Set at the apex of a tree-lined drive a large house was ablaze with light.

'This?' He leaned forward slightly. 'I thought the Gallery was a place where antiques were sold, but this is hardly a shop.'

Leaving the carriage in the hands of a groom Sheldon led the way up wide fan steps, a heavy oak door swinging open as he reached the top.

Acknowledging the quiet greeting of a uniformed footman he ushered Edmund inside.

This was what Sheldon thought he could purchase? Edmund stared. The light from a huge gasoliere danced a myriad colours from crystal droppers, running fingers of light over graceful statues set in niches about the semi-circle of walls, they in turn adorned with portraits and landscape paintings in heavy embossed frames.

'Sinclair, glad you could come.'

Detaching himself from a group of men, each wearing an identical carnation, Philip Sandon came up to them, wineglass in hand.

'I would not miss a special showing, Philip, you know that.'

'And you too, Shaw.' Sandon held out his free hand. 'I thought you might have gone back to . . . to where was it you said?'

'Wednesbury.' Edmund shook hands briefly.

'Eh! Oh yes. Don't know the place myself. Come, meet the others.'

Following after the stocky figure Edmund was caught up in a round of introductions, names he could not remember and conversation he could take no part in. Feeling like a fish out of water he glanced around the room Sandon had brought him to, his sigh of relief almost audible as he saw Sheldon sitting talking to three other men.

'There you are, Sandon, we were ready to think you already left for your stately home.'

'Not yet, Lawton, not yet. Shaw here had to meet everyone . . . takes time, you know.'

Taking a seat Edmund caught the look directed from small ferret-sharp eyes before they turned away. This one he had remembered. He let his glance rest on the slight figure, noting the quick restless movements of the hands, the seemingly uncontrollable twitch of the head. Something in Stafford Lawton left him feeling disturbed.

Waiting until each man's glass was replenished Sheldon said quietly, 'Gentlemen, I know this evening is one when talk of business is prohibited, but at the risk of incurring your displeasure . . .' He smiled, his handsome face every bit as beautiful as the portraits hanging from the walls. '. . . I must tell you Edmund here is considering taking over the Gallery.'

'Eh! Shaw is buying this place?' A bald head bobbed as Unwin Thorne removed his spectacles, rubbing vigorously at the lenses with a pocket handkerchief. 'That will put your nose out, eh, Hutton!'

Dark hair turning to grey, a distinguished-looking Melville Hutton raised his glass, his smile cool above the rim. 'The purchase I think is not made yet, am I right, Sandon?'

'Nothing signed.' Philip Sandon turned from the sideboard, decanter in hand. 'But I've given my word and a gentleman's word be as good as ink on paper any day.'

A gentleman's agreement. Edmund's soul laughed. He had come across one of those before. But Edmund Shaw would make no such agreement . . . ink on paper? He would have a contract written in blood if need be.

'I'll have no more talk of it.' Setting the decanter back on its silver stand Sandon waved his glass towards the door. 'Tomorrow is for business, tonight is for pleasure and that pleasure awaits. I hope your bank balances are healthy my friends, for this collection is truly extraordinary and truly expensive.'

His laugh deep and loud, he led the way back to the spacious hall where now chairs had been placed at intervals between several closed doors set into graceful curving arches.

Catching Edmund's arm Sheldon drew him to a seat a little apart from the others. 'This is what I wanted you to see before you make up your mind totally about buying this place; tonight you will get a taste of the money to be made. There could be more than one item will catch your eye and your fancy but keep a hold on your money, for if the Gallery does come to you then you have first choice for only a fraction of what these fellows will pay.'

'But if it is so commercially sound why . . . ?'

'Shh!' The sound just loud enough for Edmund to hear, Sheldon turned to watch as Philip Sandon took the centre of the floor.

'Gentlemen . . .'

Only as that word rang across the wide semi-circle of the hall did it register with Edmund that there were no women guests. Why? Was it that their womenfolk had no interest in antiques? Whatever, only men occupied those chairs, it was only men, men in a variety of jackets and waistcoats but each wearing an identical purplish-edged carnation in the lapel.

'*The buttonhole will be necessary if you are to be allowed into the Gallery this evening . . .*'

The words Sheldon had smiled at him as they left the house returned to his mind. Every single man in the room had the same flower, it could almost be a badge of some sort . . . a symbol.

'Gentlemen . . .'

Watching Philip Sandon set his glass on an ormolu side table, Edmund found his attention caught by the audible ripple that ran between the listening guests.

'. . . tonight the Gallery has a superb collection to show. I am certain that once you see the items you will agree they are some of the finest ever to come on to the market; once more in keeping with the policy of this house I offer you only the very best.'

On the far side of the room a door opened and a figure, dressed in a demure, empire-line, white voile dress carrying a white statue group, walked gracefully into the light of the gasoliere.

Was this why no women were present with the men? Edmund watched the poised, elegant creature smile and dip, moving from guest to guest, black hair coiled in ringlets resting against creamy skin. Were the wives acting as showroom attendants . . . ?

'This is Sèvres.'

'Which is her husband?'

Hiding the smile the question urged, Sheldon whispered back, 'Sèvres is the name of the factory that produced that group; as for the person carrying it, no one here is married to any of those who will be presenting the pieces.'

'It is called *The Lovers*.' Dark-brown eyes looking deep into his, the delicate porcelain was held for his inspection.

'And very beautiful it is.' Sheldon answered, covering Edmund's awkwardness. 'Almost as beautiful as you are, my dear.'

'A hundred.'

'Two.'

'I'll make it three.'

Around the room bids began to be called.

'Five!'

'Do they mean pounds?' Edmund caught a delicate whiff of perfume as the woman moved on, circling the rest of the buyers.

'Six fifty!' A man in a dark-fawn jacket raised a hand.

A slight shake of the head prefacing his answer Sheldon sent a glance towards the latest bid. 'No,' he murmured, 'it means guineas . . .'

Glass once more in hand Philip Sandon raised it, but did not drink.

'. . . That means the bid is accepted.'

Six hundred and fifty guineas for a piece of china! Edmund blew softly through pursed lips. Why the hell didn't Sandon hold on to this business and get a manager to run it for him?

As the figure in white disappeared, another door opened and the slight figure that emerged was dressed in a bronze silk kimono edged with a tracery of pearls woven into a design of gold chrysanthemums. Hair, ebony-black and piled high on the head, sparkled with emerald-tipped jade pins protruding from each side. Greeted with a few loud-caught breaths the figure bowed low, small white hands holding an elaborately gilded and enamelled Japanese vase.

Clever . . . ! Edmund's eye followed the figure, gold leather-topped sandals pattering on the marble floor as the vase was carried around for inspection . . . Dressing the presenters to match the items they showed.

The glass lifting at seven hundred and fifty, Philip Sandon glanced at Edmund, the look asking clearly did he now think the Gallery worth the asking price?

'A masterpiece of Satsuma art; beautiful, don't you think?'

Beautiful and expensive! Edmund turned to answer, then felt his insides harden as he saw Sheldon's glance was on the tiny delicate figure rather than on the vase.

One after another, each figure exquisitely coifed and gowned in a shade complementing the antique presented, the auction went on but it was not the breathlessness of the prices paid had Edmund's throat in a vice, it was a thought he could not shake. Did the look Sheldon gave that woman mean what he thought it to mean? But it couldn't . . . Sheldon had made love to him only a few hours ago, he could not be a man who played both ends of the field.

'This will be the last.'

Sheldon's vivid-green gaze slid past him to a door opening from the left. Standing perfectly still beneath the arch a golden-haired figure, robed in palest azure tulle crossed over the chest with violet satin bands that circled the waist, held a tall urn. Black figures wrestling or throwing spears ornamented the brown body of the two-handled pot but it was the body of the woman supporting it gracefully on one shoulder drew every man's eye.

Golden hair, roped with gold chain interlaced with tiny diamonds, gleamed beneath crystal-shed light as she moved to the centre of the floor, eyes violet as the sash that circled her waist moving slowly over the face of every man present.

'Greek, fourth century BC. Thought to have once belonged to Alexander the Great.'

Edmund listened to Sheldon's description, his own eyes following movements as graceful as a gazelle as the urn was carried to every chair, and once more wondered why Philip Sandon was willing to part with so lucrative and pleasant a business.

Listening to the spate of bids, watching the tension on the faces of the would-be buyers as they were outbid then bid again, he resolved that by hook or by crook the Gallery would be his.

'Eight twenty-five.' Sheldon Sinclair's cultured tone slid across the room, met by the raising of Sandon's glass.

'Eight hundred and twenty-five guineas!' Edmund turned a disbelieving look to the man beside him. A shake of his head showing his incredulity he blew softly through his teeth. 'I only hope that urn is worth it.'

'That is of little consequence.' Sheldon smiled, watching others begin to drift away. 'What really matters is will *you* think it value for money?'

His brow creasing, Edmund raised an amused glance.

'What does it matter what I think, it is not my eight hundred and twenty-five guineas going into Sandon's pocket.'

'Whether you feel the money well spent matters to me, Edmund, you see the urn is my gift to you.'

Amusement turning to incredulity Edmund almost gasped. 'Me! But why . . . I mean, what for . . . why should you give me such a gift?'

'Do I have to have a reason?' Sheldon watched the last of the buyers leave the hall then turned back to Edmund. 'Ah, I see that I do. My reason is simple, I want to give you something beautiful, something you will enjoy. The price is immaterial so long as you *do* enjoy it.'

'But eight hundred . . .'

'Would you rather I declare no sale?'

Seeing hurt and disappointment fill those velvet eyes Edmund felt a tremor of guilt. How could he be such a boor as to throw a man's gift back in his face!

'No, no of course not. It was just that the money . . .'

The smile returning, Sheldon stood up. 'Forget the money, Edmund, it exists only to give pleasure and that is what I hope you will get from my present.'

'Thank you, Sheldon.' Edmund returned the smile, quelling

the still-niggling thought that it was still a hell of a price to pay for an old pot, regardless of who had once owned it.

Sheldon pointed towards the door through which the woman showing the urn had come.

'Time to collect your gift. Inspect it well. I will be in the library with Sandon, join us there for a drink when you are finished.'

A Grecian urn! He could have done with the money instead, he could do with every penny if he was to raise the thousands needed to buy his share of this place. The thought returning to his mind, he opened the door.

The hall was elegant but the room he stepped into now was one of exquisite grace and charm. Chairs and roll-end day bed upholstered in pale-blue silk damask sat on one huge carpet of exactly the same shade, while drapes of watered silk flowed like miniature blue waterfalls to the floor. How his mother would have loved this. Edmund's gaze travelled the room, resting first on one lovely object then another.

'Good evening, Mr Shaw.'

The voice seemed to flow, touching against his ears like some hushed melody, and as he turned towards it Edmund caught his breath. The woman in blue had been magnificent in the hall but here, the gilding on picture frames echoing the gold of her hair, the sparkle of diamonds dulled by the brilliance of smiling amethyst eyes, she was superb.

'A glass of wine before you take your purchase.'

Folds of tulle accentuating every move of the body beneath, she laid an ornate silver tray on a small table.

Breath still caught in his throat, Edmund watched soft white hands pour wine into a glass. With such exquisite creatures as this to staff the Gallery, no wonder people came here to buy their antiques. Philip Sandon was a smart business man.

'*I want a wife who is beautiful . . .*'

Accepting the wine, those incredible eyes drawing him into themselves, enfolding him in those soft lustrous depths, the words he had spoken to Laura Cadman took on a whole new dimension. With a woman such as this at his side where couldn't he go in the business world?

A hand touching against his as he took the glass, a smile curving a lovely rouged mouth, the woman pressed the wine gently towards his lips.

'I hope you get great pleasure from your purchase, Mr Shaw, even more I hope it will not be the last you will make from the Gallery.'

Withdrawing her hand with an exquisite stroking slowness that sent fire along Edmund's every nerve, she straightened but did not release him from the captivity of those enchanting eyes.

Taking first a sip, feeling the warm sweetness on his tongue, Edmund swallowed the rest of the wine, not refusing when the decanter was offered again.

Around him the beautiful blue room widened into a wonderful summer sky. Relaxed as he had never been, it seemed he floated in its great blue void.

'Your purchase is ready for you, Mr Shaw.'

Wrapped in a feeling of comfort and well-being he glanced towards the soft melodious voice. Beside the day bed that beautiful face smiled at him as long fingers released the violet bands that held the dress. Watching it slide to the floor Edmund breathed loudly, the glass slipping from his hand as the smiling mouth closed over his.

It had been wonderful. His senses once more fully his own, Edmund lay naked and relaxed. The whole experience had been one he would not forget. The passion and the pleasure, the thrill of excitement churning his insides as those hands had stroked his body, lips that had left his to trail the length of his stomach, the mouth opening to take his flesh. The memory of it stirring him again he turned his head to look at the graceful urn stood on a table. No, he would not forget his first visit to the Gallery.

Chapter Eighteen

Glancing at Sheldon's profile etched sharp against the night, Edmund frowned. He had not asked what had happened in that room, neither he nor Philip Sandon making any comment as he had joined them in that book-lined library. Was that because he had known beforehand?

Calling softly to the horse, Sheldon guided the carriage away from the Gallery.

'Do you still think eight hundred and twenty-five guineas too much to pay, Edmund?' He laughed softly. 'Can you really have any doubt?'

'You knew!'

'Of course. Did you enjoy collecting your gift?'

He had enjoyed it, what was more Sheldon knew it too, and this realisation turned the pleasure sour in Edmund.

'It doesn't matter whether I did or not, it is not my eight hundred and twenty-five guineas Sandon has in his pocket!'

'No, it is not, so why be angry?' Sheldon flicked the reins, setting the horse to a trot.

'I still think it a hell of a price to pay for a pot, regardless of who it might once have belonged to.' Edmund remained truculent. 'And as Jabez would have said, "a whore can be got anywhere for five shillings".'

A shaft of moonlight reaching from the cover of cloud

touched Sheldon's face, highlighting eyes glittering like twin gem stones as he replied.

'And that would no doubt be true, but did Jabez ever have a whore such as that one you had tonight? Not to mention a fourth-century Grecian urn.'

His anger evaporating, Edmund chuckled. 'What about that urn, what am I to do with Alexander the Great's fancy pot?'

'Place it in the next auction. Sell it on and tonight's little romp costs nothing.'

'You mean I could do that?'

Beside him Sheldon nodded. 'Once you hold a stake in the place, yes; call it a perk of ownership. Anyone else adopting such a measure would pay for the service that went with the collecting of their purchase.'

'What!' Edmund met the other man's words with an astounded stare. 'You mean other men have . . . that every man who purchased an antique this evening also bought the services of a woman?'

Beneath the cover of darkness Sheldon smiled. 'No, Edmund, I do not mean that. I mean that like yourself they bought the services of a man.'

Astonishment curling about his tongue Edmund could not answer. Silent, he stared at the man beside him, hearing the soft laugh break from his lips.

'Yes, Edmund. Every presenter you saw tonight was for sale along with the artefact they carried, and every one of them was male.'

'The men bidding . . . they knew?'

'Yes, they knew.' Sheldon nodded, touching a finger to the carnation pinned to his lapel. 'That is the reason for these. Such occasions as that tonight call for extra privacy, the world we live in is not yet ready to accept the freedoms we prefer to enjoy, therefore only those especially chosen to attend such an auction are given one of these, without it you would not have been admitted. Cream carnations signify that men are on offer, pink ones say it will be women. Simple, but effective.'

Prostitutes! Edmund was stunned by what he heard. Those beautiful creatures with their lovely hair and elegant gowns were prostitutes, male prostitutes! Philip Sandon was running a brothel. An elegant house filled with costly furniture, the Gallery was no more than a front for an expensive high-class brothel and Sheldon had suggested he put his money in it.

'Are you disgusted, Edmund?' Sheldon asked quietly. 'You need not be, after all a house of ill-repute can be found anywhere, a room in some filthy back street serves the same purpose; the Gallery simply caters for a wealthier, more discerning clientele.'

Discerning! Edmund stared at the handsome profile. Sheldon had known the pedigree of each of the antiques offered, describing their history with an accomplished surety . . . did he know the presenters equally well? Had he bought the services of any one of them for himself?

Almost afraid to release the words scorching his tongue he swallowed hard, forcing himself to ask the next question racing to his mind.

'Why, Sheldon, why did you really buy that urn for me?'

Why the hell couldn't Shaw take what had been given, enjoy it and leave it at that! Annoyance clawing at his stomach, Sheldon forced the feeling aside. Keeping his voice low and as caressing as a loving hand he answered.

'Now you and I are the same, Edmund. We have both made love with another man; we are equal, one can have no jealousy of the other's past, no recriminations.'

'But you did not bid for any other article, you bought nothing for yourself.'

Passing the reins into one hand, Sheldon ran the other painfully slowly along Edmund's leg.

'There was no need,' he murmured. 'Why bid for something that would hold no pleasure for me? I have all I want right here beside me, Edmund, I have you.'

Lungs tight as steel bands, every nerve screaming as Sheldon's body pressed him back against the seat, Edmund could only whisper.

'Yes . . . yes, Sheldon, you have me.'

Hands cracked and smarting from the sting of washing soda, Laura took the heavy flat iron from the hob. It had taken her a whole day to launder the linen from that house and almost the same to iron it, and all for a shilling.

Fingers too sore to grip the iron handle firmly, it slipped from her grasp, brushing against her other hand in the process.

Tears pricking her eyelids, she laid the iron on the upturned saucer placed beside the folded blanket used as an ironing pad. Going into the scullery she rubbed the burned spot with soap, holding her breath against the bite of it.

She had tried every place she could think of, every part of the town that might hold a job she could do, but in every place she had met with the same answer: no help needed.

But with the very last of her money gone and no food left in the house she knew she had to find something, no matter what that something was.

Returning to the kitchen she finished ironing the last frilled pillow-case, glancing at the clock as she folded it. If she returned the laundry now there would still be time to look for some other work.

Every flexing of her fingers causing her to catch her breath with pain, she fastened her shawl about her waist.

'Will I put you a cauliflower aside for your coming back, they don't be pappy.'

Coming abreast of the greengrocer's shop Laura forced a smile.

'Thank you, Mrs Griffiths, I am sure the cauliflowers are beautifully firm but I will not be needing one today.'

'A few tomatoes then.' Mary Ann Griffiths glanced at the huge bundle balanced on Laura's hip. 'Put 'em in the oven with some salt and pepper and a bit o' toast and they be fit for the Queen. Take 'em when you comes by, Laura wench, they will just go to the pigs if you don't.'

The woman was simply trying to be kind. There was never a great deal left for the Griffiths' pig, not with the likes of the Baileys grateful for any leftovers; and she would not take any of the little they might get, even when it meant going hungry.

'Perhaps tomorrow, Mrs Griffiths, I have a beef casserole I must eat first.'

Mary Ann Griffiths watched the slight figure walk quickly along Dudley Street as Henry joined her in the doorway of the shop. 'Beef casserole,' she said, her voice loaded with sympathy. 'That wench ain't seen a bite of beef since they took her father away, no nor a decent meal neither! How long her can go on like that the Lord only knows!'

'Her has only to ask, Heaven knows we wouldn't see the wench starve.'

Her dark head bobbing, Mary Ann watched the hurrying figure cross the junction at Holyhead Road. 'Ar, Heaven knows that, Henry, same as it knows the pride of Isaac Cadman's wench. I think that one might pass beyond death's doors afore accepting any man's charity, even though her was never slow in giving it herself.'

Breathless from hurrying Laura almost ran along Wood Green coming to Myvod House. The housekeeper there had agreed for her to take the laundry for one week while the regular washerwoman was sick. Making her way to the back entrance she tapped at the door. Leaving her standing there whilst every inch of the linen was scrutinised, the woman at last grudgingly held out a single coin.

'A shilling is what we agreed.' She spoke sharply, her look sour.

'Yes.' Laura held out a hand, seeing the other woman glance at the burn mark now risen into a blister.

'Who is that, Walters?' A voice thin and high-pitched

sounded from beyond the kitchen. 'What do they want?'

''Tis the washerwoman brought the linen, Ma'am.'

'Washerwoman? But didn't you tell me the woman was sick?'

'So I did, Ma'am, and so her is, this be a temporary one, just for this week like.'

Shoving the shilling into Laura's palm the woman made to close the door, but her employer snatched it open. Running a quick look over Laura's patched skirts and woollen shawl, her thin nose wrinkled.

'Who are you?'

The question rapped out like an order took Laura by surprise and she stumbled over her answer.

'I . . . I am . . .'

'I am . . . I am!' Beady eyes snapping, the woman looked her up and down again. 'Anybody who can't say their name be up to no good, they be either thieves or gypsies.'

Her clothes were patched, her boots were worn, but this woman's accusation was unfair. Laura drew herself up. Eyes flashing like blue ice she snapped in return, 'I am neither a thief nor a gypsy. I have performed a task for which I ask payment, that is my only reason for coming to this house.'

'Hmmph! A likely story; but be it true, then say your name as I asked.'

'As you *demanded*,' Laura returned. 'But seeing perhaps that is the only way you know *how* to speak to people, I will answer. My name is Laura Cadman.'

'Cadman . . . Cadman.' Eyes narrowing, the sharp-faced woman rolled the name around her tongue. 'I know that name, I read it in the newspapers some weeks ago. Cadman! Yes, he was jailed for theft.' She paused, her look becoming one of suspicion. 'Cadman . . . not a common name . . . are you the same Cadman?'

It was bound to be asked sooner or later that question, now it had. Her tone icy calm Laura met the woman's look, 'Isaac Cadman is my father.'

'There, I knew it! I knew it!' Bony hands flapping, the woman screeched, 'A thief . . . a thief on my doorstep!'

'I am no thief . . . !'

Laura tried to speak, but the bit well and truly between her teeth the woman gave way to her tirade.

'Isaac Cadman is a convicted thief and you be one too. Like father, like daughter; if one is a thief then so is the other one.' She turned to her housekeeper, spittle flying from her mouth as she raged on. 'Did you let her into this house . . . did you take your eyes off her? Lord knows what she has stolen.'

Tiredness, hunger and worry suddenly combined in Laura. Mixing into an anger she had not felt before, it flooded through her veins. The smarting of her hands forgotten she reached forward. Clasping a thin arm she spun the woman about. Holding her so she could not move, Laura stared into eyes suddenly glazing with fright.

'I am not a gypsy,' she said, anger keeping her words soft. 'Had I been you would know my curse. As for a thief *you* are the one guilty of that . . . to pay a shilling for laundry that takes two days to complete! But if you are so in need of money then take this!'

Raising the hand that held the coin Laura threw it to the kitchen floor, flinging the woman from her; then with a quiet 'Good evening', turned and walked away.

The shilling had been her last hope. Shawl held close, Laura crossed into Dudley Street. Should she accept the offer Mary Ann Griffiths had made, take the cauliflower or tomatoes? They would at least provide a meal of sorts. She felt the rumble of hunger roll around her stomach. A meal of anything would be better than nothing; but what she took would be less for the others, folk like the Baileys who depended on such handouts.

But how long could she go on without food, how long before she was forced to stand in line for other people's charity?

Nearing the Griffiths' shop she pulled her shawl further over her face, her steps almost running as she hurried past. She could manage a little longer, maybe tomorrow she would find work.

Coming from the entry into the yard closed about by neigh-
bouring houses, she glanced towards the brewhouse. She always
kept a spare box of candles in there; she could light one of those
to sit by in the kitchen, that would save the last few drops of oil
left in the lamp, the gas lamps now going completely unused.

Use telling her feet where to tread in the shadowed darkness
she lifted the latch and stepped inside. Reaching the box from
the shelf beside the copper, she froze as her ears caught the slight
shuffling sound.

Instantly her mind carried her again to that back street, to the
filth of that floor, a man's foul breath in her face. Her whole body
trembling she clutched the box, forcing her brain to centre on it,
using it to prevent herself giving way to the hysterical fear racing
through her veins.

The door was just a few yards away. She knew the brewhouse
better than anyone, if she kept her wits she could be through the
door and down the entry before . . .

In the darkness the shuffle sounded again, more pronounced
this time. Catching her breath Laura turned for the door, but as
she took the first step a hand closed about her wrist.

'Did you find out what you wanted to know?' Seated in his office
the Governor of Winson Green watched his visitor closely. Rafe
Travers was an astute man and not one to be easily fooled.
Knowing him, as he had, since childhood he also knew him to be
fair, in judgement as well as in business.

'He said no more than he did the first time we spoke.' Easing
his long frame in a chair, Rafe Travers refused the proffered cigar.

Lighting his own cigar the Governor blew a stream of smoke,
watching the grey swirls rise towards the ceiling. 'You think the
man is lying?'

'Someone is. But I am not sure who. Tell me, Stephen, what
do you think of the man?'

Stephen Carter stretched his legs across the hearth, giving the impression of a man more interested in the comfort of the moment than in discussing an inmate of the prison; but across from him Rafe knew better. There was no man he would rather trust with a confidence, and none he knew more able to make sense of a situation.

'I have spoken no more than a few words to him.' Carter blew another stream of pale smoke, watching it intermingle with the first. 'But I have the reports of my warders. They all say the same. Isaac Cadman is a quiet man with a gentle disposition, we do not have many of his sort in here. To my mind it is a pity the man's theft caught up with him.' He paused, his head shaking slightly. 'Oh I know that is not quite the right thing for a prison governor to say but to you, Rafe, I can give an honest opinion, knowing it will stay with you; and between you and me I say that man is more sinned against than sinning.'

'Meaning?' Rafe Travers watched over hands folded together and resting against his chin.

Taking time to draw deeply on his cigar then to slowly exhale the plume of smoke, Stephen Carter answered.

'Meaning that if Isaac Cadman stole that money, and it seems he did, then he did not steal it for himself nor for that daughter of his. He stole it for someone else, someone he is still protecting. That leaves two questions, who and why? Two questions he refused to answer at his trial.'

'And still refuses to answer.' Rafe tapped his folded hands slowly against his chin.

'It might have gone better for him had he done so.'

Watching the other man flick ash from the end of his cigar, Rafe thought so too.

'Do you think perhaps the girl knows something?'

The Governor shrugged. 'Who can tell? But she seems to love her father well enough, so had she known then surely she would have said so. It can't be easy for her seeing him caged in here.'

No it could not be easy. Rafe had a mental vision of that face drawn with worry, despair filling what should have been bright blue eyes. The girl was no more than eighteen, twenty at the most. Lord, what was Cadman thinking of to put her through such torture!

'Will you buy that works?'

Hesitating for a few seconds Rafe Travers lowered his hands, the answer he gave one of long consideration.

'The works? That I have not decided as yet. There appears to be no deed of ownership, and that can prove hazardous to any sale; apart from which I have talked with several of its former employees and they are each prepared to swear that works was held in joint ownership by two men: one of whom lies in a church-yard, the other lying in your infirmary.'

Throwing the remains of the cigar into the fire, the prison Governor looked across at the man sat opposite.

'Are they prepared to swear because what they claim is the truth or to get revenge for being dismissed? For a man dependent upon a job for a living, to provide food for his family, to be sacked provides a powerful incentive for lying.'

'I thought of that too, Stephen.' Rafe Travers rose to his feet. 'But having talked to them I would say they are not the type to lie.'

'So what next, if one friend is allowed to ask another?'

'The house on Squire's Walk is already mine, the transaction went through a week ago.'

'You bought it then!' Stephen Carter walked his visitor to the door of his office. 'I can't imagine you living in Wednesbury.'

Pulling on hand-tailored leather gloves Rafe avoided the other man's eyes. 'It will be suitable for a while, until I decide about that engineering works. I shall need to be near the place should I buy it.'

His goodbyes said Stephen Carter closed the door, a brief smile hovering about his mouth.

'You need to be close to that works, Rafe?' he murmured, walking back to his chair. 'Or is it Cadman's daughter you need to be near to?'

Chapter Nineteen

'No . . . o . . . o . . . !'

Laura's scream split the silence as she jerked her arm, sending candles spinning everywhere among the shadows.

'Let me go . . . let me go!'

She jerked her arm again, freeing it from the hold about her wrist, a sob breaking from her as she ran for the door, almost tumbling into the yard.

'I'm sorry . . . I'm sorry. I never meant . . .'

Fear screaming in her brain, drowning all but the terrified pounding of her heart, Laura did not at first hear the voice behind her; only when it called again, itself throbbing with fright, did her footsteps slow.

'I'm sorry. I didn't think anyone would be going into that place 'til morning and I would have been gone by then.'

Overhead the sky turned a dull red then blazed to a full glowing crimson, lighting the yard with its glory as the furnaces of nearby steel works were opened.

'I didn't mean to scare you.'

Already at the mouth of the entry that ran between the block of houses, Laura turned but every sinew of her remained poised for flight.

Silhouetted against a background of brilliant red-gold

reflecting from the evening sky, a young girl stood just beyond the doorway of the brewhouse.

'I'm truly sorry for giving you such a turn,' she spoke again. 'I'll be going right away.'

The throb in her throat only marginally less than moments ago, Laura glanced nervously back at the figure.

'What . . . what were you doing in there?'

'I weren't trying to steal nothing.' The silhouetted shape raised its hands, holding them out. 'See . . . I ain't took nothing. Please, Mrs, please don't call for the bobbies!'

The police. She had not thought of them or even of shouting for help, her one thought had been to get away, as far as possible from the man trying . . .

But it was not a man. Laura drew a long breath, forcing her mind to accept what her eyes saw. It was a girl, a girl who by the sound of her was as frightened as she was.

'Who are you . . . why are you here?' Laura remained still, keeping the distance wide between them.

Above the girl's head the sky flamed its borrowed beauty.

'My name is Livvy . . . Livvy Beckett. I only wanted a place out of the night, a place to sleep. I would have been gone at first light. I'm sorry I frightened you, Mrs, I truly am, but I'll be gone now.'

A place out of the night, a place to sleep; fear that had held her almost paralysed faded enough for Laura to think. Did that mean the girl was on the street, perhaps sleeping under hedges?

'Wait!' She raised a hand as the girl began to move.

'It be all right, Mrs, I wouldn't harm you none.' The girl came to an immediate halt.

The glow of the sky threw the figure into sharp focus but the face remained shadowed, and though Laura knew she should chase her away the voice, so young and frightened, caught at her good nature.

'Why do you need a place to sleep, what about your home?'

Deprived of the glow of furnaces the sky began to lose its

grandeur. Scarlet and gold gave way to purple and then, its loss complete, the night was once more grey, robing the yard with shadows.

Across from her the figure seemed to melt into them, becoming almost one with the encroaching night as if using its darkness to hide, and when at last the girl answered Laura caught the sob beneath the words.

'My home be halfway to Liverpool by now.'

Despite the warning of her brain Laura stepped forward. 'Halfway to Liverpool . . . I don't understand.'

A sniff audible in the pause between the clang of metal bars being loaded and unloaded and the blast of steam whistles from the railway station, the figure raised a hand, touching it to the hidden face.

'I live on a narrow boat, least I did up to a week ago. Now I live nowhere, not even the poor house will take me in. But you don't want to stand listening to me, so if it be all right with you I'll be gone.'

'No, it is not all right with me.'

'Please, Mrs! I've done no harm, I ain't took nothing . . . please don't call the bobbies.'

Laura heard the fear behind the gasp and stepped closer to the girl.

'I am sure you had no intention of stealing anything and I have no intention of calling for the police. A cup of tea is all I can offer you, but you are welcome to it if you will come into the house.'

Not waiting for an answer Laura let herself into the scullery, lighting the candle kept just inside. Behind her there was no sound of footsteps but an anxious breathing told her the girl followed.

Ignoring her own promised saving of her precious lamp oil Laura removed the glass funnel, holding the candle flame to the wick until the lamp gleamed softly.

Removing her shawl she hung it on the back of the door before crossing to the fireplace, giving the sleepy fire a nudge with the iron poker.

Awakened flames lending extra light to the kitchen she turned to the figure stood beneath the arch that gave on to the scullery.

'You can sit down, Livvy.' She smiled. 'It is warmer here next to the fire.'

Perched nervously on the edge of the chair the girl watched the quick deft movements as Laura brewed a pot of tea.

'I am sorry I have no food to offer you.'

'Don't let that worry you, Mrs, tonight only one of many I've slept on an empty belly.'

'It is not "Mrs".' Laura smiled again as the girl took the cup from her. 'I am not married, and my name is Laura . . . Laura Cadman.'

'Cadman!' The girl looked up from her cup. 'That be a name I've heard. My father has taken cargo from a works that has that name, Shaw and Cadman. They sends bolts and screws to towns the barge passes on the way to Liverpool. It be a coincidence you having the same name.'

It was no coincidence. Laura stirred sugar into her own cup, watching the liquid swirl in circles.

'You said you have a home and a father, so how come you are alone and sleeping rough?' Perhaps it was rude to ask that question but it evaded the need to expand on what the girl had called coincidence.

'No, miss.' The girl slipped rapidly at the hot tea. 'I said I *had* a home. A narrow boat, the *Lady Margaret*. Narrow be the right word for the barges, there be hardly room to swing a cat and what with four more besides me and me parents, well,' she shrugged, 'there just weren't enough room. It meant one of us had to go and what with me being the oldest and a girl into the bargain then that someone had to be me.'

'You mean your parents just let you leave . . . with nowhere else to go?' Laura's tone relayed her disbelief.

Gulping the last few drops of tea the girl set the cup on the table then looked squarely at Laura, her eyes filled with a matter-of-fact honesty.

'They didn't want to, miss, they didn't do it gladly. My mother cried for days but I knowed it was what I had to do. Times be bad on the canals, there isn't always a cargo to be had and that means food be hard come by. That often meant the little uns went hungry. One less mouth for my father to feed would be a little more in theirs and a little less ache in their bellies. I had to go, miss, it were the only way.'

Looking at the small face pinched with hunger and drawn with fatigue, Laura felt her heart swell with pity. The girl was barely out of childhood yet already she carried burdens that would defeat many a man.

'But what will you do, where will you go?' Laura's concern was genuine.

'Well it won't be the poor house that be certain, for they wouldn't take me in, said I was too old being gone past the age of their keeping pauper children; that only stretched to fourteen, and I be sixteen turned.'

Sixteen years old and already the world had turned its back on her. Laura refilled the girl's cup sharing the only thing she had to give.

'I thought I was like to get work hereabouts so I could see me mother and father should they pass through, but everywhere I went they turned me away. I stood in the line along of the market place every day but nobody wanted a girl, not for work anyway!'

Colour sweeping her drawn face, the girl stared into her cup and in that same instant Laura felt those hands snatching at her clothes, the body pressing against her own, and from the deep reaches of her mind that awful laugh echoed.

Had the same thing happened to this young girl, that or worse? If it had not happened yet then it would if she were left to sleep under hedges. The shiver reaching her fingers, the cup rattled as she laid it aside. It was the truth the girl had told her about finding no work, for she herself had tramped the town looking for the same, so why should not the rest of what she had said be just as true? She could have got into the house as easily as she had got into the brewhouse for neither were ever locked, she could have stolen anything but she had not, she had simply tried to find a place to sleep; a place where she might feel safe.

Taking the silence as a signal for her to leave, the girl put her cup beside Laura's and rose. 'I thank you kindly for the tea miss, and for not calling the bobbies. I'll be on my way.'

Thanks only half registering in her mind Laura made no reply, leaving the girl's words to fall into the silence that still lay between them.

The wench be no further through than a kipper between the eyes! The comment Abbie Butler would have made came now to Laura as her gaze followed the girl. Leg of mutton sleeves of a faded cotton blouse hung loosely over her wrists; a patched grey skirt that once had been black ended at mid-calf, the waist held between button and buttonhole by a long loop of elastic, it could only have once been bought for a small child, just as the boots might once have been for a man; but worse than all of this was the hopelessness in those young eyes. It was too soon in life for such despair. The girl must have been loved. Brown hair shining in the lamplight, the hands and face washed clean attested to that. Loved as her father loved her . . .

'Wait!' The click of the door latch breaking her thoughts, Laura called out. 'You can stay here for the night. It will be warmer than the streets,' she added as the girl turned to face her.

Brown eyes flooding with tears, the girl held herself straight. 'That be a kindliness I can't be taking, miss, thank you all the same, but this be your home and I'll not intrude upon it.'

'It would be no intrusion.' Laura thought of the long hours to come spent lying awake, too afraid of memories to sleep. It would be reassuring to know someone else was in the house with her.

'Then I will take a corner in the brewhouse and be gone at first light.'

'Livvy,' Laura smiled, 'if you will, I would rather you slept here in the house.'

Swallowing hard the girl came slowly back to the hearth. 'I won't forget your kindness to me,' she said softly, 'I won't ever forget.'

'*I won't ever forget.*'

Watching the moonlight shaft into her bedroom, Laura said the words over in her mind.

Nor would she. She would not forget one man's kindness to her. She would not forget Rafe Travers.

The girl was gone. Laura glanced about the kitchen. She had said she would leave at first light, but now the reality of her leaving left a taste of disappointment. She had been so polite, so un-imposing, a girl you could come to think of as a sister. But had all of that been a deception, had the girl left at dawn or crept away as soon as they had said goodnight? Crept away, taking with her . . .

A pulse beating rapidly in her throat Laura reached into a drawer of the dresser, taking out the box that had held the house-keeping money. All that had been left was just enough for her fare to Winson Green prison, if the girl had taken it . . . !

Fingers shaking she removed the lid, a low gasp leaving her lips as she stared. It was there. A flush of warm guilt rising to her cheeks she stared at the coins in the box, then set it back in the drawer. How could she have thought the girl a thief, judged her so unfairly? Was that what these last few weeks had done to her, turned her into a false accuser as ready to lay blame as Edmund Shaw had laid blame upon her father?

Closing the drawer she started at sound of a knock to the scullery door. No one in the square knocked on each other's scullery door. A loud 'Be you in?' was all that was needed as they let themselves inside. Was it Edmund? Laura hurried to open the door. Had he come to tell her it was all a mistake after all, that her father was no thief?

Flinging open the door, his name already leaving her lips, she halted abruptly, staring at the pale young face.

'Livvy, I . . . I thought you had gone!'

Seeing the hope die in Laura's eyes the girl turned to where a bucket stood filled with coal.

'I brought this first. I've set a marker beside the lock of the canal, it will be seen by all the cut people that passes through and tells them a kindness has been done to one of their own. There will be a lump or two of coal left there by every bargee so you need never be short of a fire. I thank you again for that kindness.'

'Livvy.' Laura held out a hand as the girl began to walk from the yard. 'Livvy, I want you to stay. We can look for work together.'

'You be sure of this, miss?'

Livvy watched Laura pour boiling water into the teapot.

'Yes, Livvy, I am sure, and I know my father would approve.'

'Your father? He wasn't here last night nor did he come afore I left the house, and it was already five by that clock when I did. Is he working a double shift?'

'No, Livvy.' Laura stood with the kettle in her hand. 'My father is in prison.'

Letting the tea mast, then pouring it into two cups, Laura told all that had happened including her near-rape and the assistance of a tall darkly handsome man, spilling out her heart as she thought never to do since Abbie's death.

'That day in Brummagem, was that the reason you was so feared last night when you found me in the brewhouse?'

Drawing a breath, holding it in her throat, Laura nodded. That encounter in a Birmingham back street would stay with her for a long time.

'It can be rough in that place. My father would not allow Mother or us kids to leave the barge while we were tied up in Gas Street Basin. He said it were not safe for women, now I knows what he meant. 'Twas good of that man to help you though.'

'Yes, it was very good.' Laura watched the picture form in her mind. Clear grey eyes regarded her from strong features finely cut above a firm jaw traced by a slender line of beard.

'Call it my second good deed.'
The picture faded, but not before the full mouth smiled.

The house had been sold. In the room he had taken at the George Hotel, Edmund Shaw once more counted his assets. Including the money he had saved over the years, the cash in hand came to less than fifteen hundred pounds. Fifteen hundred, and he needed five thousand at the very least, maybe more if Hutton or one of the others refused to join a consortium.

If only he hadn't spent so much on clothes, if only he had waited! Clothes were something that could have come later, after he had bought into the Gallery.

Pushing angrily to his feet, he crossed to the window looking over the Five Ways towards the market place. Below him the streets were busy with carts and wagons, and in the space where the ancient Butter Cross had once stood there was now a group of people waiting in the hope of a day's labour.

Ought he to have kept the works going instead of closing it, sacking men on the spot as he had? Would it have sold more quickly as a still-operational concern?

Maybe. He stared at the women, drab skirts flapping about ankle-high boots, black bonnets perched on hair so tightly scraped back they might have been scalped; and the men in threadbare jackets and worn-through trousers. He could have let the ones at Shaw and Cadman work on . . . but it had given him so much pleasure handing them their tins!

Touching the fingers of one hand to the fine velour jacket, he smiled. He could have saved that money Jabez had so unwittingly left but, dressed as he had been in clothes so like the ones worn down there in the street, he would never have been given access to the Gallery, he would never have had the pleasure of that exquisite creature in a pale blue gown.

'Are you turning in your grave, Jabez?' He laughed softly. 'Are you wishing you had kept your mouth shut about marrying

Laura? If you had you might still be telling me what to do. But you will never tell me anything again. Wherever you are, *father,*' he laughed again, the softness added to by hate, 'watch me. Watch me spend your money!'

But first he had to get it. He turned from the window, his brain moving rapidly. Documentation, that buyer had said. Produce documentation proving ownership of the works and he would buy it.

Taking hat and gloves he made his way downstairs, a nod of the head acknowledging the landlord's greeting. Since there was no document to be found then one would have to be drawn up and Isaac Cadman made to sign it.

Making his way to the offices of Messiter, the solicitor who had handled the sale of the house, he had the document drawn naming him sole owner of Shaw Engineering, signing it in the presence of both solicitor and his clerk. Tucking it in his pocket he bid the men a pleasant good afternoon. Crossing the street to the Turks Head, he went inside.

First dinner and then a visit to Great Western Street. Laura would write an addendum to the document and take it to that prison for Isaac to sign . . . and sign it he would, if he valued his daughter's safety!

Chapter Twenty

'I see you on this train last month.'

Laura glanced across the crowded compartment towards a middle-aged woman, red poppies flopping over the brim of a navy straw hat, a basket balanced on her knees.

'I were none too sure when you got off at Snow Hill but I be pretty certain now; you be going to Winson Green prison.'

Beneath her own plain bonnet, Laura's face turned pink. The woman glanced in turn at the rest of the passengers. All ages and shapes, they had one thing in common, except for children they were all women.

'There be no need of blushing.' The woman returned her glance to Laura. 'Though every one of us in this here carriage have done the same in our turn. I be right don't I, you be going to Winson Green?'

Nodding her head at the whispered yes, the woman smiled showing a line of crooked teeth. 'Then you would do well to stay on the train 'til it reaches the station at Soho, that way you don't need to take the tram, you can walk to the jail from there.'

Walk along those narrow streets and dark alleyways? Every step would be a nightmare!

Seeing her face blanch of its sudden colour the woman smiled understandingly.

'All of us women walks together, you would come to no hurt

with us. In fact Bertha hopes every week that some bloke will try it on, her ain't had a good tussle since they took her Simeon inside, that's right ain't it, Bertha?'

Along the wooden bench a plump woman laughed. 'That be right, Sarah. A roll in the hay or on the ground would set me up 'til old Simple be turned loose.'

'Now you got the wench all pinked up again.' The woman called Sarah smiled at Laura. 'Don't go taking offence at Bertha, we all gets a bit excited when we be going to see our menfolk.'

'Well I won't be coming no more after next month be gone by.' Bertha grinned. 'Me and my Simple will be living in clover.'

'You be wondering why her calls him Simple 'stead of his proper name.' Sarah caught the tiny bewildered frown that flitted across Laura's brow. 'Tell her, Bertha, go on tell her, the wench can be trusted, her's got one of her own in that place.'

'Tell her, Bertha, we can all do with a good laugh.'

At the urging of the rest of the passengers Bertha hoisted her own basket high on her knees, holding it against her ample stomach.

'It be this way . . .'

'Telling the tale again, Bertha?' Smartly dressed in the green and gold of the Great Western Railway Company, the ticket inspector halted in the doorway of the compartment.

'Ar, that I be, Joe Wilkins, but it ain't the same one you likes to hear whispered in your ear when you be getting your tail pulled on a Saturday night!'

Shaking his head genially the inspector took Laura's ticket, punching it once with what looked to her like a pair of her father's pliers.

'You wants to steer clear of this mob, miss,' he smiled, handing back the ticket, 'a week or two of their company and you'll finish up as bad as them.'

Pretending offence, Bertha glared at the smiling official. 'We'll have less of your old buck, Joe Wilkins, unless you wants to part with them bloody posh trousers right now!'

With a wry pull of his whiskered mouth the man appeared to contemplate the good-humoured threat.

'That be an offer I find hard to refuse, Bertha me love, but then much of a treat lies in the thinking of it, so I'll leave it 'til our usual time Saturday night.'

'Cheeky bugger,' Bertha laughed after him. 'You'll have my Sim kick your arse when he gets out.'

'. . . and that will be next month,' she added as the inspector moved on into the adjoining compartment.

Free next month. Laura felt a tug at her heart. If only her father were to be freed, if she could take him away from that awful place, bring him home . . .

'You was telling the wench why your man be called Simple 'stead of his christened name.'

'Oh, ar!' Bertha answered, the wide smile still spread across her plump face. 'It were like this. My Simeon were in the Bear, that be an inn stood at the corner where Shires Oak Road touches against the Bearwood Road . . .'

The explanation meant nothing to Laura but she nodded, willing to listen to anything that would take her mind from that prison.

'. . . he were playing cards with some of his mates when in walks a group of toffs, all silk hats and fancy waistcoats talking so bay-windowed you needed a three-acre space for each to stand in. Well they stops by where Sim were sitting and one of 'em says in that posh voice, *"You are not playing those cards frightfully well, my man!"* Well!' Bertha chuckled, 'that didn't go down well with old Sim. *"Ho! H'ain't I?"* he says, all pork pie and lard, *'H'in that case p'raps your Lordship will h'oblige me by showing how the game be played proper."'*

'And did he?'

Turning her glance to the young lad who had called the question, Bertha treated him to a scorching glance. 'Little pigs who have big ears finishes up getting them chopped off, me lad!'

'Sure and get on wi' it, Bertha, or we'll all still be waiting when your Sim be playing his next game in the Bear!'

Bertha's remonstrative glance swung to a stringy woman dressed in a dun-coloured coat and brown bonnet.

'Hold on . . . hold on!' She glared, not taking kindly to yet another interruption. 'This be my tale and the telling of it will be done in my own good time. Trouble wi' you, Kate O'Connell, is you be too quick for your own comfort, you'll move so fast one day they'll find you disappeared up your own arse!'

'At least there will be room for me in there so there will, not like your fat self, Bertha Wooten; there wouldn't be room for you inside of an elephant so there wouldn't!'

'Leave off, you pair, we hear enough of that cat calling without listening to it today!' Sarah cut in testily. 'Go on with your telling, Bertha, it always brings a smile if nothing else.'

Sending one more glare to her travelling companion Bertha resumed her story.

'"*Always prepared to give a little instruction to the lower clarsses,*" says the toff, "*their education like themselves is so appallingly pathetic; I doubt if they could recognise 'A' from a bull's foot!*" Well my Sim touches his cap all polite like and answers, "*It be a kindness of your Lordship to bother, I'm sure I will try my best to get my dim wits about the proper way of the playing of pontoon.*"'

Pulling the basket closer against her stomach Bertha drew in a breath, assuming a haughty expression before continuing.

'"*What was that you called the game?*" asks another of the toffs. "*Pontewn? Hi say, how frightfully droll!*" So the game is played, Sim at first losing every hand until his money were almost gone. Then having the lah-de-dah firm on his line he began to reel him in and by the time he was finished that bloke were not only skint but looking like a right 'Erbert into the bargain. Slipping the winnings into his pocket, my Sim stands up and touches his cap again, all polite. "*I thanks your Lordship,*" he says with a bow, "*for your h'instruction h'and your money.*" At that the toff up and shouts he has been robbed, that Sim cheated. In the skirmish Sim got away home but tells me the bobbies will be sure to be banging on the door in no time. So he shoves the money in his favourite hiding place and I skips off round the corner to my sister's; I reckoned if I weren't there when the bobbies called then they couldn't involve me.'

'But they was there in your house when you got back, that be a fact, eh, Bertha?'

'Oh they was there!' Bertha laughed. 'Truncheons out and buttons shining but though Sim was arrested and sent down they never did find them winnings. The judge said that Sim was too simple a man as to hide the money, it had to be as he said, he had thrown it into Thimblemill Pool. But it were the bobbies were simple. They searched all right but not in the right place, they didn't think to look in Sim's favourite hidey-hole.'

'And where is that?' Sarah waited for the answer, her own smile wide.

'Where, where my Sim often pushed his hand, up my bloomer leg!'

A chorus of laughter drowning the call of the conductor he tapped the punch against the wooden bench.

'Soho!' he called again. 'Soho Station. This be where you ladies get off.'

'They would not let me see him.'

Seated in her own kitchen, Laura cried bitterly.

'. . . I begged them but they would not let me see him. I . . . I said I had been to the infirmary on my last visit but it made no difference.'

'Did you ask to see the Governor?' Livvy asked gently.

'Yes, but I was told he was away.'

'The warder, then, the one who went with you to the infirmary last month.'

'He was very kind.' Laura pressed a handkerchief to her eyes. 'But he said visits to the infirmary were only allowed on the Governor's specific instruction and since he was not there to give permission then I could not be allowed in. Oh, Livvy, what will

Father think not seeing me today, how can I wait another month not knowing how he is, whether he is getting over his chill?'

'He can't be worse, that be certain.' Livvy tried to sound cheerful. 'Had he not been getting over it they would have let you at least peep in on him, that being a merciful thing to do, so try not to worry on that score.'

Merciful! Laura felt all the hurt of that refusal rise again in her throat. What was merciful about refusing a man a visit from his daughter, a few minutes in a month when they could talk and she could feel his hand in hers? Where was the mercy that said when one man was absent then no other could give permission for her to sit with her father?

'They would not even let me leave the linctus and the herbal soothers. The warder said they could not let them be taken to him without the consent of the Governor; he said to take them next month.'

'Your father will enjoy them just as much.'

'No. No, the soothers may not be as good, the sugar coating is sure to have softened in that time.'

'Then you must make him a fresh batch.'

Watching the girl bend to the oven, Laura shook her head. 'With what, Livvy? I used my very last penny going to the prison today; if I do not find some work . . . any work . . . soon I will not be able to visit at all next month, much less make herbal soothers to take with me.'

'Well we have four weeks to sort that, right now you are going to eat one of these.'

Laura's eyes widened as she saw the large baked potatoes Livvy held in a cloth.

'Where did you get them, you didn't beg from Mrs Griffiths?'

'I certainly did not!' Livvy looked indignant. 'I went up to the Shambles and Maggie Cartwright offered these and a bag of tomatoes for loading her cart. It were no problem stacking them boxes of fruit and such, not when you've spent years helping to load every manner of stuff on to the deck of a narrow boat, but

I puffed and blowed as though the job were killing me. It must have made her feel guilty 'cos when I was done she gave me a swede and carrots and a few parsnips. If we had a bit of meat we could make a broth.'

The girl's pleasure at providing at least a couple of meals shone in her brown eyes, and Laura answered it with a smile.

'And if we do not get a bit of meat we will have a vegetable soup, and enjoy it every bit as much.'

The girl had found a way to feed them for a few days and she must do the same. Laura dried her eyes. But her labours must bring money, how otherwise could she visit her father? Picking at the steaming potato Laura racked her brain for the answer.

'It ain't much I know, but I thought it to be better than nothing.'

'What?' Laura looked up from her plate.

'Your potato. You ain't eating it, you be playing with it, pushing it about as though it were some toy. I know you are used to better but it were all I could get.'

'Livvy. I'm sorry.' Contrition and guilt both together in her answer, Laura was apologetic. 'The potato is very good, my father and I often . . .'

Tears rising in a swift tide she got no further.

From the opposite side of the table Livvy Beckett watched the thin shoulders heave as sobs racked the girl who had become a friend. Why should such sadness be brought to anyone as kind and good-natured as she was? What sort of man was this Edmund Shaw? Going to Laura she put her arms about her, cradling her until the sobbing died, and when it had Livvy had made herself a solemn promise. Should ever the chance be given to repay him in kind then she, Livvy Beckett, would make that payment in full!

His meal finished Edmund leaned back in his chair, a brandy glass in his hand. Around him the dining room buzzed with the conversation of other diners, some of them former associates of

Jabez, all of them business men of one sort or another.

Business men! Swirling the liquor around the glass he hid a deprecating smile. Like Jabez, they would live and die without ever knowing true money, money such as business like that of the Gallery could bring. But he knew and he would have it.

'Mr Shaw?'

Edmund looked up at the man come to stand at his table. Dark-haired, a slender line of beard edging a strong chin, he stood tall and easy in a well-cut, ash-grey jacket, a touch of darker grey silk edging the lapels.

'Forgive my interrupting your dinner but I have tried several times to contact you and tonight is the last chance I will have for some time to speak with you.'

Looking relaxed in his chair Edmund gave no indication of the sudden increase his pulse rate had taken, the feeling of wariness touching his nerves. Was this something to do with Isaac Cadman, did Laura after all hold an agreement their fathers had made . . . had she decided to use it? Questions rocketing in his brain he replaced the glass slowly on to the table, his eyes holding to clear grey ones.

'My dinner is finished, Mr . . . ?'

'Your pardon.' The tall figure bowed slightly. 'Allow me to introduce myself . . . Rafe Travers.'

'Travers!' Edmund's lower lip thrust forward as if he were searching his mind for recognition, whilst in reality it gave him a breathing space, a moment for his nerves to calm. He knew the name if not the man.

'The same Travers that bought the house at Squire's Walk?'

'The same.'

Had he found some fault with the property? Edmund lowered his glance. That would be too bad, the contract was signed and legally binding, and there was no way that money would be returned.

'You have found some problem?'

'I have no problem . . .'

Indicating the other man to take a chair, Edmund heard the faint emphasis behind the words.

'. . . but it appears there is one with the other property you have placed on the market. To be brief, Mr Shaw, I am interested in the purchase of your engineering works but it must come with a document showing original ownership. This, it appears, is not in the hands of your solicitor.'

'A glass of wine . . . brandy?' His outward appearance calm, Edmund's brain raced for a plausible answer. His offer refused, he picked up his own glass, savouring the drink on his tongue.

'No, it is not.' He swallowed the liquid, feeling the smoothness of it pass his throat tightened once more with apprehension. 'There are several papers as yet still deposited with the bank, my father felt they would be safer there. The deed of ownership to the works is among them.'

'Then perhaps we can do business.' Rafe Travers watched the face opposite him, saw the glance slide sideways.

'This is not the most appropriate time or the most convenient place, but as I said my time is limited. If you will place the necessary paper with your solicitor he can contact me, and then perhaps we might agree a price.'

'The price has been stated.' Edmund looked back sharply to the eyes watching him with the same cool calm.

'That would be the price commanded by a going concern, your works is no longer in production.'

'That is due simply to pressure of time. There is still a great deal of call for a well-turned bolt and screw.'

Watching the brandy glass being refilled, Rafe nodded. 'Obviously, or I would not be interested; however, the onus is on a *well-turned* bolt.'

The implication of the heavily accented words, together with an already strong influence of brandy, brought a hot reaction from Edmund. As he banged the glass to the table, his usually insignificant eyes held a pale fire. Voice thick with anger and almost a shout, he glared at Rafe.

'If you are saying . . .'

'I am saying nothing . . . yet!' Calm as the other man was angry, Rafe Travers rose to his feet. 'Except that if you wish a sale between us then have that paper to me within a week!'

Within a week! Brandy and anger hot in his veins Edmund watched the tall figure stride from the hotel. Who the bloody hell was he to give Edmund Shaw an ultimatum! Waving a hand he fumed silently as his glass was filled yet again. Some bloody smart-arsed upstart who thought he could put one over on him. Throwing the liquor into his throat he signalled for another. Well, Mr Rafe bloody Travers would need a much smarter arse than that to shit on Edmund Shaw!

Legs as well as face showing the effects of the several glasses of brandy, Edmund stumbled slightly as he weaved his way past other diners. Ignoring their voiced irritation as he knocked against them, he stepped out into the street, distaste thickening on his tongue as he looked first one way and then the other. The facades of once-elegant Georgian houses now disguised bank, hotel and pithy little shops; pork butchers, ironmongers, drapers and pie shops, they were all there sandwiching the medley of market stalls that leapt startlingly into sight as the night sky flared with the light of furnace openings.

Wednesbury! He turned toward the Shambles. The sooner he was out of it for good the sooner he would be happy, and for that he needed the paper in his pocket to be signed.

'*Perhaps we might agree a price . . .*'

Mindless of the traders packing carts and boxes, their business done for the day, Edmund smiled to himself as he thought of Rafe Travers' words.

They would agree a price but that price would be one dictated by Edmund Shaw!

Coming to the end of the Shambles, his head somewhat cleared by the night air, he glanced at a stretch of empty land darkening as the sky lost its crimson glow. He would reach Dudley Street much quicker by cutting across there than by going the way of Camp Street.

Sure of his way, knowing it since childhood, he began to walk across the rough ground pockmarked by large clumps of yellow broom. Laura would be home and she would be alone. He smiled, and this time the smile spread openly across his narrow face.

Laura Cadman would take that paper to Isaac . . . and in a few days the works would be sold and together with what he had made on the house the first payment on the Gallery could be made.

Touching a hand to the pocket that held the document he had had the solicitor draw up, he felt the envelope filled with five-pound notes. He had taken payment for the house in cash, as he would take that from the sale of the works in cash. The smile deepening, he savoured the feeling he had harboured all day; the pleasure of strewing Philip Sandon's desk with white bank notes, and the more infinite pleasure of celebrating with Sheldon . . . in their own special way.

Chapter Twenty-One

A cup of tea all the breakfast they had to share, Laura rinsed the cups, drying them on a huckaback cloth. Livvy had already left, her smile confident as she spoke of being sure to find a day's work.

A day's work! Laura felt a cold misery settle over her. Not so many weeks ago she had been happy, her days filled with the task of caring for her home and her father. She had never had to think of where the next penny might come from or worry over where to find the next meal. Her father had not brought in an exceptional wage but it had been enough to keep them and allow for her to make the odd tray of sweets.

But her father was no longer with her, nor would he be for fifteen more years. A lenient sentence, the magistrate had called it. Tears rising swiftly Laura leaned dejectedly against the brown stone sink. It might as well be a sentence of death, for that was what it was like for her father locked away in that dreadful prison.

She had pleaded with Edmund again last night. She had promised to repay every last farthing of that money, if only he would tell the magistrate there had been a mistake, have her father released.

He had laughed at that, a vicious laugh that had sent shivers along her spine. *I have not come here to talk of your father's possible release,* he had said, *but to have you take this to him.*

Dabbing her apron to her eyes Laura walked into the kitchen. Glancing at the table she seemed to hear again the threat in Edmund's voice as he had slammed a folded paper on to its centre.

'*I have come here to give you this. Take it to Isaac, be certain he signs it or it could be he will never come out of that prison.*'

Had he been there, been to Winson Green, seen for himself the atrocious conditions men lived and worked in, smelt the foulness of the air, felt the chill of damp strike into his bones?

She had looked from Edmund's cold eyes to the paper, asking what it was he wanted her father to sign.

'*You know well enough!*' he had almost shouted. '*That paper gives me legal right to what is mine already, the engineering works.*'

'*Stay away from Edmund Shaw . . . Let him take the works . . .*'

The words her father had spoken as they had taken him away sounded even more like a warning as she had looked back to Edmund, his narrow face drawn with tension as he waited for her answer.

Let him have the works her father had told her. But he had already taken his revenge. Sinking to a chair, she remembered the surge of defiance that had swept over her. Edmund Shaw had taken fifteen years of her father's life . . . he would not have the works as well.

'*If the works is already legally yours then there is no need to bother my father with any paper.*'

She had said it quietly but the effect upon Edmund acted like an explosion. Pale, usually insipid, his eyes blazed, his narrow face draining white. Grabbing the paper in one hand he had caught her arm with the other, snatching her almost off her feet.

'*Think!*' he snarled. '*Think carefully before you answer further. The punishment for theft is imprisonment, the punishment for murder is death!*'

She had stared at him, the moment dragging at her senses. What new trick was Edmund playing?

'*I know what you are thinking,*' he had gone on, his fingers biting into her arm, breath heavy with alcohol filling her nostrils. '*You are thinking that murder is one accusation that could never be brought against*

Isaac Cadman . . . but there you would be wrong.' He had laughed again, his eyes filling with cold hate. *'You think that accounts clerk was sacked, but he wasn't, Laura. It was not I found the deficit in the works' accounts it was that clerk and once it happened then Isaac knew he had to be got rid of; not just the sack, Laura. Oh no, that way he could talk, that clerk had to be killed. Now!'* He had flung her from him, at the same time throwing the paper once more on to the table. *'Either you get your father to sign that paper, or I will see him swing!'*

'It's a lie!' She had felt her senses swirl. *'My father did not kill anyone . . . he couldn't.'*

'Couldn't he!' The answer had rung around the kitchen bouncing against her ears, thudding into her brain.

'Couldn't he, Laura? Then don't take that paper, let Isaac be brought back into court, let him face the charge of murder!'

Eyes closing against the pain of it Laura threw back her head, drawing air into her lungs on a long, shuddering breath. How could she do that to her father? Even with the verdict unproven, as it must be, the stress and strain of again answering to a court of law could only prove too much for a man already worn out with worry. She had been forced to agree, forced to promise to take that paper to her father. But it must wait, she had explained to Edmund, she was allowed only one visit per month and the next was not due for three weeks.

She would be allowed to see him then, but first she must get money to pay her train fare; but that she had not told the furious Edmund, she would not give him the satisfaction of seeing the state his spite had reduced her to.

'I will try to get my father's agreement . . .' she had begun to answer but he grabbed her, his mouth drawn back in a snarl.

'You had better do a whole lot more than try, Laura,' he breathed, *'or it won't be only Isaac will suffer . . .'*

He had released her as Livvy's call had sounded from the scullery and she had come into the kitchen carrying a bucket of coals, but the threat in his angry eyes had continued as he murmured, *'It will be you, too. Two days and no more. That paper will be signed and here for me in two days or Isaac Cadman will feel the noose about his neck!'*

The force with which he had grabbed her then flung her away, had torn the sleeve of her blouse. Laura glanced at the garment she had laid aside for repair. It was her one last good blouse, the one she wore with her Sunday suit, the one she wore to that prison.

Fortunately her needlework was adequate, the repair would hardly show. Reaching for the box that held needles and threads, she paused. Her bottom drawer! It was full of linen she had made herself; maybe someone would buy a table-cloth or a pair of pillow-slips.

Placing the box back in the dresser she ran up the stairs to her room. Taking the linen from the chest of drawers she spread it out on her bed.

Delicately embroidered in soft pastel shades or edged with pretty white lace she stared at them, all that was left of her dreams.

Packing them carefully into a Gladstone bag she carried them into the kitchen. Dreams were like flames, beautiful but fleeting, and when they were gone . . . she threw her shawl about her shoulders . . . all that was left were the ashes.

Carrying the bag she hurried along Dudley Street, waving an answer to the greengrocer's cheery call but not stopping. She could try the market place but the women who shopped there did not often have call or money to buy fine linen. Maybe she would have more luck if she tried at one of the finer houses.

Deciding to do just that she made her way along Springhead, passing the stone mounting-block from which Wesley had preached his sermon before being tossed into the brook. Gaining the crest of the sloping street she turned to her right. The villas here were large, maybe one of the ladies would like her work.

Hours later, the Gladstone bag packed and repacked, she moved dispiritedly to the next house but met with the same reception. Yes, they would look at what she had for sale but, after fingering it each had politely declined to buy.

Arms and back aching she rested the bag on the footpath. The clock of the parish church chimed four. It was no use trying any further, she had knocked on every kitchen door the length of Wood Green and beyond, but sold nothing.

Picking up the bag, the weight of it seeming to want to drag her arm from its socket, she traced her steps back towards Springhead. Coming to Squire's Walk she glanced along its familiar rise. She had known some happy times here, trailing in Edmund's shadow. But those times were gone as Edmund was gone, Jabez' house sold.

Jabez' house sold. She looked to where graceful brick chimneys rose from behind screening trees. Whoever had bought that house might need household linen. Gritting her teeth against the pull of the bag she walked determinedly to the house she had known so well and tapped at the rear door.

'I don't think the master be needing more linen.'

'Please, if you will only look at it, the stitches are very fine and . . . and I don't want very much for them.'

Across the yard in the stable block the man saddling a horse paused, listening to the women's voices.

'That's as maybe.' The housekeeper's firm tone floated out to him but it was the other voice he listened for.

'Please . . . it will not take very long.'

'Well,' the firmness faltered, 'I be ready for a bit of a break and a cup of tea wouldn't come amiss neither. I'll not promise as how I can buy any of your linen, finely stitched as they may be, but I can give you a cup of tea.'

Turning towards the stable entrance the man watched the figure, patched skirts beneath a faded shawl, lift her bag into the kitchen.

Laying the saddle back on the rail, he ran a hand over the shining black flank and strode out of the stable. Ignoring the trail dusty boots left on the rich red Turkish carpet in the hall he strode into the sitting room, going at once to the fireplace and tugging sharply on the tapestried bell-pull that hung beside it.

Moments later the housekeeper entered, hand smoothing a snow-white apron.

'I thought you were gone, sir.'

'Not yet, Mrs Cromwell.' Rafe Travers gave a shake of the head. 'Tell me, who is the woman came to the door just now?'

'I don't know, sir.' Amy Cromwell looked and sounded bemused. How did he know anyone had called, there had been no front-door bell sounded, of that she was sure.

'What does she want?'

He had heard what the woman had said but asked the question anyway.

Amy Cromwell smiled a small pitying smile. 'She be wanting to sell linen but it seems that be something she's not used to, traipsing a bag from one house to another; poor girl be just about all in.'

'What sort of linen?'

The question taking her by surprise the housekeeper's smile slipped away. Why would he be asking that? A man didn't usually enquire after such.

'It be table-cloths and pillow-slips and the like,' she answered, 'and very nicely stitched they be an' all. Between you an' me, sir, I thinks it might well be her very own bottom drawer the girl be selling, and any woman must be on her uppers to do that.'

Down to her last penny, maybe no penny at all! Rafe made a pretence of looking at the watch attached to his waistcoat pocket. Or could it be an intended marriage were no longer intended?

'No woman would part with her bottom drawer even had she no marriage to look forward to . . .'

Rafe almost smiled. The woman must have read his mind.

'. . . no, I say she be selling it 'cos it be that or starve.'

Replacing the watch he looked at his housekeeper.

'Buy the lot! Give her whatever you know that linen to be worth and make it a fair price.'

'What did you say, sir?'

'You heard me, Mrs Cromwell, buy the lot.'

Dumbfounded Amy Cromwell opened her mouth to speak, but Rafe Travers was already gone.

'I told you yesterday, miss, you can't go in there without the Governor's say so.'

'But please, you don't understand, I . . . I have to go in, I have to see my father.'

Not unkindly the guard looked at the young woman. Scrupulously clean, her clothes neat and well-pressed and boots with a shine only continuous use of shoe polish created, she made a picture not often seen presented at the gates of Winson Green.

'It be you don't seem to understand, miss. I can't let you into that infirmary, I would if I could; Lord knows I ain't refusing out of spite.'

'But it would only take a moment.'

Looking into wide eyes turned to blue crystal by the sparkle of threatened tears, the guard felt his heart soften. The wench must genuinely feel for that old man lying in the infirmary. It would only take a moment . . . maybe, but then it would only take the same to sack him and there would be no maybe about that.

'I'm sorry, miss,' he shook his head, 'but the rules be the rules and to break 'em means to lose my job. Do that and my kids don't get fed. Understand, miss, I don't refuse from choice, you get permission like I says and I'll whisk you over to that infirmary like a shot out of a gun.'

Two days Edmund had said. Laura clutched the basket that held linctus, herbal soothers and the paper he had flung on to the table before slamming out of the house. One of those days had been spent walking half the town trying to sell her linen; today was all she had, she must get her father's signature on this visit if she was to save him from the shame and trauma of another trial.

Frustration bringing the threat of tears fully into her throat, she swallowed hard. Bringing the paper from her basket she held it towards the guard.

'I need my father to sign this, please will you take it to him, tell . . . tell him Laura asks him to sign it.'

The look in those brimming eyes, the trembling mouth, pulled on the man's sympathy and he reached a hand towards the paper.

'Watch it, Charlie, the superintendent be about!'

At the warning from a second guard come to stand at the small narrow door let into massive wooden gates, the man's hand snapped to his side. 'If you wishes to see a prisoner in the infirmary you has to get permission of the Governor.'

'Then let me see the Governor, please, it is very important.'

'So be our jobs, miss.' The second guard edged further into the doorway, his glance running over Laura. 'Now you be a sensible wench and get along 'ome. You can see who it be you wants to see next visiting day.'

'But that will be too late!'

Laura's cry halted the swing of the door being closed, sympathy showing clear on the face of the first guard.

'I can't take that paper, miss. It would be the end for me if I was caught. Wait 'til the Governor be back and take it to him; that be my advice. Like I says it ain't out of choice.'

'Wait, please!' Her hand on the door, Laura tried to prevent its closing. 'Let me see the Governor.'

The door swinging back so quickly it had Laura stumbling forward, the second guard caught her, roughly setting her back on her feet.

'Now look 'ere, you've been told there be no admittance and you've been told the Governor be away . . . and afore you asks, we don't get told when he will be back! What you won't be told again is to get yourself off, two more minutes and you'll find yourself run in for nuisance.'

'Hold on, Bert!' The first guard intervened. 'The wench don't mean no harm, you can't blame her for asking.'

'And we can't be blamed for answering. How many times of telling does it take afore it sinks in!'

Elbowing his colleague aside, the guard called Charlie smiled briefly.

'You ain't hurt are you, miss, that stumble . . . ?'

'No.' Laura shook her head. 'Please, will . . .'

'Sorry, miss, there be nothing I can do except to say it be most likely the Governor will be back next week.'

Next week! Laura stood staring at the closed door set in towering gates, their very height adding to their impassiveness. By that time it would be too late. It would be no use appealing to Edmund's better nature, it seemed that had died along with his father.

Turning away, her steps slowed by the weight of fear pressing on her heart, she walked along Bacchus Street taking the right hand fork that was Benson Road and led into Soho Railway Station.

If only she knew what had changed Edmund so maybe she could help, but it was as if he couldn't bear to look at her; and the night he brought that paper he had wanted almost to strike her. He had never done that before, not even as children when she had plagued him had he raised a hand against her.

Reaching the platform she took a seat on a low wooden bench set outside the third-class waiting room.

Something had happened that had changed more in Edmund than his choice of clothes; he had become a spite-filled, vicious man, one prepared to see another man die for what he knew to be a lie.

The man Edmund said her father had killed, the clerk who had kept the works' accounts, if he had a family then there was every chance he was still in Wednesbury.

The thought bringing hope in its wake, Laura began to think logically.

Jonas Small, the foreman at the works, would surely know and if not him then one of the other hands. They were no longer employed at Shaw and Cadman, Edmund had closed the business down a few days after Jabez' death.

Teeth worrying at her bottom lip she did not see the tall dark-haired figure watching from the furthest end of the flower-decked platform.

But she knew where many of the men lived and they knew her and, best of all, they respected her father. If that clerk still lived in the town then they would tell her, and once she found him then Edmund would have no new case to bring.

The thought acting like a tonic she breathed out slowly, the touch of a smile enhancing her mouth.

'Now that is much better, I thought for a moment I would have to perform my third good deed.'

Her head lifting sharply, Laura stared into a pair of cool grey eyes. 'I beg your pardon. I did not hear what you said.'

'My third good deed.' Rafe Travers smiled. 'I thought you about to cry any moment, I was well prepared . . . see!' Pulling a handkerchief from his pocket he held it towards her.

'No, no I was not about to cry, I . . . I was thinking about my father.'

Slipping the handkerchief back into his pocket, Rafe nodded. 'I guessed you had been to Winson Green, but this is not a visiting day?'

Dropping her glance to the basket on her knee Laura took a moment in answering.

'No. Visiting day is not for three weeks but I hoped I would be allowed a few minutes with my father.'

'But you were not?'

A shake of the head her answer, Laura looked up.

'Were you not aware of times for visiting?'

'Yes. But I thought . . . I hoped . . .'

Resisting the urge to take her hand, Rafe waited for the stifled breath to be loosed and the sob he had heard to be swallowed.

'The Governor is a friend of mine. I happen to know he will be returning to prison on Friday of this week, if you wish I will tele-phone him . . .'

Fingers closing about the handle of basket Laura stood up, the glance she raised to him sparkling with unshed tears.

'That is very kind but it will not be necessary.'

'Like my third good deed.'

The eyes looking directly into hers holding her like a magnet, Laura was relieved when a steam whistle screeched the imminent arrival of her train.

'Like your third good deed.' She smiled. 'But both offers were appreciated.'

Watching her climb into a carriage Rafe Travers turned towards the front of the train, choosing a first-class compartment. What had urged him to come to Soho rather than Snow Hill station? As he leaned into his seat he knew the reason sat some yards further along the train.

Chapter Twenty-Two

Putting her basket on the kitchen table Laura stared at the shadows already beginning to collect. It had been another wasted journey, the document Edmund had brought was unsigned. He would come for it . . . at what time she did not know . . . but he would come.

Removing her shawl she hung it on the peg behind the door.

And when he did, what then? Would he truly cite her father as a murderer? Perhaps if she told him what that man on the station had said, that the Governor would be returning to the prison on Friday, would he wait that long . . . give her another chance to try to see her father, to get that paper signed?

Maybe she should have agreed for that man to make his telephone call, after all he had helped her twice before. Laura bent to the fire, poking out the ash between the bars of the grate. But she could not do that, she could not ask a perfect stranger . . .

The poker still in her hand she straightened, staring into the short dancing flames of the awakened fire. That is what he was; that tall dark-haired man with compelling grey eyes was a perfect stranger, she did not even know his name and yet in the three times of their meetings she had felt no unease.

Replacing the poker in the hearth she turned. What had she felt? The grey eyes smiled from deep within her memory and Laura felt the sudden sting to her skin. Why should she feel anything? Her movements unaccountably rapid she began to empty her basket, carrying linctus to the larder. The man was a stranger . . .

Setting the jars on the cool stone slab she felt the colour blaze in her cheeks.

. . . so why did it feel so right when he was with her? And why did she see his face, hear his voice so many times before she slept?

'Oh, you're back. I thought I would be first in . . .'

Coming in through the scullery Livvy hung her shawl beside Laura's.

'. . . how did you get on, did they let you in this time?'

Questions coming over her shoulder she fetched the coal bucket, tipping its contents on to the fire.

The image of that strong face faded from her mind but somehow the smile remained, holding her heart.

'No. No they would not let me see Father.' Laura took the empty basket to the scullery, returning to the kitchen in time to see the other girl scowl.

'Miserable sods!' Livvy swung the kettle over the fire. 'Wouldn't have caused the end of the world to let you pop into that infirmary.'

'Rules have to be kept, Livvy.'

Laura defended the prison guard's action. He was a man with a family to keep, a man like her father whose job meant security for those he loved. He had been right to refuse. But where did that leave her and the father she loved?

'We all have to keep to rules,' Livvy answered tartly, 'but it don't hurt to bend one now and again! Them guards must have known you have a fair distance to travel . . . and for them to go turning you away.'

'The Governor was away . . .'

'Still away!' Livvy turned, hands on her slight hips, her eyes bright with reproach. 'Some folk have good jobs! The money he must be paid and he ain't there doing the job when he should be, that be what I calls criminal!'

'The man said he would be back there on Friday.'

'What man?'

The colour tingeing her cheeks as swiftly as before, Laura turned to the dresser, reaching cups.

'The guard told you that?'

'No, not the guard.'

'Who then?' Livvy was not to be put off. 'Who else would know when that Governor were due back?'

Taking a moment to fetch milk from the scullery Laura tried to push back the blush that stained her cheeks. Livvy's question had her pulses increasing as if she had been caught in some misdemeanour. But how did she explain riding in the carriage of a man she did not know? And worse, how could she tell of accepting money from him even though that money had been repaid?

'I don't know how he knew about the Governor . . .'

Feeling the query ready again on the other girl's tongue, Laura busied herself brewing tea.

'But how did he know in the first place . . . that you had been to the prison, I mean? Not every woman in Hockley be visiting Winson jail.'

'I . . . I met him there before . . . he gave me a half-crown.' Glancing up Laura saw the astounded look that came to the girl's face and she laughed. 'There is no need to look like that, Livvy, perhaps I should have said he loaned me half a crown and that it is now paid back.'

Flames sending spurts of light into the room as if seeking furniture, and faces becoming veiled in shadow, Laura carried her cup to a chair. There was no need for secrecy, Livvy was welcome to hear the whole story, little though there was to tell.

Having held her silence, listening intently as Laura spoke, Livvy answered at last.

'That were right kind-natured of him, but who is *him*, I mean what is his name? You ain't once said it.'

'That is because I do not know his name.'

'You mean you didn't ask!'

'Why would I? I will never see the man again.'

Laura rose, carrying her cup to the table, and as she set it down the smile that held her heart died.

She *had* to have got it signed.

In his room at the George Hotel Edmund lay on the bed watching the play of shadows on the ceiling, but his mind played constantly on the question of that paper.

Isaac must have put his signature to it. He knew by now that Edmund Shaw did not make empty threats. If he refused to sign, refused to say he had no claim whatever on the works, then he would face a charge of murder. There would be none to prove otherwise . . .

Catching his breath Edmund held it behind his teeth.

None to prove otherwise! There would be if that accounts clerk showed up, and it was more than likely he would if only to get his own back for being sacked. But then again it was Isaac had given him his tin, Isaac that had told him he was finished at Shaw and Cadman. That being so he might not come forward, he might keep quiet and see Isaac go to the scaffold; what better revenge could he ask?

Breath released in a soft swoosh, Edmund smiled. He would bless every nail that went into the building of that scaffold!

Closing his eyes he reached his hands behind his head as the smile returned. If Isaac had not signed he was a dead man! Unless . . .

Coming quickly to a sitting position he stared into the thickening gloom. Laura too would know of the accounts clerk and she was no longer the child who followed at his heels or the young woman who had once thought to become his wife. Laura Cadman was nobody's fool, what if she found the man first, played on his sympathy?

It wouldn't work. Getting to his feet Edmund walked to the

window, staring out on to the darkening street still busy with carts and hurrying people. That clerk had been given the sack, turned off the premises at a moment's notice . . . a man did not easily forget such a thing, forget or forgive.

But a woman in tears? Laura was certain to resort to tears pleading for her father's life. How easily could a man resist that?

A realisation of the element of risk to his plans had Edmund turn angrily from the window. He had to be sure, he had to make certain there would be no testimony in Isaac's favour. Touching a hand to a pocket in his jacket, he felt the wad of banknotes nestled inside. A few of them would make sure the man kept his mouth closed.

Thankful that he had chosen to wear a plain jacket and matching black trousers that did not mark him as different from many other factory and colliery owners of the town, he left the hotel, moving quickly along Union Street.

The clerk had lived more towards the centre of the town than the other employees, perhaps it was the feeling that he was just a little better than the rest. However the man felt, it was to be hoped he still lived in the same house. It took only minutes to reach the junction that led to Loxdale Street. There were not so many people here but still it would not do to be seen to loiter. Glancing quickly right then left, Edmund walked on.

Reaching the row of houses where he knew the clerk had lived, he halted. If the man were not home? Even should that not be so did he want to discuss business with a wife and family looking on? He could give a child a farthing to go knock on the door and ask for the man to come outside . . . no, that would not do either, it was just another mouth to talk.

Unsure of what to do for the best Edmund turned away. It was at that moment the hunched figure of Edwin Hagley turned the corner.

'Hagley.' Edmund stepped forward as the figure made to pass. 'I would like a word.'

'Eh!' A finger pushing rimless spectacles up along a narrow

nose, the man stopped. Peering at Edmund, drawn mouse-like features displaying quick anxiety, the man took two steps backward.

'There be no call for alarm, Hagley, it be me, Edmund Shaw.' Edmund adopted the speech he had used when on the workshop floor.

'Who?' The man peered again but kept his distance.

'Edmund . . . Edmund Shaw.'

'Oh, ar!' The sharp mouse-like nose sniffed. 'And what be you wanting with Edwin Hagley, you can't sack me twice!'

Suddenly the whole thing seemed to click into place in Edmund's mind. It was going to be so easy.

'The reason I be here is because you never should have been sacked at all. Since Jabez died I've found out you were not at fault, it was no error of yours that had them books show the figures wrong.'

'That don't make it any the better for me!' The spectacles slipping as he brought his head sharply upward, Hagley sniffed again. 'I still ain't found a man to take me on. The answer be the same no matter where I asks, we ain't in need of no 'counting clerk; what they means is they ain't in need of one thought to be a thief. Oh they knows Isaac Cadman were convicted, but there be no smoke wi'out fire be the creed they goes by.'

The man had no job! Edmund felt his confidence deepen.

'That be a creed not shared by everybody.' He smiled at the hunched figure peering at him from shadow that had the street in blackness. 'I know of a businessman who is looking for a competent accounts clerk. I recommended you Hagley and he agreed to offer you the post but said he must speak with you himself.'

'You recommended me? That be right good of you, Ed . . . Mr Shaw.' The man's attitude changed instantly. 'If you just says where it is I have to go then I will see this fellah first thing tomorrow morning.'

'That will be too late.' Edmund kept the note of satisfaction from his voice. 'He leaves for London on the morning train; however he did say he would see you tonight if you got there before eight, after that he will be tied up with dinner guests.'

Taking a match from his pocket Edmund struck it against the wall, using the light of its flame to read the time on his pocket watch.

'It is after seven now.' Shaking the match and extinguishing the flame he tossed the watch back into his waistcoat. 'I doubt there would be time for you to reach him now. I'm sorry . . . I did try to find you afore this but nobody seemed to know where you were.'

'That be 'cos since my being sacked from Shaw and Cadman I be like a blue-arsed fly, here, there and every bloody where!' Edwin Hagley shrugged his bent shoulders. 'But there be no job in any place no matter where it be.'

'There might still be time . . . if we took the train.'

Shaking his head Edwin Hagley pushed his spectacles back into place. 'That be a non-starter. I ain't got a halfpenny for the tram let alone the price of a train ticket.'

'I'll see to the fare, but you have to go now, no time for expla-nation to your wife.'

'Dora will keep.' Hagley smiled. 'Maybe by the time I gets home tonight we will have something to celebrate.'

The man's steps rapid to keep up with Edmund's lengthy stride, they walked in the direction of the station. Coming close to Great Western Street Edmund prayed for his luck to hold and not to come face to face with Laura.

Telling the clerk to wait as they entered the station he crossed to the ticket office, returning with a solemn expression on his face.

'No Birmingham train until morning, the last one pulled out less than two minutes ago.'

In the yellow glaze of gas lights Edwin Hagley's crestfallen face seemed to become narrower and even more mouse-like. 'That be it then, my thanks to you for trying.'

Drawing a quick breath, making his words tumble out as if only now thinking of the idea instead of the well-laid plan already formed in his mind, Edmund walked quickly from the station.

'It need not be the end, trains are not yet the only form of transport.'

'There be the tram but if time be limited . . .'

'No, no, not the tram.' Edmund turned off towards the livery stable. 'A carriage will do almost as well as the train. Hurry, man, we can still make it!'

Settled in the hired carriage Edmund flicked the reins, sending the horse into a swift trot. Beside him the man's profuse and repeated thanks made no inroads into his mind. That held only one thought, and it was not about employment for Jabez' ex-accounts clerk.

She would not see the man again.

The thought returned as Laura finished laying the table for the evening meal. Livvy had brought home a fillet of cod from Tedd's wet-fish shop. She had worked hard for the piece of fish, scrubbing out the gutting shop with soda and disinfectant, yet it was the smell of fish lingered on her clothes.

'I'll take the kettle out to the brewhouse and give meself a scrub down.' Livvy grinned. 'I smell worse than a hot holer's shimmy.'

'A what!'

'Ain't you ever heard that before? Hot holer's shimmy.' Livvy's grin flashed again. 'Hot holer be a bargee who loads slag and cinders from the ironworks and his shimmy be his under-vest, and sometimes you can smell them coming a mile off, like folk must have smelt me coming down the street after scrubbing out that gutting room.'

Resting the fork she was using to whisk flour, salt and bi-carbonate of soda into water to make a crisp batter for coating the fish, Laura turned towards the stairs, her own smile adding to Livvy's.

'Scrubbing yourself down won't get rid of the smell, you will have to change your shimmy too. Wait there and I will get you some fresh clothes.'

Running back down the narrow stairs she handed clean garments to the girl stood with steaming kettle in one hand.

'Put yours in the copper, we can wash them tomorrow.'

The girl gone to the brewhouse Laura turned back to preparing the meal. Dipping each of the two pieces of fish into the creamy batter she lowered them into the pan of hot fat.

There had been no need for Livvy to scrub out that shop, no need for her to work so hard for a meal, not now they had the money from selling her linen.

Fish sizzling in the pan Laura set to slicing bread, the memory of the look the girl had given her as fresh as the crumbling crust.

'I don't eat what I ain't worked for,' Livvy had said quietly and when Laura had made to object she had shaken her head. 'I know what you be about to say, Laura,' she had added gravely, 'and that be something else I'll not forget. But neither will I forget the teachings of my mother and my father. Eat only what you pays for and take the bread of no man's charity 'less you gives in return. Those were the words I was reared on and they be the ones I will live by. I have you to thank for the roof over my head and one day, given the Lord's help, I will pay you back for that as well.'

'Livvy . . .' Laura had started to voice her protest but the girl's hand had come up sharply.

'No, Laura. I won't take what you have earned, I puts my share of food on the table or I leaves.'

The determination had been more than pronounced.

Returning to the fish she flipped each piece over, leaving it to cook through from the other side. She had put the money away, taking only enough to pay her train fare to the prison. That was all she would use it for and nothing else; if Livvy could find work to bring in a meal, then so could she.

Lifting the fish and placing them in a colander to drain she carried the pan of fat into the scullery, leaving it on the bench beside the sink to cool, and was turning back to the kitchen when a banging on the door halted her in her tracks.

Edmund? Instantly her mind dismissed the notion. He would come, but that was not him; Edmund would not bang on the door in that fashion.

Like a moving picture, the memory of what had happened in that dirty little back street in Birmingham flashed across her brain. Her whole body trembling, she stared at the closed door. Maybe it would go away, if she stayed quiet maybe the nightmare would go away.

'Missis Laura, be you in, Missis Laura!'

Almost sobbing with relief Laura opened the door, a frantic Teddie Bailey almost knocking her from her feet as he rushed in.

'Teddie!' Her own panic barely under control Laura caught the sobbing boy. 'Teddie, what is it, what is wrong?'

Burying his untidy head in her skirts, his shoulders heaving, he sobbed.

'It be me mother, Missis Laura, it be me mother!'

Hopping on one foot, blouse only halfway buttoned up, Livvy came scurrying from the brewhouse, and even in the gloom of the scullery Laura could see the concern on her young face.

'I heard the commotion from the brewhouse, what on earth be the matter?'

Before Laura could answer the boy lifted his head, his voice cracking with panic.

'It be me mother . . . that be the matter!'

Glancing over his head to see Livvy closing the scullery door, Laura led the boy into the kitchen and by the light of the lamp saw the streaks tears had marked along his cheeks.

Taking his arms, holding him, she shook him gently.

'Teddie, Teddie tell me what has happened, where is your mother?'

'In the nick! They've put her in the nick. Please Missis Laura, you have to 'elp!'

'Of course I will, Teddie, of course I will help.' Pulling the crying boy closer into her arms Laura glanced again at Livvy.

'The nick!' The girl mouthed silent astonishment. 'What for?'

A slight shake of her head the answer, Laura held the boy several moments, her hand stroking the tousled head. Mary Bailey arrested! It could not be, Teddie must have it wrong. But even as she told herself so she knew it was she who was wrong, Teddie Bailey was already too shrewd to make mistakes like that; but for her own assurance she had to ask again. Her voice still gentle yet nevertheless firm she sank to her heels, holding the lad at arm's length, bringing her eyes level with his.

'Teddie . . . Teddie, listen to me. You say your mother has been taken to the police station?'

'That be what I says and I ain't coddin'.'

'I know that, Teddie, I know you would not joke about your mother . . . but her being arrested!'

'It be the truth.' His eyes wide and honest, the boy sobbed. 'God's honour, Missis Laura, it be true . . . cross me heart and 'ope to die.'

'But why?' The last button firmly closed in place Livvy stood with hands on hips.

'Yes, Teddie, why . . . what is it the police think your mother has done?'

'They don't think, they knows what 'er done.' The boy sniffed. 'They could see the blood on that bastard's 'ead!'

Laura frowned at the word but did not chastise. The boy was much too upset for her to add to his plate of suffering; admonishings could wait.

Pushing to her feet she led the boy to a chair beside the fire, but when she tried to press him into it he shook off her hand.

'I can't sit here, Missis Laura, I have to go 'elp me mother.'

'Hold up!' Livvy caught him as he made to dart from the kitchen. 'We want to help an' all if we can but you have to tell the whole story if we ain't to go marching off on the wrong foot. Now! You just hold yourself still and tell it all, everything you know . . . and I mean everything.'

Staring at the girl he had not seen before, the boy's lips closed, his brown eyes blazing with defiance.

'It's all right, Teddie.' Laura recognised the look. 'Livvy is my friend and what she says is true also. We want to help, but first we have to know the circumstances.'

The term far above his vocabulary Teddie stared from one girl to the other.

'Guess that means you needs to know why her bosted that bloke's 'ead.'

Mary had broken a man's head! Laura felt her anxiety increase.

'. . . It were 'cos he walloped our Alfie.' The boy sniffed again. 'Two of 'em there were, two bum bailiffs. They turned up about an hour ago demanding the rent, or else . . . Mother said as how her didn't have the money today and that her would pay next week. Well, the fat 'un he got nasty at that, said as how the landlord had waited too many weeks already and it was either pay up or get throwed out. It were then, when Mother said again that her didn't have the money that the second bloke grabbed her and said there was another way her could pay. Mother tried to push him off and the fat 'un he said for us kids to bugger off. Then he grabbed Mother an' all pushing her down on to the floor. Then our Alfie picked up a chair and hit him over the back with it, laying him out; that were when the other bloke hit Alfie, give him a right cockheaver to the side of his face, sent him spinnin' it did. But the bloke weren't satisfied with that, he grabbed Alfie and was set to give him a belloiling when Mother jumps up from the floor, grabs the tater pot and bosted him on the 'ead with it.'

Attempted rape and seeing her son about to be beaten senseless! No wonder Mary Bailey had cracked that bailiff over the head. But still she had been arrested.

Taking her shawl from the peg, Laura flung it about her shoulders.

'Where is your father, Teddie . . . does he know of this?'

Wiping a finger under his nose the boy shook his head.

'He ain't been in the whole day, he be looking for work.'

Above the small fiery head Livvy looked at Laura tying the shawl beneath her breasts.

'What you going to do?'

'I don't know, but I have to do something.'

'Her will get sent down for sure.'

Prison! Laura stared as the kitchen faded, its place taken by a picture of that visiting room in Winson Green, the awful reek of carbolic drenched with misery and men's tears, the smell of hopelessness and the cold of so many empty hearts.

Mary Bailey could not be put through that, the children . . .

That thought snapping her back, Laura touched a hand to the boy's shoulder.

'The others, Teddie, what of the others?'

'The babbies,' he looked up at her, 'they be all right, our Alfie be with 'em and her next door come in as well.'

Her brain moving so swiftly one thought rolled into another, pushing each aside before she had chance to analyse them clearly, she knew only one thing: those children needed their mother even more than she needed her father. Glancing at Livvy she said tersely, 'Wait here!'

Running across the kitchen she raced up the stairs.

Chapter Twenty-Three

'This be right good of you, Mr Edmund.'

His mind elsewhere Edmund made no reply to Edwin Hagley's thanks. He must turn the carriage around; but to go where . . . to Sheldon's house . . . to the Gallery? No, not to either of those places, it must be a more public place. A hotel? Yes a hotel . . . but in which town? Not West Bromwich, that would place him on this road; Dudley? Not far enough away.

Pulling slightly on the right rein he guided the horse into Potter's Lane. The timber yard over towards the railway, what more promising a place for a job.

'I won't forget this, Mr Edmund, truly I won't.'

'No, you won't forget it, Hagley, but then again you will not remember it!'

Bringing the whip in an arc above his head Edmund brought it cracking down on the other man's skull.

Repeating the blow once, he set the whip back in its holder. No blood, there must be no blood on the carriage!

The timber yard was shrouded in darkness as he knew it would be. The carriage almost invisible in a pool of black shadow he jumped down, pulling the half-conscious man after him. The few houses that made up Potter's Lane were far enough away for them not to be heard but should, by chance, someone be knocking about . . .

Better to make sure. Reaching for the whip he once again

brought the heavy stock crashing against Hagley's temple. Never do things by half. That was another of Jabez' favourite sayings. Well this job would not be skimped, this would be well and truly finished.

An arm about the senseless figure Edmund blessed the strength the years of working steel had given him. Half carrying, half dragging he hauled Hagley around the side of the timber yard. He must be quick, any minute now the night-time opening of the furnaces would begin and the whole place would be lit up in a glow like crimson daylight.

Breath becoming tight in his lungs he pushed on, hauling himself and his burden away from the timber yard. Halfway across the bridge that spanned the railway line, he propped the man against the low stone parapet. From the darkness of the distance a train hooted mournfully.

'That be for you, Hagley.' Edmund smiled. 'It will be the only hymn that will sound.'

Listening to the rhythm of wheels on lines, Edmund's smile deepened. In one more minute there would be no one but Isaac Cadman to testify that engineering works did not belong entirely to Jabez Shaw's only son; and who would believe a convicted thief?

Beneath his feet the ground seemed to vibrate from the rush of the oncoming train, the scream of its steam whistle slicing into his brain.

Laughing softly to himself he waited two more seconds . . . then heaved the moaning Hagley over the bridge.

Seeing the boy to his home Laura pushed him gently towards the door.

'Go help your brother with the children.' She smiled, though in the shadows made darker by the scarlet glow fading from the skies it could not be discerned. 'I will do all I can for your mother, I promise.'

Giving him another gentle shove as he made to protest she added, 'If your father gets home before I . . . we return then at least you will be here to tell him someone is already with your mother.'

'Do you think you can do anything?' Livvy watched the boy go into the house.

'Mary will have to appear before a magistrate, that will not take place until morning,' Laura answered. 'If I can persuade the man to drop his charge . . .'

'More chance of seeing a pig fly over!'

'It is unlikely, I know, but I have to try; though there is no need for you to come, Livvy, police stations are not the nicest of places to be in.'

'Nice or nasty that be where I will be just as long as you be there . . . and I'll take no ifs and buts.' Catching Laura's arm the younger girl held tight to it as they hurried towards Holyhead Road.

'She walloped him with the tater pot.' Livvy's voice held more than a hint of satisfaction.

'Oh God, I only hope she has not killed him.'

The worry etched into Laura's answer made little impression on Livvy. A definite chuckle colouring her tone, she came back drily, 'I only hope there were no potatoes in the pot, be a waste of a good supper!'

Walking on in silence Laura felt the grip of worry return strongly despite Livvy's attempt at lightening the situation. If the bailiff refused to drop what was at best a charge of assault what would become of Mary Bailey's children, who would take care of them whilst her husband worked?

'. . . *The court is prepared to combine mercy with justice . . .*'

Laura felt her heart trip. Fifteen years! Was that the mercy of the court, would it be the same mercy for Mary Bailey?

'How much further is the police station?'

Wrapped in her own thoughts Laura had not noted the route, familiarity guiding her steps. Now, hearing the catch of the girl's

257

breath, she looked about. Rising black against the deep grey of night, the art gallery and town hall reared on her right.

'It is just a little further, we are almost there.'

As good as her word, a few yards more bringing them to the station, she paused.

'Wait here, Livvy, there is no need . . .'

'We had this conversation a while back, I ain't going over it again.'

Mouth clamped firmly shut, it was Livvy pushed open the door, glaring at the young constable who asked politely could he help.

'Somebody can.' Livvy's tight mouth signalled determination. 'You have Mary Bailey here, so I believe.'

The young constable consulted a book, its page half filled with neat handwriting.

'You don't have to go looking at that,' Livvy said sharply, 'you knows Mary Bailey be here and so do I.'

'And so do I, young woman.'

All three glanced to where a door had opened off to the left, framing the stocky figure of Walter Potts.

His eyes resting first on Livvy then on Laura he smiled, bushy whiskers lifting.

'Now then, Laura wench, what be you doing here?'

Before she could answer he nodded to the younger man. 'All right lad, I'll deal with this.'

Recognising his dismissal, the constable first glanced at Livvy then left the room.

'So, Laura, what is it you be here for?'

'It is Mary Bailey, her son tells me she was arrested earlier today.'

Walter Potts nodded his head. 'He told you right.'

Being here brought memories of the night her father had been arrested, memories so intense Laura found herself struggling for breath.

'On . . . on what charge?'

'Assault and battery. Her walloped a bailiff over the head with an iron pot.'

'Is he badly hurt?'

'Now come on, Laura wench, you knows I told you more'n I should already.'

'Please, Sergeant Potts, I . . .'

Her eyes closing Laura swayed on her feet.

Catching her beneath both elbows the sergeant lowered her to the bench that ran along one wall.

'You should be home, not traipsing about the town after things that don't concern you.'

He turned, calling for the constable to bring two cups of tea. Busying himself behind the table that served as a reception desk, he waited until both girls finished drinking. Taking their cups, passing them to the constable who stole another sideways glance at Livvy before carrying them away, he spoke gently.

'Off you goes now, Laura, what would Isaac say if he knowed you was here?'

Her senses calmer now, Laura looked at him with a steady gaze. 'I believe my father would say I am doing the right thing by trying to help another as equally ill done by as he himself was. Mary Bailey should not be in that cell.'

'You know what you says be wrong, you both knows it.'

His glance switching to her, Livvy answered tartly, 'We both knows what that lad told, and having heard we say Mary acted to save herself and to save her son.'

'Save her son,' the sergeant frowned, 'what you going on about?'

'Sergeant Potts, one of those men attacked Mary then the other one joined in, they were about to . . . to . . .'

'They thought to have themselves a good time, they was going to rape her!' Livvy felt no compunction to hold back the word.

Her gaze dropping to her hands twisting together in her lap, Laura's cheeks tinged pink at the other girl's outspoken way.

'When Alfie saw his mother being attacked he naturally tried to help her, that was when one of the men turned on him. Mary did the only thing she could, she grabbed the nearest thing to hand and struck out with it . . .' Laura's gaze lifted back to the policeman, '. . . she was protecting Alfie as much as herself, Sergeant, surely you see that!'

'It ain't what I see, you knows that, Laura wench, it be what the magistrate says tomorrow, and I can't see him letting her off light, assault and battery be no laughing matter.'

'What about attempted rape!' Livvy flashed. 'Be that a laughing matter, be it something for men to chuckle over! Or is it that women don't count, be that it?'

'We don't want no shouting, young woman.' Bushy grey eyebrows drawing together, Walter Potts looked at the young face bright with anger. 'This be a police station not a music hall! Mary Bailey will have her chance to speak up when her appears before the court in the morning. Now my advice be for you two to get along home.'

'Sergeant Potts.' Laura made one last try. 'Please are you allowed to say whether the man Mary struck is badly hurt?'

His chubby face relaxed into a smile, Walter Potts led the girls to the door that gave on to Holyhead Road. 'He ain't near death's door if that be any consolation, though I reckon he'll have the devil of a headache for more than one day.'

'Serve the bugger right!'

Ignoring Livvy's muttered comment the sergeant touched Laura's hand. 'How be that father of your'n, is he keeping well?'

Laura's smile died before being born. 'A broken leg, but they say it will mend.'

His nod saying more than his tongue the sergeant pressed her fingers lightly. 'Remember me to him when next you sees him.'

'I will, Sergeant Potts, and thank you.'

Beyond the door the darkness was dimly lit by a hooded moon. Pulling her shawl well over her head Laura shielded her face.

'I cannot help but think of that man, of how badly he may be injured. If I knew where he lived I might be able to help, or at least offer some assistance.'

Walter Potts, too, used the darkness to hide a smile. He wasn't as green as he was cabbage-looking, he knew what Isaac's wench was about.

'You don't want to go offering no help to that man, he might try to do to you what he tried to do to Mary Bailey!'

'The wench be right, Laura, you take a mind of what her says.' Walter nodded. 'But should you bump into him as you pass number eight Russell Street you might mention that Sergeant Potts says for Sol Cooper to be sure and turn up at that magistrate's court in the morning, for he wouldn't want to have the trouble of fetching him.'

'That sergeant might just as well have told you to go see this Sol Cooper.' Livvy's grumble was motivated by concern as they walked quickly from the station. 'Don't he know the bloke be dangerous?'

'That was the reason he said to give that message. Sol Cooper will know that Sergeant Potts is already acquainted with the knowledge that I am going to see him, therefore he will not dare try his tricks.'

'Wish I could be sure of that. Seems a risk to me, why not leave it to the Justice?'

Leave it to the Justice. Laura's determination hardened. The Justice that took fifteen years of a man's life without thought of his family or the promise to repay; was that the justice waiting for Mary Bailey?

'I can't leave it, Livvy, at least not without trying.'

Livvy's head turned in the darkness. 'Trying what . . . what can you do except possibly get yourself hurt?'

'I don't know.' Laura stopped before a house caught in a row of others. 'But then I have not tried yet.'

'Sol be lyin' down, he ain't feelin' himself.'

The woman who had opened the door to them looked closely at Laura, her dull eyes wary.

'It will only take a moment, Mrs Cooper. Please would you ask him to come downstairs for a moment.'

'I already be downstairs.'

At the further end of the shabby kitchen the stairs door banged open and a man in grease-stained trousers and shirt open at the neck stood with hands raised to the wall either side of him.

Feeling Livvy tremble as she stepped closer, Laura tried to hide her own nervousness.

'Who do you be?' Voice as rough as his appearance, the man glared.

'Sol, they say they be from . . .'

'I ain't talking to you,' the man snapped viciously. 'Get away out, and take these bloody kids wi' you!'

The woman scooped a baby from a drawer and with three toddlers clinging to her patched skirts scurried towards the stairs, the door missing the last child by a hair's breadth as it was slammed shut behind them.

Grabbing a bottle from the table he drew the cork with his teeth, spitting it into the remnants of a fire in the dusty grate. Taking a long swig he wiped his mouth on his sleeve.

'You two deaf!' He sneered, drinking again from the bottle, 'I said, who do you be?'

Meeting the beady eyes as they travelled the length of her before coming to her face, Laura tried to stay calm.

'No, Mr Cooper, I am not deaf, neither of us is. My name is Laura Cadman, and this is my friend Livvy . . . Olivia Beckett.'

The bottle empty he slung it away, sending it smashing against the unpolished black cast-iron grate. Swaying slightly he moved to the one chair. Wind breaking noisily from his backside he lowered himself into it, touching a grubby hand to the rag tied about his head.

'So what be you wanting with Sol Cooper?'

'I wish to speak with you regarding Mary Bailey.'

'That bitch!' He roared, holding his head again. 'Don't talk to me about her, talk to the coppers . . .'

'I have spoken to the police.' Laura interrupted in the calm voice that threatened to desert her as Sol Cooper's vicious little eyes turned on her. 'Sergeant Potts asked me to tell you not to be late for the magistrate's hearing tomorrow morning, he said he would not want the trouble of having to fetch you.'

'Huhh!' Sol grunted, settling back into the chair.

Drawing a long breath, taking the hand furtively feeling for her own, Laura began again.

'However, Sergeant Potts' message is not the only reason Livvy and I are here. I understand you are not badly hurt.'

'Not badly 'urt!' He lurched forward in the chair. 'Not bloody badly 'urt, what does he call a crack on the 'ead with an iron pot . . . a bloody pat?'

'*I* call it self defence and acting in defence of an eight-year-old child.'

A few yards from her the small eyes narrowed and the body seemed to tense. Laura's hand closed more tightly about that of Livvy, but still she did not move.

'That be what you calls it is it?' Almost hidden by tobacco-stained whiskers the man's lips drew back in a snarl.

'Yes it is, and that is what I will tell the magistrate. You and your associate tried to rape Mary Bailey in her own home, and when her son tried to go to her assistance he was beaten . . . beaten for protecting his mother. How do you think the court will take to that, Mr Cooper?'

'They won't bloody believe you.'

'Won't they?' Surprised at her own calmness, yet knowing it was vital if she were to achieve what she had come for, Laura smiled coldly. 'Are you certain of that, certain enough to take the risk?'

Pushing clumsily from the chair he lumbered to the one cupboard in the dreary room. Snatching open the front he rummaged towards the back of it, bringing out another brown glass bottle. Repeating the process of opening it, he stood with it in his hand while again relieving himself of wind.

'What are you sayin'?' He held the bottle to his lips.

Taking a handkerchief from her pocket Laura held it beneath her nose, trying not to breathe the foul air released from the man's backside.

'Simply this. The only thing you stand to gain by prosecuting Mary Bailey is to see her sent down.'

'It'll be no more than her deserves.'

'And her children?'

Swallowing a third of the bottle's contents, Sol Cooper burped loudly. 'They be no concern of mine.'

'But your own are, or should be.' Laura glanced pointedly about the room. 'It seems they have little enough comfort here, but even this is preferable to the workhouse.'

'Workhouse!' He lowered the bottle. 'What do you mean? My kids be going to no bloody workhouse.'

'Then where will they go, once you are so crippled you can no longer work to support them?'

'Crippled.' He laughed, swallowing half the remaining ale. 'I ain't bloody crippled!'

'Not at the moment, but tomorrow or the next day. Have you forgotten Mary's husband?' Laura paused letting the fullness of the words sink into his mind, adding, 'How long do you think it will be before he gets a hold of you, and how much life do you think he will leave you with knowing his wife is serving time because she tried to prevent you possibly killing her son . . . because he in turn was trying to prevent her being raped? Ask yourself the question, Mr Cooper, see what answer you come up with.'

Lowering the bottle he sank into the chair. 'He won't come after me, the coppers will know . . .'

'And so will you, supposin' you still be alive after he be through.' Her courage returned, Livvy stepped forward. 'Do you still think it worth the risk, the risk of being done in or maybe crippled for life, just to see Mary Bailey sent along the line?'

'Her hit me with a bloody iron pot, do her get away wi' that?'

'Do you get away with attempted rape and child-beating?'

Laura asked quietly. 'Or do you both suffer when this affair could so easily be settled?'

'Settled?' The beady eyes narrowed instantly. 'I ain't lettin' that bitch go scot free, not when her nearly killed me I ain't.'

'There won't be any nearly about it when her husband lays into you, you'll be killed for sure.'

'Livvy is probably right, Mr Cooper. Gabriel Bailey can be a violent man when roused.' Laura shook her head as though accepting his final word. 'You must, of course, do as you think fit but I would have thought a cash settlement far preferable to a severe beating.'

Releasing her hand from Livvy's grasp she drew her shawl more firmly about her shoulders.

'You think you can pull that on me,' he scoffed as Laura turned away. 'That bitch couldn't pay the rent so how come her can find money to buy me off?'

Her hand on the door latch, Laura answered as she lifted it. 'She can't, Mr Cooper, but I can.'

'Hold on!'

Refusing to let her relief show, Laura glanced back over her shoulder. Sol Cooper was on his feet, a hand stretched towards her.

'Hold on. How much . . . how much be it worth to you to see that woman go free?'

'Five pounds.'

Seeing the glint that sprang to his small eyes, Laura felt her hopes rise.

'Five . . . pah!' His hand dropping he laughed while his other hand raised the bottle once more.

'I regret that appears to be an insufficient sum but that is all I have. Goodnight to you, Mr Cooper.'

Ushering Livvy protectively before her, Laura stepped out into the street. She had failed. She had tried to save Mary Bailey from prison but she had failed.

Overhead the bowl of the night sky turned from deepest grey

to blood red, a great scarlet robe thrown across the heavens as the doors of many furnaces were lifted. Her father had always admired the strange beauty of the scene emerging from the night, two church spires rising from the hill, buildings tall and low etched black, creating a ragged almost surreal landscape. But her father would not see this sight for fifteen years; and Mary . . . how many years would pass before she too saw such a sight again?

'Don't feel too bad.' Nestling her hand in Laura's, Livvy murmured consolingly, 'You tried your best. It's not your fault the man is a swine.'

'What will I tell Teddie? He came to me for help.'

The calm she had maintained since leaving home threatening to crack, she pressed the handkerchief she still held to her lips.

'Teddie is a sensible lad, he will know you did all you possibly could.'

Had she? Following as Livvy urged her away Laura went over the whole scene in her mind. Had she done all that could be done, would the man have agreed had she offered a higher sum?

'Wait!'

The shout bringing them to a halt, she turned as the figure of Sol Cooper lumbered up to them.

'Five pounds,' he wheezed, 'you said five pounds. Hand it over and the bitch can go.'

Laura stepped back as his hand lunged towards her. Give him the money and what was to stop him reneging on his word?

'Come with me to the police station now, withdraw all charges against Mary Bailey and then I will give you the money.'

The glow of the sky lit his face, turning his eyes to tiny burning coals. 'If you should be lyin' . . .'

Lifting her head Laura looked squarely into the venomous stare. 'Should I be lying then you may treat me as you treated Mary's son.'

His laugh deep and evil, he lowered his face to hers.

'I won't treat you to that, not until I've treated you to what I intended for his mother!'

Chapter Twenty-Four

Standing in the garden of the house he had purchased at Squire's Walk, Rafe Travers looked on to the chimneys and buildings of the town silhouetted black against the crimson sky. Seeing it like this one might almost call it beautiful. Beautiful enough to live in? He had not thought so on first coming here. He had thought to acquire the property he had seen advertised in the *Express and Star* newspaper, to set it to his standards but leave the day-to-day running to a capable manager.

But acquiring that engineering works had not transpired. Any other time he would have written off the idea, told the seller he was no longer interested. So why not this time . . . what was special enough to hold him in this place?

The house here was pleasant, but Ladywood was beautiful. The works could prove a profitable investment, but there were properties to be had elsewhere. Two days he had told Shaw, two days to show proof of ownership. Why had he done that?

Above him the sky was losing its battle for light, shadow mounting ever larger forays to capture its scarlet glow, enfolding and smothering, absorbing it into its own dark body, advancing relentlessly until at last the sky was won.

In the sharp blackness that was the legacy of this nightly war Rafe breathed deeply, catching the delicate perfume of the rose garden. Up here on the rise above the smoke-covered town the air was clearer, or was that simply another of the excuses he knew he was making for staying on?

But nothing ever came of excuses!

Suddenly impatient, he turned back to the house.

Tomorrow he would see Shaw, tell him the prospect of buying the further piece of property was no longer of interest to him. Then he would leave this town, go back to Ladywood. He need feel no regret, he had stated his terms, now any refusal . . .

'. . . *Like your third good deed, but both were appreciated . . .*'

Appreciated yet unaccepted!

Under cover of darkness Rafe's fingers curved tight into his palms. He knew which offer held most importance for him, and which refusal.

Sergeant Walter Potts pretended not to see the slip of folded white paper pass from one hand to the other. Laura Cadman had paid the varmint, paid him five pounds so he would drop the charge against Mary Bailey.

'You put your mark here, Sol Cooper.' Waiting while the man put an X against the passage his finger indicated, the policeman first dried the ink mark with a sheet of pink blotting paper then placed it in one of a tall set of drawers stood against the wall behind the table desk.

This done he turned again to the group of people stood in his tiny station.

'Now, Sol Cooper!' Eyes hard below bushy eyebrows, he fingered the keys dangling from a broad leather belt about his ample waist. 'I have a mind to run you in for wasting police time.'

'Eh!' Sol Cooper's narrow eyes widened, his nerves jangling louder than the keys now in Walter Potts' hand. 'You can't do that!'

Leaning his head a little to one side, allowing the merest fraction of a smile to work its way between generous whiskers, Walter lifted the keys, holding them on a level with Sol's ferret eyes.

'You calling me a liar, Sol Cooper?'

The nervous shuffle that had suddenly taken control of Sol's feet developed into a jig.

'No, no I ain't at all, Walt . . . er, Sergeant, that were never my intention, I was only trying to do a good deed.'

'How very Christian of you.'

The sarcasm of the remark was lost on Sol as he tried to further his own ends. 'That was what we was taught as kids, weren't it, to do a good deed wherever we could.'

'And to tell the truth.'

'Yes, Sergeant, to tell the truth.'

'You was taught always to speak the truth.' Walter Potts turned the keys, seeming to inspect each one. 'Then how come you never mentioned the blows given to the Bailey boy or the attempt to rape his mother, that you told only of the bang to your own head?'

'If you says, then that be how it was.' Sol wanted no more argument than was necessary, this place gave him the jitters, it was only one step removed from jail.

'I do say so, I also says I'd like to know why it was so much slipped your memory.' Walter Potts glanced over the top of the keys, a sharp look challenging the man hopping nervously from foot to foot.

'That be it, the rest slipped from my mind. I suppose it was that clout on the 'ead, after all it were no silk fan her hit me with. I'm like to be suffering from that concussion.'

'Maybe, but I have my doubts, after all your head be no silk purse either.'

Placing the keys on the desk the sergeant spread them, giving each a small separate place of its own. His eyes still holding to those that were now bright with fear, he touched a finger to each key in turn.

'There be half a dozen of these, each opens one of them cells out the back there, opens or locks! You can take your pick, Sol.'

'But I withdrawed my complaint!' Sol's voice throbbed with pent-up fear.

'Exactly.' Walter Potts selected one key, using that to pick up the bunch. 'Which means you either made a false charge at the start or else you had deliberate intent to waste police time.'

'Sergeant Potts.' One arm supporting Mary Bailey, Laura intervened. 'As long as Mary is free to go home to her children couldn't the whole thing be forgotten?'

'What say you to that, Mary Bailey?'

Trembling like a leaf in the breeze the woman nodded, her whispered 'Yes . . . yes, let it be forgot' hardly audible.

Flipping the keys together into his palm, the sergeant looked long and hard at the man he knew was gagging for his answer.

'This be against all regulations,' he said as the other man jigged so fast it became a stationary run. 'Rules be made to be kept; however, seein' as it has yet to be brought to the attention of the magistrate . . .' he paused dramatically and Sol Cooper's breathing paused with him, '. . . I be inclined to humour you women.'

'Thank you, Sergeant Potts.' Laura smiled the gratitude of the three of them.

'However!' Bushy eyebrows lowering, the police sergeant glared at the shaking man. 'Let me hear no more of this, and you, Sol Cooper, you be very careful I hears no more of you for if I does I will make use of these . . .' He rattled the keys. '. . . and I will make sure you gets put away for more years than you knows how to count!'

Leaving a tearful Mary with her children, the feel of a grateful Teddie's arms still warm about her waist, Laura turned into Great Western Street, the quick steps of Livvy echoing her own.

'You gave that toe-rag five pounds!' Livvy still could not believe what she had seen.

'It was worth it to have Mary home.'

'Worth it!' Livvy's indignation rang clear in the deserted

street. 'The only thing that shit-bag is worth is a good pummelling.'

Darkness hiding the smile Laura could not, she tried to add a sternness to her voice.

'Livvy Beckett, that kind of language is not only unbecoming, it is unpleasant!'

'Sorry, Laura.' Livvy drew her shawl shamefacedly about her head but that did not lessen the disgust in the rest of her reply. 'But that is what that man is. To try to rape a woman and then take money for saying *he* would bring no charge . . . it ain't right, Laura . . . it just ain't right. He was the one should have been charged, he should be sent along the line!'

'Yes, Livvy, he should. But that would not have saved Mary, she would have been sent to prison the same as he.'

'I know . . . I know.' Livvy shook her head. 'But it all seems so unfair. He not only gets away with what he done, he makes a fiver out of it.'

Her hands holding the shawl beneath her breasts Laura felt the spot in her bodice where she had tucked those notes. She had raced upstairs, grabbing all of it from the drawer in her room, tucking it into her bodice as she raced down again. Now there were no notes.

'Life is not always fair, Livvy, you know that without my telling you.'

'Ar, I do, I knows it well. But that five pounds was part of what you was paid for your linen, wasn't it?'

Common sense telling her the silence that met her question was a yes, Livvy tutted angrily.

'And you left what remained of it with Mary Bailey . . . tell me I be wrong and I'll say no more . . . but I ain't wrong am I?'

'No,' Laura answered quietly. 'You are not wrong, Livvy, I gave the rest of the money to Mary.'

'But why . . . ?'

Speaking quickly, Laura cut through the other girl's enquiry.

'She needed it more than I do. If the arrears of rent were not paid there would be other bailiffs hammering on her door, others who might prove even more despicable than those who called today, and next time Mary might not be so lucky.'

'But you kept enough for the train fare . . . you kept enough so you could get to see your father?'

Another silence her answer, Livvy caught at Laura's arm, drawing her to a halt.

'You didn't, did you? You didn't keep a single halfpenny. Oh, Laura, what have you done!'

The barrier of her strength breaking, Laura felt the hot tears sweep down her cheeks.

'I could not stand it,' she sobbed, 'I could not stand the thought of Teddie and the others without their mother, I could not stand knowing the heart-break that would bring; do not blame me for that, Livvy, do not blame me for what I have done.'

Her arms going about Laura, the young girl drew her close.

'I don't blame you for it, Laura,' she murmured, 'I only love you for it.'

Stood in the darkness, hearing the muffled sobs of the girl who had become her friend, Livvy stared over the bent head, her mind showing her a picture of a narrow boat, its deck holding a sobbing woman and a group of tearful children waving to a young girl walking away across an empty field.

Drawing a long breath Livvy allowed the vision to fade.

Laura Cadman had shared all she had with her, now she had given her last penny to save another woman from prison, given that which would have ensured a visit to see her father.

Pulling her shawl tight about her as Laura drew away, she clenched her fists tight.

Laura would have that train fare. Livvy stared ahead. She would have it, even supposing Livvy Beckett had to steal it!

'The fish will be cold by now.' Laura sniffed back the last of her tears. 'And you worked so hard for it.'

'Cold or hot it will still eat.' Livvy glanced sideways, her good humour returning. 'And if it ain't satisfying I'll go catch old

Weaver's horse and we will both take ourselves a bit from its ar . . . from its rump.'

The weight of the worry of the past two hours lifting from her, Laura joined the other girl's giggle. It was over now and she could relax. Tomorrow would be soon enough for more worry. Tomorrow she would see about earning enough money for a visit to Winson Green.

Relief warming her she pushed open the scullery door, picking up candle and matches from the shelf before passing through to the kitchen.

Striking a match she held it to the candle, allowing the wick to take flame. The glow spilling a small circle of pale yellow light she set the candle in a holder, turning with it towards the fireplace and, as the light caught the chair her father had always used, she felt the blood turn cold in her veins.

Edmund! In the tension of the evening she had forgotten Edmund, forgotten the paper he said he would return for.

'I will set the kettle to boil . . .'

Livvy broke off as her eye caught the figure sat in the chair. Quick as a flash she was beside the fireplace, the iron poker ominously raised in her hand.

'What you want here . . . get out before I break your head!'

Coming to her side, Laura pressed down the hand holding the poker.

'It's all right, Livvy, Edmund is a frie . . . is a man my father once worked with.'

Reluctantly laying the poker aside, Livvy made no move or gave any sign of a smile as Laura made a brief introduction. Edmund Shaw, that was the name Laura had used of the man who had caused her father to be sent to prison. How she wished she had hit him with that poker before waiting to find out who he was.

His glance at Livvy fleeting and disinterested, Edmund flicked a dismissive hand.

'Laura and I have private business to discuss. Leave us alone.'

Dislike showing as clear on her face as the candle flame would allow, Livvy rested a hand on each hip.

'You don't live here, mister, it ain't for you to give orders, and no matter where you hails from, Livvy Beckett don't take none neither.'

For a moment it seemed Edmund would spring at the young girl so brazenly defying him.

'There is no need for Livvy to leave, she knows the situation between us, Edmund.'

Laura's words diffused the moment but the air still bristled with tension.

'As you wish.' He shrugged. 'But at least let us have some light!'

She had not meant to use the remaining lamp oil. Money had not stretched to buying more and now she had given away. . . Pushing aside the reserve Laura reached for the lamp, setting it in place of the candle.

'I came nearly two hours ago.' Risking being caught in the lie Edmund calmly consulted his pocket watch and when neither of them challenged it, went on. 'I thought perhaps you would rather I wait in here than on the street, tongues wag so effortlessly in this part of town.'

First swinging the bracket with its kettle over what was left of the fire, Livvy hung her shawl and Laura's on the pegs behind the door, but her eyes were never far from the man sat beside the hearth.

Slipping the watch into the pocket of his waistcoat Edmund looked up, his glance cold.

'The paper, Laura. I have been here long enough to miss an appointment already.' That too was a lie but she was not to know. Edmund held out a hand.

'The paper is here, Edmund.' Taking it from a drawer in the dresser she held it in her hand. 'I took it to Winson Green but they would not let me in.'

'It isn't signed?'

The words hissing viciously through set teeth had Livvy grabbing the carving knife from a hook screwed into the dresser side.

'No.' Laura felt the shiver touch along her spine. 'The guard on the gate said I could not be allowed into the infirmary without the written permission of the Governor.'

'Did you ask him?'

Forced between teeth clamped together with anger, the question slithered threateningly into the quiet kitchen.

Behind Laura the other girl held the knife in tightly clenched fingers.

'. . . Did you ask him?'

The menace underlying the repeated words playing over taut nerves, Laura had to swallow hard to free her throat of the lump that rose to it.

'I . . . I could not . . .'

'What do you mean you could not?'

Anger erupting into a shout he sprang to his feet. As quickly, Livvy moved, the lamplight bouncing off steel as she raised the knife.

'The Governor was not at the prison. The guards told me he had not yet returned. I asked if one of them would take the paper to my father, tell him Laura asked that he sign it but I was refused, the guard said his job . . .'

'His job!' Edmund spat, his face almost as white as the paper he snatched. 'Half a crown would have seen it signed, why didn't you offer the man half a crown!'

Too proud to own that she had not had half a penny, much less half a crown, Laura faced the fury in the eyes of the man who only weeks ago she had thought she loved.

'Her did.' Knowing pride would not let Laura lie, Livvy felt no such constraint. 'Her did,' she said sharply. 'Her offered what you said but the guard told her half a crown would be little to keep his family on should he be caught. He told her to keep her paper 'til visiting time proper, in three weeks.'

'Three weeks.' Edmund's hand crushed the paper. 'It will be too late in three weeks' time.'

'I can try again on Friday,' Laura answered quickly. 'That man said the Governor would be back at the prison on Friday of this week.'

Eyes cold with anger swung to her. 'Man, what man?'

'Her don't know his name.'

'Livvy is telling the truth,' Laura said when his glance did not move. 'A man spoke to me at Soho Station, he asked had I been to Winson Green prison, that maybe I was not familiar with regular visiting times.'

'You did not tell him of this?' Edmund raised the fist clutching the paper.

Laura shook her head. 'I said I wished to see my father who was in the infirmary, that I thought maybe special allowance might be made. It was then the man told me the Governor would be there on Friday.'

'That was all?'

'That was all. He walked away without saying his name or enquiring after mine.'

Holding her gaze several moments before being satisfied she had told him all, Edmund dropped his hand to his side. He had to be careful, the fewer people knew of this paper the easier he would sleep at night.

Friday! He turned to stare at the fire. Would Philip Sandon wait that long? And if he did what of the others, those Sheldon had been so sure would join in the buying of the Gallery; they would not wait a few days for his share, they had made that very plain at that meeting at the Periwig Club. They had been in favour of joining a consortium but his money had to be on the table with theirs.

A coupe of days! Edmund's fingers cracked with the pressure with which he gripped the paper. A couple of days was all he needed and for that he would lose the Gallery, lose the life he wanted so badly . . . lose Sheldon . . . !

Anger becoming a tide of iced fire that ripped like fury along every vein, he flung the paper into the fire.

'Friday!' Turning he looked at Laura, all the emotion of an iceberg drawing his narrow features. 'Friday will see Isaac Cadman facing a charge of murder!'

In the darkness of the street, Edmund breathed long and slow. Isaac Cadman had robbed him of his true inheritance, of that which was rightfully his, and now he was set to rob him of the one thing he wanted more than he had ever wanted anything in his life . . . Sheldon Sinclair.

Snatching at the reins he brought the carriage about, taking the road to Wolverhampton. The train had gone over that body almost before it hit the rails, there probably would not be enough of it left in one piece to make a satisfactory identification. But even should there be, there could be no link with him; such a dreadful accident as falling beneath the wheels of a train could not be placed at the feet of Edmund Shaw, how could it when evidence would show he was miles away in another town?

A life for a life! Edmund followed the man who showed the way to the mediocre little hotel room.

Isaac Cadman had seen fit to ruin the life of Edmund Shaw.

Left alone he smiled, a slow malevolent smile that left his eyes cold and dead.

It was only fair that Edmund Shaw take the life of Isaac Cadman.

Chapter Twenty-Five

'There be no use in you going on like this.'

Livvy stared at the girl who had not moved all night. Laura had sunk to the chair as Edmund Shaw had delivered his final blow and she had neither moved nor spoken since.

'Very well!' Livvy's patience finally snapped. 'Be as selfish as you please, indulge yourself, sit there 'til the cows come home, your father won't mind; he won't mind your doing nothing to help him . . . after all he won't know, will he? He won't know you be sitting on your backside while they be building the gallows that will hang him!'

'I can't . . . !' Moving for the first time in hours, Laura dropped her head into her hands. '. . . I can't help him, Livvy, there is nothing I can do . . .'

'Of course there be something you can do!' Livvy stamped her foot impatiently. 'Your father is going to need a lawyer, somebody to speak for him.'

'You know that is impossible.' Laura looked up, her face white as the apron folded on a corner of the dresser. 'I have no money to pay a lawyer, you know I gave every penny I had to Mary Bailey.'

Determined not to lose the ground she had gained, Livvy tossed her head. 'O'course I knows, so we have to go out and earn some more.'

'Just like that?' Laura gave a hopeless shrug of her shoulders. 'Yes . . . just like that!'

'We found it difficult enough to find employment that would pay for us to buy a meal, it would take a miracle to find that which would bring enough to buy the services of a lawyer, and miracles like that don't ever happen.'

'How do you know?' Livvy snapped, her brown eyes flashing. 'Are you such an authority on miracles, Laura Cadman? Be you in the know . . . does the Lord send you word as to when and for who the next miracle will be? Stop making excuses for yourself . . . you want a miracle then get up and work for it!'

The outburst taking her by surprise, Laura could only stare at the young face so alive with emotion. She had seen Livvy angry before, heard it in her choice of language, but this Livvy was quite new, one she never guessed existed.

'Well!' Livvy's boot came down hard again on the quarried floor. 'Be you going to sit there and let that swine Shaw get your father hanged, or be you going to do something about it?'

Glancing at the clock Laura read the time. Six-fifteen. She could be in the line on the High Bullen for six-thirty.

Bones crying out with weariness she reached for her shawl, her lips already forming a prayer for a miracle.

'You be healthy . . . I don't want no wench who ain't healthy. You go falling sick on me and you gets no money, you understand me, wench? You don't get a solitary halfpenny.'

Meeting the penetrating stare of the roughly dressed man who had walked the line four times before stopping in front of Livvy, she bobbed a brief curtsy.

'I ain't sick, sir, I ain't never had a day's sickness in me life.'

'You better be sure and not have one while you be working for me neither, I don't pay for work as ain't done. I carries no dead weight, you gets what you works for and no more. The pay be twelve shillings for the week take it or leave it.'

'I'll take it, please, sir.' Livvy bobbed a second curtsy grinning at Laura before following the man striding away towards a cart.

Potato picking. Livvy walked behind the cart. A whole week's employ, she had been in luck. Now if Laura too was given work then this was the start of their miracle. Twelve shillings was a good wage even for a hard job like lifting potatoes. Following the cart as it lumbered past Wood Green Cemetery she glanced at the memorial stones standing bleak in the greyness of the morning, and her thoughts flew immediately to Laura's father. If they could not raise enough money to defend him then he might soon be lying beneath the earth; but it would not be here. A murderer hanged for the crime was not allowed a place in a public cemetery nor in the hallowed ground of any church, but was buried without marker in a place unknown to all bar the authorities.

Shivering at the awfulness of the thought Livvy drew her shawl tighter about her thin body. They would earn the money, when this job was done she would find another and then another; she would not let Laura suffer even more than she suffered now.

'That be the field needs picking, sacks be there in the barn.'

Five minutes' further walking had brought them to a house surrounded by fields, words painted in black proclaiming it as Upper Bescot Farm.

'You works 'til seven, the church clock will tell you when that time be.' Climbing down from the cart he pointed towards one corner of the field. 'Start there and make sure each sack be full, I pays for no half measures. Listen for the chime that tells midday for that be the time you eats your meal, a full half hour you gets for the doing. Now get yourself started and mind . . .' he glared, 'don't go packing no soil in them sacks, I empties the taters from each afore I pays any wage, a sack has soil in it then that one you don't get paid for.'

Glad to get away from that accusing stare Livvy collected a sack from the building he pointed to and set off for the field. One week and she would have twelve shillings.

The last of the prospective employers had long since gone and the men and women hoping to be given work had drifted away, some in ever hopeful search, others in resigned dejection, only Laura still stood head bent against the thin drizzle of rain.

'You seeking a day's work?'

Glancing up at the question she nodded to the elderly woman dressed head to foot in black, the ribbons of her bonnet tied in a bow beneath her chin.

'I am, ma'am.'

Nodding at the polite answer the woman ran a swift eye over the patched clothing.

'Let me see your hands.'

Bringing them from beneath the shawl Laura held them out, turning them palm upward at the woman's sharply spoken request.

Leaning towards her the woman sniffed several times before stepping away.

'Your hands be clean and there be no stale smell about your clothing.' The woman nodded again. 'Where you be from, girl?'

Dipping a short curtsy Laura answered, 'I live in Great Western Street, my name is Laura Cadman.'

Unblinking eyes regarded her steadily, giving no sign the name meant anything, as the woman replied, 'I asked for no name, why did you give it?'

Brushing the rain from her cheeks Laura held her head high. 'Because my father is Isaac Cadman, he is serving a prison sentence for theft.'

Crossing both hands across her stomach the woman stared at the face of the girl who stood young and proud, head held high despite the stigma of a father who was a convicted thief.

'I did not ask you of your family either.'

A film of raindrops glistening like tears along her thick lashes Laura gave a slight shake of her head. 'No, ma'am, you did not. But I would not wish to accept employment knowing my background is likely to cause offence.'

'It be like to cause offence all right!' Skirts swishing, ankle-high boots kicking up a shower of drops from a puddle, the woman turned. 'But it don't cause me none. Follow me, wench, if you wants a day's work.'

Her brisk step a contradiction to the years showed by the grey peeping beneath the black bonnet, the woman made her way into Ladbury's Lane and past the smoke-blackened parish church to the further side of Church Hill, stopping at a tiny cottage nestled at its foot.

'Rose Cottage.' She pushed open the gate, leading the way to a door almost smothered in lovely pink-coloured blooms, their perfume heady after the touch of rain.

Inside the kitchen the windows were hung with flowered chintz and the plain wood dresser sparkled with china delicately painted in matching russets and pinks. Laura found herself smiling. The kitchen was as pretty as the garden.

'Hang your shawl over there.' The woman pointed to a row of hooks set into the wall beside the door, turning at once to the kettle hissing softly over the fire burning in a grate so polished with black lead it gleamed silver. 'We both be near soaked, but a cup of tea soon has the damp gone from a body's bones.'

Scalding tea leaves left ready in a large rose-patterned teapot warming on the hob, the woman flicked a nod towards the dresser. 'Don't stand about like a mawkin, Laura Cadman, reach two cups and sweeten them with milk, you will find a jug in the dairy out the back.'

Following the line of the woman's glance Laura walked out into the yard. A low white-washed building ran the length of the cottage, the inside boasting a long shallow stone sink set amid two long trestle benches while the walls held a variety of pans and sieves, every one as gleaming clean as the dairy itself.

Taking a small jug from a shelf above the sink and filling it from a wooden churn, Laura carried it indoors.

'You found your way about the dairy, that be good. Now let's have that tea, I be gasping for a cup. Betsy Simkin enjoys naught more than her cup of tea.'

'If you will tell me what it is I am required to do, ma'am . . .'

'The first requirement be for you to stop calling me ma'am.' Betsy Simkin's button eyes twinkled. 'I ain't one of them fancy housekeepers down along of Wood Green or on the hill there, they have more airs and graces than the woman of the house herself and that don't be my style. Plain Simkin does for me, wench, you just call Betsy Simkin by name and we will do fine.'

Laura smiled. 'Then what will I do, Mrs Simkin?'

'First you best wipe yourself down with this cloth, the water be dripping from your face, that done you joins me in a warming drink, a body can't work satisfactory be her cold and wet.'

Taking the cloth the woman held out, Laura dried her face then accepted a steaming cup.

'The fruit be heavy this year.' Betsy stirred sugar into her own cup. 'There be too much for me to handle on my own and letting it bide on the trees means the wasps has the bigger share and I count that as waste, though I shouldn't for all the Lord's creatures deserves a part of His bounty. So I wants you to help with the preserving of some and the making of jam with the rest.'

Laying aside her cup, Laura glanced at the basket she had seen beside the door and made to pick it up. 'Which do you want picking first? I will get it now before the rain comes on again.'

'No rush, wench.' The woman smiled, cheeks as colourful as her roses merging with the generous folds about her chin. 'A drop of rain will do no great harm for I have most of the fruit brought in yesterday. P'raps if we gets through the lot today then tomorrow we can fetch in the rest.'

Tomorrow! Laura fastened the straps of the large white apron handed to her, the promise of another day's work adding to the pleasant warmth of the small house.

Following the woman's instructions Laura worked steadily, stoning plums and damsons, fetching jars from the storage shelves in the scullery, sterilising them in hot salted water before setting them out in long lines on the well-scrubbed table. Then as Betsy filled them with fresh boiled jam she lifted another pot of water to the bracket above the fire, adding fruit and sugar before carrying the used pot and ladles to the scullery and scrubbing them clean.

'You've worked well, wench.' Hands on her hips, Betsy stretched her spine. 'You have earned your coppers.'

'I have enjoyed the work, Mrs Simkin.' Laura's smile was genuine.

'And I've enjoyed your company, it has been a pleasure having you here.'

'Thank you.'

Reaching for a tin box patterned once more with her beloved roses, Betsy hesitated before raising the lid.

'We set no wage for the day.' Her bright eyes suddenly shrewd she kept them on Laura's face. 'Nor did we say the pay for each hour.'

'No.' Laura removed the apron, stained now with fruit juice and the marks of fingers sticky with jam.

'Then what be you expecting?'

Folding the apron Laura held it along with the cloths the woman had had her put aside for the wash, and when she looked again into the woman's face her eyes were clear and honest as before.

'I expect what I know you will pay, Mrs Simkin. The wage you think my work for you is worth. Whatever that should be, I thank you for giving me the chance to earn it.'

Raising the lid of the box Betsy listened to her thoughts. This girl reckoned her father to be serving time for theft, but how could a rogue raise a wench so honest and hard-working as this one?

Counting out several coins she handed them to Laura.

'Be that satisfactory to you, wench?'

Glancing first at the silver in her hand, Laura looked quickly back to the woman now putting the box away.

'Three shillings . . . this is too much . . .'

'I don't count it too much.' Betsy glanced at the line of jars, each filled to the brim with rich fruity jam. 'I shall get that back and more from getting most of the crop into jars, and that I couldn't have done without a pair of hands as willing as yours have been. I be well satisfied with your labours, so much so I be willing to pay the same tomorrow should you want the work.'

Tying her shawl beneath her breasts Laura nodded. 'Yes please, Mrs Simkin.'

Watching the slight figure run quickly away up the hill Betsy Simkin shook her grey head. Such a nice girl. Whatever had turned her father into a thief?

'Thank God!' Edmund Shaw flopped into a chair in the sitting room of the private apartment of the Gallery. 'Thank God they agreed.'

'God?' Sheldon Sinclair smiled. 'I rather thought it due more to my powers of persuasion than to God's powers of intervention.'

'You were marvellous.' Edmund glanced up at the handsome face. 'I could never have talked them round without your help.'

'We haven't quite talked them over yet.' Sheldon draped himself elegantly in a facing chair. 'They agreed to wait a week for your share, should that not be forthcoming by then chances are they will withdraw.'

He had been given one more chance to raise the money. Five thousand pounds. Edmund watched the other man light a slender cigar. Lawton, Thorne and Hutton had each agreed to loan five thousand at a rate of twelve per cent interest a year. They were not interested in a partnership but each had agreed to a loan. It was a hell of a debt to go into!

'You are still worried at the prospect of taking on such a loan?'

'You have to admit it is a daunting one.'

'Agreed.'

The smile reaching through the lavender haze played over Edmund's face. 'But it is not an impossible one. The whole amount could be paid in nine months, maybe less.'

It sounded so confident, but deep inside Edmund felt the same doubt he had felt since the whole business of buying the Gallery had been mooted.

'I don't see how. With that paper not being signed then the sale of the works will not go through, and without that money I have nowhere near five thousand.'

'Maybe it could be raised without the sale of your factory.' Sheldon blew a cloud of lavender-grey smoke, watching it curl towards the delicately moulded plaster ceiling.

'Huh!' Edmund laughed sarcastically. 'I would like to know how.'

'Then, my dear Edmund, I shall tell you how.' Getting up from the chair Sheldon went to stand before the fireplace.

'A select showing here at the Gallery, let us say the white carnations, they always ensure a clientele more than willing to part with their money. You would easily clear enough profit to make your down-payment. One night and you would have their signatures and this place would be as good as yours.'

Three thousand! Edmund swallowed hard. Could that much money really be made in one night?

'Well?' Sheldon lifted an elegant eyebrow. 'What do you say?'

'Could it be done . . . I mean, really?'

Throwing the remains of the cigar into the grate Sheldon laughed. 'Why would I say it could if that were not the case? It needs only to be handled properly.'

'That's a stumbling block in itself.' Edmund frowned. 'I hardly know an antique from a pint pot . . . and as for the presenters, where do I find them?'

The smile returning to his full-lipped mouth Sheldon shook his head, the faint movement sending darts of bronze light spearing into the room.

'You don't. I will take care of that part of the proceedings. All you have to do is take the cash. However, there is one thing that would most definitely swing events in our favour. Melville Hutton has a penchant for the new.'

What the hell did that mean? Edmund averted his glance. It was going to take a long time to ease comfortably into Sheldon's style; wines, antiques, even words he used went over his head.

'I thought he preferred antiques.'

'Not in women . . .'

Sheldon laughed, the answer seeming an obvious right one. A lucky strike? Edmund returned his glance to the handsome face.

'. . . He prefers them to be new to the art . . . Melville likes his fillies to be unbroken; in other words he likes virgins. Now get him one of those pretty enough and he would *give* five thousand, let alone make a loan of it. But . . .' he shrugged, '. . . where do we get such a prize? A girl from the slums would never do, Melville is particular in his choice, the woman must be presentable in speech as well as looks.'

'There must be one somewhere . . .'

'True, Edmund, there must be such a woman somewhere, but unfortunately for us the only ones I know of are most carefully guarded by their mamas. Pity . . .' He shrugged again, an eloquent dismissive lift of the shoulders. '. . . it would have halved your problems, as it is we must concentrate on those assets we *can* bring into play.'

'When do you think the best time might be for another . . . auction?'

Edmund hesitated over the word, still uncomfortable with the activity it covered. Against the fireplace, watchful despite his air of nonchalance, Sheldon recognised the reason behind the other man's slight falter. Picking up a small enamelled box from a side table he turned it over in his hand, admiring the intricate workmanship.

'One can never say with absolute certainty when the best time might be, but let me put it this way . . .' He replaced the pretty trinket box. '. . . each one held so far has been very well attended.

We will go to the Periwig Club tonight and I can make a few enquiries, and you might wear this.'

Reaching into his pocket Sheldon drew out a small box, tossing it to Edmund.

'What is it?'

Like quiet music Sheldon laughed softly. 'Why not open it and see for yourself?'

Lifting the lid Edmund looked at the small gold object nestled on purple velvet. Unschooled as he was in all things arty he recognised the skills involved in creating a thing of beauty, and this small object was beautiful.

Taking it between his fingers he admired the small golden beetle, then smiled as he recognised the ball held between its front legs.

'The button,' he glanced up at the smiling Sheldon, 'it's the button from my waistcoat.'

'Not any more. The beetle is a representation of Khepri. The ancients thought it a deity who was given charge of rolling the earth across the daytime sky; the button is the world and that is what I am offering you Edmund, a new world, my world, all you have to do is take it.'

'Khepri.' Edmund ran a finger over the tiny golden insect. 'I have so much to learn, Sheldon.'

'And I so much to teach.'

Green eyes locked with brown darkened to deep enticing pools that lapped at Edmund's senses. Sleek and sinuous as a hunting cat, Sheldon crossed the elegant room to stand a foot or so from him.

'So many things, Edmund,' he said throatily, 'so many delightful things, why not begin now?'

Leaning forward he placed his mouth full over the one raised to him. His hands slowly releasing waistcoat and trousers he smiled as Edmund slid to the floor.

So many delightful things, and he wanted them all. Pulses beating like drums, his senses reeling in a vortex of pleasure,

Edmund moaned as the touch of hands and lips scorched across his chest and slowly, so very slowly, down the central line of his stomach to halt at the mound of silky brown hair.

The pain of longing so excruciating, he almost cried out. Edmund clenched his teeth against the sweet pain of fingertips curled into the fine hair.

'You have to tell me, Edmund . . .'

Sheldon's voice was low, a voluptuous torment that rippled along Edmund's tight nerves like fire.

'. . . tell me what it is you wish to learn.'

Moving his hand slowly as before, Sheldon trailed a path upward to pull teasingly at each nipple.

'Is it this?' he asked. 'Or is it this?'

Agile as a leopard he moved to kneel at Edmund's feet.

Both hands stroking skin that seemed to sing beneath his hands, he drew them lingeringly over ribs and hips, sliding them sensuously over thighs and legs.

His eyes closed, Edmund moaned, helpless against the emotions ripping through him.

'Is it that, Edmund? Is that truly all you want?'

The sound thick in his throat, Sheldon Sinclair laughed softly as he looked at the naked man lying before him.

'. . . I think not. I think perhaps it is this.'

Placing a hand on each knee he pushed the legs wide, smiling at the gasp that tore from Edmund's lips.

Sliding both palms along the insides of the spread thighs, bringing them slowly to the pulsing crotch, he smiled once more, then dropped his face to the silky mound.

Chapter Twenty-Six

'The work is too heavy for you, Livvy, please don't go to that farm again, we can manage.'

'On what you works for. I told you, Laura, I eat only if I puts my share and that I can't do by sitting here.'

Tired though her face was, Livvy's obstinacy was more clearly marked.

'Then take what you have earned up to now. Tell that man you will not be picking any more of his wretched potatoes. We will find work somewhere else, there is no use in killing yourself.'

'Today be the last of it.' Livvy reached for her shawl, setting her teeth against the ache of every muscle in her body. 'I were told at the beginning that should I stop afore the week were up then I would get nothing.'

Fastening the shawl about her waist she looked at Laura with determined eyes.

'I got the feeling he would like that, like to have me work my roe out and pay nothing for the labour, but he can go on hoping. It ain't been easy work but it will be worth it when I see the pain it gives the old Scrooge to pay me my twelve shilling.'

'Then come straight home tonight, do not go to the canal.'

'I have to, Laura.' Livvy shook her head. 'It were a number three scratched on my marker, that were put there by none but my father and it showed the barge would moor there on the third night. That be tonight, Laura, I can't miss the chance of seeing my family.'

She could understand that being of paramount importance. Laura fastened on her own shawl. Nothing would deter her from seeing her father should the chance be given . . . but would that chance come as he faced a jury, faced a charge of murder?

Following Livvy from the house she felt the dread she had felt since Edmund had stormed out that night he had come for the paper that had not been signed, a dread that lay heavy on her heart.

Reaching the High Bullen she glanced at the men and women, some with children in their arms or clutching their skirts, collected in the open space at the foot of the hill from which rose two churches.

Two churches built so closely together, bringing the comfort of God to the town; but where was the comfort for these people? How many of them would find work that would bring them the comfort of a meal?

'I hope you gets offered something.' Livvy too had eyed the gathering.

'I shall not need any offer.' Laura turned to the girl who had walked with her to the High Bullen as she had each morning before taking the road that led to Bescot Farm. 'I am coming with you. Two pairs of hands does more than one. Between us we might finish that field by midday then you can tell that farmer goodbye.'

'There'll be no more money, you picks if you likes but I'll pay no more.'

Her smile added to the covert laugh with which Livvy mimicked the farmer's answer to their proposal, Laura bent to the work of lifting potatoes from the heavy clay soil, her mind wandering almost immediately to her father.

Once his leg was mended he would be back in the main prison. That infirmary was miserable enough but at least it afforded him a little space, it could not be as awful as sharing a cell with two or three others . . . no privacy, every moment of his life on view to another, robbing him even of his self respect. But that was not enough for Edmund, he wanted her father's life.

From the hill rising above the town, the clock of the black-spired parish church rang twice.

Two o'clock. Laura straightened, every bone protesting at the move. Livvy had worked like this for five days, five days of scrabbling in the damp earth. If only she had known how back-breaking the task she would never have agreed to the girl's accepting the job. She glanced at the thin figure away at the further end of the field. No matter how badly off they might become, she vowed silently, never again would Livvy do this work.

'That be the lot of 'em . . .'

Lifting her feet high against the sucking mud, Livvy came across the field.

'. . . can't say I be sorry.'

'Nor I.' Laura wiped a hand across her brow leaving a dark line in its wake. 'I can't think how you managed to do such a job, it would break the back of a donkey.'

'Well thank you, Miss Cadman!'

'I didn't mean . . .'

'I know.' Livvy answered the apologetic look with a grin. 'But you be right, this job would break a donkey's back, but it be finished now . . .' Her grin widening, she touched a tentative hand to her spine. '. . . but I think my back be all in one piece, so what does that make me?'

'Jabez would have said it made you a gutsy wench.'

'This Jabez was a good friend?'

Laura nodded.

Swinging the sack she had filled with potatoes on to her back, Livvy waited as Laura struggled to lift her own.

'This Jabez,' she asked as they staggered through the clinging mud, 'be it the same one you told me about?'

Bent beneath the weight of the sack, the pressure of it forcing the words to come one at a time, Laura answered.

'Yes, he was the same, he was Edmund's father.'

✻

His meal finished, Edmund Shaw glanced at the watch attached to his figured silk waistcoat.

Two o'clock! Slipping the watch back into his pocket he pushed away from the table, going to stand at the window. Blue and silver, pink and cream, flowers and foliage edged sculptured lawns that rolled away to a ribbon of water gleaming in the distance, skirting a small island that held a building such as he had seen in a book his mother showed him as a child. The temple of Apollo she had called it, though Sheldon had laughed and said this was just another folly, that there were several such dotted about the grounds, Japanese pagodas, Egyptian obelisks, even a minute version of a Siamese Wat, all erected by Sandon's grand-father after doing the grand tour.

Follies! Edmund stared out towards the small replica temple rising from its bed of glittering water. Fantasies created to satisfy one man's fancy, money spent without thought of where the next might come from; there had been no worry here, no fretting over a paltry five thousand pounds . . .

The thought brought him up sharply. He had given no heed to the fact that this house still belonged to Philip Sandon, that any money raised by another special auction or by legitimate sale of an antique would belong not to him but to Sandon.

Why hadn't he thought of that before, thought of it before Sheldon had left? But then why couldn't he think straight about anything when they were together?

Two men . . . two men making love to each other, passion strong and tearing, lifting them to the same heights it lifted man and woman. But what did he know of the passions that enfolded a man and a woman? He had never made love to a woman.

Turning away from the window he felt the quick jerk of desire as Sheldon Sinclair entered the room.

No, he had never made love to a woman, and now he would never want to!

Glancing at the remains of the meal still on the dining table, Sheldon wrinkled his nose. Pulling the bell cord that hung beside the elegant Adam fireplace he smiled at the manservant who answered its summons.

'A bottle of the Canard Duchene please, Mason, and we will take it in the sitting room.'

Minutes later, glass in hand, Edmund waited. Was the champagne a celebration or a wake?

'The ball is rolling nicely.' Sheldon raised his glass. 'Here's to your first special showing.'

'It's on?'

'Did you doubt it?' Twisting the stem of the glass, Sheldon watched the bubbles rising in the pale golden liquid.

'No.' Edmund shook his head. 'I had no doubts on that score.'

'Then what score? You do have doubts, that is quite plain.'

'It . . . it's just that . . .'

'That . . . ?' Sheldon raised a well-shaped eyebrow.

'What about Sandon?'

His smile languid, Sheldon eyed the elegant champagne flute in his hand.

'What about Sandon?'

An exasperated breath shooting between his teeth, Edmund set his own glass down hard.

'He still owns this place, that's what! Until my name be on a deed of purchase the Gallery is still his, that means any money made on auctions or any other way is legally his.'

'So?' Languid as the raising of his eyebrows, Sheldon let the one word hang in the air.

Raising a hand then letting it fall, Edmund stared at the other man. Why did he not see what was hitting him in the face? 'So! The auction will do me no good, I still won't get the money I need, it will go to Philip Sandon.'

'You supplied your own answer to that small problem. The answer lies in that one word, legally. Remember, Edmund, the type of auction we speak of is highly illegal. That being so Sandon would not make official complaint should we hold one; besides, whilst he is away he cannot know what goes on here.' Sheldon lifted his glass, smiling over its rim. 'While the cat's away and all that . . .'

Everything was so easy for Sheldon Sinclair. Edmund drained his glass. It seemed nothing bothered him, everything was passed over with a wave of the hand or a shrug of the shoulders. He had simply smiled on hearing the sale of the works had not yet gone through, and again when he was told that paper remained unsigned. 'Give it time,' was all he had said, 'give it time.'

But time was something else he did not have. He watched the pale liquid tumble into his glass.

Time and money! It seemed his whole life had been a matter of time, years spent waiting . . .

'But you are still not sure.' Putting his own glass aside, Sheldon rose. His movements fluid, his smile easy, he crossed to Edmund. Leaning downwards he brought his face close, his voice falling to a throaty murmur.

'I have a very good solution for that problem too.'

Reaching a yard caked with mud and animal droppings, Livvy set her sack on the ground then helped Laura lower hers.

'You go wash the muck from your boots while I take these to the barn.'

'You can't carry both.'

Laura bent to the sacks but Livvy's quick hand stopped her.

'Let me take them. No sense in us both listening to that man moan. Clean your boots and wait for me at the gate. I'll just get my twelve shillings and we'll be off.'

'I would rather come with you.'

'Tut . . . tut!' Livvy wagged her head slowly from side to side. 'Did your mother never tell you that little girls should never be given everything they ask for . . . no matter how pretty they be. Now do as I say, only . . .'

'Only what?'

Her light laugh floating behind her, Livvy took up a sack crossing with it towards the tumbledown barn.

'Only wash your face, it be streaked like a licorice humbug.'

Slipping off the sack Livvy had tied for protection across her back, she yanked the handle of the pump in a corner of the yard, holding each foot in turn beneath the trickle of water. Then, after rinsing the soil from her hands, she caught a little of the water, using it to bathe her face. The touch of it cold against skin heated by heavy labour, she gasped; then douched her face again. It was the one thing she did not mind touching her, the only really clean thing she saw in the whole yard.

Shaking the droplets from her hands she drew a handkerchief from her pocket, dabbing it against her face. She might not be truly cleansed of the mud of that field but she felt better.

Glancing towards the barn she looked for signs of Livvy. The second sack of potatoes was gone and the barn door closed. Laura shifted her glance to the house. Livvy must have gone there to be paid.

Removing her shawl she shook it, wary of dust the sack might have left on it. Livvy had been careful to choose two that appeared new and as yet unused, but even so she shook her shawl twice more before draping it about her shoulders.

Walking to the gate she stood watching the bevy of brown hens scratch among the refuse that littered the yard. Her mother had once kept hens, but then her mother had died and Abbie had declared the hens 'nobbut a noosance, forever laying away so a body had to go searching for they eggs!' So the hens had gone, one more thing taken from her young life!

First her mother, then Abbie. At least their deaths had been the cause of nature, but her father . . . Staring at the fussing hens she felt the tears rise warm behind her lids . . . was he to be taken from her as they had been, would he die also, executed to satisfy another man's spite?

Closing her eyes against the horror of the thought she

reached a hand to the gate, then froze as Livvy's screams cut the quiet air.

'I don't know how to thank you.'

Laura looked at the man sat in her kitchen. It had been a miracle his being there as she half carried, half dragged Livvy to where the cart track gave on to the road that led along Wood Green.

'I have told you I do not require to be thanked, I am simply glad I was able to help.' Rafe Travers watched the girl, her face pale as churchyard marble, her eyes still dark with shock. She had not yet said the cause, but he would find out; yes, by God he would find out!

'The doctor has said she has no broken bones?'

Laura nodded, her lips trembling too much to give a verbal answer.

'Tea!' He stood up, swinging the kettle away from the fire. 'My mother always reckoned tea the best medicine to treat a fright, now . . . where do you keep the caddy?'

'I . . . I'll do it . . .'

'No! You will not!' Teapot in hand he looked at her. 'I have to tell you, Miss . . .'

'Cadman,' Laura supplied, 'Laura Cadman.'

'Rafe Travers,' he smiled. 'I have to tell you, Laura Cadman, I turn quite nasty when my offer of a good turn meets with repeated refusal, I have even been known to shout, not to mention stamp my foot.'

Despite the trauma of the past couple of hours, Laura smiled at his effort to amuse her.

'I do not think I could cope with a tantrum right now, so maybe I had best let you have your way.'

Watching his deft, assured movements she found herself calmed by his presence. He had come upon them as she helped Livvy away from that farm, and at once he had taken charge. But not in a domineering way. She glanced down at her hands folded in her lap, remembering the gentleness of his touch as he had helped her into the carriage.

'Is there anyone will come and sit with the girl while you get some rest?'

'Livvy, her name is Livvy . . . Olivia Beckett.' Laura accepted the cup held for her to take. 'Yes . . . we have friends who will be willing to help.'

One more friend than you know. Rafe hid the thought, lowering his glance to the tea he had poured for himself. A friend who intended to do as much as he was able to end her problems.

'Then I should leave, they are probably waiting to see my carriage drive away before coming to see what is wrong.'

'No, don't go . . . !'

Colour rising in her pale face as her quick words brought his glance, she finished lamely, '. . . at least finish your tea first.'

'Laura . . . may I call you Laura . . . ?'

At her nod, he laid his cup aside. '. . . Laura, will you trust me enough to tell me what happened this afternoon, how Livvy got those injuries to her back?'

Realisation that she already had trust in this man coming as no true surprise, she spoke quietly, telling how they had picked the last of the potatoes then carried the sacks to the yard.

'Livvy took them into the barn while I cleaned the mud from my boots, then washed my hands and face. She seemed to be taking more time than I would have expected but I told myself that was due to the farmer tipping out the sack to inspect the contents. Livvy said he did that every evening, inspecting what she had picked; he had told her should the sacks contain soil then she would not be paid that day's work. I noticed that the barn door was closed and presumed she had gone to the house to collect her hire for the week so I went to stand at the farm gate.' Her mouth trembling violently she paused. 'That . . .' She paused again, sobs throbbing on a long-drawn breath. '. . . that was when I heard Livvy scream!'

Still watching her, Rafe made no sound. He needed to know all.

'She . . . she went on screaming, one after another as I ran to the house. But Livvy was not in the kitchen nor in any of the downstairs rooms. It was then I realised the screams were not coming from the house, they were coming from the barn. I don't remember running from the house or even calling her name, the only thing was her screams . . .'

Still offering no word he watched Laura's head tilt backwards on her neck, eyes closed and teeth clenched against the memory.

'. . . I tried,' she spoke again, the effort of doing so clearly marked in her eyes as she opened them. '. . . I tried to open that barn door but it seemed to be stuck, and all the time I could hear Livvy screaming. At last . . . I don't know how . . . I opened the door. Livvy was face down on the floor, the back of her blouse torn and soaked with blood and . . . and the farmer was lashing her with a whip. Bringing it down one blow on another . . . and all the time he was muttering that no chit of a wench called him a liar. I yelled at him to stop and when he would not I caught at his arm . . .'

'Is that when you were hit across the face?'

Rafe felt his fingers tighten as he glanced at the red weal so startlingly clear against the pallor of her skin.

'I caught his arm . . .' Laura continued as if she had not heard the question. '. . . he shook me off and struck out with the whip, knocking me sideways. When I looked up he was raining more blows on Livvy, that was when I saw the pitchfork. It had blood on it . . . and . . .' She broke off, a massive shudder shaking her from head to toe. '. . . I asked him to stop . . . I asked him to stop . . . I asked . . .'

Her strength breaking, Rafe stepped to her, drawing her into his arms, holding her while the sobs took their course.

'I asked him to stop,' she sobbed against his chest.

Had Livvy killed that swine of a man? Rafe held her in the circle of his arms.

If she had not, then he most certainly would!

Chapter Twenty-Seven

'I have to go back there, Laura, I want my twelve shilling!'

'You will do no such thing, go back to that farm and you could get yourself killed. The man is not to be trusted.'

Laying a cloth over the bed-sheet Laura handed the girl a bowl of broth.

'There was never a truer word spoken. That farmer can't be trusted, he is naught but a thief; but I mean to get my hire, twelve shilling was agreed and twelve shilling he will pay!'

Wincing from the smarting of the weals cut into her back, Livvy put the soup aside.

She had not asked the reason for that man taking a whip to Livvy, she had thought only of getting her out of that barn and away to safety. Now, looking at the determined young face, the question rang loud in Laura's mind. What had gone on in that barn?

'He up-ended both sacks of 'taters on that barn floor . . .'

Seeming to read the question on Laura's face, Livvy explained.

'. . . then when I asked for my pay he said he didn't pay for soil, he said that there was more of that in the sack than there was potatoes, that it had been the same with half the sacks I had picked so he was paying no more than five shillings. I said that was a lie, and when he argued further I called him a liar and a cheat; that were when he took the whip and began beating me. It was lucky for me you were there.'

'And lucky I am here to prevent your returning. You are not going to that farm, Livvy, not if I have to tie you to that bed . . .'

'But my money!'

Hands on hips, Laura stared hard at the younger girl. 'Forget the money,' she said fiercely. 'No amount of money is worth the risk of having you more seriously injured than you are now.'

Livvy's mouth dropped and the glint of tears nestled in her brown eyes. 'But it was to be for you, Laura. It was to be put aside against the train fares you are going to need to get to see your father. I ain't bothered for myself . . . it was for you.'

'I know.' Sinking to the bed Laura took the girl's hands in hers, her own eyes bright with moisture. 'I know and I am grateful, but I could not stand the thought of that man hitting you again. Promise me, Livvy . . . promise me you will not go there. I have the money to get to Birmingham and I can earn more, so please . . . promise me.'

'Do I have to? Twelve shilling be awful important.'

Looking into that small face Laura smiled. 'Not nearly so important as you are. Put the loss of your earnings down to experience and remember never again to take work like that unless I work with you.'

'I'd like to kill that cheating bugger!'

For once not remonstrating with her friend over her choice of words, Laura felt her face pale. She had struck that farmer with his own pitchfork, stuck it into him as he bent over Livvy, then had dragged her away without looking to see how badly the man might be injured; it could be he was already dead, that *she* had killed him!

Caught in the worry of the moment she was unaware of Livvy's intentions until the girl swung her legs from the bed.

'Livvy! Please, you must not . . .'

'I ain't going to Bescot Farm.' Livvy saw the alarm leap to Laura's face and despite the sting of her back she smiled, '. . . so you need have no worries on that.'

'Then what are you doing? You know what the doctor said, a few days' complete rest, try to forget that man's cheating you.'

'Losing that money to him, I won't say it don't bother me 'cos it does.' Pushing up from the bed, Livvy's mouth tightened with pain. 'But the real bother would not be meeting with my family, that would be the really hard bit to swallow, Laura. I've counted every minute from seeing that number scratched on my marker, every minute 'til I see my mother again; ain't nobody taking that from me, that be why I have to get up from this bed, I have to go to the cutside afore the boat leaves.'

She wanted to say no, to insist upon the girl remaining in bed, but the determination stamped about Livvy's mouth told Laura that would be useless.

'I could go. Tell me exactly where the boat will be moored and I will fetch your family to you. That way we would all be satisfied.'

Livvy hesitated, then, her legs still shaky, sat down on the bed.

'It will be better that way. We are not likely to meet with another man who will ferry us home if you find you can't make it.'

'That is something else I should do.' Livvy made no protest as Laura helped her into bed, covering her legs with the bed clothes. 'I should thank the man who helped you bring me home. Who is he . . . do you know him?'

'His name is Rafe Travers.' Laura handed the bowl of soup once more to Livvy. 'Now eat all of that while it is still warm.'

'So how do you know this Rafe Travers . . . you do know him, don't you?'

Spooning soup into her mouth, Livvy watched the play of colour on Laura's cheeks.

'I don't really know him.' Laura busied herself tidying the small table Livvy already had immaculately tidy.

'So how come you know his name?'

Her back to the bed and the other girl's inquisitive stare Laura answered.

'He . . . he introduced himself before he left.'

Not satisfied she had heard all, Livvy spooned her soup before asking. 'But you had met him before today?'

Disturbed by the question yet without knowing why, Laura stood a moment without turning. The sound of his name on Livvy's lips had brought colour surging into her cheeks and somehow her pulses raced at mention of him.

'Is he the one helped you that time you were . . . you lost your purse?'

'Yes.' She turned slowly to face the bed. 'It is the same man. He gave me money to get home that evening, I repaid it when I saw him again at the railway station.'

'Does he live in Wednesbury?'

Taking the dish from Livvy, Laura shook her head.

'I have no idea where he lives or who he is; and you, young woman, should not ask so many questions. Now tell me where along the canal to find your parents' barge then you have to rest while I go find them.'

Giving the necessary instruction, Livvy watched as Laura turned to leave the bedroom then, as she reached the door, said softly, 'You like him don't you, Laura? You like this Rafe Travers.'

Holding her shawl against the cooling evening breeze, Laura picked her way across open heathland towards the canal that linked the Black Country towns like a great winding artery.

'You like him don't you, Laura?'

The words circled her mind demanding, as they had since leaving the house, an answer. Beneath the touch of the breeze her cheeks glowed warm. She had not had the courage to face that question even though it had crept surreptitiously into her thoughts many nights before she slept.

But then so many thoughts invaded her mind before the blessing of sleep finally overcame her, so many nights of staring into the darkness of her room, thinking of her father and of Edmund; wondering why one had been so cruel to the other. But always after these thoughts came others, others that asked why had Rafe Travers bothered himself with the problems of a girl visiting a prison, why had he bothered yet again, taking her in his carriage to the railway station? And always those thoughts ended with the question, why did thoughts of him bother her so much?

Now Livvy had brought the question into the open, brought her face to face with it.

Holding her shawl across her mouth and nose Laura sought once more to evade her answer, but as the blush stained deeper into her face she knew she had to admit to the truth. Yes, she did like the man who had given his name as Rafe Travers, she liked him more than she cared to admit.

The sharp staccato bark of a dog bringing her back to the task in hand, she glanced across the remaining yards to the ribbon of green water lying still and somnolent between dark trodden towpaths.

A brown patched white bull terrier regarded her from the deck of a narrowboat.

'What be it, Kitchener . . . what be up?'

A flat cap covering most of his brown hair, a muffler knotted at his throat then tucked beneath a ragged jacket, a tall lean man emerged from the tiny cabin, going to stand with one hand on the dog's broad shoulder.

'Don't come no nearer.' He glanced to where Laura stood. 'Stop you there. Kitchener 'ere don't be partial to whether he sinks his teeth into man or woman, it be all the same to him.'

Feeling her throat tighten as the dog growled, Laura swallowed hard.

'Is . . . is this the *Lady Margaret*?'

'What if it be?'

The lack of either acknowledgement or denial only adding to her nervousness, Laura shivered as the deep warning-note rumbled once more from the dog's throat.

'I . . . I am looking for Mr Beckett, would you be he?'

A sharp word had the dog silent yet its eyes thundered a warning as they stayed locked on Laura.

'My name is Laura Cadman,' she said, hearing the tremble in her words. 'I have a friend, Livvy, Olivia Beckett, she said her parents would be here, they operate a narrowboat called the *Lady Margaret.*'

'Livvy!' The man stepped to the edge of the deck, peering across at Laura. 'You say you knows my Livvy?'

'If you are Mr Beckett, then yes.'

'Mother.' The man stamped a boot on the timbered decking. 'Mother, come up 'ere quick.'

The door to the cabin swung back and a woman climbed out, followed closely by a group of children, the smallest clinging to her skirts.

'Whatever be up with you, Jem Beckett? You fair frighten a body with your stamping and shouting!'

'Stop your blethering, woman, and listen.' Jem Beckett reached a hand towards the bank, pointing as she came to stand beside him.

'That there wench says her be friend to our Livvy.'

'My Livvy . . . !' The woman clenched a hand to her mouth, the words trembling between her fingers as she asked, 'You knows my little wench . . . my Livvy?'

Standing in the quiet of the fading evening, Laura could almost feel the emotion of the woman. Nodding her head she answered gently, 'Livvy Beckett is my very good friend, are you her mother?'

Keeping the hand to her mouth the woman looked up at the man beside her.

'It be my wench, I said t'would be her marker, I said it would.'

'Ar, you did, and it seems you was right as always, Sarann.' He put an arm comfortingly about her shoulders, then glanced again to Laura. 'So where be our Livvy then, why be it her ain't here 'erself?'

How could she tell these people their daughter had been whipped, tell them that she may have only just escaped with her life? Yet somehow, however difficult, the telling had to be done.

'Livvy is . . . is resting, she asked me to come . . .'

'Resting!' The woman's cry was sharp, bringing a rumble to the dog's throat.

'. . . My wench ain't needed not a day's rest in her life. It would take more than the need for rest to keep her from her mother . . . you don't be telling me the all of it . . . there be summat wrong, summat very wrong to keep my wench away and I wants to know what it be!'

'Steady, Mother.' Jem's arm tightened about his wife's shoulders, then looking at Laura he asked quietly, 'Be there summat ailing our Livvy, be that why you be 'ere in her stead?'

Across the towpath that separated her from the barge, lengthening shadows touched the woman's face but did not hide the pleading that filled it, or disguise the silent prayer Laura guessed filled her heart.

Finding words that would not cause the woman heartache yet at the same time were not lies was not easy, and Laura found herself hesitating.

'Livvy met with . . .' That would not do, that whipping had been no accident.

'Livvy was hurt this afternoon,' she began again. 'But she is all right, the doctor says she will recover fully.'

Breaking free from her husband's arm but keeping her glance on Laura, the woman called for her shawl grabbing it from the child that scrambled to fetch it from the cabin.

'None of you leave the boat, you hear me? You stays where you be, the lot of you . . .'

Giving her children their instructions she flung the shawl about her head. '. . . I will be back afore long, and your sister with me.'

'You heard your mother.' Jem turned to the watching youngsters. 'You wenches put yourselves to bed; you, Jack,' he turned to the boy of about fourteen, 'you will stay on deck 'til we returns.'

Following his wife down the narrow strip of wood that formed a makeshift gangplank, he glanced behind to the dog watching his every move with bright alert eyes. Pointing to the hatch that led into the tiny living quarters he snapped, 'Kitchener, guard,' and as the bull terrier took up its position he turned to follow Laura across the heath.

In the first-class compartment he had reserved on the train to Birmingham, Rafe Travers went over the day in his mind.

He had talked again with the solicitor handling the sale of that engineering works and made a final offer, if it were not met then he would look elsewhere than Wednesbury for premises; and if he did that how would he manage to see Laura Cadman again?

Glancing through the window he watched the passing landscape leave behind the tiny smoke-blackened houses pressed close together on every side as if seeking protection, and give way to open heathland bordered by fields newly shorn of their crops.

Much as that farmer's field had been harvested of potatoes. Rafe felt the sinews of his body tighten like whipcord. How could a man treat another human being as that one had treated that girl? That brought him close to wanting to beat the man senseless, yet how would he have felt if it were the other girl who had been whipped? It could so easily have been! The thought had his fingers curling into clenched fists. It could have been Laura Cadman who felt the bite of that whip.

'Leave it, please, it . . . it is over now.'

The words she had spoken as they had reached her home came back to his mind, while her image seemed to stare back at him from the glass of the carriage window.

He had eventually agreed not to go straight back to that farm, yet as the image faded from the window he knew his answer would have been very different had it been Laura was injured.

Even so he had agreed only not to visit that farmer today, tomorrow was another matter . . . as the swine would discover.

Reaching for his bag as the train pulled into the station, he stepped down on to the quiet platform pretty with boxes of late summer flowers. He had first seen *her* on a station platform. A girl in grey coat and bonnet, pale golden hair peeping beneath it and eyes, when she looked up at him, eyes like vivid blue gem stones, eyes he saw every night when he went to his bed, eyes that kept him awake to the small hours.

And he had seen her again today coming from that farm track, stumbling along, her hand covered in blood. His heart had seemed to stop beating as he caught sight of that blood.

The memory still raw in his mind, he passed a hand across his brow. If it had been her own . . .

'Carriage, Mr Travers, sir?'

'What?' Lost in his own thoughts, Rafe looked blankly at the smiling man collecting his ticket.

'A carriage, sir. Will you be wanting the hansom to Ladywood or is your own a comin' for you?'

'A hansom . . .' Rafe returned the smile of the station attendant he had known from boyhood. 'Yes, I will require the hansom if it is still here.'

'It still be here, Mr Travers, it waits for this last train.'

Giving his thanks once more to the man who was station master, ticket collector and porter at the small station, he gave the driver of the hansom his instructions.

He would not dine at home this evening, he had no taste for being alone, thoughts had too strong a habit of being his company since first meeting that girl.

On the steps of the Periwig Club the liveried doorman effected a respectful bow. Inside the chandelier-lit reception hall a footman, in pale green velvet heavy with gold braid, smiled beneath an elaborate powdered wig.

'A gentleman asked after you a little while ago, sir, a Mr Innes.

He said he would wait an hour and if you had not come into the club by the end of it he . . .'

'Where is he now?' Shrugging out of his coat Rafe glanced towards the dining room.

'He is not a member, sir.' The footman draped the coat expertly over one arm. 'Therefore I asked him to be seated in the visitors' room. Will I ask him to join you?'

'No need.' Rafe turned in the opposite direction. 'I will join him there, and we will dine later.'

'There you are, Travers, I was about to give up on you.'

Shaking the hand extended as he entered the room, Rafe smiled. 'I got held up, remind me to tell you about it later. You got my telegraph?'

'Yes.' Greville Innes tapped a pocket of his jacket. 'Three o'clock this afternoon, are you sure it's on?'

'Something must be.' Sinking to a chair Rafe rang a small silver handbell, ordering two glasses of Madeira from the answering footman. 'Why would my informant tell me otherwise?'

Greville Innes shrugged his shoulders. 'Contacts have been known to prove false.'

Waiting until the wine was served and the footman withdrawn, Rafe answered.

'Not this one, not so far at least. I have no reason to doubt him this time. We have no way of being certain this is what we are after but . . .'

'But you never know if you never try.' A glance more grey than blue watched Rafe over the rim of the glass. 'Let us hope our efforts bear fruit, that I get what I want and you get what you want.'

What did he want? Touching his glass to that of his visitor Rafe glanced at the clear red wine, but his eyes saw only a small frightened face framed with golden hair, a lovely mouth trembling beneath crystal-blue eyes that shimmered beneath a film of tears, and silently he drank to what he wanted.

Chapter Twenty-Eight

Some swine had whipped his little wench!

Sat on the deck of the narrowboat, one hand resting on the neck of his dog, Jem Beckett stared across the moonlit heath to where chimney stacks rose tall and black against the sky.

Some bastard of a man had cut his daughter with a whip!

His hand folded in the skin of the animal's neck, bringing a whimper.

It had taken every power of persuasion to turn Sarann from bringing Livvy from that house, but he could see the wench had a home there, that she was happy as she was like to be anywhere without her mother; and that other one, the one come to bring them to Livvy, she had said they must visit on each occasion the boat passed through Wednesbury. In the end Sarann had agreed Livvy should be left where she was, but had cried every step of the way back to the canal.

Tears had not been far from his eyes, neither. He stared harder into the dark-shrouded emptiness. But they were not tears of parting, hard though it had been for him also to leave Livvy behind. Though tears had filled his eyes they had not blinded him; there was a matter to be settled.

An eye for an eye. That had been the teaching of his father, but for Livvy he would take both eyes!

'Kitchener, guard!'

He spoke softly, watching as the bull terrier settled at the door of the hatch. There would be no living creature, human or otherwise, would pass that dog.

That part of his family would be safe 'til his return. His tread light as any cat, he sprang the few feet to the towpath.

Livvy had said she had stuck that farmer with a pitchfork, now she must be made safe. There must be no comeback made on her, no law court to condemn her. The man had got only what he deserved.

Knowing the canal as well as he knew his hand he followed the glittering trail, leaving it where it turned away from Bescot to wind on to Willenhall.

Crossing the fields at a quick run, using the hedges for cover, he came to the farm gate. The house lay in darkness. Jem waited. There was no bark of a dog, no sound of any sort. The man would be sleeping but would there be another body p'raps watching over him, a wife . . . a son?

But then neither Livvy nor the other wench had mentioned there being a soul other than him about the place.

From deep within the heart of the silent darkness a church clock rang twice. Leaping the gate, avoiding the possibility of its creaking, Jem moved towards the house. Dawn would come with the next striking of the clock. What had to be done must be done quickly.

Lifting the sash of a window that looked on to the yard he slid effortlessly over the sill. Waiting until his vision became accustomed to the new darkness, he guessed at a door that might give on to stairs. An injured man would be in his bed.

The house was empty! Jem left the way he had entered. A hospital? Had the man been taken to hospital, was that why the house was empty?

She had stuck him with a pitchfork . . . in the barn. That was what Livvy had said . . . in the barn; could he still be in there? If he was dead then the charge would be murder, and there had been folk standing in the line would have seen him give her the work for a week.

Drawing breath hard through his nostrils, Jem turned towards the barn. He had to be sure!

'Are you sure you wanted to stay here, Livvy? If you were saying that because you think I will be too much alone here then you must not. I have friends in the street, I will manage well enough. It is not too late, I can bring your parents here before they sail tomorrow.'

Resting on pillows that had been smoothed out for the tenth time, Livvy smiled.

'Laura, for the sake of my mind will you give over fretting. If I've said it once I've said it a dozen times, this is where I want to be. Now that I've seen my mother and her has seen me and knows where I be then I'm satisfied. Had I wanted to be back on the barge then that's where I would be right now, not lying here listening to you blethering on.'

'But you were near heart-broken the night I found you in the brewhouse.'

'Ar, I was.' Livvy nodded. 'I won't even try to argue against that, but that was then and this is now. I miss me mother and father and misses the kids, but I 'ave to learn to live life with broken apron strings, and I want to learn that here, Laura, here with you.'

'Then we will learn together.' Smiling her goodnight, Laura left the tiny bedroom. It has been difficult asking the girl if she truly wanted to remain here, knowing the loneliness that an empty house would bring; but she had had to do it for Livvy's sake as well as her own peace of mind. She knew for herself the pain of missing a parent.

But Livvy had opted to stay. Slipping into her calico night-gown she loosed the hair kept pinned at her neck. They had both assured the girl's parents that they were managing quite well, that they would go on managing. But would they? Pulling a brush slowly through thick strands of hair, Laura thought of the silver shillings she had put into the box kept in the drawer of the dresser. She had hoped that half of them could be kept for train fares, but that hope had already been dashed. Two shillings for the doctor's visit and ninepence for the ointment for Livvy's back had left threepence, and that had been spent on meat to make broth.

That had accounted for one day's earnings. Replacing the brush on the small washstand she climbed into bed. The money paid for the second day would go the same way; Livvy must have proper care, even supposing it meant she walk to Winson Green prison.

Turning off the lamp she stared at the darkness that leaped into the room. Walk some ten miles? Yes, if she had to! Laura answered her own question with determination. Nothing would keep her from visiting her father, only this time there would be no help from Rafe Travers; his quota of good deeds was all used up.

Coming to the door of the barn Jem stood and listened. By the thin light of the moon he could see it stood a few inches ajar. Carelessness? Or was there someone inside? A bloke on the road would never make the mistake of leaving open the door of a barn in which he made a bed for the night, farmers' eyes were sharp and so were their pitchforks.

Pushing the door a few inches further he waited, listening for any sound, and when none came he slipped like a shadow into the barn.

Seconds ticked on, sliding away into the silent blackness, and still Jem waited, tense, wary, poised like a cat with a mouse in its sights.

Minutes later, satisfied no attack would come, that he was alone in the barn, he turned to leave and as he did so the hairs on his neck rose.

Half-turned he froze, the racing of his pulses the only movement of his wiry body. He had heard something. Years of nights
sat on the deck of the narrowboat, with only the moon and a dog
for company, had keened his hearing like a razor's edge.

Fingers inching slowly to the sacking knife kept tucked in his
belt, he held the breath locked in his throat.

Caught in a silence that was almost vibrant, his ears stroked
the quiet darkness, probing, feeling, waiting . . . and then it came
again, but this time the sound was louder, more identifiable.
Drawing out the knife, Jem held the bone haft firmly in one hand,
the other raised palm outward. Whoever was in the barn with him
was in pain, the long drawn-out moan had told him that; but pain
made an animal more dangerous. Jem allowed the breath freedom.
That also went for a man!

'If . . . if you be here to steal then I don't 'ave the preventing
of it.'

The voice came from the well of blackness that was the centre
of the barn. The knife tight in his grip, Jem turned to face it.

'I be injured,' the voice went on, 'I be 'urt bad, help me to my
bed and I'll bring no charge against you.'

Bring no charge! Jem almost laughed at the ludicrousness of
the situation. The man, for it was a man's voice, had said he was
hurt bad, that was an invitation to any thief.

But he was no thief, and if this was the man he sought then it
was he who had a charge to answer.

'In God's name . . . I needs your help!'

In God's name. Jem slipped the knife back into his belt. Then
in God's name he would give it!

'Be there a lamp?'

Loosing a gasp of relief, the voice answered, 'Beside the door,
on your right hand as you comes in.'

Pulling a box of matches from his pocket and striking one,
Jem used the flare of light to locate the paraffin lantern. Touching
the match to its wick he held it on a level above his eyes.

Taking a moment to adjust his vision he glanced about the

barn, following the rim of the pale gleam to where it became lost in shadow.

'Don't stand gawping, get me across to the house.'

The voice had come from the floor. Swinging the lantern in a wide arc Jem saw a figure lying face down on the hard-packed earth, a darker stain spread on the back of a dark jacket.

Every instinct telling him to take the figure and choke the very life from it, Jem had to fight with himself to hold on to his self control.

'What happened?' He set the lantern on an upturned barrel.

'I were attacked.' The man moaned again.

'Why would a man attack you, was it another you thought set to rob you?'

'It were no man.'

Jem caught his temper, caging it behind set teeth as he spotted a pitchfork lying inches from the wounded man. Going to him he rolled him on to his back, paying no mind when he shouted with the pain of it.

'It were no man you say, then who?'

'It . . . it were a wench.' The man gasped with the pain of being moved. 'A bloody lying, robbing bitch. I took her on as casual labour, tater picking was what her was paid to do but her half filled every sack with earth . . . but I can't tell you this now, I needs taking to my bed and a doctor calling.'

'I will get you to your bed, but I have my needs as well as you; call it inquisitiveness if you likes, but I needs to know who be the wench stuck you with that pitchfork? For I thinks it be that were used on you.'

'For Christ's sake the telling can wait!'

Meeting the flash of the other man's eyes, Jem smiled.

'Oh, ar, it can wait, it can wait 'til you bleeds to death or 'til some other body comes across you, whichever be the quicker makes no odds to me.'

'The bitch were called Livvy summat or other,' he groaned again, 'I told her I didn't pay for sacks half filled with soil pulled along with them taters. That were when her stuck me with a pitchfork, but her'll pay, I'll see her sent down for a stretch so long her will have forgot what the world be like by the time her gets out! Attempt to murder be a serious crime and that vicious bitch be going to get what her deserves.'

'Maybe the wench were frightened, maybe you struck her.'

Jem's words, spoken so softly, were met with a groan of denial, the man's head shaking.

'I raised no hand to the bitch . . . that fork was stuck into my back and her away with twelve shilling afore I could say Jack Robinson. I been unconscious most of the time since then, now help me to my bed afore I blacks out again.'

'I say it were you was lying.' Jem stared down at the man lying at his feet. 'Same as I says you was the one was vicious. That wench asked only for what her had rightly earned, a twelve shilling you never paid, instead you paid her with a hoss whip, you lashed the girl half senseless; she be going to get what her deserves you says, and so be you, mister . . . so be you!'

'It ain't true . . . it ain't true!'

'It be true all right!' Unable to hold the anger that burned torch-like in every vein, Jem lashed out with his boot. 'The bloody lying, robbing bitch you spoke on be my wench and her ain't never took from nobody in her life; it were you was the liar, you the robber, and when her spoke up you took a whip to her back.'

Seeing the anger in Jem's face the farmer tried to get to his feet, but his legs buckled beneath him and he sprawled to his back.

'Her stuck me with a pitchfork!' he gasped. 'Her stuck me . . .'

'Ar, her stuck you but not hard enough, now her father be here to finish the job.'

Grabbing bales of straw Jem placed them either side of the man watching with staring eyes.

'What . . . what you thinking to do?'

Jem laughed softly. Breaking open another bale he breathed the fragrant aroma as he pushed some beneath the useless legs and more beneath shoulders and head.

'You asked for your bed, but why have yourself dragged across to the house when you can lie just as easy here, after all there be naught sweeter than a bed of soft dry straw; and you will be well warmed against the cold dawn air.'

Dropping the remainder of the straw on to the man's stomach, Jem turned back to the barn door.

Lifting the drum on which the lantern had stood he removed the bung. Returning to the man lying on his straw bed he smiled, then slowly and methodically tipped paraffin over the bales.

'What you doing . . . be you bloody crazy . . . !' Scrabbling at the straw, trying to push it away from his body, the farmer screamed; but Jem carried on throwing the oily liquid over walls and door, spreading it until the drum was empty.

Throwing the drum aside he looked with cold eyes at the whimpering man.

'You should never have done what you did.' The words held no heat of anger but a soft iciness that cut fear into the farmer's soul. 'No man takes a whip to Jem Beckett's wench.'

His eyes keeping to the terrified face he reached for the lantern, flinging it on to the soaked straw.

'Get me out . . . for pity's sake get me out!'

Watching the flames rise blue and gold, dancing their colourful dance of death, listening to their whisperings rise to a roar, Jem stared at the figure writhing in the heart of the glow.

'I have shown you pity,' he said quietly, 'the same pity you would have shown my daughter.'

Half an hour later, the great bowl of the sky already turned to pearl, Jem Beckett walked beside the horse pulling the narrow-boat along the path of water that led past Bescot. Toward the horizon the greyness was relieved by a vivid red glow.

The first of the day's furnace openings?

Clucking softly to the horse, Jem's mouth set in a firm line. That glow came from no steel workings. It came from a funeral pyre, the funeral pyre of a swine who deserved to die.

And in its flames lay Livvy's safety. There would be no charge of attempt of murder brought against her. His wench was safe, there would be no prison cell to lock her away from her mother . . . and no swine of a farmer to whip another man's daughter.

Why had he never thought of it before?

Lying in his bed in the private apartment of the Gallery, Edmund Shaw smiled widely.

It was all so simple . . . so bloody simple! Lord what a dolt he had been; all these weeks when it could have been over in days . . . after all there was no longer any Edwin Hagley to put a spoke in the works, no one who could speak against the venture.

He would do it tomorrow. He turned on to his side, nestling his head more firmly into the pillow.

Shaved and dressed next morning, he took a leisurely breakfast. This was the life he would enjoy from now on, he and Sheldon together.

But they must not be together all the time, Sheldon had warned. The love they shared was frowned upon by society, they did not understand. But soon perhaps they would go to live abroad, in a country more amenable to their preferences; let the Gallery make them enough money to keep them in moderate comfort, then they would leave. Sheldon was so competent, so able. Edmund pushed away from the table. It was he who even now was away somewhere arranging the finer details of a private auction. How much money would that really bring, a thousand, two . . . or would it truly be the three Sheldon predicted?

Three thousand pounds! He walked slowly from the dining room to a smaller room across the landing, seating himself behind an elegant Georgian desk. Could so much profit really be made in one night? And, if so, for how many more nights?

It was no longer a dream, no longer a fantasy. The dream he had dreamed for so long was coming true, he would be the master. But not of any tuppenny-halfpenny engineering works. He was going up in the world, he would take the place more suited to him, a place among the gentry.

Reaching for pen and paper he began to write.

Two hours later he left the solicitor's office, a sworn affidavit in his pocket and next to it the letter he himself had written that morning.

I, Edmund Shaw, do swear and affirm . . .

He smiled. It had been so easy. He had sworn the works belonged solely to Jabez Shaw, showing the letter that backed his claim, a letter seemingly signed by Isaac Cadman. But who could say the signature was a forgery? None but Isaac himself or his daughter, and neither of them was likely to make any accusation; they would not even see the letter.

'What do you think now, Jabez?' Seated alone in a first-class compartment on the train taking him to Wednesbury, he spoke the words with a soft laugh. 'What do you think now of the son you never could like? The son who is about to sell your paltry little life's work!'

Chapter Twenty-Nine

Taking lunch in the Turk's Head Hotel Rafe Travers listened to the men at the next table, wine adding zest and volume to their speech.

'Seems that were the cause of it, knocked the can of paraffin over and then does the same wi' a lantern; bloody careless if you asks me.'

'That be summat you can't say about his dealings wi' his money.' The second man took a long drink from his glass, wiping his lips with the back of his hand. 'Skin a fart for a halfpenny would Farmer Madeley, men standing the line on the Bullen have to be nigh on desperate afore they accepts a day's labour from that one.'

'Well he'll be hiring no more.' The first man drank a little more delicately, holding his glass as his companion refilled them both from a carafe. ''Tis to be hoped the line he be standing don't have the devil as hirer.'

'Serve the bugger right if it do be Old Forktail. After all Madeley would know that one for a fellow, for he played hell with enough folk on this earth.'

'That's right and it ain't wrong!' The first man nodded gravely. 'If he do be in line for a hot reception it'll be no more'n he deserved.'

Farmer Madeley! Rafe was suddenly more attentive. Were

they discussing the man who had whipped Livvy Beckett? He had returned to that farm the next day, determined to give the man the same beating he had given that girl, but he had found only a still-smouldering barn.

'And no more'n he already got.' Lifting his glass the second man grinned over its rim. 'The taters picked from that field weren't the only ones got roasted in that fire, his own two was done to a turn or so I hears.'

'That were the best warming they'll 'ave had in a long time.' His companion spluttered wine over the white cloth. 'His missis buggered off long since and Madeley were too much of a miser to pay a shilling a tumble wi' a doxie, an' there be none willing to give it him for nothing, not wi' a face as ugly as sin and a smell that told you of his coming a mile off.'

Their laughter subsiding, the first man spoke again, his words drifting clearly to Rafe sat in the alcove of the fat-bellied bow window.

'Ar, well mayhap his wife will be back once her gets wind of what happened, but one thing can be said for certain, there'll be no more harvesting on Bescot Farm for this year.'

Bescot Farm! That had been the name painted on that gate. Rafe signalled a waiter, asking that his carriage be brought to the front entrance. The man had perished in a fire caused by his own carelessness. It was not a fate he would have wished upon the man, but then fate was not always given into any man's hand. The Lord had seen fit to punish in His own way.

Outside, the late summer sun had given way to rain. Stepping quickly into the carriage hired from the stables adjoining the railway station he flicked the reins, guiding the horse in the direction of the office of the solicitor handling the affair of the sale of that engineering works. He had received word that all was now ready to proceed, a signed affidavit attesting to the seller's ownership being in the solicitor's possession.

It would be over and done in an hour. Rafe felt the sharp twist to his stomach. In a few minutes from now he would have a valid reason for spending time in this town, there would be no cause for him to fabricate a reason. But he would have done so, and gone on doing it in the hope of meeting Laura Cadman.

He had called twice at that poky little house sandwiched between smoke-blackened replicas of itself, and twice he had been politely received. He clucked quietly to the horse, soothing it as a steam tram rattled noisily past going in the opposite direction. Politely, but not with enthusiasm. His visits were not really wanted, he was a stranger and a stranger's calls at a house sheltering two young women on their own . . .

It did not need more thinking on. Rafe reined the animal to a halt. His visits caused them embarrassment, that being so he should not go there again, but not to see Laura . . . the thought brought another twist, this time to his heart.

Should she buy a half a pound of sausages? If she were quick Mr Hollington might have a few left. The meat sold on his stall in the Shambles was the tastiest in the town, and he always had a smile and word of welcome for her when she called there.

Looking at the few pennies lying in her hand, Laura caught her lower lip between her teeth. The four pennies were the very last left from the money she had earned helping to make jam, ought she to spend it on sausages? Once it was gone how was she to get more? The sensible thing to do was to buy a stale loaf from Purslow's bakery, that would cost only a penny and leave her with enough to buy food tomorrow. But Livvy needed more than dry toast if she were to get well, and at least sausages would give dripping to dip slices of bread into.

The argument resolved she crossed the market square, making her way quickly along the Shambles to butcher Hollington's stall.

The sausages tucked into her basket, she glanced towards the patch of empty heath that lay immediately behind the

Shambles. That was the quicker way home but . . .

Almost at once the memory of that deserted back street in Birmingham rose chokingly to her throat. He had led her deeper and deeper into that maze of narrow streets, further and further from the busy heart of the city and then . . . fear almost live within her drove strongly to Laura's mouth, only her knuckles pressed hard against her lips held it back.

She could not take that way, she must go back to the market square and on home by way of the streets. It would take longer but that would help allay Livvy's suspicions. She had hated lying to the girl by pretending she had found work each day, but it had been the only way to prevent Livvy seeking employment herself and she was not yet well enough for that.

Holding her shawl tight against rain that minutes before had been a mean drizzle but now lanced against her face pricking her skin like needle points, she turned along Lower High Street.

Tomorrow was the day for visiting the prison. Tucked beneath the shawl her fingers closed tight about the one penny left to her. She had hoped to save enough of her second three shillings to pay for a tram ticket, eked it out day by day by buying only those vegetables set aside as waste, and bread that was at least two days old; but without finding a single day's labour her money had gradually dwindled away.

'You here again, me wench?'

Coming to stand at the side entrance to the bakery, Laura caught the eye of the baker. White twill apron reaching to his boots, face and hands covered in a fine film of white dust that clung to his lashes and side whiskers, he looked as if he had been rolled in flour.

'Do you have a penny loaf, please?'

Glancing at the girl, rain sliding long fingers over a face pale and drawn from hunger, the man shook his head.

'The stale 'uns all went hours ago.'

Disappointment that was almost despair blocking her

throat, Laura drew the shawl closer as she turned away.

'Hold up, wench!' the baker called after her. 'I said as the stale 'uns was all gone, I d'ain't say as I had no loaf at all.'

Catching up to Laura the baker shoved a loaf into her basket, shaking his head as she held out the penny.

'You take that penny up to Maggie Connell in the market place and get yourself some nice fat taters. Roasted in the ashes of the fire they will make a few fine hot suppers.'

'Thank you . . . thank you very much.'

Eyes brilliant with tears, Laura tried to smile.

'Ain't no need for thanks, wench, just you get along and do as I says then off home outta this rain.'

Tears blinding her eyes she turned from the bakery. Stepping into the road, she was halfway across before she heard the shout of a passing carter. Half turning in its direction, rain and tears robbing her of vision, the clatter of wheels and horses' hooves, the shouts of people drumming in her ears, she threw up a hand as the steam tram lumbered down on her.

Looking down at the figure laid on the plain wooden settle, Rafe Travers felt the pulses still race in his body. He had hoped to find a legitimate excuse to see Laura Cadman again, hoped to find a way he might speak with her, but not this way . . . Christ not this way!

Unaware of the emotions that danced across his features, the volumes revealed in his fine eyes he glanced at Livvy.

'I think the doctor . . .'

'No!' Lowering her feet to the floor Laura sat up, fighting the wave of dizziness threatening to draw her down again. 'I have no need of a doctor, I am not hurt.'

'And that's a miracle!' Anxiety making her answer tart, Livvy spoke sharply. 'You might have been killed. What on earth were you doing crossing that road without looking, don't you have more sense than that!'

'I should have been more careful, Livvy, I know that, but I was in a hurry to get home.'

'That hurry nearly got you to your maker!'

The brusque reply masking her true feelings, Livvy turned to the fireplace.

'Well, if you won't have the doctor, you'll have some hot tea. Will you take a cup, Mr Travers?'

Reluctantly Rafe drew his glance from Laura, resting it instead on the slight brown-haired girl filling a teapot from the bubbling kettle. He wanted to stay, Lord knows he wanted to stay, but it was not seemly, tongues wagged in any district; rich or poor there were always those ready with a wicked tongue.

'No, no thank you, Miss Beckett,' he answered, taking up the soft leather gloves he had snatched off and thrown on to the table after carrying Laura into the house. 'If you are sure I cannot help in any way, then I must leave. However,' he turned back to Laura, 'I am staying the night in Wednesbury and will call tomorrow, if I may; I would like to reassure myself you are truly unhurt.'

Feeling the warm flush creep to her cheeks, somehow unable to meet that glance, Laura kept her eyes on the hands she had clutched together in her lap.

'I will not be home tomorrow,' she said quietly, 'it is the day I visit my father.'

'He is still there, in Winson Green prison?'

Shyness fading as quickly as it had formed, Laura lifted her head, her eyes meeting his holding no trace of shame.

'Yes, Mr Travers, my father is still in that prison, and will be for fifteen years.'

Whatever the man had done, whatever his crime, Laura Cadman loved her father, it shone in her eyes, throbbed in her voice. If only she could love him the same way.

Surprised by the thought Rafe turned quickly, afraid that what he had just realised might show on his face. Livvy at his back he walked to the door, then turned to face Laura once more.

'Miss Cadman.' He hesitated momentarily, lost for a way of putting what he wanted to say, then as she looked across to him went on, 'Miss Cadman, I shall be returning to Birmingham myself tomorrow. If you would do me the honour of travelling with me in my carriage I would be happy to take you to Winson Green.'

It would save her hours of walking, and this man had helped her several times without even touching her or saying an embarrassing word to her.

'Thank you, Mr Travers.' Laura felt the smile curve her mouth. 'I will be happy to travel with you.'

Hours later, shawls draped over calico night-gowns, chairs drawn close to the last of the fire, both girls sipped cups of steaming cocoa.

'But you don't know him, Laura,' Livvy voiced her concern, 'so how can you say you will be happy to travel with him?'

Her glance on the glowing embers, Laura seemed to feel again the arms that had lifted her into that carriage, the voice that had cracked as it whispered her name.

'No, I suppose I don't know him, but I trust him.' She smiled, holding the tenderness of his arms deep in her heart. 'I will be safe with him, Livvy, I know I will.'

'Hmmph!' Livvy snorted. 'You would be better off taking the train. You do realise you will pay almost as much for a single ticket getting the train back as you would for the return journey . . .'

The swift turn of Laura's head stopping her in full flow, Livvy laid her cup aside.

'. . . Laura, you do 'ave the money to buy a ticket?'

The shock of being almost caught in the path of the tram, the strange emotions caused by Rafe Travers' arms about her, was suddenly all too much. She had not the strength to lie again. Her glance still on the crimson coals, she shook her head.

'Oh, Laura, you should 'ave said!' Livvy was on her knees, her arms about Laura's waist. 'You spent all that money getting food for me, you shouldn't 'ave done that . . . it's my fault you can't go to see your father . . .'

'It is not your fault!' Laying her own cup down so sharp as to send cocoa dribbling a brown stain the length of the prettily patterned cup, Laura caught the girl's head between her hands, forcing it upward. 'I spent that money the way *I* wanted to.'

'But I didn't need the doctor to call twice!'

'That too was for me to decide.' Laura answered the protest firmly. 'I was taking no risk of those cuts becoming infected.'

'But now you ain't got the money to get you to the prison.'

Looking into brown eyes bright with guilt and concern, Laura smiled comfortingly, dropping a kiss on the other girl's brow before releasing her.

'No, I do not have the money to purchase a train ticket, but then with Mr Travers' offer I do not need one.'

'Oh no?' Returned to her chair, Livvy stared at her friend. 'Then how be you to get home again, walking?'

'Yes.' Laura nodded. 'That is exactly what I shall do.'

'But you can't!' Livvy gasped unbelievingly. 'You remember what happened that last time you walked through them streets, you can't risk that again!'

Yes, she remembered. Remembered every time she turned a darkened street corner, every night she lay in her bed; she would never forget being thrown to the floor, that hand fumbling beneath her clothes, the smell of that man's breath as he tried to rape her. It still brought terror to her soul, but it would not prevent her visiting her father.

'I will not forego the chance of seeing my father.'

'Then I shall go with you!'

Gathering both cups Livvy carried them into the scullery, washing them with a clatter that told of her own determination.

It was sweet of Livvy. Lying in her bed, Laura watched rain clouds scud against the moon. But they could not take advantage of Rafe Travers' offer, he could not be expected to take them both. When he called tomorrow she would make some excuse, refuse his offer of a lift to the prison.

Yes, it was sweet of Livvy to say she would go with her, but the sweetness was dulled by the knowledge she would not after all have the pleasure of being with Rafe Travers.

Sat on the late evening train returning him to Edgbaston Edmund touched a hand to the pocket that held the letter he had written that morning. He had often practised copying both Jabez and Isaac's style of writing, practising over and over in the privacy of his room at Squire's Walk, telling himself he could never tell when the need to forge either or both hands might arise. That practice had stood him in good stead. It would take a sharp eye to detect the flaw. Even had that solicitor been well used to Isaac Cadman's hand he would have been unable to say with certainty the letter of was not written by him. But Lawyer Messiter was not familiar with Isaac Cadman's handwriting, nor had he given more than a cursory reading to that letter. Accepting the affidavit he had completed the transaction and Travers had paid over a cheque for two thousand five hundred pounds for the works and all the machinery along with it.

Two thousand five hundred. Edmund stared through the window to the darkened landscape. Together with what he had got for the house he had four thousand pounds. Only months ago that would have represented a fortune, promised a life he would have been satisfied to live; but now it meant almost nothing. He had seen how Melville and the others lived, tasted their world, and four thousand would not even buy him the dregs.

He was still a thousand pounds short of the initial down payment. But an auction would solve that, the kind of auction held at the Gallery would solve all of his problems.

Nodding to the conductor who had politely announced their imminent arrival at the small Ratton Park Station, Edmund touched his hand once more to the pocket that held letter and cheque. That auction would swell the amount he had to near enough six, maybe seven thousand. More than enough to settle with Melville, and after that . . . ? Alighting from the train Edmund hailed the one hansom the station boasted, giving the address of the Gallery. After that it would be no time before his creditors were paid, and the Gallery his.

Chapter Thirty

'Mrs Griffiths said to tell you there would be half a crown in it for you.'

Two shillings and sixpence for scrubbing out the store room. Laura looked at the tousle-headed lad who had brought her Mary Ann Griffiths' message.

'Did Mrs Griffiths say anything else?'

Alfie Bailey sniffed, his freckled nose wrinkling at the effort.

'Her said as it 'ad to be done today, afore the fresh supplies was brought around four o'clock.'

Glancing at the clock ticking rheumatically above the fireplace she noted the time, it was a quarter to three. It was too late to start scrubbing now, she had to leave at once if she was to reach that prison by visiting time and it would be after five before she left again.

'Her said to come right away in case the deliveries be earlier, her says they does that sometimes.'

Two shillings and sixpence! Laura nibbled her lip uncertainly. It was half as much again as Mary Ann would need to pay to have the store room scrubbed, the woman was being kind, and that money would buy food for two weeks if she were careful. But she could not disappoint her father, once a month was all the chance they had to see each other and she would not forego it.

'Alfie,' she looked at the lad stood waiting for her answer. 'Tell Mrs Griffiths thank you, but I cannot do the work today. Tell her I am going to see my father.'

'Can't do what work?'

Livvy had come in from the brewhouse. Stood in the doorway she had heard Laura say she could not work.

'Mrs Griffiths wants the store room scrubbed out afore they takes in fresh stuff.' Alfie had the words out while Laura was still thinking how to reply.

'It is no use, Livvy, I must be at the prison for four o'clock. It does not leave me time to scrub that room now, and Alfie says it must be finished by four so I cannot even do it when I get back.'

'How much be her willing to pay?'

'Half a crown.' It was Alfie spoke again.

'Half a crown! To scrub one room.'

'I know.' Laura heard the amazement in the other girl's voice and nodded. 'Mary Ann is offering far more than she need do, if only it had been tomorrow she wanted the job done, I . . .'

A knock at the front door interrupting her she glanced quickly at Livvy. 'That will be him, please would you answer the door.'

Hearing the deep melodious voice answer Livvy's higher pitched one she glanced at the boy, his own gaze turned inquisitively towards the parlour.

'Tell Mrs Griffiths what I said, and be sure to thank her . . .'

Brown-toffee eyes swinging back to her, the boy drew his brows together in a frown of incredulity.

'You ain't turnin' 'alf a crown down! Bugger me . . . 'alf a crown . . .'

'Alfie!' Laura answered sharply. 'The soap I have for scrubbing floors works equally well on boys' tongues.'

'Sorry, Missis Laura.' His frown disappearing the lad dropped his head. 'It . . . it were just that . . . well, 'alf a crown, it be a fortune.'

'And who is short-sighted enough to turn down a fortune?'

Unaware of the man watching them Laura swung around, colour sweeping into her cheeks.

'It be Missis Laura,' the boy answered, no hint of intimidation in his voice as he turned to look at the tall figure, seeing a half-smile playing about the mouth. 'Her's been offered 'alf a crown to scrub Henry Griffiths' store room, that be a fortune, mister, and her's turned it down though her needs it bad.'

'Alfie!' Laura's colour deepened. 'Please go tell Mrs Griffiths I am sorry, I appreciate her kindness but . . .'

'So what about Livvy, her don't 'ave to go to no prison, why can't her do the scrubbin'?'

The lad did not give up easily. His bright glance quizzical he looked squarely at the two women. The only thing would satisfy him was a full explanation, but she could not explain, not in front of this man watching with keen eyes.

'I *am* going to that prison today.' Livvy caught the boy by the shoulders, shunting him towards the scullery door. 'Laura will need someone to walk home with.'

'Walk home?' The deep voice cut across the kitchen. 'Did I hear you say Miss Cadman intends walking home?'

The flush on her face now as red as the coals slumbering in the grate Laura reached for her shawl, using the draping of it about her shoulders to disguise the flurry of her nerves. She could have been already gone before he came to the house but that was a route she would not follow. She would not answer kindness with rudeness.

'Mr Travers, I . . .' she stumbled, finding the words difficult to say. 'I thank you for your offer to take me to Winson Green but . . . but Livvy and I . . .'

'Will walk?' The half-smile faded, leaving his mouth a tight line. 'Have you any idea how far it is to that prison?'

'It be a good way don't it, mister?' Alfie wriggled free of the restraining hands.

'Quite a good way,' Rafe Travers agreed, looking at Laura.

'Too far for a woman to walk and much too far for her to walk back.'

'Livvy and I will manage.'

'Am I having yet another of my good turns thrown back at me?'

Looking up quickly Laura's heart tripped at the sight of those clear grey eyes regarding her now, amusement gleaming in their depths.

'Please don't think that.'

'Then what am I to think?' The amused gleam faded. 'You prefer to walk such a distance rather than ride with me, that has to tell a man something. You now refuse an offer you accepted yesterday evening. What am I to think except you find my company unwelcome.'

'Laura don't think no such thing . . .'

It was Livvy now joining in, her tone sharp with protestation. '. . . her decided to walk because of me.'

Rafe Travers looked at the younger girl, waiting for her to go on.

'I said I would not let Laura walk all that way back, not after . . .' She hesitated hearing Laura's quick gasp. '. . . well anyway I said that if her was to walk back to Wednesbury then I was going to walk with her!'

'But why should she walk back?'

''Cos her ain't got the money to buy a train ticket nor a tram ticket neither. I knows 'cos I heard Henry Griffiths tell 'is missis as much!' Alfie skipped sideways avoiding the swipe of Livvy's hand.

'Alfie.' Her face burning, Laura felt mortified. She did not want this man to know their circumstances. 'Alfie, please go tell Mrs Griffiths what I ask.'

Gathering the shreds of her dignity she lifted her glance as Livvy bundled the lad out into the yard, closing the scullery door firmly behind him.

Her glance unwavering as it met those grey eyes once more, she spoke with quiet pride.

'Mr Travers, neither Livvy nor I would take advantage of your kindness. We felt we could not ask that both of us ride with you, that is the reason we shall walk.'

Part of what she said was true. Rafe Travers continued to hold her gaze. This girl would never take advantage, not of him, not of anyone. But the true reason for her being determined to walk so far lay in what that boy had blurted out. She did not have the means to purchase a ticket. Sliding his glance to Livvy he gave a slight bow.

'Forgive my rudeness, Miss Beckett, in not inviting you to share my carriage last evening, had I known you wished to accompany . . .'

'I didn't, not then anyway,' Livvy said quickly. 'But I couldn't be here thinking of Laura coming back, the streets don't be all that safe for a woman on her own.'

'I agree, Livvy. But Miss Cadman would not be alone, neither would she be walking. I will of course see her back home, you too if you will allow it.'

'Mr Travers, there is really no need . . .'

'You would bring Laura home?' Livvy ignored Laura's protest.

'But of course.' Rafe Travers too ignored it.

'Then I could go scrub the Griffiths' store room.'

'No.'

This time Laura turned, her head already shaking.

'But it would be perfect, Laura, you can get to see your father and be brought back safe and sound, and I could do that job for Mary Ann.'

'Perhaps Miss Cadman feels she would not be safe and sound with me.'

Grey eyes swung to her. Amusement or accusation? Laura could not define which caused their gleam.

'That is not so,' she answered truthfully.

'In that case, the choice lies with Miss Beckett.' He smiled at Livvy, a deep honest smile that had her instantly in his hand. 'Will you come or will you stay?'

'I'll go scrub that floor.' Livvy grinned.

'But your back!' Laura tried again, but again her protest was brushed aside.

'My back be healing nicely, a bit of scrubbing will do it no harm; and Mr Travers,' she looked at the face still wreathed with a smile, 'if . . . if it don't be impolite or anything . . . if . . . if you would like there will be a supper waiting when you gets back.'

The smile dying away, taking with it all trace of amusement from his grey gaze, Rafe Travers repeated the slight bow given earlier and when he answered his voice held a deep respect.

'It is not impolite, Miss Beckett, and I would like, I would like very much.'

They did need that half-crown, they needed it very much, but she would still rather walk home alone than have Rafe Travers wait to take her back.

What must he have thought . . . still be thinking? Laura felt the blush tingle in her cheeks.

What Alfie had said had been nothing if not true, but to blurt it out as he had . . . and Livvy, she had been so quick to follow it up, to suggest she take on the job of scrubbing out the store room.

She could have flatly refused. Laura glanced about the large square room, windows set high along the bare grey-painted walls, its doors locked and barred. She could have said she did not want him to bring her to this prison. That would have settled matters, he would offer no more good turns had she been firm; she would not have been bothered by him again.

The thought struck like a blow, and it took a moment before Laura realised a woman who stood at her side was speaking to her.

'I looked for you on the Soho train. I thought as p'raps you wasn't visitin' this month.'

'I did not travel by train,' Laura answered, her mind still partly dazed by the thought that had leapt so quickly into it.

'That were obvious enough!' The woman's reply was terse and Laura realised she felt snubbed.

'I was offered a lift by a . . . a friend.'

'I know, I seen his carriage.' The woman smiled, placated by her own supposition. 'Ain't no other woman 'ere a toff would be seen dead with let alone drive her in his own carriage. Christ did you ever hear the like! Driven to Winson Green in a private carriage, now I've seen everythin'! You must 'ave that one by the tackle, me wench, so squeeze it 'ard, take the bugger for as much as you can get afore he kicks your arse!'

The woman laughed, a harsh cackling sound that played on Laura's nerves, and she was glad when the woman turned her attention to a middle-aged, gaunt-looking woman to her other side.

Coming here in that carriage must have drawn everyone's attention, set every tongue talking; what when they found it waiting for her when the visiting time was over . . . how many remarks would be passed when next she came, and that time by train or tram as the rest of the women did?

She should have been firm, she should have told him she did not want him to bring her here!

But that was a lie. The thought as stunning as before, Laura held the breath tight in her mouth. She had wanted it, deep down she had wanted to be with him, and deep down she realised she would always want to be with Rafe Travers.

The rattle of keys and the increased buzz of voices cleared the thoughts from her mind and she was thankful to let them go, as she would be thankful to see him go. The man had shown her kindness, she must not let her silly imagination present it as anything more than that.

At the further end of the room a pair of double doors swung

wide. Two uniformed warders, heavy wooden cudgels in hand, led prisoners flanked by yet more warders into the grey dismal space, no chair or table offering hospitality. It was not the aim of Her Majesty's prisons to make their inmates comfortable.

Laura watched the line of silent men shuffle into the room. She had not been told whether her father was still in the infirmary, the guard at the gate being one she had not seen before he had not wanted to hear her enquiry, only telling her brusquely to 'get on to the visitors' room or get out of it altogether, there be folk other than you wants to pass inside'.

Her father must be in the infirmary, where else with a broken leg? That meant valuable minutes wasted while waiting to be taken to him.

Scanning each face as men filed into the room, seeing the light leap into dead eyes as they spotted their womenfolk, hearing the cries of those women as they elbowed through to their men, Laura could not prevent emotion clogging her throat.

Her father was not here. She turned to look for a warder who might have helped on her last visit, then turned back as a thin voice called her name.

Teeth sinking painfully into her lower lip she stared at the shrunken figure, a crude wooden crutch under each arm. What had happened to him . . . what was it had him looking so dreadful, was he ill, in pain?

'Laura.'

He spoke the name again, inching himself towards her, one leg dragging along the cold stone floor.

'Father . . . Oh, Father!'

Her reply a sob Laura flew to him, wrapping her arms about his wasted shoulders, holding him as their tears mingled.

Releasing him at last she dabbed at her cheeks with her handkerchief.

'I will ask for a chair . . .'

'No.' Isaac shook his head. 'Don't waste what bit o' time we have, the answer will be no.'

'But Father, you cannot be expected to stand, your leg . . .'

'What I can't expect be treatment different to any other prisoner.' Isaac's tired smile met his daughter's protestation, and when she would have gone on with it said, 'Tell me how you've been, you have kept well?'

Feeling her heart lurch with each shadow of half-hidden pain that crossed his face Laura spoke quickly, telling him only of the good things like getting Mary Bailey freed from the police station, and the jam making she had so enjoyed, leaving out any mention of Edmund's threat or of Livvy being whipped.

'But you, Father, why are you here and not in the infirmary?' she finished, looking anxiously into eyes that had once been bright and alert but now seemed so desolate.

'There be work even a man with a broken leg can do.'

He leaned against the grey-painted bricks, letting them support what little weight he had left. 'A prisoner capable of moving hand or foot has to move them, he has to do work of one kind or another, he is not left to lie abed.'

'But surely anyone can see you are not . . .'

'Anyone can see the delight I have in my little wench,' Isaac interrupted again. 'Oh Laura child, it be so good to see you, to touch you, your coming be all I longs for, all I wants.'

But not me. Laura fought the surge of tears rising chokingly into her throat. It is not all I want, I want your freedom . . . I want Edmund Shaw to say your stealing was a lie.

Edmund! Laura looked with new, even more frightened eyes at the man leaning against the wall, the skin stretched over sunken cheeks was almost yellow, the lines about his eyes seeming to have been scored by a knife. Was Edmund the reason he looked so ill, had Edmund been here to threaten him with a new trial, a trial for murder?

'Has . . . has Edmund been to visit? I . . . I have not seen him here.'

Seeing the flash of pain cross his haggard features Laura felt guilty for the asking, but she knew her father would not tell her if she did not ask; he would keep it to himself for fear of causing her yet more heartache.

'You wouldn't see him, me wench.' Isaac eased the crutches more comfortably beneath his arms. 'Men visitors don't be allowed same day as women. It be policy of the Governor. He reckons if a fight broke out women couldn't be harmed if they wasn't here, but judging by the looks of some o' these they could give any man a run for his money.'

Meeting the wan fleet smile that died almost as it was born, Laura answered, 'They do look formidable but most of them are kind hearted, though I think as you do, a man accosting one of them would go home with more than one black eye.'

For a wild moment she felt those hands pawing at her breasts, tugging at her clothes.

'Laura . . . Laura wench!' Isaac's voice was anxious. 'Be you all right? Edmund Shaw, he ain't threatened you?'

Forcing the memory away, Laura shook her head. 'I have not seen or heard from Edmund.' It was a deliberate lie but then she was prepared to do far more than lie to protect her father against more worry. 'Have you, Father?'

Shifting again on his crutches he answered with a sadness she found strange.

'No, no I've seen or heard nothing of Edmund Shaw.'

He had not yet made good his threat. But the paper, the one he had thrown into the fire, why had he changed his mind about its being signed, and what had he meant by saying Friday would be too late?

Thoughts whipped through her mind demanding answers, yet not waiting to receive them. That had been three weeks ago, three weeks in which she had waited for Sergeant Potts to show on her doorstep, to hear her father was to answer a charge of murder. But Edmund had not brought that charge, not yet . . . though he would not give up the idea, he was biding his time. But why . . . ?

The shrill blast of a whistle cut over the animated buzz of

conversation and at a stroke men began to file like so many automata back through the wide double doors.

'Laura wench, don't cry . . .'

His own voice pulsing with sobs, Isaac kissed the face of the daughter he could not hold without losing his balance.

'. . . don't cry, my little wench, I won't be able to stand it if you cries.'

'I . . . I'm not crying, Father.' Through the thick veil of tears Laura looked at his face, the pain of standing for an hour combined with that of their parting painting the yellow skin as grey as those empty walls.

'You'll come again next month . . . you will come?'

A second, longer, more commanding blast of the whistle followed by a shout from the guard that blew it drowned her words, but Laura's eyes told them as clearly as ever her voice could.

'Yes, Father . . . yes I will come.'

Chapter Thirty-One

She had not spoken on the way back from the prison, sobbing quietly the whole time.

Rafe Travers fastened the buttons of his plain dark waistcoat.

He had waited for her as he had said he would. She had not emerged in the mainstream of visitors and he was already out of the carriage and halfway to those tall gates when she had come out.

Her head had been bent almost to her chest, a hand to her mouth.

Rafe's fingers tightened, becoming awkward as they strung the chain of his gold pocket watch through a buttonhole of his waistcoat, an echo of the fear that had surged through him then surging through him now.

Was it something to do with her father, had something happened to him in that prison . . . or to her? The blood had run cold in his veins at the thought, she would not be the first young woman to be propositioned behind those walls.

He had helped her into the carriage, having to accept the shake of her head that said nothing had happened; but the trembling of her slight body as his hands had touched her seemed to say otherwise.

But he had not pressed her, nor had he touched her again though he had wanted to.

He reached for his jacket, slipping his arms into the sleeves.

God how he had wanted to! It had taken all he had not to take her in his arms, to kiss away the tears, but that would have been unforgivable. Instead he had driven her back to Great Western Street, leaving her with Livvy.

He had intended to have supper with them both, had looked forward to it, but his presence in that house could only have been an embarrassment to Laura Cadman.

But he would visit that house again. It would simply be observing good manners to do so, to ask if Miss Cadman were recovered and to offer his help in any way they might ask.

Leaving the house Rafe looked out over the slight rise of Squire's Walk to the smoke-grimed houses of the town at its foot.

His business in this town was done. The house he intended to sell on; the small engineering business he had bought, it was all signed and settled. There was no more need for him to stay, a manager could oversee the employment of men and the running of the works.

But he would stay for a while yet. He turned towards the stables.

And yes he would visit that house again, but the call would not be prompted by simply good manners. For a brief moment he seemed to feel that soft young body tremble against him as it had when he had helped her into the carriage.

Good manners were one thing, but it was not good manners had his insides in a vice.

Climbing into the carriage harnessed ready for him, he guided it from the yard.

Miss Cadman!

Rafe's lips came together in a determined line. He did not want to tell her that. He wanted to call her Laura, and help was not all he wanted to offer her.

'They say he be going to set the place gooin' agen.'

Stood in line on the High Bullen, Laura listened to the talk of the men around her.

'Folk says a lot o' things as has no substance.' A second voice sounded disconsolate. 'I'll believe that works be startin' up agen when that theer new owner gives me a job, though I reckon that'll never be for he ain't showed his face on the Bullen yet.'

'That be right you knows, Joby, that bloke ain't took no men on as I've 'eard tell.'

Shawl pulled well over her head, Laura listened to the conversation flitting between the men. They were speaking of Shaw and Cadman. Edmund had sold it, sold the property half of which rightfully belonged to her father!

'That be as it might,' the first man answered testily, 'but you don't 'ear everythin', Meshac Timmins. I been told, and by a reliable source, that that theer new owner be in that works most every day sortin' and a sizin', and that same source reckons that any day now that works will be openin' its doors.'

'Ar, it will,' the disconsolate voice replied. 'It will open its doors to carry out jigs an' tools, not to let men in. You be daft for listenin' to such tales, Joby Clines, daft as the bloke who be tellin' 'em.'

A new owner! Laura pulled the shawl closer about her shoulders, shivering against the cold morning air. How would she tell her father . . . how did you tell a man his life's work was gone?

She had vowed that money would be paid back, promised herself in the dark reaches of her sleepless nights that somehow the debt to Edmund would be repaid and somehow the works would be given back to her father.

But in all the weeks since her father's imprisonment she had not managed to save a penny; if it were not for Livvy she would have gone hungry for most of those weeks. To repay Edmund. Empty words, empty promises! She would never be able to repay.

'There will be something soon, there has to be work of some sort needs doing, we just has to wait, that's all!'

They had returned home together and now Livvy poured boiling water into a basin already a quarter filled with cold. Coughing as steam curled into her nostrils she stood the kettle on the hob.

'Me mother always says "everything comes to him who waits".'

Smiling she turned towards the stairs but, as she ran quickly to Laura's bedroom, the smile faded. 'Only him as waits too long gets nothing,' she murmured, catching up the white calico night-gown from the foot of the single narrow bed.

Downstairs she bustled about the kitchen though her mind played over the fact that the last of the two shillings and sixpence was spent yesterday, and neither she nor Laura had managed to find work.

'How can I tell him, Livvy?' The heat of the water on her foot doing little to drive away the cold of what she had heard those men say, Laura looked with hopeless eyes at her friend.

'You don't have to tell him!' Teapot in hand, Livvy answered firmly. 'Least not yet you don't. By all you tells me, that father of your'n has enough on his plate at the moment, why give him more to cope with? Bad news gets no worse for the keeping.'

No, it could get no worse. Watching the deft movements of Livvy's hands Laura could not lift the despair that sat like a stone in her heart.

But neither did it seem to get any better. It wanted no more than a week to the time she could visit Winson Green again and, as before, there was no money with which she could purchase train or tram ticket.

She had not a penny, while Edmund . . . he had sold the works, sold it and never offered her father so much as a shilling from the proceeds.

Laura took the cup offered by Livvy, clasping her fingers about the warm china.

How could she ever have thought she loved him? Staring into

the creamy brown depths of the tea, she seemed to see a boy's face smile up at her, a hand reach towards her.

Edmund Shaw had not always been the man he was now.

'Drink that tea then get yourself out of them damp things and into your night-gown, it will do no harm for you to eat supper in your night clothes.'

Looking up as Livvy broke in on her reverie, Laura sipped from the cup.

'We . . . we could have visitors, how would it look to anyone calling to find me in my night-gown?'

Bending to the slow oven Livvy pressed the tip of one finger to the potatoes she had placed there earlier in the day. How would it look to anyone? But it was not anyone Laura was thinking of, it was one man, it was Rafe Travers. She had said almost nothing of him since that time he had taken her to the prison, but somehow Livvy knew that was not the case with her thoughts. She had tried bringing him into their conversations, but each time Laura shut it out, each time refusing to speak of the man who seemed only too ready to help her.

Could that be the reason? Using the toe of her boot, Livvy swung the plate door of the oven shut. Did his quick offers worry Laura . . . did she think some motive other than help was behind his visits?

Whatever it was, her reception had grown cooler with each call and now they had stopped altogether. Yet with their stopping she had not seemed relieved, just the opposite; Laura had been, if possible, more depressed.

'There be nothing wrong in being caught downstairs in your night-gown . . . it's being caught without one a girl need worry about.'

'Livvy Beckett, you surprise me sometimes. Really, the things you say, your mother would be horrified!'

Finishing her tea Laura laid the cup aside, proceeding to dry her feet on the cloth spread over her knees. Warmer now, she managed a smile.

Slipping bare feet into her boots she picked up the basin of water, carrying it outside into the yard and emptying it into the shallow drain that ran between the houses.

Refilling the bowl she placed it on the hearth before turning to the girl busying herself with plates and knives and forks.

'Your turn, Livvy, your feet were as wet as mine, and no arguing . . . !' She met the other girl's denial before it could be made. 'Neither of us can afford to take the influenza, so do as you are told, I can finish preparing supper.'

Dressed in night-gowns, shawls tucked comfortingly about their shoulders, their feet resting on the hearth, both women sat staring into the fire.

It had been worse than usual standing the line today. The wind had been bitingly cold, the touch of rain freezing against their faces, but most miserable of all had been the looks of desolation passing over the faces of men as they had been passed by for work, the look that told of yet another night their women and children would go to bed with naught but hunger in their stomachs.

Was her father being given enough to eat? He had looked so thin and ill, his face grey with . . . with what? Hunger, illness . . . or mistreatment? Each time she visited he looked more tired, more ill, were those people at the prison ill-treating him?

He had virtually dragged himself along on those crutches, the foot of his broken leg scraping the floor. A fall they had told her, but had it been a fall?

'I'll fetch the coal from the outside in the mornin' and then I'll have a look about the town, there 'as to be work of a sort somewhere. It seems useless to stand the line, there's been nothing from there in over a week and we be down to our last crust, 'sides which you'll be needing the means of getting to Brummagem.'

The means of getting to Birmingham. Laura felt the tug of depression. It was like looking for a rose in winter . . . an impossibility.

'You shouldn't 'ave been so quick to say no to Rafe Travers' offer.' Livvy turned to making the evening cocoa. 'It would 'ave been a certain sure way of getting to Winson Green.'

'I cannot take advantage of the man's good nature.' Laura glanced away from the other girl's quick eyes.

'He wouldn't offer if he didn't mean it, and it ain't as if you don't need help.'

'I know he meant it, Livvy, but I would hate for him to feel he had any sort of obligation.'

Spooning sugar into each cup Livvy added a drop of milk, mixing the contents to a creamy paste.

'What do you mean . . . obligation?'

'I mean Rafe Travers does not seem a man to turn his back, no matter how often his help is asked; he would give it even supposing his own life-style were to suffer. I will not be the one to cause that, Livvy, I prefer to make my own way.'

'Even if that way be to walk to Brummagem and back,' Livvy grumbled beneath her breath.

If only circumstances were different . . . if she had met Rafe Travers some other way . . . but it would have made no differ-ence. Falling silent, Laura stared into the fire. He would not look twice at her were it not for that one simple fact she was a woman in need of assistance.

'You are not even pretty . . .'

The words struck home, each a stabbing blow.

No, he would not look twice at her.

Coals shifting in the bed of the fire sent a rainbow of sparks shimmering into the blackness of the chimney, but buried deep in her thoughts Laura was oblivious to the fleeting beauty.

'I said there be somebody at the door.'

The tap of Livvy's hand to her arm causing her to start, Laura looked up from the fire's gleam.

'The door,' Livvy said again, seeing the far-away look still resi-dent in the other girl's eyes, 'there be somebody knocking at it.'

A caller. Her cheeks instantly stinging, Laura pushed to her feet. Rafe Travers?

'We . . . we cannot be seen like this.'

'So what do we do, tell whoever it be to sling their 'ook?'

She did not want to have to see him again, to add to memories still so very strong within her; memories of his smile, his strong yet gentle voice, the touch of his hand on hers, she did not want the pain of going over that again . . . but she did not want him to go away.

'Well?' Livvy demanded, watching emotions scud across her friend's face and knowing the reason for each. 'What's it to be, you can't keep a body standing out in the night air.'

'I . . . we . . . are not dressed for callers.'

'Then I'll shout for whoever it be to go away.'

'No!' The blush on her face deepening as she realised she had spoken too quickly to be seen to be wishing their caller gone, Laura searched for an escape. 'It . . . it might be your parents.'

'Ain't them.' Livvy turned towards the scullery. 'They won't be back from Liverpool for two more days yet; anyway, it don't matter who it be, you don't want to see 'em so I'll just tell 'em to go.'

'Wait.'

Snatching her skirt and blouse from the airing line strung above the fireplace, Laura struggled quickly into them. Smoothing her hands over her hair she nodded to Livvy.

'You get dressed, I . . . I will keep the caller in the scullery until you are ready.'

'It be me, Miss Laura, it just be me.'

Recognising Mary Bailey's voice coming from the back yard, Laura felt the sharp stab of disappointment. She had told herself so many times that she did not want to see him again, but it had been a lie, each time it had been a lie.

Opening the scullery door Laura welcomed the woman inside, glad of the darkness that veiled her face, hid the disappointment in her eyes.

'I 'pologise for knockin' on your door so late, but I 'ad to wait for that man of mine to get 'ome, I couldn't go leaving the babbies on their own; it be this one I've come about.'

Giving a shove to Alfie's back she sent him before her into the candle-lit kitchen.

'Is something wrong, Mary, Sol Cooper, he hasn't . . . ?'

Her disappointment swallowed, Laura followed the woman and the boy.

'No, no we ain't seen hide nor hair of 'im,' Mary shook her head, ''e knows my Gabriel would break his back if he comes within a mile of me or my kids. No, Miss Laura, it be another matter entirely.'

'Sit you down.'

Livvy had already placed a chair beside the table and was reaching for more cups.

'It be this way.' Mary sat down, her son standing beside her. 'You minds them there suck you give to 'im and Teddie?'

'I remember the sweets.' Laura gave a puzzled look. 'They were perfectly fresh, Mary, I only made them the evening before, they were to have been for my father but the prison officials would not allow me to give them to him.'

'Oh I knows they was fresh, it ain't nothin' to do with that.'

Smiling her thanks to Livvy, Mary Bailey accepted the proffered cocoa, a hand helping her son remember his manners as he too was given a steaming cup.

'Then what is it to do with?'

'It be this little toe-rag, him and our Teddie.'

In the pause while Mary sipped the hot cocoa, Laura caught Livvy's questioning glance, her own equally perplexed.

'Well, he only up and done with that suck what he done with the other trayful you give 'im.'

'He promised to share them, Mary.'

'Oh he shared 'em all right . . .' Mary put her empty cup aside, a nod telling Livvy she had enjoyed the drink. '. . . only not with the babbies.'

'Not with your brothers and sisters, but Alfie you promised. Surely you and Teddie . . .'

'We d'ain't eat 'em all, Missis Laura!' Toffee-brown eyes reflecting the pale gleam of candles lifted to Laura's. 'Fact be me and Teddie d'ain't eat none of 'em, not a single one.'

'Then what . . . ?'

'I'll tell you what.' Mary resumed the telling. 'He done with 'em what he done with them jars of cough syrup you sent against my kids going down with cold, but then p'raps the little sod best be doing the tellin' hisself.'

Feeling his mother's palm against his shoulder blades the boy answered flatly.

'We sode it! Me and Teddie, we sode the lot.'

'Sold it!' Laura gasped, sinking to her chair.

Alfie's head came up and in the weak light his freckled face wore a look of unmistakable pride.

'Ar, every drop, and we could 'ave sode more if we'd had it.'

'But to whom did you sell it?'

'Loads of folk.'

Laura shook her head at the impossibility of the answer. 'There was not loads to sell, Alfie.' She said, rebuke in her voice, 'I gave you just four jars. Even if you had sold the linctus you could only have sold to four people.'

'We could if we had sode a jar to each but we d'ain't.'

Realising he was thought to be lying the boy dropped his glance.

'Why not just let him tell it, leave the questions until he be done.' And the recriminations too! Livvy's quick shake of the head carried the message clearly. 'Go on, Alfie, say what it is you and Teddie have been up to.'

The lick of candlelight catching unruly red hair he turned to his mother, then at her nod he faced Laura.

'We took the jars to Granny Bird's. Her don't mind Teddie and me using her brewhouse and with her being too old now to do her own washing her never goes in there, so there was no chance of her finding that cough cure. Next day we divided the suck, putting a few in paper cornets we made from some sheets o' greaseproof we got from the grocer's shop when old Longmore weren't lookin'.'

Her mouth open to remonstrate at his method, Laura caught Livvy's glance and closed it again.

'When it were all wrapped we left one each for the babbies . . .'

'Ar, they did that.' Mary nodded as her son went on.

'. . . the rest we carted around the town giving them to every shopkeeper we could find, and a few to the cut folk an' all.'

Why on earth would those boys go to so much trouble, wrapping her sweets and carrying them all over the town to get rid of them, why not just dump them on the tip if they did not want them? Laura posed the questions in her mind only to come up with a deeper mystery. The Bailey children had never *not* wanted her sweets, so why now, why did they not want them now?

'When the last of 'em was gone we went round some of the big houses, you know, them along of Wood Green and the Myvod, then we did Squire's Walk and Hollies Drive. We asked if they 'ad any little bottles as they might not want, we said we was collecting 'em to be sold back to the glass bottle works along of West Bromwich.'

'Another lie, Miss Laura.'

Mary Bailey looked despairingly at the young woman sat opposite her.

'Well Teddie an' me could 'ave took 'em there if we 'adn't used 'em,' Alfie answered defensively. 'Anyway the 'ousekeeper along of Oakeswell Hall gave we a dozen or more and her said if our mother was thinking of keeping a couple for lemonade then they 'ad to be st . . . st . . . cleaned proper.'

'Sterilised.' Laura supplied the word he could not remember.

'Ar, that.' The boy nodded. 'Her give we some powder and said to mix it with boiling water and when it were cooled to use it to scour the bottles good and proper, then rinse them with plain boiled water.'

Wondering where the tale was leading, Laura brought her brows together but remained silent.

'Me and our Teddie we done all that, just as the woman said to do,' Alfie went on, 'then we filled the little bottles with cough syrup from the jars and done with them what we 'ad already done with them 'erbal soothers and the other suck you gied we.'

The telling done he stared at Laura. In the silence that rested she felt the eyes of both Mary Bailey and her son on her.

'You gave that away also?' Confused, she glanced at Livvy but Livvy was watching the boy. 'But why, Alfie, why not just take it all to the tip and bury it . . . if you thought it not good enough for you family?'

'Take it to the tip, not bloody likely!'

Mary's hand catching him across the back of the head Alfie tottered a couple of steps before regaining his balance.

'I begs your pardon, Miss Laura.' Mary looked glaringly at her son. 'His father will 'ave the skin off him when I tells 'im the language this one has just turned out.'

'It were a slip of the tongue, Mrs Bailey.' Livvy was quick to defend the boy. 'We be sure Alfie 'ad no intention of being offensive, don't we, Laura?'

Seeing the look in those brown eyes Laura could bring herself to do no other than to add to Livvy's defence of the boy. 'I am certain he did not.' She smiled at Alfie. 'Though I am still far from certain why it was you went to so much trouble.'

'Tell 'er, son,' Mary encouraged quietly. 'Tell Miss Laura the rest of it.'

'It were for you.' Pride fading swiftly, the lad's glance dropped and when he spoke again there was a trace of shyness beneath the apology in his tone.

'It were done for you, Missis Laura. Me and our Teddie we knowed as you 'ad no money and well . . . well we decided we was going to get some for you 'cos you be always so good to we and to our mother. So we sode the cough syrup and . . . and we got this.'

Reaching into the pockets of his ragged jacket he placed two heaps of coins on the table.

Gave away . . . sold? Laura looked blankly at Mary Bailey.

'I know, Miss, it took me that way first time I heard it.' Mary interpreted the look correctly. 'What Alfie be saying is this. Him and Teddie handed out them sweets and that linctus asking naught but that folk try them for theirselves. A few days later they went back to each of the folk and asked if they thought what they tasted worth the buying. Where the little bugg... where they gets their cheek from I often wonders, but ask they did and that be the fruits of it.'

'Teddie and me, we 'opes it will 'elp, Missis Laura.'

There had to be several pounds there. Laura stared at the coins. But it could not have come from her sweets.

'We would 'ave liked it to be more, Missis Laura, but that was all we got.'

Tears springing to her eyes, Laura shook her head slowly. 'I . . . I can't take this . . .'

'But it be for you!' Alfie's eyes, too, glinted moist in the mean yellow glow of candles. 'Me and our Teddie we tried so 'ard to get more but . . . but . . .'

He tailed off, turning his face to his mother so Laura would not see his threatened tears.

'I do not mean the money is not enough.' She was out of her chair, holding the boy close before the words had cleared her mouth. 'Please, please do not think that. I simply meant the sweets and the linctus were a gift to you and that if you chose to give them away or to sell them then whatever they realised belonged rightfully to you; that money is yours, Alfie.'

'Miss Laura.' Mary took her son, her face wreathed with a tender smile. 'Me an' Gabriel we supports both of them, we are proud that Alfie and Teddie brought that money 'ome and asked it be given to you, and we asks that you take it, it be little enough 'gainst what you 'ave done for us in the past.'

'I never did anything I wished payment for, Mary.'

'No more you did,' Mary answered softly. 'But my lads done what they done with the same good heart, don't deny 'em the pleasure it brings to see you accept.'

Tears spilling on to her cheeks, Laura looked at the boy stood at his mother's side. Taking his hands she smiled.

'Thank you, Alfie,' she whispered, 'and Teddie also. You don't know what this means to me . . . you don't . . .'

Sobs catching in her throat she broke off, turning her back as she dashed at the tears with her hand.

'Laura means that money be a Godsend,' Livvy stepped in, her own face creased with smiles. 'It means her can go see her father and not have to walk there and back. You be a wonder, Alfie Bailey, make no mistake about that, you be a real boster.'

His face beaming from the praise, he glanced to where Laura stood dabbing her eyes with a handkerchief.

'That ain't all, Missis Laura, there be these an' all.' Digging into each pocket of patched trousers he deposited a number of crumpled pieces of paper.

Picking up one of the pieces, holding it to the candle Livvy had placed on the mantel, Laura read the neat writing, doing the same with another and another until she had read them all. Holding them in her hands she sank to the chair, her face totally devoid of colour.

'Eh, Laura wench!' Mary Bailey glanced anxiously at Livvy then back to Laura still sitting in silence. 'Me and my Gabriel we looked at them papers but we couldn't read all the words, they . . . they ain't nasty am they?'

'No.' Laura laughed, a small unbelieving laugh, while her eyes showed their happiness. 'No, Mary, they are not nasty, they are wonderful, absolutely wonderful.'

Chapter Thirty-Two

It was more than she had ever dreamed possible.

Walking home through the market place, a large wicker basket heavy on her arm, Laura thought again of that evening Alfie had brought her the pile of coins. But wonderful as that money had seemed, it was the crumpled scraps of paper was the truly wonderful part.

Laura smiled, remembering the delighted cries of Livvy and of Mary Bailey as she read them out. Each one had proved an order for various amounts of sweets, herbal soothers or cough linctus.

That had been three months ago and each time she visited her buyers the orders increased; so much so she and Livvy were hard pressed to keep up with demand. Livvy had been such a help, never flagging even when tiredness showed pale in her face. If only she would take a break now and then, but to argue with Livvy was like arguing with a brick wall, it achieved nothing but headache.

Perhaps the young constable might be prevailed upon to call at the house more regularly; now that would take no great argument. Laura's smile deepened. P.C. Matthew Haynes needed no encouragement to call on Livvy. That the young man was in love was obvious, and Livvy . . . her blushes when he did ask her to walk on the heath on his days off from duty said volumes, she too was in love; pray God theirs would be a real and lasting love, not the sort she had once imagined herself to have.

She had thought herself in love with Edmund Shaw. But then again she had never truly thought about her relationship with Edmund, it had merely drifted along, familiarity becoming mistaken for love.

Could love, real love, ever be mistaken? But a question such as that was irrelevant for she would never have the answer.

'You are not even pretty . . .'

The words stung as keenly as they had when they had first been flung at her.

Not pretty enough for Edmund Shaw . . . not pretty enough for any man.

Huddling into her shawl she waited for a carriage and several carts to rumble past before crossing the road to Jackson's chemist shop.

'I 'ave it all ready for you, Laura wench.'

The bewhiskered chemist she had known from babyhood smiled benignly behind a counter so polished his reflection looked up from it.

'Let me see, there be oil of eucalyptus and of peppermint, essence of vanilla and of mulberry and four ounces of cherry bark extract.'

Smiling, he took the coin from Laura. Handing her change he asked, as always, after the health of her father, shaking his head at the reply that Isaac had not seemed to completely recover from his broken leg.

'It don't be so much the breaking of his leg as the locking up.' The chemist placed each purchase carefully on top of other pack-ages that had the basket almost filled. 'It were a bad business . . . a bad business altogether . . . but that be the way the world is today. But at least you be keeping well and we must be thankful for that.'

The change in her purse, Laura took the basket on her arm.

'Afore you go, Laura,' the elderly man smiled again, 'I wants to order some more of that linctus of yours, it be selling really well, I suppose that can be seen as one good thing to come out of this cold weather; and, Laura . . .' he hesitated, '. . . if you don't mind a word from an old friend.'

'I have always valued anything you have told me, Mr Jackson.'

He lifted a hand, curling the edge of a long white sideburn about one finger as he looked at her.

'I wish I could say that of everyone I serves in this shop.' He shook his head again. 'But this be a bit of advice you might find beneficial. That linctus of yours be selling real well as I told you, so why not make another with a different flavour? Add essence of raspberry or strawberry, try that there cherry extract; there be all kinds of essences you could use that would appeal to children, you'll lose little for the trying.'

'I had not thought of that,' Laura said, genuinely pleased at the advice. 'Thank you, Mr Jackson.'

It was certainly worth a try. Head down against the driving rain she made her way to the herbalist in Lower High Street. But how could she and Livvy cope with the extra work the making would entail?

Leaving the herbalist shop, shawl drawn against the sleeting rain, she stepped back, catching her breath as a heavy dray cart sent muddy water spraying high across her skirts. Struggling to hold basket and shawl in one hand, brushing at her skirts with the other, she did not see the carriage that came to a halt a little way along the street.

'Can I be of assistance, Miss Cadman?'

The voice, low and slightly musical, surprising in its closeness, startled her and she started, almost dropping the basket.

Without waiting for an answer Rafe Travers took the basket in one hand and her elbow in the other, propelling her towards the carriage.

'Sorry.' He grinned as he took up the reins and set the horses to a walk. 'I knew you would decline the offer of being taken home and I had no taste for standing in the rain while you turned down yet another of my good deeds.'

Surprised by the sheer swiftness of his action, Laura felt the colour burn into her cheeks as she realised that surprise was turning into pleasure.

It seemed she thought of this man more and more in those quiet moments before sleeping, imagined what she might say to him should she meet him again; and now that had happened she could think of nothing except how wonderful it felt to be with him.

'I did not pause to think, maybe you have not yet finished your shopping. Is there any place you would have me take you?'

He had drawn the carriage to a stop and now he watched her with enquiring eyes.

'I . . . I have no more shopping to do. The herbalist was my last call.' She looked away, finding his look disconcerting.

'Then it's home.'

Afraid to glance at him for fear he should see the pleasure in her eyes, not wanting to speak in case she could not keep it from her voice, Laura sat in silence, her head turned towards the passing houses of Dudley Street.

She had ridden several times in this carriage and on each occasion she had wanted only for the journey to end; now she would be happy for it to last, to go on and on so she would not have to be parted from Rafe Travers.

The thought added to the flame in her cheeks and she held her shawl across her face as he handed her down from the carriage, her thanks a shy murmur.

Taking the basket, Laura's whole insides turned a somersault as his fingers brushed her, and she drew back quickly.

In the chill of the winter evening she saw the line of his mouth tighten.

'Be so kind as to convey my regards to Livvy.' He spoke tightly, sudden anger seeming to choke his throat as it had when she refused his offer to take her to see her father. 'Good night, Miss Cadman.'

Rain drops slithering down her face mixed with the warmer drops of tears she could not hold back. She had wanted . . . she had hoped . . .

Turning her back on the departing carriage she stumbled blindly through the covered entry separating the string of tiny terraced houses.

What was it she wanted . . . what was it she had hoped?

Unhappiness weighing down her soul, Laura looked at the pages of her life. They were empty. Laura Cadman would never know her dream fulfilled.

He had paid Sandon five thousand pounds and Melville Hutton the same. Glancing out across the grounds from which the Gallery rose tall and beautiful, Edmund Shaw smiled with complete satisfaction.

It had all happened exactly as Sheldon said it would. The auctions had been an all-out success, the profit from both being more than the predicted three thousand each time.

Lighting a cigar he blew a stream of smoke towards the ceiling. Two of his creditors were paid in full, a few more of those special evenings and they would all be paid off and then this lovely house would be his.

His house!

He breathed deeply, feeling the pleasure of the words course through him.

His house. The house he would share with Sheldon.

'You should have been more careful, Jabez.' He laughed softly. 'You and Isaac Cadman, you should have been more careful, you should have made a contract; but then you were never good businessmen, were you?'

Not like him. Drawing deeply on the cigar he watched a gardener go about the business of protecting the more tender plants against the winter frosts.

Another year. He nodded to himself. Another year and this business would belong solely to him, and he had a contract to prove it.

'Are you not ready yet?'

Turning from the window Edmund let his glance slide over the man entering his room.

Sideburns reaching below the line of earlobes, emphasising finely wrought features, sage-green eyes brilliant beneath eyebrows winging over a clear unlined brow, he smiled.

'We should get started if we are to make it in time for lunch.'

Meeting that jewel-bright gaze Edmund felt his insides trip. Sheldon Sinclair was so handsome, were he a woman he would be called beautiful.

Beautiful was what he was, and he was his.

His insides tripping again Edmund returned the smile. Sheldon Sinclair was beautiful and he was in love with Edmund Shaw.

Shrugging into a beaver-trimmed beige mohair overcoat, he watched the other man slip elegantly into his own coat then smooth fine leather gloves over long fingers, every move graceful as a cat.

He had been so lucky, so damned lucky meeting Sheldon the way he had. All his life he had felt that something was missing from it, but since being here at the Gallery, sharing it with him, life had become complete; Sheldon had made it complete.

Meeting those wonderful eyes, reading the meaning resting in their gleaming depths, Edmund felt his senses swirl. They had gleamed that same way last night at supper; gleamed green fire as Sheldon had taken his hand, drawing him slowly to the bedroom, turned to living emeralds as those beautiful hands slowly stripped away his clothing, then had melted to soft green lakes as they had fallen on to the bed, mouth to mouth, flesh moulding into flesh.

'I got these for Lawton's wife.'

Downstairs in the graceful reception hall Sheldon picked up a small bouquet of flowers. Handing them to Edmund he went on, 'Charm Grace Lawton and any dealings you might have with Stafford Lawton will become admirably more easy.'

'Dealings?' Edmund watched the other man take up an oblong box from an onyx side table. 'I don't intend having dealings with Lawton.'

'Maybe you have not thought of it but you still owe him money. Get his wife on your side and he might agree to wait, agree to be the last creditor to be paid.'

Sheldon was right of course. Edmund followed to the waiting carriage. He could not hope to make ten thousand pounds all at once, therefore it would be impossible to pay off his debts to the two remaining creditors at the same time; they would each have to wait a while, but one was going to have to wait longer than the other.

Climbing into the carriage he laid the flowers on the seat, taking up the reins as Sheldon climbed in beside him.

'I thought you might present her with these also, Grace is quite partial to sweet little things.'

Letting the reins rest again on the brass rail fronting the carriage, Edmund smiled at the innuendo before taking the box, the tasteful pale mauve and silver decoration glinting in the daylight.

'It's certainly pretty enough, what's inside?'

'It will tell you, should you bother to read it.'

Reaching a hand to the box Edmund caught his breath.

Slowly his eyes read the words:

CADMAN'S CHOCOLATES — Exclusive to the better taste.

'I can still hardly believe it.'

Sat at the kitchen table, Laura checked the figures for the third time before looking up again at Livvy sat across from her.

'It is less than a year since Alfie brought in those first orders for sweets and linctus and already I have enough to pay back what my father took from the works' accounts.'

She had gone over the dream of having the money to repay that debt many times, but never once could she think of it as being stolen, of her father being a thief. But that was what Edmund and the magistrate had called him and that was the reason he was serving fifteen years in prison.

'Comes to the same do it?'

Closing the book in which she diligently recorded every item she bought and each sale she made, Laura nodded.

'This month shows a profit of one hundred and two pounds five shillings and tuppence.'

'And everything be paid for, them fancy boxes?'

'Fancy boxes and everything beside.'

Squealing with delight Livvy caught her by the hands, sweeping her from her chair and whirling her around the kitchen.

'Wait until that swine sees you hand him that money,' Livvy laughed. 'That'll wipe the smirk from his spiteful face, I only wishes I could stuff every sovereign up his ar . . . down his throat.'

Dizzy from the girl's mad whirling, Laura steadied herself against the table.

'Eh, Laura! It's going to be a fair pleasure for you to pay that man back.'

'Yes it will, but it would be more of a pleasure were I able to bring my father home. No matter how much profit my business makes I can never do that.'

Taking up the small ledger she carried it to the dresser. Placing it in a drawer she leaned against it, her shoulders drooping.

'Oh, Livvy, if only there was something I could do. I would gladly work the rest of my life for nothing if only I could free him.'

And me alongside, I would work for the same wage and glad to do it if only I could help. Livvy kept the thought to herself as she turned to the kettle always kept steaming over the fire.

'No, you can't,' she said, pouring boiling water into the

earthenware teapot. 'The law be the law and it will 'ave its pound of flesh. But once that debt be repaid to Edmund Shaw you can see to making life pleasurable for your father once he do be free.'

'In what way?' Laura turned, her glance following the other girl's quick efficient movements.

'Well for a start I reckon he would like that engineering works back, and this time with hisself its only owner.'

'Buy the works!' Laura was astounded. 'That would take hundreds of pounds!'

Teapot in hand Livvy stared at the girl who had become such a dear friend, but there was little gentleness now in her level gaze.

'So it will take 'undreds of pounds! You've already made over seven 'undred.'

'Yes but . . . to buy the works . . .'

'Would take a lot more,' Livvy interrupted brusquely. 'But then you 'ave a lot more time in which to make it, fourteen years more time; you can do it, Laura, I know you can.'

'The money will be repaid.'

Standing in the kitchen, the light of the paraffin lamps spilling their soft glow, Laura remembered the words she had said to Edmund over a year ago. It had seemed impossible then that they would ever come true, impossible as those Livvy had just spoken could ever come true; but the money was there to repay, all seven hundred and eighty pounds. Could it be she could earn enough to buy back her father's business, or was that one dream too many?

Dream or reality, it must take its turn. Livvy had worked long and hard while taking nothing but board and keep in return. It was time that state of affairs was remedied.

Seating herself back at the table she accepted the cup the girl passed to her. Stirring sugar into it, she watched the creamy brown contents swirl in a tiny whirlpool.

'Livvy, I could never have managed it without you.' She spoke quietly, every word laced with feeling. 'You have worked so very hard for such a little, but now I feel . . .'

'I know what you feels, Laura, and I knows what you be about to say, but you might as well keep quiet. I've got a roof, a meal and a good friend; my folks know where I am and that they can call here whenever they gets the chance, I don't need no more than that.'

'But that is not good enough, Livvy,' Laura protested, 'you must take a wage, we can afford it now.'

'When I be ready to accept money I will ask for it, 'til that day I'll take none, and if you feels you must argue the toss over it, Laura Cadman, then argue away, I be quite good at fighting my own end.'

'That I know very well.' Laura smiled. 'So I will not argue, at least not for a while, but I would ask one thing, Livvy, should your family need anything . . .'

'Then I will ask, there be no two ways about that.'

Sipping her tea, Laura stared at the flames curling into the dark void of the chimney. If only she could buy back the works. But Edmund had sold it a year ago, sold it to Rafe Travers.

'Why the hell did you let them do it?'

Eyes blazing with fury, Edmund Shaw glared at the manservant he had retained in his employ when taking over the Gallery.

'Sir Philip claimed the articles as his property. Not knowing the terms under which you purchased the property, I could not argue, sir.'

Anger choking him, Edmund waved the man away. The place was virtually empty, stripped almost totally bare, Christ it looked like a bloody barn! Pictures, furniture, carpets, mirrors, even the chandeliers were all gone! Throwing open doors he strode from room to room, seeing each left almost devoid of everything it had held.

Racing up to the first floor he snatched open the doors of his own apartments and stood staring at a room empty except for the bed.

Sandon! The bastard had taken the lot!

Rage freezing the blood in his veins he crossed to the dressing room. That, at least, had not been touched.

Turning back into the now desolate bedroom he struggled to control the ice-cold anger surging in waves through his body. The contract, the one he had signed when buying the Gallery, what exactly were the terms? He had read the high falutin' words but the meaning of them, couched in equally high-blown legal phrases, had gone beyond him most of the time.

But Sheldon had read the contract, he would have understood the fancy words, he would have said if Sandon had any claim on the things taken.

Taking the stairs two at a time he ran to the stables, shoving aside the elderly groom. Throwing a saddle on to his horse he sent it galloping from the yard.

Sheldon had dropped him at the Gallery less than an hour ago, saying he was returning to his own house and not the Periwig Club.

Heading the horse towards Thimblemill Brook Edmund kept it at the gallop. Sheldon would be at the Bell House. They had to discuss this matter tonight.

'All of it?' Sheldon glanced from the guests seated around his supper table to the man burst into his dining room.

'Almost every stick!' White with fury, Edmund snapped his answer.

Raising an exquisitely chased crystal glass, Sheldon held it beneath his nostrils, breathing the rich bouquet before smiling. 'How very like Sandon!'

'But the stuff he took, it's mine!' Edmund looked from one face to another, all were smiling . . . no . . . no, they were smirking, these bastards were smirking! His own face white with raw anger, he swept aside the offer of wine.

'I have to talk to you, Sheldon,' he said tersely, 'in private!'

His movements languid, Sheldon replaced the glass on the table before lifting his glance to Edmund. 'If it is anything to do with the Gallery, then you can say what you have to here, these men do, after all, have a stake in that venture; if it is not the business of the Gallery then it must wait for another time, I will not have my guests inconvenienced.'

Inconvenienced! Inwardly Edmund fumed. He had just been robbed of God knew how much, and Sheldon could not have his guests inconvenienced!

'Very well, if it has to be said in front of them then it must!' Pulling out a chair he sat on its edge, hands rolled into fists on its brilliant white cloth. 'When you dropped me back at the Gallery I found it almost totally stripped of its contents, rugs, furniture, the lot! Seems Philip Sandon had been there in my absence and made away with everything worth the taking!'

Sheldon smiled again. 'I repeat, how very like Sandon.'

"Ow very like!' Edmund exploded, anger dragging the carefully cultivated pronunciation from his tongue, "ow very bloody like! Be that all you 'ave to say? I've been bloody robbed and all you says is 'ow very like.'

'Robbed?' Sheldon raised an elegant eyebrow. 'You should take care what you say, Edmund, allegations such as that, heard in the wrong quarter . . .'

'Wrong quarter, I don't give a bugger what quarter they be 'eard in!'

'Then you are a fool.' Sheldon's smile returned. 'Philip Sandon is a powerful man . . .'

Edmund's fist came down hard, setting fragile glasses bouncing on the table. 'Philip Sandon be a bloody thief!'

Not even blinking at the outburst, Sheldon's smile remained fixed. 'As I was saying, Philip Sandon is a powerful man, one who does not take kindly to having his name subjected to slander; I would advise you think very carefully before making any libellous accusation against him, Edmund, I would hate to see you hurt . . . in any way.'

Had he been more rational Edmund would have understood the implications behind the words, but as it was they passed him by.

'The man be a thief,' Edmund banged the table again. 'He entered my house and stole my property, and I'll see him in jail for it!'

'Your house?' His smile fading, Sheldon Sinclair straightened in his chair. 'Not quite, Edmund, there is a matter of ten thousand pounds to be paid before you can call the Gallery your house. In fact we were discussing that very fact when you came in. Lawton here, and Thorne were asking when they might expect settlement.'

Edmund glanced briefly at the small ferret-eyed man watching him across the table, his head twitching in time with the quick movements of his fingers drumming on the table.

'You know 'ow long, Lawton, I told you that t'other day when we met for lunch in the Periwig.'

'I remember.' Stafford Lawton's head twitched more violently. 'I also remember thinking it might not be soon enough.'

'It'll be paid soon as I 'ave the money!' Edmund snapped. 'But right now I 'ave a bloody robbery to consider.'

'Are you so certain that Sandon has committed a robbery?' Unwin Thorne removed his spectacles, wiping them thoroughly with a spotless handkerchief before settling them on his dab of a nose. 'You are certain he is not simply removing his own property?'

'Removing his own property!' Edmund whipped to the plump man whose bald head was shining beneath the light of the gasoliere. 'That Gallery be mine!'

'The Gallery, yes.' Thorne pressed a finger to the bridge of his spectacles, pushing them from where they had slid to the end of his nose. 'The contents . . . I fear not.'

'What do you mean?' Edmund's reply hurled itself at the podgy face.

'You read your contract, Edmund.'

It was Sheldon Sinclair who spoke. Turning to look at him, Edmund felt a flicker of apprehension touch his throat.

'. . . You *did* read it?'

Sage-green eyes held to his, Edmund felt the apprehension

turn to doubt and doubt to fear. He had read those pages but how much had he really understood? His throat closing, he nodded.

'Then you know Philip has done nothing that is not legal. It stated quite categorically that the building was the subject of the sale agreed between you, the *building*,' he emphasised the word, 'was what you agreed to purchase, Edmund, not the contents. Those remained the property of Philip Sandon.'

The property of Philip Sandon! The reins lying loose in his hands, Edmund let the horse find its own way home. The property of Philip Sandon!

'You should have been more careful . . .'

The words coiled like a snake in his mind.

'You never were a good businessman . . . not like me . . .'

The words slithered around his brain.

'I have a contract to prove it.'

A contract! He swiped the whip viciously across the horse's shoulder, sending the frightened animal into a wild gallop. Yes, he had had a contract, one he couldn't bloody understand!

Striking the horse again and again he set it racing towards Thimblemill Brook gleaming silver among the black heathland.

Sheldon had known, known and said nothing! Why? Applying the whip he shouted into the wind, but only the image of deep green eyes, smiling eyes, returned in the darkness.

Chapter Thirty-Three

'I really don't understand you sometimes, you want him to show an interest . . . oh yes you do, Laura Cadman, I sees that for meself so don't lie . . .'

Livvy's mouth was tight as she sprinkled powdered sugar on to the surface of a large sheet of greaseproof paper.

'. . . then when he brings you 'ome like he did last night you up and turns your back on 'im.'

'I did not turn my back, Livvy.'

'You didn't invite 'im in, neither!' Grabbing a pinch of cream of tartar between finger and thumb, Livvy dropped it into the pot of sugar and water she had bubbling gently over the fire, stirring with a long-handled wooden spoon. 'No wonder he stopped calling, wouldn't you if you was treated like you had summat catching every time you showed up!'

Reaching for the small bottle of peppermint oil, Laura carefully added a few drops to her own mixture of boiled sugar and water. Leaving the pot on the hot side-hob of the fire grate, she stirred.

'I did not mean to treat him uncivilly . . .'

'I didn't say you was uncivil,' Livvy answered, adding ground almonds and a touch of lemon juice to her mixture, then quickly grabbing an egg yolk she had separated earlier and dropping that too into the pot.

'. . . but you was cold enough to freeze the arse off a polar bear!'

'Livvy!'

Looking up from where she was cooling the bottom of her pot in a basin of cold water, Laura shook her head.

'Well I feels like a good cuss!' Livvy brought her own pot, holding its base in the water as Laura moved to the table. 'Same as I feels like shaking you. Anybody with half an eye can see Rafe Travers be interested in you.'

Pouring her thickened mixture on to the sheet of sugar-coated paper she had laid opposite Livvy's, Laura worked quickly, using a broad-bladed knife to lift and fold the mixture in on itself.

It was foolish what Livvy had just said. She folded the cooling mass, the warm flavour of peppermint drifting into her nostrils. Rafe Travers had merely wished to help her get to see her father, it was no more; now she did not require that help he did not come. What could be more self explanatory than that?

'You should 'ave asked 'im in, Laura.'

Moistening her hands in a bowl of fresh water, Laura began to knead the fondant.

'No, Livvy, I should not. I do not want Mr Travers to feel . . .' she paused, searching for the right word but then said only, '. . . to feel he is under an obligation to be friendly.'

Across the table Livvy pressed her knuckles viciously into the marzipan that had cooled to kneading temperature.

'Obligation my ars . . . my foot!'

Catching Laura's frown, Livvy's own face found its more usual smile.

'Well . . . !' she laughed. 'You be enough to make a priest swear.'

Their fingers moving quickly they worked in companionable silence for several minutes, both concentrating on the task of slicing the cooled mixtures and rolling each small section into a ball. Placing each in a small paper case Laura carried her tray to the cold shelf in the larder, Livvy rolling all of her sweets in grated coconut before doing the same.

'Phew!' Rinsing her hands and drying them with a cloth pulled from the airing rail, Livvy let out a long breath.

Following suit Laura reached for the teapot, they had both earned a cup of tea.

'You put your feet up.' She smiled at Livvy. 'I will see to clearing the kitchen.'

'I'll be bugg . . .'

'Ah . . . ah . . . ah!' Laura wagged her head though her eyes were smiling. 'You keep that up, young lady, and I will ask P.C. Matthew Haynes to run you in for using unsavoury language on the Queen's highway.'

'We ain't on the Queen's 'ighway,' Livvy grinned, 'and all I was about to say was I will be blowed if you will, we ain't finished making suck . . . sweets . . . yet.'

'No, I think . . .'

A knock at the door trapping the rest of the sentence, Laura felt her mouth suddenly dry and her fingers seem to lose their strength. It might be . . . maybe he . . . but then she realised the knock was at the scullery door; Rafe Travers would not come to that door.

'That'll be Gabriel, I'll go let 'im in.'

Livvy had seen the colour surge to Laura's face. Knowing the hope behind it and the heartache that followed when each knock brought a visitor that was not Rafe Travers, she walked slowly to the scullery, giving Laura time to regain composure.

'They be all there, miss, the new orders and the money for the last lot. I 'ad each bill wrote on to say paid in full, but I got the money afore I asked.'

'Thank you, Gabriel.'

Laura smiled at the tall man who went with his son once a week to collect payment for sweets and linctus. She would not have Alfie walk the streets alone in the evening and this way it left her free to concentrate on her work while providing the Baileys with an extra few shillings.

Handing him several coins she asked, 'Where is Alfie, is he not with you?'

'He was 'til we got as far as the George atop of Union Street, then he was offered a tanner to keep an eye on a bloke's hoss and carriage. I told 'im, give the bloke five minutes and if he still weren't outta that 'otel by that time then he was to get hisself along 'ome.'

'I know Alfie, sixpence is a sum he would find hard to pass up, but I would feel more at ease had he stayed with you, the town can become a little rowdy on a Saturday evening.'

'No call worryin', Miss Laura.' Gabriel pocketed the coins. 'My lad be used to the ways of the town, 'sides it be soon yet, the market still be full o' folk. Alfie will do as he be tode, he'll be 'ome again afore I gets there.'

Following him to the door Laura stood as he turned, the cap he had placed in his pocket now in his hands.

'I'll see you next week?'

Tipping her head upwards, her face catching the pallid glow of lamplight, she smiled.

'Yes, Gabriel, I will see you next week.'

'And what good deed did he do? One you found more accept-able than mine was easy to see!'

A small startled cry freezing in her throat, Laura spun around. Rafe Travers stood just inside the scullery.

'What . . .'

'Am I doing here?' he cut her off angrily. 'Asking you a ques-tion, what is he doing for you that you will not allow me to do?'

'Laura!'

The large knife she had used minutes before now held above her shoulder, Livvy rushed into the scullery.

'It . . . it is all right, Livvy.' Managing to breathe, Laura turned to the girl whose face had paled with fear. 'I . . . I did not see Mr Travers, the yard is quite dark when there is no moon.' Glancing back at him she went on, 'Will you come into the parlour, it is lighter in there.'

'I don't need light!' he snapped, anger vibrating through every word. 'I need an answer.'

From the corner of her eye Laura saw the knife lower and heard the swish of the other girl's skirts as she left the scullery.

'Very well.' She stared into the angry face. 'I will give you an answer. Whomever I entertain in my own house, and for whatever reason, is no concern of yours but as you ask I will tell you. Gabriel Bailey is a friend to me and a husband to yet another friend, Mary Bailey. Their son works for me and once a week Gabriel accompanies him on his rounds to collect money due to me and brings it here to this house.'

'That is all?'

Crossing her hands over her skirts Laura drew in a long breath.

'That is all, Mr Travers. Though if you wish I can invent more.'

'Miss Cadman . . . Laura . . .' He took a step forward then checked himself and when he spoke again the anger was replaced with coldness. 'I apologise. I can offer no excuse for entering your home uninvited. I ask you to forgive my rudeness.'

Waiting a moment he turned when Laura did not answer and was at the door when Livvy bounced into the scullery.

'You will take a cup of tea afore you leaves? I 'ave a pot fresh brewed.'

Following with him as Livvy led the way back into the kitchen, Laura felt her nerves sing.

But was it due to her wanting to slap Livvy, or wanting to hug her?

Sheldon Sinclair had known the terms of that contract.

Tipping back the brandy he had ordered, Edmund called for another.

That fall he had taken last week when putting his horse to

leaping the brook had broken the animal's leg, but at least it had cleared some of the anger from his mind.

Tipping off the second brandy he shook his head as the barman asked would he be requiring another. Laying a coin on the counter he swung away.

'You read the contract . . .'

The words flickered against his brain. He had wanted to kill Sheldon then, wanted to kill the man he felt had betrayed him.

But later, calm and in Sheldon's arms, he had realised the truth. Sheldon Sinclair loved him and would never betray him. Sheldon had genuinely thought he understood every word in that contract.

Unused to drinking brandy quite so quickly, a little unsteady as a result, Edmund muttered an apology as he bumped into another man leaving the hotel at the precise moment he did.

Weaving slightly as the crisp evening air bit into lungs heated by brandy, he watched the man slip a coin into a boy's hand before climbing into a carriage.

'Hansom, mister?'

The boy was at his side, a face pinched with cold turned up to his.

'Can I fetch you a hansom, mister?'

At his nod the boy was off, darting across the busy road junction to the space in the market where once the Butter Cross had stood.

Moments later, fumbling with a handful of coins, Edmund flipped one to the boy then settled himself in the cab. The Gallery needed furnishings, he could not entertain clients in an empty house. It had taken him some time to think how to get them, but now he knew.

It had been a stroke of luck in that other hostelry earlier in the day. Wine loosened the tongue and increased the volume of voices of some men. Luckily he had heard what he wanted to hear.

Cold air clearing the effects of the alcohol, he went over in his mind what had happened some two hours ago.

He had waited on the rough heath that stretched behind the Shambles. Away on Church Hill the clock of St Bartholomew's had rung eight. That was the time that shop owner had said the money was collected. His was the last of the round, he had only to call at Jackson's chemist and after that he was finished.

He had been finished tonight right enough! Edmund felt the prickle of moisture on his palms. It had been a gamble thinking the man would cut across the empty ground instead of taking the longer way of the streets, but the gamble had paid off.

He had been a sizeable fellow and his tread had been easy to hear on the almost frozen heath. It had been easy. Edmund smiled. The man had obviously had no thought he might be robbed. He had strode past the gorse bushes that fringed most of the empty heath and it had been a matter of moments before the heavy stave had knocked him senseless. But senseless had not been enough. Senses could be recovered. The moisture in his palms becoming sticky Edmund rubbed them together. The blood on that stave had been sticky as he had clubbed the man again.

No one had seen him. The money bag under his coat, he had gained Union Street in a quick dash, then walked briskly along its length, stopping several moments to stare into the window of the tobacconist before proceeding.

Now the money was safely hidden in his valise at the George Hotel.

Laura must be doing well. Cadman's chocolates was obviously a lucrative business if tonight's takings were anything to judge by. It would pay him as well as Shaw and Cadman engineering had, and for as long . . . say some fourteen years!

Having the driver of the hansom wait, he walked through the entry that divided the line of houses.

'Edmund!'

Shock robbing her face of its smile, Laura stared at the face revealed by the light of the lamp held in her hand.

'Good evening, Laura.'

Expecting the knock to be Gabriel's, Laura stared bemusedly.

'May I come in?'

'Yes . . . yes, of course.' Flustered at the unexpectedness of his being there, Laura stammered the words.

In the brighter warmth of the kitchen Livvy looked up as he walked in. She had heard the name Laura had gasped. The broad-bladed knife held prominently in her hand she stared at the narrow features. Whatever Edmund Shaw was here for, it would hold no benefit for Laura.

Ignoring the customary practice of offering tea, Livvy carried on with the process of cutting a slab of raisin fudge into shapes using a tiny star-shaped metal cutter.

'This looks like every lad's Aladdin's cave.' He glanced at the trays of assorted sweets set in every possible space in the kitchen. 'Are you thinking of giving a party or are you giving every child in Wednesbury a Christmas box?'

'Neither!' The abrupt reply was Livvy's.

Glancing at her, Edmund kept the sudden urge of temper under control.

'Forgive my mistake, Miss . . .' He deliberately refused to use the name the girl had once flung at him.

'Beckett.' It was Laura answered. 'Olivia Beckett.'

Inclining his head in a carbon copy of Sheldon Sinclair, Edmund continued, 'Forgive my mistake, Miss Beckett, though I am used to seeing Laura making sweets I have not before seen her do so on quite such a scale.'

'I make sweets for a living now, Edmund.' Laura too made no offer of tea.

'A sweet way to live.' The quip was such as Sheldon would have made, but unlike the other man's humorous comment this brought no smiles.

Feeling the animosity steaming from Livvy yet knowing that to ask for her to leave would give rise to speculation, and possibly more animosity from Laura than was already present judging by the cold stare on her face, he went on.

'Laura, I have had time to think on what happened

between us . . . time to realise that none of it was your fault . . .'

'Will I go upstairs?' Livvy interrupted, not wanting to embarrass Laura by being present if unwanted.

Her own glance firmly on eyes as pale and indiscriminate as she remembered them, Laura answered with a quiet firmness.

'Unless *you* have an objection, Livvy, I would prefer you to stay.'

The snub felt as keenly as any slap to the face, Edmund's nostrils flared then, anger controlled, he managed smoothly, '. . . none of it was your doing, Laura, I . . . I am sorry you were hurt.'

He be sorry she were hurt! Livvy's thoughts were furious as she set raisin fudge stars between layers of greaseproof paper. He fair broke her heart, almost ruined her life and he be bloody sorry her felt hurt!

'I know I can't undo what has been done, I can't give you back the months that have passed but I can undo some of the harm I brought to you.'

He sounded so different. Laura's mind registered the delivery that had had the rough edges of dialect smoothed away. The voice matches the clothes, she thought, both are an improvement; but the eyes, the eyes were the same as almost two years ago, cold and impassive, like a reptile about to strike.

'Undo,' she said quietly. 'Only my father's release from prison could undo the harm and you cannot free him.'

'No.' Edmund shook his head. 'But I think I may have found a way for you to.'

For a moment the kitchen whirled in a crazy sweet-filled circle and Laura grabbed a chair, holding on to its curved back.

'I can't be absolutely certain, Laura, but it's a possibility and that's worth a try if no more.'

Worth a try. Laura's heart pressed painfully against her chest. Anything . . . anything was worth a try.

'I have a friend,' Edmund went on quickly. 'He is coming to dinner on Friday of next week and bringing an acquaintance with him. The man he is bringing is a judge, a very well-respected judge. I intend asking if he will review Isaac's case. If you could be there, Laura, if he could see you, see what a respectable woman you are it might help persuade him Isaac's taking that money was . . . well a mistake. That is what I shall tell him anyway, and I shall say the funds have been repaid . . .'

'That at least will be the truth,' Laura broke in quickly. 'I was hoping to find where you live, Edmund, so I can give you back the money my father took from yours. The debt can be cleared, then you and I need not meet again.'

Glancing at Livvy she nodded and the girl ran lightly up the stairs returning with a tin box.

Edmund watched the rhythmical counting. One by one the white five-pound notes were placed neatly on the edge of the table.

'Three hundred and ninety.' Laura closed the empty box. 'Take it, Edmund, now you have everything you wanted.'

'Laura, it doesn't matter about the money!'

It was a lie but he knew she would not take it back. Letting the notes remain he caught at her hands.

'Don't you see, we have a chance to get Isaac a retrial and this time I could say there was a discrepancy in the figures, that the numbers had been miscounted; and the time to ask that judge could not be better.'

'Time?' Laura frowned.

Looking into her puzzled face he gave a slight impatient toss of his head.

'Christmas, Laura. The season of goodwill to all men, so why not to Isaac?'

Why? Laura's mind was dazed by what Edmund said. Why after all this time, after all he had said, after all he had threatened did Edmund Shaw want to help her father now?

'He could be freed by the new year.'

Watching the brilliant gleam of hope sweep the dazed look from her eyes, catching the tremble of fingers still caught in his,

Edmund almost smiled. The Gallery would be re-furnished, maybe not with antiques but how many of the clientele cared about antiques?

Freed by the new year. Laura felt her heart lift. Her father could be freed. Lifting her eyes to his she asked tremulously, 'Where shall I come?'

The debt was repaid!

Lying in her bed Laura watched the winter moon play in and out of silver-edged clouds.

Next time she visited the prison she could tell her father he was free of the shame of debt. But she would not tell him of asking for a retrial, then if it did not happen . . .

Livvy had said not to set her hopes too high and she was right, yet she could not help but wish.

That Livvy did not trust Edmund had been plain in her argument that Laura did not go to that house alone but asked Rafe Travers to accompany her.

'He would do it, Laura, even if it meant sitting outside in his carriage 'til that dinner be over.' Livvy had said.

Staring at the moon-filled windows Laura remembered the relief that had swept through her when Rafe had accepted Livvy's offer of tea, of how that relief had turned to happiness as, after begging to be allowed to help with the sweet-making, he had seemed as happy as she felt. But out of all her memories of that evening the one she cherished most was his softly murmured 'May I come again . . . Laura?'

Clouds sweeping away, the moon released dark shadows into the room.

'Don't set your hopes too high!'

The words seemed to taunt her from the velvet darkness.

Rafe Travers had shown her friendship, she must not hope for more.

Chapter Thirty-Four

'Gabriel, I am so sorry!'

Laura looked anxiously at the man sat beside the fire, his wife hovering close.

'Ain't your fault,' Gabriel Bailey answered the girl who had come running to his house. 'I just be sorry the swine got away with your money.'

'The money is unimportant, Gabriel, it is you that matters, are you sure you are not injured?'

'Doctor says he be all right apart from a knock on the 'ead.' Mary touched a hand to her husband's shoulder.

'You . . . you could have been killed. Oh Gabriel, I feel so awful.'

Seeing tears gleam at the back of Laura's eyes, Gabriel gave an embarrassed smile.

'Tek more'n a couple of bangs on the 'ead to kill Gabriel Bailey. A couple of them pills of Jackson's and I'll be right as rain, and then,' the smile faded, 'I means to look for the bloke as done this and when I does then nothing will save 'im.'

Laura glanced worriedly at Mary.

'He must not do that, he must rest. Leave the one that took the money for the police to find.'

Mary shook her head despairingly but her answer held more than a hint of pride. 'I've tried talking to 'im, Miss Laura, but you can talk 'til Kingdom come and it'll make no difference once his mind be set.'

'Gabriel, please . . .'

Gabriel Bailey shook his head, trying not to show the pain that shot through it.

'No, Miss Laura, I won't leave it lie. I intends to look for the one as robbed me and I tells you plain, if I finds 'im then I'll do for 'im. He won't rob no other poor bugger . . . if you'll pardon me words.'

'You 'ave told the police?'

Having been silent up to this point, Livvy put the question.

'Ar.' Mary nodded. 'I went to the station meself and that young constable come here with me and asked Gabriel for full particlers; he said as 'ow he would be calling on Miss Laura later. I suppose police will want to know how much were in that money bag. Eh . . . when I thinks of it!'

'Well you are not to think of it, Mary, nor Gabriel neither, we must just be grateful he is not seriously injured.'

'Laura is right.' Livvy spoke again. 'That Gabriel suffered no lasting hurt be the main thing, money can always be earned again.'

'But it will not be earned the same way. We will find some other way to make a living, a way that does not involve collecting money.'

'Eh, Miss Laura!' Mary gasped. 'You can't give up your business, not on our account.'

'It is not on your account, Mary, it is on mine. I will not have anyone run the risk of being injured . . . possibly even killed . . . through working for me.'

His hand closing over his wife's where it touched against his shoulder, Gabriel shook his head slowly.

'Then that swine took more than money, he took your livelihood. He has done to you much the same as were done to your father, robbed you of what you worked 'ard for. But I ain't one to sit by and let that 'appen. That suck business will go on, even though I 'ave to send my Mary along to mek it;

and the collecting of them payments will go on same as before only from now on there will be two men doing the round, me and me brother Seth, and we'll both be carryin' more'n a cloth bag!'

'I still says you shouldn't go off with 'im by yourself.' Livvy's voice held a worried note.

'Stop fretting.' Laura smiled, stepping into the wedding gown that had graced a much slimmer Mary Ann Griffiths. 'I will be away no more than a few hours, Edmund said he will bring me home the moment the dinner is over.'

'Ar!' Livvy grumbled. ''E also said as he was sorry you had been hurt but I didn't believe that neither.'

'It was so kind of Mary Ann to lend me her wedding gown.' Laura changed the subject. 'Lucky for me it fits.'

Doing up the last of the tiny buttons that closed the waist-to-neck bodice of the hyacinth-blue georgette dress, Livvy stepped to look at Laura from the front.

'It is pretty,' she breathed, 'you look beautiful, Laura.'

'You are not even pretty . . .'

The words said so coldly returned. Like an icy douche to the face they washed away the pleasure of the moment. Mary Ann's wedding gown was pretty but its present wearer was not.

'No, no I am not beautiful.' She smiled, fastening the cheap necklace of blue-glass beads that had been a childhood gift from Abbie Butler. 'Edmund told me that a long time ago.'

'He told you that did he?' Livvy snorted. 'Edmund Shaw told you that. Then the man is not only a spiteful bugger, he be a spiteful bugger with shit in his eyes!'

'Livvy!'

Laura's exclamation merely served to bring a mutinous line to the other girl's mouth.

'I'll not watch my language!' she declared hotly. 'Not when I be referring to a louse that needs to be trod on! Come here.'

Catching Laura's waist she pulled her towards the mirror that sat above the washstand. 'Now tell me Edmund Shaw don't be a fool, tell me you ain't beautiful.'

In the light of the extra lamp Livvy had carried upstairs, Laura looked at the image staring back at her.

Enhanced by the lovely colour of the gown, wide and deeply blue eyes regarded her from a creamy high-cheekboned face while pale wheat-colour silk hair gleamed in coils, holding in their satiny folds the tiny blue flowers Livvy had fashioned from a narrow ribbon.

It was not her. Laura gasped. The woman in the mirror could not be her.

Afraid to breathe in case the image shattered and was gone, she stared at the face she knew was hers yet could not believe it so.

'See, I told you.' Livvy laughed delightedly. 'I told you you was beautiful, now see what Mr Edmund Shaw has to say when he looks at you!'

The face in the mirror remained still but her heart jolted sharply. It was not Edmund Shaw she wanted to see her looking like this, it was Rafe Travers.

Picking up the blue silk gloves that had cost tuppence from the pawn shop next door to Jackson's chemist shop, Laura followed carefully down the narrow stairs, holding the folds of the gown high above her feet.

'Eh, wench, you looks beautiful.' Mary Ann Griffiths let herself in through the scullery door.

'So long as I remember not to lift my dress above my feet.' Laura giggled, raising the dress to display worn leather boots. 'Not quite the classic glass slippers.'

Lips pulled together Mary Ann shook herself. 'I see what you means. These be no glass slippers neither but they might serve better, supposin' they fit.'

She held out a pair of pale blue satin shoes, diamante buckles sparkling in the lamplight.

'Cost my mother all of a shilling and sixpence did these and not a soul but us two knowed they come from old Alfred Bloomers pawn shop along of Russell Street; but the frock, that were new, my mother sewed every stitch herself.'

'It is lovely, Mary Ann, but I am still not sure I should borrow it, it must be very precious to you.'

'Ar.' The woman nodded her dark head. 'It be precious but that don't mean it shouldn't be worn; I hopes one day my own girls will wear it to their weddings but right now I wants you to wear it, and these an' all.'

Shoving the slippers into Laura's hands, the woman beamed when they slipped easily on to her feet.

'There now.' She smiled. 'The Princess Royal could look no more beautiful; you be going to have that judge eating out of your 'and.'

It was a good house. Edmund Shaw glanced about the reception hall he and Sheldon had re-furnished. The paintings and statues were the works of no great artists but the men gathered here tonight would not be looking too closely at what was on the walls.

He looked around again, satisfied at the flood of mauve-frilled carnations set in every buttonhole. Touching the one firmly bedded in the Khepri lapel-pin fashioned from his waist-coat button, he caught Sheldon's smile. After tonight Thorne and Lawton would be paid off and the proceeds from the next auction would be theirs to spend as they wished.

'Your guest is quite comfortable?'

Edmund glanced towards the curving staircase. He had shown Laura into the private apartment, excusing himself on the pretext of welcoming his other guests' arrival.

'Quite comfortable.' He nodded. 'Are Thorne and the others coming?'

'They are already here.' Sheldon nodded to where two men

stood in the shelter of an alcove. 'I suggest we begin; will you conduct the sale, or will I?'

'I have to spend some time upstairs, I don't want Laura coming down here, and she might if I am gone too long.'

'She is a lovely woman, Edmund.' Sheldon followed Edmund's glance to the stairs. 'I wonder you did not claim her for your own, but then we both know your taste does not follow that direction.'

A soft feline laugh following him, Edmund made his way towards the men in the alcove as Sheldon began to introduce the first of the artefacts offered for auction.

Once more in his private sitting room Edmund watched the faces of the two men he had introduced to Laura. She had obviously charmed them. Thorne especially. Taking Laura's hand and placing it on his arm he led them to the dining room.

The meal passed slowly for Laura; aware of the glances of Edmund's guests, of their over-attentiveness she felt stifled, and rose gladly when they suggested they withdrew to the sitting room. She could not have expected the question of her father's retrial to be broached during dinner, but now surely Edmund would raise it.

The men served with brandy and Laura with coffee, Edmund stood beside a small white porcelain figurine.

'Forgive me if I turn to business for a moment.'

Laura breathed an inward sigh of relief. He was going to speak of the real reason for her being here. A few more minutes and she could leave.

Edmund touched a finger to the delicate figurine. 'You have seen what is on offer, gentlemen, are you prepared to name your bid now or shall I return it to the sale room?'

Glancing at the beautifully modelled figure of a woman leaning against the bole of a tree, a veil draped over one naked breast to trail chastely between her legs, Laura admired the skilful beauty of the piece, but, beautiful as it was, she would rather Edmund did not speak of it now.

'Remember it comes in absolute pristine condition.' Edmund repeated the phrase he had so often heard Sheldon use. 'I could quite easily sell elsewhere, Hutton has already shown an interest.'

Why did he have to sell his statue now? Laura felt a twinge of annoyance. Surely that could wait for a more opportune moment. Placing her cup aside she caught the glance of shifty, darting eyes. She did not like Stafford Lawton, nor for that matter did she like Unwin Thorne or the way both of these men looked at her, almost as if they were hungry.

'Five hundred more.' Stafford Lawton's ferret eyes flicked from Laura to Edmund.

'Are you done?' Edmund passed his glance to the partly balding figure.

Stafford Lawton passed the tip of his tongue over puffy lips, peering with small ferret eyes.

'I take it you have.' Removing his finger from the figurine Edmund smiled. 'Sold for . . .'

'Wait!' Thorne shoved a pair of spectacles from where they had slid to the tip of his blob nose. 'Six . . . six hundred more . . . that be my final bid.'

Breath loosed in an exasperated snort, Stafford Lawton got to his feet.

'Prize be yours, Thorne.' He glanced at Edmund. 'I will say goodnight, Shaw.'

Seeing Edmund follow the irate man striding from the room, Laura rose.

'Edmund . . . what of my father?'

'Thorne knows all about your father.' He smiled. 'I am sure he will be glad to discuss it with you while I get a receipt for his money.'

Three thousand six hundred pounds! A smile of satisfaction curving his thin lips, Edmund Shaw walked slowly down the stairs.

*

'And now, gentlemen, we come to the last item of the evening, a piece I know you will agree is absolutely priceless; but the Gallery is hoping you will not abide by that agreement.'

Sheldon's voice, soft and persuading, floated across the wide reception hall followed by a burst of laughter. Halfway down the stairs Edmund paused.

The lowering light from the huge central gasoliere plunged the room into sudden shadow with the effect of silencing everyone in it.

Edmund's hand gripped the carved-oak banister. Sheldon had mentioned nothing of amateur dramatics.

Moments passed. Edmund listened to the expectant rustle slip through the shadows. What the hell was Sheldon up to?

'Gentlemen,' the voice came softly from the darkness. 'Allow me to present Michaelangelo's *David*.'

At the precise moment of the word 'David' the gasoliere was turned up, flooding the room with new light.

The great pull of breath into each throat sounding like a wave rushing against the shore, brought Edmund to the foot of the stairs then held him there, every muscle of his body temporarily paralysed.

Directly beneath the gasoliere a figure gazed unsmiling towards men it seemed had forgotten how to breathe.

Golden hair curled tightly above a wide brow, sweeping into the nape of a strong neck. Left leg placed casually apart, left hand holding a short leather strap over the same shoulder whilst the right remained loose at his side, he stood completely naked.

No carrying of a statue, no trick or deception this time. Edmund moved to a side alcove. There could be no mistake as to what was being offered; and everyone present in the room knew it.

He looked again at the figure stood in the centre of the light. Curls rested above fine-lined eyebrows arching above a strong aquiline nose; the unsmiling mouth, full-lipped, echoed the strong line of jaw and chin.

A beautiful face. Edmund almost felt the ripple that ran

around the room as every man wrestled with his own thoughts, his own desires.

Skin lightly oiled and dusted with bronze powder, the figure gleamed like a golden god. Broad shoulders and tight waist gave on to narrow hips and taut flat stomach. Long legs rippled with muscles, while between them golden curls nestled above the gleaming genitals.

A beautiful face on a beautiful body! Edmund breathed slowly as Sheldon called for an opening bid.

Listening to the rapid calls he could guess the thoughts behind the reckless scramble. Once bought this magnificent piece would not be offered for auction again, he would be kept for one man's pleasure.

'Gentlemen . . . gentlemen . . .'

Switching his eyes to Sheldon he saw him raise a hand for silence.

'. . . I see you are all interested but time is short so I will tell you I have a reserve bid on this item. The offer is ten thousand pounds, will anyone go higher?'

Ten thousand pounds! Edmund heard the gasp that went up from each man. Who on earth would pay such a sum, even for a prize such as this?

Drawing further into the shadows of the alcove, he waited. One by one the buyers began to drift away, those who had made a purchase leaving via different doors while those who had not left at the main doors.

But who had bought the golden David?

It was as the last man walked to the door that the question was answered.

Blood pounding in his veins, Edmund watched as Sheldon kissed the beautiful mouth.

'Mr Thorne, I . . . I have to talk to you.'

Pushing spectacles along his squat nose Unwin Thorne

moved closer, his plump leg pressing against Laura's.

'We will talk, my dear,' he smiled, showing gapped teeth, 'but later. Right now there are other pleasures to be had.'

'Please!' She pulled her hand from beneath his. 'Edmund told me you might be able to help my father.'

'Oh!' Unwin Thorne's eyes slid to her breasts, his tongue licking wetly over puffy lips.

Laura glanced towards the closed door. Please God, let Edmund come back quickly.

'He said you were a judge, that . . . that you would consider a retrial of my father's case, my father was imprisoned . . .'

'Oh I be a judge all right.' Thorne's podgy hand whipped like a fat snake, clamping itself on one breast. 'But it don't be no law court judge. I judge a woman's flesh and now I am ready to judge yours.'

'Don't you dare touch me, you . . . you have no right . . .'

The hand moved upwards, fastening on the neck of her gown, his eyes narrowing behind the thick spectacles.

'Right!' He snarled. 'I have three thousand six hundred rights, that be the number of pounds I paid for you and I be going to take value for every one of 'em!'

Paid! This man had paid for her! Suddenly the whole thing became clear. Edmund knew no judge . . . he did not want to help her father . . . but to do this! Did Edmund hate them so much he would sell her to a man?

Eyes wide with horror, Laura grasped the wrist of the hand fastened about her dress, trying desperately to force it away.

'I . . . there has been a mistake, I . . . I am not a prostitute.'

A laugh low in his throat, Thorne's free hand came up to stroke her face.

'So it had better prove,' he said thickly. 'I paid for a virgin and a virgin is what I get if Shaw values his neck.'

'Please.' Laura's eyes followed as he stood up. 'Edmund must have meant some other woman.'

Thick fingers fumbling with buttons Unwin Thorne grinned viciously as he peeled away coat and waistcoat.

'Maybe, but then I have a fancy for the one that be here and I don't think I shall be disappointed. Now be a good girl and get undressed, I don't like being kept waiting.'

The fear that had come to her so many nights came again now, cold all-devouring fear that stole her breath and locked her throat, and once again she was being dragged through that narrow back street.

'No! No . . . please . . . !'

It was no more than a terrified whisper but it acted like a roar of triumph on the plump, balding man. Spectacles clinging precariously to his nose he lunged at Laura, dragging her to her feet, snatching at the delicate fabric of her gown so it ripped open to the waist. Tongue licking over his lips, he touched a fat finger to the whiteness of her breasts.

'Nice,' he muttered. 'I shall enjoy sucking them.'

In her mind his thick laugh became the one she had heard before, his face the one that had bent over hers as she lay on that filthy floor. A cry breaking from her lips she struck out at the grinning face, running for the door as the plump figure reeled backwards.

Was this the place he had brought her to?

Rafe Travers' eyes moved slowly about the reception hall.

It had to be here. The girl had been quite definite about the name. He had gone to Great Western Street in answer to the invitation to supper but Laura had not been there. He had listened to Livvy's explanation of how Edmund Shaw had taken her in a carriage to his home, promising to bring her back seeing as there would be no late-evening train from Ratton Park Station.

Judge . . . retrial . . . better if he could see what a respectable woman she was. His teeth coming together like a vice, Rafe moved silently across the room. A respectable woman would be the last thing the men who frequented this place would want . . . Christ if any harm had come to her he would tear Shaw apart, piece by piece!

'He said 'is house were called the Gallery,' Livvy had insisted. 'I remember 'cos I thought it a queer sort of a name to give to a 'ouse.'

It had not been difficult to fathom. At the stairs Rafe paused to listen. Ratton Park Road railway station served the Bearwood area of Birmingham and a so-called Gallery stood close to Thimblemill Pool. But if this was the place, where was Shaw, and more importantly where was Laura?

Glancing up the curving staircase, he stiffened as the sound of crashing china filled the silence.

Slowly, one stair at a time, he moved upwards. Then a cold stab of anger sliced into him. If the stories he had heard about this place were true she was likely to be up there somewhere.

When he was halfway to the landing a sharp, terrified scream, a woman's scream, rang out curdling the blood in his veins.

Taking the rest of the stairs two at a time, he heard a voice raised in anger.

'I paid for you, you bloody bitch; ain't nobody takes Unwin Thorne's money unless they deliver the goods, and you be going to deliver. You be the virgin I paid for but you'll be no virgin when I be finished with you.'

Rage swallowing him whole Rafe raised one foot, sending it crashing against a closed door.

'What the bloody hell!' Spectacles releasing their grip, a startled Unwin Thorne turned towards the intrusion, his plump body gleaming naked in the gaslight. At his feet Laura lay against a fallen table, a thin trickle of blood oozing from one temple, a cheap canvas bag clutched in her hand.

'You filthy swine!'

The words grit between his teeth, Rafe was across the room. Grabbing the other man's arms he frog-marched him from the room, propelling him down the stairs and out of the main doors.

'Tell Shaw I'll find him, wherever he goes, I'll find him!'

Letting go Thorne's arms he placed a boot against the bare buttocks, sending him sprawling down the wide stone steps.

Heart pounding, anger still vibrant in every pore, he turned back to the house. He had been too late to save Laura.

Chapter Thirty-Five

Edmund Shaw watched the three men walk towards him across the hall of the Gallery. Last night he had followed Sheldon and his golden god, seeing them enter Bell House together. Sheldon did not know he had witnessed the reserve bid that finally purchased the beautiful 'David' or seen the man who had walked from the room with him. Nor had he seen the way in which Edmund had spent the next few night hours.

'I am glad you could come, my note gave you little time I'm afraid, but then I would rather get my debts paid quickly.' Leading the way up to his private sitting room he waited until the men were seated. 'Your money, Thorne, and yours too, Lawton.'

Taking two envelopes from his pocket he set them on the table.

'Five thousand each.' He smiled. 'That, I think, settles your loans, the Gallery is now mine.'

'Hardly!' Stafford Lawton's quick fingers scooped up one envelope. 'Five thousand barely covers the interest.'

'Interest?' Edmund's brows drew together.

'Twelve per cent was what we agreed.' Lawton's fingers rifled the white banknotes. 'Plus fifty per cent if the loan was not paid in full on the time set down in the contract. You did not settle on time.'

'Fifty per cent!' Edmund swung to the smiling Sheldon. 'You knew about this?'

'Of course, so did you if you read the agreement you signed. It is there, stated quite clearly; and it was you who asked for an extension of the time.'

Still smarting from being kicked naked on to the streets, Unwin Thorne sought revenge in the only way he could. Fat fingers closing about his own envelope, he smirked, 'Took you by surprise has it, Shaw? Well we all has surprises at one time or another, we just has to get over 'em.'

'Exactly.' Edmund smiled. 'And I shall get over this one. In the meantime, gentlemen, perhaps you will join me in a drink.'

Going over to the sideboard he took up a silver tray set with four glasses and an unopened bottle of wine.

'Chateau Tayssier St Emilion!' Lawton raised an approving eyebrow.

Drawing the cork, Edmund smiled. 'Sheldon has a weakness for expensive wine . . . among other things.' Filling each glass he held his own towards them. 'I was thinking of proposing a toast to the ongoing prosperity of the Gallery, but on the face of it I think, perhaps, the Queen. Gentlemen, I give you Her Majesty the Queen.'

Rising to their feet each man repeated the toast then swallowed the contents of his glass.

All except for Edmund. Seizing the bottle he brought it crashing down on Sheldon's head, knocking the untasted wine from his hand as Thorne and Lawton fell writhing on the ground, hands clawing at their throats.

'Arsenic trioxide, so very potent, and so very reliable. Unlike you, Sheldon, my beloved friend!'

Stepping over the unconscious figure he caught up the coil of rope he had placed behind a chair, tying it about Sheldon's hands and feet.

'I wouldn't worry about Thorne or Lawton, the poison in that wine was tasteless, it would not offend their palate and they would be dead in minutes. But not you, my dear Sheldon, I wouldn't dream of poisoning you.'

Laughing softly he draped the sleeping figure over his shoulder, carrying him from the room.

Minutes later, a huge winter moon turning the shadows bright, he smiled as Sheldon stirred.

'What . . . what the hell . . . !'

Catching him by the collar Edmund hauled him to his feet.

'Let's not talk of hell, Sheldon,' he murmured, 'we will both be there soon enough.'

'What are you doing, where are the others?'

'A little way in front,' Edmund laughed again, 'just a little way, we will soon catch them up.'

Trying to twist away, finding himself bound hand and foot, Sheldon gave way to panic.

'You bloody maniac, what do you think this will get you?'

Gathering the tail end of the rope Edmund passed it about the body of the jerking man.

'Revenge, Sheldon,' he said quietly, 'it will get me revenge. It was deliberate, wasn't it? The Gallery, rich men, beautiful women, it was all there for the taking; but I was the one taken, lock, stock and every last halfpenny.'

Knotting the rope tight, he looked into the face of the man he had loved so much; sage-green eyes, silvered by moonlight, staring back at him.

'What did you do with your share of that interest, was it that money you used to buy your golden whore?'

Stretching what was left of the rope out to its end, Edmund looked at the trembling figure, his own voice rising over that of the terrified pleas.

'Tell me, Sheldon, did he please you as I did, was his body on yours sweeter than mine, did he love you the way I did . . . love you enough to die with you?'

Laughing softly he twisted, wrapping himself tightly into the rope. Then, locking his arms about the screaming Sheldon, he walked them both to where the waters of the brook emptied into the gleaming silver waters of Thimblemill Pool. Still laughing, he walked on into the cold glittering depths.

'If you will stay with Laura, I will return this to Mary Ann.' Livvy took the dress, wrapped in layers of blue tissue paper. 'It was very kind of you to have it repaired.'

'It was kind of you, Mr Travers, I was afraid the dress might be ruined. I would have hated that after Mrs Griffiths was good enough to lend it to me.' Laura smiled. 'But really there is no need for you to sit with me, I am perfectly all right on my own, in fact I should be the one to return the dress.'

'I have never yet managed to get the supper Livvy offered, perhaps tonight . . .'

'The minute I get back.' Her smile wide, Livvy caught her shawl and was gone.

'Livvy gets a little over anxious.' Laura rose from the chair, a shudder passing through her as her eye caught the cloth bag her hand had clutched as she had fallen against that table; the same cloth bag Gabriel had used to collect payments.

'Are you asking me to leave?'

The eyes looking directly into hers as she glanced up seemed suddenly to hold a darkness, one she had seen before. It was the same dark look of pain that had lurked in her father's eyes the day he was taken away from her. But that was understandable, her father loved her.

'Are you, Laura?'

The shadow in his eyes seemed to deepen with the question. Unsure of its cause, unsure of the emotion it had roused deep within her, Laura dropped her gaze.

'No . . . No, I . . .'

'Then don't!'

Suddenly she was in his arms, his mouth against her hair. 'Don't ever ask me to leave you. I love you, Laura, I have loved you from the first day I saw you on that railway station. You looked so lost, I wanted to snatch you up there and then.'

It could not be true. Rafe Travers simply felt sorry for her, now as he probably had then; he certainly could not love her. But it had been wonderful to hear, just once in her life to hear a man say he loved her. Wanting desperately to stay locked in his arms yet knowing she must not, she pushed away.

Unable to look at him lest he saw the hurt that was in her face, she forced the words to come.

'You do not need to feel sorry for me, Mr Travers . . .'

'Sorry for you!' The explosion rang around the tiny kitchen. 'My God, Laura, *I* am the one I feel sorry for, *me*, I feel sorry for myself. I love you so much I don't know which way to turn.'

He had said it again! Her heart in her throat, Laura felt the world swing dangerously.

'Look at me, Laura.' Drawing her gently to him he tipped her chin with one finger, lifting her face to his. 'Each time I saw you, each time I came to this house I wanted to tell you I loved you, I loved you so much it was like a pain tearing my heart in pieces; all I want is to share my life with you, yet if you wish it I will go and never bother you again.'

'You . . . you can't really love me,' Laura whispered. 'I am not even pretty.'

The short laugh like a gasp in his throat Rafe held her at arm's length.

'What! Where on earth did you get that idea?'

Eyelids lowered, the memory still painful, she answered quietly, 'Edmund, he told me, he said I was not the kind of woman he would want for a wife.'

'Thank God he did!' Rafe laughed openly now. 'Thank the Lord for that or I might have been too late. Much as I intend to kill that man for what he has put you through, were he here now I would shake his hand, thank him for being a fool.'

'I . . . I don't understand.'

Looking down at her as she raised her lids, threatening tears shining like dawn mist on summer-blue lakes, Rafe felt his whole body quiver.

'He was a fool not to ask you to marry him, but he was correct in saying you are not pretty; you are beautiful, Laura Cadman, a very beautiful woman and I want you to be my beautiful woman, my beautiful wife. I am asking you, my darling, will you marry me?'

The answer in her eyes, Laura lifted her mouth to his.

'You know my father is in prison . . .'

His mouth releasing hers, Laura tried breaking free of his arms. He had asked her to marry him, told her he loved her, but had he thought of the social consequences of marrying a woman whose father was a convicted thief?

'I know.' He kissed the tip of her nose. 'What of it?'

Wanting to give in to the feelings engulfing her, wanting only to have his kisses on her mouth, it took all of her strength to answer.

'Don't you see? Having a convict for a father-in-law . . .' Stopping her mouth with his, kissing her long and hard, Rafe held her pressed against him.

'I want you for my wife,' he said when at last he released her mouth, 'that is all I care about . . . except one other thing bothers me.'

'One other thing bothers me.'

Laura felt the words stab into her, did he think she had submitted willingly to that man Thorne, been glad to accept him if it meant freeing her father, did Rafe Travers not believe what she had told him?

Lips trembling, she forced herself to look at him. She would face his accusation even though it would devastate her to have him voice it.

Meeting her gaze, his own deep and penetrating, his voice soft, he went on.

'The thing that bothers me is that you have not yet answered my question. If you cannot be my wife I must live with that, if you cannot love me . . .'

'But I do love you . . .'

The words rushed from the deepest part of her soul, lifting the shadows from his eyes, leaving them clear and gleaming.

'Then say it . . .' he smiled, 'say you will be my wife.'

Her whisper lost beneath his mouth, Laura gave herself up to the waves of happiness surging in every vein. Rafe Travers loved her, he loved her despite the terrible stigma of her father's conviction.

'Rafe.' Shyly using his first name, loving the sound of it on her tongue, she pushed from his arms, leading him to the chair that had been her father's favourite seat. 'Before I answer you must hear everything about my father . . . about me . . .'

'There is no need . . .'

The quick shake of her head cutting his words short he sat down. Kneeling beside him Laura told the whole story, leaving nothing out.

'I was stupid,' she ended, 'stupid to believe Edmund was sorry for what he had done to Father, stupid to believe he now wanted to try to get him freed; yet even now I cannot believe he sold me like a common prostitute . . . if you had not come in time . . .'

'But I did, my darling. Nothing like that will happen to you again, as for Edmund Shaw he will pay for what he's done. Now I have listened to you,' he stood up, drawing her close in his arms, 'it is your turn to listen to me. I love you, Laura Cadman, and I want an answer to my question. Will you marry me?'

This time he waited to hear her whispered 'Yes' before his kiss drowned the rest.

'I wanted so much to help Father, if only there was a way.'

Holding her to him, Rafe felt the sob she tried so hard to hide.

'We will try, my love.' He touched her hair with his lips. 'We will never stop trying, but at least he will have the comfort of knowing you are cared for by a man who loves you.'

'Who loves who?'

Livvy's bright eyes smiled from the doorway, a delighted smile curving her mouth.

'You don't have to be saying a word, I knowed it of you both weeks ago.'

After hugging each of them she hung up her shawl, then turned to laying plates on the table.

'We might not be at the George Hotel but we can celebrate here just as well.'

'Do you mean I am at last going to get that supper you have so often tempted me with?'

Turning to the teasing smile Livvy grinned as she flung an apron across at him.

'You be almost one of the family now, and in this family folk be expected to help wi' making supper.'

Bending to the oven Laura froze as a knock echoed through from the front of the house. Straightening she turned to where Livvy was standing, dishes held in her hands. The front door . . . Laura's limbs had become suddenly leaden. The only time front doors were ever used in Great Western Street was to carry out a coffin or to let in bearers of bad news.

'Father . . . !' The word broke quietly from her mouth, every vestige of colour draining from her.

Glancing from one girl to the other, Rafe strode silently into the front parlour, a gasp breaking from Laura as he returned, a tall young police constable behind him.

'Sergeant Potts said to be sure and apologise for disturbing you.' He glanced across to a blushing Livvy then back to Laura. 'But he thought as you should see this right away. I have to take it back to the station when you've read it.'

Taking a paper from his pocket he held it out to Laura.

'It were delivered with the last post this afternoon, but Sergeant Potts had to wait on me finishing my rounds before he could send it. He said you would understand he couldn't leave the station unmanned.'

Hands shaking, she unfolded the single sheet.

My dear Laura,

Words dancing with the trembling of her hands, she read on.

> *I am sending this to Sergeant Potts so it can be clearly understood you have no part in the compiling of it.*
>
> *First I want to say I lied when I swore on oath that your father had no claim on the business formerly known as Shaw and Cadman; he was Jabez Shaw's full partner. The money he is accused of stealing can, I think, be legally termed his own. I hope so, Laura, especially seeing as you have repaid every penny. So why am I telling this now? It is because I will have no chance after tonight. I shall not see you or Isaac again and I would set the record straight.*
>
> *The night my mother died she told me what I had long suspected. She told me Jabez Shaw was not my father, the surprise being that my father was Isaac Cadman. Jabez had never known and I did not enlighten him; but the pain of what I had heard bit deep. Isaac Cadman had robbed me of my inheritance, robbed me of the life and the love I should rightly have had. He knew my parentage before I was born and yet had never owned to it.*
>
> *From that night I vowed revenge, and you know well how I achieved it. I forced Isaac Cadman to defraud the business then give the money to me. Only in one thing did I feel remorse. I told you you could never be the sort of wife I wanted. That was a lie, Laura, you are a woman any man would be proud to call his wife, but now you see, little sister, that man could not be me. You told me once you would forget I ever existed, I hope that was your lie, Laura.*
>
> *Goodbye, little sister,*
> *Edmund*

Taking her in his arms as Livvy saw the constable to the door, Rafe held her close.

'It is all over, my love,' he said soothingly, 'nothing will ever hurt you again, I promise. When the magistrate sees that letter he will order your father released. Soon you will have both men who love you here to take care of you, now you can be happy.'

They had talked together long after the constable had left. Livvy, being assured she was very much wanted to stay on in this house, had been bright and bubbly, Rafe understanding of Laura's own quietness.

Now, lying in her own bed, Laura stared into the pearl-grey shadows of dawn, watching a young girl, wheat-coloured hair hanging loose to her waist, laughing with delight as a tall gangly youth swung her round in a circle.

Edmund had been so kind to her, then.

The picture sliding back into memory she turned her face towards the window, staring at the dying moon.

Edmund her half brother!

If only she had known, if only she could have told him then the feeling she had now, the joy of having a brother. Edmund had hurt them both, her and her father . . . his father . . . but that was forgiven and in time the hurt would fade.

. . . You told me once you would forget I ever existed . . .

The words written on that paper danced in her mind. Closing her eyes against them, Laura smiled into the stillness.

'No, Edmund,' she whispered, 'I will never forget my brother.'